Goodfellas

Goodfellas

Carl Weber, Ty Marshall,
and Marlon PS White

www.urbanbooks.net

Urban Books, LLC
300 Farmingdale Road, NY-Route 109
Farmingdale, NY 11735

ISBN 13: 978-1-945855-19-1
ISBN 10: 1-945855-19-3

First Trade Paperback Printing August 2018
Printed in the United States of America

10 9 8 7 6 5 4 3 2 1

Distributed by Kensington Publishing Corp.
Submit Orders to:
Customer Service
400 Hahn Road
Westminster, MD 21157-4627
Phone: 1-800-733-3000
Fax: 1-800-659-2436

Goodfellas

Carl Weber, Ty Marshall,
and Marlon PS White

Sibling Rivalry

Chapter 1

Faye

"You can't leave me now. You can't . . ."

Her voice cracked, and she was the only one who heard how much she meant the words she'd spoken. Faye Jackson's heart was frozen over as she sat watching the only person who cared about her in the whole world as she lay still in a hospital bed, dependent on a breathing machine. It was the hardest thing she'd ever done in life, and Faye could feel her mental deteriorating right along with her heart. She grabbed the woman's warm hand and put it to her lips.

"Please don't leave me, Mama," Faye whispered. "Not like this. I haven't been alone in so long. You've always been here since the beginning."

Hot tears streamed down her face as her words fell on deaf ears. It had been a week, and it was becoming evident to Faye that her mother, Chrishelle, wasn't waking up anytime soon. She had no idea what had happened the night her mom was placed in the hospital. All she knew was what the detectives told her. That someone brutally attacked her, mugged her, and left her brain dead to the world. It just didn't make any sense to Faye because her mom didn't have any enemies. She was in her late forties, but she was healthy as an ox and sweet as she could be. Everyone in Bed-Stuy loved her, and she was definitely the heart of the apartment complex that they lived in. Faye kissed Chrishelle's hand again wishing that she could hear her voice one last time.

"Who would do this to you, Mama? You have never done nothing to nobody."

The silent tears turned into sobs, and soon, Faye's vision was so blurry that she couldn't see anything in the hospital room anymore. She'd quit her job at the bank the day before because her heart was so heavy. Being around people when she felt so detached from everything around her just wasn't a good mix. All she wanted to do was be by her mother's side while she still could.

"Excuse me, uh, Miss Jackson?"

Faye wiped her puffy eyes and looked up to see the tall, bald-headed detective that had been working her mother's case. He was light skinned with brown eyes and a thin mustache. Detective Winthrop was his name, and supposedly, he was working his hardest trying to figure out who had harmed Chrishelle.

"Detective," Faye's voice sounded exhausted when she acknowledged the newcomer.

"Can I come in, or is this a bad time?"

"No time right now is a good time," Faye said, tucking her long curls behind her ears and sniffling. "But, yes, you can come in."

Detective Winthrop entered the room and took a seat in a chair that faced Faye on the opposite side of the room. He wore a dark tan suit with a pair of Stacy Adams, and in his hands, he held a folder. He watched Faye gently place her mother's hand back on the bed before straightening up and focusing her attention on him. It was apparent that she'd been crying, and the tip of her nose was a bright red.

"First, I want to apologize for the delay in the case, but I want you to know that we are trying our best to uncover what happened to your mother and how she got that bruise on the back on her head."

"Trying your best? It has been five days, and the only information you have is the same information you had when it first happened."

"Once again, Miss Jackson, I apologize. These things aren't like the detective shows you watch on TV. In real life, these things take a little more time."

"I understand that." Faye glared her light brown eyes in his direction. "But each day you come to me it's the same thing. You telling me you're sorry and me feeling empty all over again. Didn't you say she was found outside of a nightclub? Don't you find it odd that a woman her age would be outside of a club for the twenty-somethings? Have you talked to the owner of that place to see if you can get access to their security footage?"

"Miss Jackson—"

"Miss Jackson, my ass! Now I know what they think is going to happen by assigning you to her case. They think that because you're a black man I am going to just trust you and believe you will have our best interests at heart. Huh, brotha? Well, you're wrong. I don't trust you, or any of the rest of you slimy motherfuckas. My mother ain't shit but a black casualty to you, and you are just waiting for her to die so she can become another cold case. Coming from where I come from, I see this shit all the time. So don't come in here with your empty-ass apologies. I bet there ain't even shit in that folder, huh? You just brought it as a prop to make me think you've done something."

Detective Winthrop's light face had slowly turned red while Faye was talking, but she didn't care. He could get up and leave the way he came in for all she cared. Each time he came to her, she held on to a little hope that maybe he had some news about what had gone down, and each time she was disappointed in a major way. She didn't know why she had even allowed him to come and do the same that day. Probably because she still had hope. She just wanted to understand why, out of all of the people in the world, why her mom? The detective cleared his throat and stood back to his feet.

"As I said before, we are working our best, and hopefully, the next time we speak, I will have a breakthrough in the case."

"Whatever," Faye turned her full pink lips up. "This case ain't gon' get you a meal with the mayor, so I doubt you are working that hard. Unlike me, you're probably still getting a full night's rest. Good-bye, Detective."

Detective Winthrop looked like he wanted to say something more; instead, he gave Faye a head nod and walked out of the room. She wished that he hadn't even come to waste her time. Checking the clock on the wall of the room, she saw that the time was nearing six p.m. She reached toward her duffle bag of clothes beside her chair and grabbed the blanket that was neatly folded on top of it. She'd brought it from home. It was the one that was always at the end of her mom's bed. The one they always curled up in when they watched movies and drank hot cocoa on the cold New York nights. Before she could get comfortable, there was another knock on the hospital door. When she looked up, she saw her mom's physician, Doctor Boswick, standing in the doorway.

"Hey, Doctor," Faye greeted the average height, redheaded Caucasian man. He entered the room and began to check Chrishelle's vitals. "Is there something wrong?"

She didn't like the way his brow was scrunched up or the concerned expression on his face. He had a chart in his hands, and he looked from it, to Chrishelle, and then back to Faye. Finally, he sighed deeply and looked directly into Faye's eyes.

"We have tried everything that we can for your mother, Faye. However, whatever she was hit with has caused so much damage that the only way for her to wake up is if she is going to do it herself."

"And what are those chances?"

Doctor Boswick's mouth became a thin line, and his expression turned grave.

"Doctor Boswick, what are the chances that my mother will wake up on her own?"

"For the past week, she has had no brain waves. She has not even been able to breathe on her own. If it was not for her being connected to that machine, she would have died days ago. I'm sorry to say that I think it may be in the family's best interest to pull the plug."

"So that's it? You're just going to give up on her? It's that easy?"

"This type of thing is never easy, Miss Jackson. We never give up on any patients that are showing signs of getting better. And, well, your mother has not gone in the direction we would have hoped for. The damage is just too grave. We can continue to wait, but that can become very expensive to the family."

"So, what . . ." Faye felt her chest tighten and her jaw clench. Talking right then felt almost impossible. She took a breath and tried again. "So, what now? You need me to sign off on some papers that says it's OK to take her off of life support?"

"Yes," Doctor Boswick said bluntly. "However, unfortunately, per policy and law, we would need someone who is related to the patient by blood to do so. And being as that you are adopted, we have contacted the next of kin to come and do so."

"W-what?" Faye's eyes widened. "Who did you call? I'm all the family she has!"

"Wrong!"

Faye heard the voice and instantly cut her eyes at the doctor before turning them to the doorway. In entered a woman in her early thirties, and Faye knew her all too well. She had a red wig on her head and was dressed head to toe as if she'd just stepped off of the red carpet. Her face was beat to the gods, and she didn't look to be a day older than twenty-five. Carmen Jackson was Chrishelle's biological daughter. The biological daughter who had run off years back after emptying all of her mother's accounts. She was the reason that Chrishelle and Faye had been stuck living in their run-down apartment in Bed-Stuy for longer than they had ever intended. Chrishelle had two accounts in her name, one for herself and one for Faye.

Faye had been working since she was fifteen and had given every penny to her mother to put up for safekeeping. By the time she was twenty-two, she'd saved up $25,000. She was going to use it to get herself and her mother out of the hood. Put a down payment on a house in a nice neighborhood and use the rest to go back to college.

Somehow, Carmen found out about the money and stole Chrishelle's ID since they looked so much alike. People often mistook the two of them as twins. So gaining access to the money, she cleaned out the account and even took the $500 Chrishelle had in her own savings account and left town. No one had seen or heard from her in three years . . . well, until then. She couldn't believe the doctor had contacted her of all people.

"What is she doing here?" Faye sneered and jumped to her feet.

She felt rage enter her heart and prepared to pounce. Carmen saw that, and at first, looked alarmed. But when she realized that the doctor was between them, she began to chuckle.

"Well, hello to you too, sis. Always a pleasure."

"To who? Not me," Faye turned back to the doctor. "You can't be serious right now. Her? This woman stole everything from us. She is not to be trusted."

"Oh please! Are you still mad about that chump change?"

"You stole $25,000 from us!" Faye tried to jump past Doctor Boswick to get at her, but he caught her just in time.

"Ladies! Now is not the time!"

"You're the one who called her! She is not good to this family, and my mother would not be happy that she is here right now! Why would you not tell me that you were going to call her?"

"We needed a blood relative and—"

"I'm blood." Carmen put her arms up in a voilà fashion. "Whether you like it or not, *foster child*. And the longer you keep her in here clinging to life, the more I'm going to have to pay in the long run."

"You owe it to her! I am not going to sit here and let you kill her!"

"You have no choice."

"What are you doing, Carmen?" Faye asked, her voice desperate. "Do you think that there is insurance money in it for you? Because she made me the sole beneficiary right after you took everything from us."

"All the more reason to pull the plug," Carmen glared at her mother. "Serves her right for loving a random more than she did her own daughter. Say your final good-byes, Regret. That woman is taking her last breath at midnight."

Without another word, Carmen turned around, whipping her thirty-two inch extensions in the air, and stormed out of the room. When she was gone, Doctor Boswick shot Faye an apologetic look before he too exited the room. Faye was defeated. She took a few steps back as the world around her began spinning.

"No no no!" She shook her head and clutched her chest. "Please, God, no. Please, no!"

She knew Carmen meant to make good on her word, and it felt like the world was falling apart around her. It felt like five nights ago when she'd first gotten the call saying that her mother was in the hospital. Her body had gone into shock, and she couldn't even cry. Instead, she grabbed the blanket that she'd dropped to the floor and went to her mother's bedside. She climbed on the bed since there was more than enough space, and curled up next to Chrishelle, placing the blanket over them. Like always. Except, that would be the last always.

Chapter 2

Kayden

"Jayden! Oh my God, baby! Why are you doing this to meeee?"

He listened to her call out as he pounded into her with his eight inches of thickness. He was completely naked, and his muscular, caramel-colored chest was wet from sweat. The two of them had been going at it for an hour, and, he had to admit, Treasure had some treasure between her legs. He had wanted her for so long, and when the chance finally arose for him to get at her, he did. She was a five foot five brown-skinned goddess. Her ass was fatter than a mug, and it looked even bigger when he gripped her small waist. His dick wanted to come badly as he watched her breasts bounce and brush against the bed under her, but he held it. He wanted to bring her to her fifth orgasm so he could see her body quiver on his shaft one last time.

"Shut up, bitch, and arch your back," his gruff voice commanded.

"OK, daddy," Treasure moaned and tooted her ass up even higher for him. "Baby, you've never talked to me like that before. I love it. Call me a bitch again."

"You dirty bitch," he told her, smacking her left cheek so hard that it rippled. "You're a nasty-ass bitch."

He thrust deep inside of her womanhood three more times, and that did the trick for them both. Right on command, Treasure's screams turned to shrieks, and he felt her juices spilling down his legs. He grunted and threw his head back as he released his seed in her love canal. He should have pulled out and come on the soft, cream-colored comforter, but her pussy was so warm that pulling out was not an option. When he pulled out, all he wanted to do was fall on the bed next to her, but he had to get out of there.

"Where are you going so soon? It's only nine o'clock," Treasure pouted. "I wasn't good to you this time?"

"Nah," he chuckled to himself. "You were good. Great, actually. I just got some shit I need to handle, ma. That's all."

Treasure smacked her lips and rolled her eyes at him as he got dressed. After he put on his Ralph Lauren T-shirt, he threw a tan hoodie over it before pulling his jeans on. He was moving fast and checking the clock on the wall. He'd definitely stayed longer than what he had wanted, but shorty was fine, could cook, and had good conversation. The smile on his handsome face never went away, and Treasure tossed a pillow his way.

"What's so funny?"

"Nothing," he said, shaking his head. "I was just thinking that I understand why Jayden made you his bitch."

The confused look on her face was interrupted by a door opening and closing in the distance. He heard the front door of Treasure's two-bedroom apartment lock and cursed silently in his head. He let out a big sigh, already knowing what was about to happen.

"Treasure!" a deep baritone voice called. "Baby girl, I got something for you!"

Before either of them could do anything, the newcomer stepped into the master bedroom with a look that said he wanted to murder everyone written on his face. Treasure's eyes widened, and her brow furrowed. Her eyes moved back and forth between the men, and when they fell on the small mole on the right cheek of the man she'd just slept with, she gasped. She gasped and put her hand over her heart as she scooted as far back on the bed as possible.

"K-K-Kayden?"

"In the flesh," he said and winked at her.

"No," she shook her head. "No. Why? I can't believe you would do something like this!"

"Like what? Fuck my brother's bitch?" Kayden laughed. "Trust me when I say you're not the first one twin and I have shared. Tell her how we used to tag team hoes back in the day, bro."

He looked at the face of the angry man who had just entered the room, and he might have been looking in a mirror. The only thing that set him apart from his brother was the mole on his face; other than that, the two men were identical. Kayden shrugged his shoulders and shook his head. Truth be told, his plan had been to dive into Treasure and dive right back out without his brother ever knowing he was there. It looked like his plans had changed, now, and he gave Jayden a sheepish grin.

"My bad, Jay. You know we have the same taste in women."

Jayden's eyes were a blazing circle of fire. He looked at Treasure, who had tears streaming down her face, and then back at Kayden.

"Yo, man, what the fuck is wrong with you? You just got back in the city, and you're already on bullshit. With *my* bitch?"

He was completely messed up in the head. He and Treasure had been dealing with each other tough for eight months, and he really thought she would be the one to get him out of the game. Now he knew he would never be able to look at her the same. He glared at her, not because he blamed her for what had just happened, but because he was not ready to say good-bye. Without thinking twice about it, he swung and connected a powerful blow to Kayden's jaw. His brother fell back and clutched his face as if afraid it was going to disconnect from his head. Treasure shrieked and clutched onto the sheets even tighter.

"Jayden, I didn't know," Treasure's voice was wavy. She sucked in air and looked at her man with fear in her eyes. "Please don't leave me. Please. I'm so sorry."

"Shut up!" Jayden yelled, looking her way in disgust. "You gon' fuck this nigga in the crib I put you up in?"

"How was I supposed to know that your sick-ass brother would do something like this?" Treasure threw her robe around her naked body and jumped from the bed. Her sobs were loud and her entire body was shaking. "Jayden, I love you. I would never do anything to cross you, baby. Please believe me!"

She tried to reach out and grab him, but he pulled away from her and stepped back. He didn't want her to touch him. He could still smell the scent of her sweet pussy in the air, and he couldn't take the thought of Kayden experiencing the bliss between her legs. He turned to his brother, who still had a smirk on his face. Jayden wanted nothing more than to knock it away from his lips, so that's what he did. His right hook came so fast that Kayden didn't have time to duck.

It was a powerful blow, and it knocked Kayden back, but not off of his feet. The next one did, though. Jayden was so mad that all he saw was red. He could have killed his brother at that second, but he felt a pull in his mental that stopped him. He blinked his eyes and saw his brother laid out on the floor with a bloody nose and a fat lip.

"You gon' put your hands on me over a bitch, bro?" Kayden asked, holding his hands like a cup under his leaking nose.

"She wasn't just a bitch to me," Jayden said, looking back at Treasure's tearful face, and then shook his head. "She is now, though. You can have her."

With that, Jayden snatched up the bag that he'd dropped at the bedroom door entrance and left the way he came.

Chapter 3

Faye

Two weeks had passed since her mother was taken off of life support. Since then, the funeral had been held, and Faye had said her final good-byes. Of course, Carmen did not help pay or show up for any of it. Faye figured she left town once she found out that there was really no life insurance money for her. Either that, or she realized that the next time she saw Faye, there would be nobody to save her from the ass whooping she had coming her way.

It turned out that Chrishelle had a $200,000 life insurance policy, all of which went to Faye. Two hundred thousand of which $50,000 of it went toward funeral and hospital costs. So now, there she was, $150,000 richer sitting in the bedroom of an empty home. Not empty in terms of furniture, because the apartment was fully furnished, but empty in a sense that there were once two people that lived there. Now there was only one.

Faye sighed from the center of her queen-sized bed. She wore a pair of shorts and a tank top over her smooth caramel skin. Her hair was pulled back into a ponytail, and she looked at the big boxes that were against the wall of her bedroom. She'd bought them days before, but still had yet to pop them open and start packing. She knew she needed to get out of that apartment, but she was not ready to say good-bye. It was the only home she'd known since she was ten years old. Getting up from the bed, she decided it was time to enter her mother's room for the first time since it all had happened.

She walked down the hall and couldn't understand how the wooden floor was cold under her feet when the heat was on. When she made it to her mother's closed bedroom door, she took a deep breath before she opened it. She took one step inside, flicking on the light, and instantly got a whiff of Chrishelle's scent. Vanilla and Sweet Pea, her favorites. The bed was neatly made, and there was an outfit laid out on the bed. The day that she was attacked, Chrishelle must have had plans for later in the evening. The tears tried to come up, but Faye willed them away. She had to be strong; it's what her mother would have wanted. She found herself walking around the room, running her hands softly on all of her mom's belongings. She already knew that she would never give anything away. She already had a storage unit ready and waiting to receive all of it. All she had to do was pack it all up. She took a seat on the edge of the bed and picked up the dress that was laid out there. She wanted to press it against her nose and inhale deeply, but before she did that, the parchment that had been under the dress caught her eye.

"What's this?" she said aloud, picking up the piece of paper on the top of the stack.

When Faye saw what it was, she let the dress go and focused all of her attention on the paper in her hands. It was her birth certificate, her original birth certificate. She'd never seen it before, and Chrishelle kept it tucked away. That, along with everything else from Faye's early past.

"Regret You Vincent." She read her birth name out loud and clenched her teeth.

She never knew her parents, but she knew that they must have hated her. They wanted her to know how much of a mistake she was, so they gave her a name that would remind her every day. Before Chrishelle came into her life, she was in an orphanage. Although she was a pretty girl, she had grown up with a bad attitude. But that was to be expected since life, so far, had not been nice to her. She was mean, rude, and a bully to everyone that she encountered. A few families tried to house her, but they always brought her back within a month. It got to the point where she truly believed that she was unlovable. That was, until she met Chrishelle. She remembered that day like it was yesterday.

"Regret! Get upstairs and make your bed this instant!"

Regret rolled her eyes to the back of her head when she heard Sister Louise's voice. She'd literally just gotten out of her last class of the day and was looking forward to being alone. She hated everything about that place. She couldn't even call St. Peter's a home. It was an orphanage. A place for kids who had nowhere to go. The moment she stepped foot out of the classroom, Sister Louise had been waiting for her. The other girls snickered as they walked past and shot Regret funny looks.

"She's always in trouble!" Regret heard one of the girls whisper.

"No wonder her parents named her Regret. She can't do anything right. Not even make her bed!"

Regret was boiling. It felt like every second the sisters got to ridicule her in front of others, they took it. She let out a small groan and took heavy steps toward the staircase down the hall. Sister Louise tried to grab her arm as she walked, but Regret snatched it away.

"Don't touch me," she glared at the older, chocolate-skinned woman. "I know the way to my room."

"I know you do," Sister Louise said, adjusting her robes before cutting her eyes down at Regret. "I am simply making sure you are headed in that direction!"

"OK, well, you don't have to touch me to do it!" Regret snapped again as she walked. "I don't even know why you want me to make my bed now when the day is over. I'm about to go lie in it as soon as I get upstairs. I want to change out of this ugly uniform. Who chose the colors blue and yellow anyway?"

"Oh no, you aren't!" Sister Louise said as she walked beside Regret. "Tonight is Craft, and Sister Aria told me that you weren't at your last knitting lesson."

"I'm only ten years old!" Regret said in an exasperated voice. "I don't want to sit under an old lady knitting for hours!"

"Your attitude is toxic," Sister Louise said when they finally reached the stairwell. "Don't you see that's why none of the other children have taken to you? Don't you see that the way you behave is the reason why these parents keep bringing you back? You have been chosen four times—four! There are children here who have not been chosen once. You are too young and too pretty to have so much anger in your heart, Regret. Nobody here is trying to hurt you."

"Then why do you always choose to chastise me when we are in front of people?"

"I chastise you the moment I see you after you have done something irresponsible," Sister Louise snapped, but when she stared down into Regret's face, she realized that, although her mouth was smart, she was still talking to a child. She could see in Regret's face that she was unsettled. Sister Louise sighed and softened her tone. "Honestly, Regret, if I had my choice, I would never chastise you at all. I just want you to be happy."

"How can I be happy here?"

"We find happiness in all that God gives us," Sister Louise smiled. *"This may not be where you want to be, but believe me when I say that this is not your last stop. I may be hard on you, Regret, but believe me when I say that the life you have here is much better than the one you could have out there. And at the rate you're going, you may never experience a real home. If that is the case, then it is my, and all of the other sisters', job to make sure you leave this place with the right values that a young woman needs to know."*

"Like what?" Regret asked curiously.

"Like how to make your bed in the morning." Sister Louise touched Regret softly on the cheek, and surprisingly, the young girl did not back away.

Although Regret felt the smile inside, she did not let it show on her face. She allowed Sister Louise's thumb to stroke her cheek only once before she pulled away and bounded up the stairs.

"And I expect to see you at Craft, Regret! We have a guest coming."

"Yea, yea," Regret said under her breath when she was at the top of the stairs and out of earshot. She walked down the hall, passing many of the other girls' rooms who were also on the west wing. When she finally reached hers, she was happy to see that nobody was in sight. They all must have gone outside after their English lesson. Regret had been looking forward to going into her room and changing into her more comfortable clothes, but if she had to go to Craft in an hour, then it was best that she left her uniform on. She didn't want or need Sister Louise down her back about another thing.

She shared a room with three other girls. The room was spacious, and each girl had a closet, a desk with a chair, and a full-sized bed. Regret had to admit, things *for her could have been a lot worse. She'd seen the way other kids lived in other orphanages. Whereas St. Peter's might not have been where she wanted to be, she was at least grateful to have a roof over her head. Regret wasn't as big of a terror as people made her out to be. However, once the other girls heard her name and saw her pretty face, they treated her differently. She was too young to understand that the other kids were just jealous of her.*

Sister Louise was right about one thing. Regret had been chosen to have a real family multiple times, while many of the other kids hadn't even been chosen once. Regret had been blessed with long, fine hair, light skin, and the face of an angel. She, in other words, was soft on the eyes. She had the kind of face that parents melted at when they saw it. However, whenever she left and got in the houses of the people who wanted to make her their daughter, she just didn't get the vibe of "home."

After Regret made her bed, the hour passed by quickly. Soon, she was back out of her room and in the hallway with a few of the other girls headed downstairs for Craft.

"Did you make your bed, little baby?"

Regret heard the voice and instantly knew who it belonged to. Carie Lacey was a year older than Regret, and for some reason hated her guts. She was a pretty brown-skinned girl who wore her hair in two pigtails. That day when Regret whipped her head to look at her, she saw that Carie was wearing blue bows in them to match their skirts. Regret rolled her eyes at the girl and kept making her way toward the stairs. She hated getting into it with Carie because everyone always took the other girl's side, even when she was wrong.

"I don't understand why you would even think it was OK to leave your room without making your bed. That's disgusting! No wonder parents always bring you back. No one wants a pig lying around their house!"

"*You know what?*" *Regret stopped and swiveled around to face Carie. She put her hand on her hip, not able to resist herself. "They say I have a nasty attitude, but if people knew the real you, they'd say you had the bad attitude. Maybe the parents can see through the Goody-Two shoes act. No wonder you have never gotten chosen to go home with anyone.*"

Carie's eyes bulged, and there were a few gasps from the other girls who were in earshot. Regret smirked at her small victory and turned her back to Carie once more, leaving her with the stupidest look on her face. Regret was tired of people being mean to her. Sister Louise said that the other kids didn't take to her because of her attitude. No, they didn't take to her because if they saw one kid being mean to her, they followed suit. None of them had their own minds. None of them would ever be her friends. St. Peter's was not a bad place to live, but she was always alone. And that was why she hated it so much.

She finally reached her destination. The Craft room was on the first level of the orphanage. It was huge and had different sections, kind of like stations, all around it. Regret assumed that she was going to walk into a room full of old people, as usual, ready to show the girls how to knit. However, that day, she was surprised with all the new faces. There were twelve girls in the Craft room, and twelve women, not including the sisters standing around. Sister Louise smiled when she saw Regret enter the room and nodded toward a table with chairs around it. Regret, curious as to what was going on, took a seat by her name tag without another word. Her eyes fell on a pretty, younger-looking lady with a pixie cut and the face of a model. Her body was shaped like the women in the magazines that Regret sometimes snuck and read. She was very stylish in her jeans, boots, and brown leather jacket. When her eyes met Regret's, Regret hurried to look away.

"Good afternoon, lovely ladies," Sister Clarise started once everyone was seated. "I'm sure you're wondering who these lovely new faces are. Well, after deliberating with a few of you girls, it has come to our attention that you did not really enjoy your knit sessions. I mean, I couldn't understand it because who doesn't love to kni—"

Sister Louise cleared her throat, and Sister Clarise paused, catching herself with a smile. A few of the girls giggled, and even Regret cracked a smile.

"Since we want you girls to be happy with your stay at St. Peter's we are going to, shall we say, switch gears a little bit. These ladies will be your new mentors! You will get to spend two hours with them every Wednesday outside of St. Peter's."

The other girls squealed with joy while Regret tried to contain her happiness. She didn't want to seem too impressed by the new arrangements. Still, it must have showed on her face because Sister Louise smirked her way.

"Now, each of these lovely ladies has already been assigned to one of you," Sister Clarise turned to the women standing behind her. "You can go find your girl, ladies."

Regret's eyes scanned the women. They all looked to be in their late twenties or early thirties. Most of the women were black, but there were a few Caucasians in the mix. She couldn't see where the pretty, young-looking lady went, and she found herself looking to see who she had been matched with. Regret was so busy watching the other girls being paired up that she didn't even feel someone coming up behind her.

"Regret?"

Regret turned around and found herself face-to-face with the pretty face that she'd been looking for.

"T-that's me," she finally said.

"Looks like I'm going to be your mentor," the lady smiled big and stuck her hand out. "I'm Chrishelle. Nice to meet you, pretty girl."

Faye snapped back to reality and realized that the birth certificate in her hands had become blurry. She willed the tears to leave her eyes as her mind wallowed in the memory of when she had first met Chrishelle. It was one that she would hold close to her heart forever. There was no way that she could ever forget the melodic smile that she'd received. No one had ever smiled at her like that.

"I miss you so much, Mama," Faye said and made to get up from the bed, but something on the birth certificate caught her eyes.

She'd never known the names of her birth parents, and Chrishelle always told her that she didn't know either. But Faye realized then that her mother, who she thought never told a lie, had lied to her. She was looking at the full name of her mother and the full name of her father.

"Taylor Elayne Vincent," she read her mother's name out loud, and then her father's. "Greyson Vinc—"

She gasped and dropped the paper. She hopped up from the bed and swallowed the thick lump that had formed in her throat. Greyson Vincent? *The* Greyson Vincent? Owner of half-a-dozen businesses in New York? However, everyone who was down knew that those businesses were used to wash a different kind of business.

"New York's kingpin?" Faye said to herself. "No. It can't be."

She rummaged through the papers on the bed, trying to get a better understanding on why her mother even had it out. There was a piece of notebook paper in the mix. It had her mother's chicken scratch scribble all over it. There was an address, the same one as the nightclub that she was found outside of. There was also a phone number.

There was an envelope underneath that piece of paper. When Faye opened it, she found a letter inside. On top of the letter, there was a printer sheet that showed Faye that the one in the envelope must have been the copy of the original.

> *Dear Greyson,*
> *As you know, I have been caring for your child since she was ten years old. You know, the child that you threw to the side as if she was nothing? The third child that nobody knows about. I'm sure there are many blogs and magazines that would love to get their hands on a story about how their dear Mr. Vincent left his child for dead in an orphanage when he had more than enough means to take care of her. What kind of dent would that put in your pockets, huh? But for a price, I am willing to keep my mouth shut. I want $5 million. Faye, who you know as Regret, is a good woman. She is smart, beautiful, and compassionate. She has deserved much more than what life has thrown her way. The least that you can do as her father is give her a decent future, and you will never have to hear from us again. My number is at the bottom of this letter. Please contact me at your earliest convenience.*

After reading the letter, Faye snatched the birth certificate up from off of the ground and ran back to her room where her computer was. She pulled up his profile and matched his date of birth to the one on her birth certificate.

"Oh my God," she said. "It is true. Greyson Vincent is my father."

She kept digging and found out that he had two sons in line to take over the family businesses after him. Kayden and Jayden Vincent. They were twenty-five years old, like her. At first, Faye thought that Greyson must have been stepping out on his wife, but that was until she saw pictures of the twins next to their birthdate. They were the spitting image of her, except they were boys, and, unless the Internet was wrong, they all shared the same birthdate. Suddenly, Faye's stomach felt as if it was about to reject the burger and fries she'd eaten earlier. The boys weren't twins . . . They were all triplets!

She had so many questions running through her head at that moment, but the main one was how long had her mother known about it all? And if her mother had known about Greyson's deep dark secret and was trying to extort money from him, then . . .

"Oh my God," Faye said again, scooting away from her computer desk.

Her mother hadn't gotten "mugged," like the police wanted her to believe. She was murdered.

Chapter 4

Jayden

This nigga is always on some bullshit, Jayden thought to himself as he blew a cloud of smoke out the window.

Whenever he was distressed about something, Granddaddy Purp always helped him ease his mind. Usually, it had a lasting effect; in this situation, it only helped numb the pain. He and Kayden had grown up with a father that had pretty much told them that it wasn't manly to have feelings. About anything. So he tried to mask the hurt with a high that was hard to come down from.

It had been a few weeks since the incident at Treasure's place, but he still hadn't completely gotten over it. Although he had many women on his roster, Treasure had been a special one to him. She was different than the rest of the women he'd come across. Someone that he wouldn't want to share with any other man while he had her. His hand tightened around the black steering wheel of his silver 2017 SL Benz as the images of Treasure's naked body intertwined in her sheets plagued his mind, shortly after the fresh memory of her cries in his ears when he broke the news that he didn't want anything else to do with her entered his head.

"Jayden, please don't leave me," she'd said. "I love you, baby. You know I don't want anyone else."

"It's fucked up, but I can't look at you the same anymore. Knowing that my brother—"

"He tricked me!"

"I know, but *just knowing that he has experienced a part of you that I wouldn't want to share with any man . . . It's just too much, Treasure.*"

"*So why not cut him off? Why are you trying to leave me, Jayden? We can work it out, baby. We can make it past this!*"

"*Look, Treasure, I can't just cut my brother off. I will handle him in my own way. But just know that if it's a choice between you and him, I gotta rock with him.*"

"Even though he went behind your back and fucked your girl?"

"*You were never my girl. I cared about you, though. But that's not enough to fuck up my money flow.*"

"*You bastard. I hate you!*"

"*Yea,*" Jayden had said right before he disconnected the call. "*Join the club.*"

That conversation had taken place minutes after he opened his eyes this morning. He knew that his words probably cut her deeper than he'd intended, but he had no choice. She had to get cut off. She wasn't the only fish in the sea, and eventually, he would get back at his brother, but for right then, he needed to clear his head and keep his eyes on the money. Anything that could detour him from what mattered the most had to get eliminated. Treasure was a big distraction, and in a way, Kayden had been right when he told him he was acting like a bitch behind a bitch. Still, Kayden needed to be put in his place.

Jayden slowed his Benz down in front of the cobblestone building in Bed-Stuy that his brother had said to meet him at. He leaned down so that he could peek outside of the passenger window and couldn't help but to wonder what his brother was doing in a place like that. Sitting on the wide porch steps outside of the building was a woman who couldn't have been older than twenty-one and two young toddlers. She had a scarf over her long feed in braids and, even though bare-faced, was very pretty. Although she was dressed casually in a pair of sweats and a coat over a long sleeved shirt, her sons were dressed like it was Easter Sunday. Their jeans were freshly ironed, and both had on Ralph Lauren winter coats over red Ralph Lauren sweaters. On their feet, they had matching red Tims. They played and laughed together while their mother was on the phone, loudly cussing out whoever was on the other end.

"Bitch-ass nigga! You laid up with a ho but can't run me the money to get Jaymar the money for his prescription? He needs his inhaler, Damien!"

Jayden heard her yells get louder when he got out of his vehicle and locked the doors. He didn't look like a man that should even be in that part of town. He was in Gucci from head to toe. Even his thick pea coat was designer. He pulled his hat down over his ears and made his way to the steps.

"Yes, he *had* insurance! But I've been going back and forth with the assistance people since I decided not to put your trifling ass on child support! If you weren't going to be a real father, what the fuck did you sign the birth certificate for?" She paused briefly. "What does me not wanting to be with you have to do with the fact that my son can't breathe at night? He's wheezing!" Another pause. "So you aren't going to send me the money to grab his inhaler? Shantae is on her way to get me right now because you said yesterday you would give me the money—hello? Hello?"

Jayden heard her voice crack on the second "hello."
She looked at the phone in her hands, baffled, and not
even knowing that she was being watched. Her fingers
dialed another number on her touch screen smart phone.
Her hands were shaking so much that she just put the
phone on speaker instead of holding it to her ear.

"Hello?" a loud woman's voice answered with a deep
Bronx accent.

"Hey, Shantae," her voice was soft then, like a mouse.
"It's OK, you don't have to come get me, girl. Damien isn't
sending me the money like he said."

"What?"

"I know."

"Lee Lee . . ." Shantae sighed loudly. "So how is Jaymar
supposed to get his inhalers and nebulizer?"

"I don't know."

"Look, I have a hundred on my card—"

"No, Tae, you ain't even gotta do all of that. You
shouldn't have to. Plus, I know you have things to do this
weekend."

"Lee Lee . . ."

"I know, girl. I'ma just keep boiling peppermints and
having him inhale the steam until I get paid on Friday.
Honestly, hopefully by then, the state calls me back and
tells me they reopened his insurance."

"All right, boo," Shantae said. "I'm still going to come
through and get y'all."

"OK, cool. We're outside waiting."

She disconnected the phone and went to put it in her
coat pocket when she suddenly noticed the man standing
in front of the steps. They connected eyes for a moment,
and Jayden could tell that she felt embarrassed, realizing
that he must have heard her whole conversation.

"Excuse you?" she said and rolled her eyes at him.

"I'm sorry you're having a bad day," Jayden told her,
trying to offer her a kind smile.

She looked him up and down before she scoffed. "I bet," she shrugged. "'Cause it doesn't look like you've had a bad day in a long time. What you doing listening to my conversation anyway? Ain't you never heard of privacy?"

"Trust me, I wasn't trying to listen in on your baby daddy issues, but you were so loud, I'm sure the entire block heard you."

She didn't mean to, but she smiled. She had a small gap between her two front teeth, and it made her ten times more attractive. Her smooth brown skin went well with the brown of her coat, and her eyes, her mahogany-colored eyes, were defiant. Jayden knew that she wasn't happy, but it didn't show. He smiled at her, and then at the two small boys. They were talking with each other and giggling at whatever they thought was funny at the time.

"They're happy," Jayden observed.

"Huh?"

"They're happy," he repeated himself. "They look healthy and are dressed better than kids I see living in mansions. That lets me know that you don't let them see you when you're down, and you do what you have to do to keep it that way."

"You know that by just looking at them sitting there?"

"And by the fact that you're upset, but I can't tell just by looking at you. You don't even show weakness in your eyes."

"Then how do you know?"

"The sassiness in your voice. Your attitude when you speak gives off everything you're feeling. Don't do that. Just believe."

"Believe in what? My son still has to go without his inhaler."

"Believe that everything happens for a reason. Like me being here at this very moment," Jayden said and reached in his pocket for his wallet. From it, he pulled out every dollar he had and handed it to her. "That could be anywhere from two to five bands. Spend it wisely, but do something nice for yourself and your kids, all right, Lee Lee? I'm Jayden, by the way."

She was so taken aback as she stared at the money in her hands. Her eyes were on all of the Ben Franklins when he walked past her and through the entrance of the building. He headed for the stairs to get to the second floor when he heard Lee Lee's soft voice sound behind him.

"Kid."

He turned around and raised an eyebrow. "What's up?"

"Kid," she corrected him again. "I only have one kid. The younger one is mine. The older one is my sister's son. I'm just babysitting today. But . . . thank you. Thank you very much."

"My bad," Jayden told her with a wink. "One or two kids, you're still fine, ma. I ain't judging, but you're welcome."

With that, he bounded up the stairs toward door number 205. Lee Lee was still on his mind when he knocked on the door to the apartment. He heard music playing loudly on the other end and lots of scattered movement.

"Yo, what's the word?" a gruff voice said.

"Ain't no word, just currency," Jayden replied.

After a few seconds, the door swung open and Jayden was greeted by a big cloud of smoke. When he entered, he passed a big man who was strapped with an AK-47 at his side. The man nodded at Jayden to show respect and stepped out of the way. Jayden didn't know what to expect, but that definitely was not it. The apartment was decked out, complete with not one, but two fifty-inch flat screens on the wall. All of the furniture inside was black, including the leather sectional his brother was sitting on with three other dudes.

"What's good, baby bro?" Kayden's cheerful voice sounded.

His lip was still a little swollen, but other than that, he looked like life was treating him well. Both twins wore their hair cut low with popping waves and a clean lineup. Their sideburns connected with their small and neatly trimmed beards. Both had a muscular body build, and that, mixed with their handsome faces, never made it hard to get women.

Jayden looked around the apartment and made a face. On the outside, one would never even think that any apartment in the building would look so nice. It even looked like there were new appliances added in it. The entire kitchen looked like one off a cooking show with a stainless steel refrigerator and dishwasher. Sitting at the high table in the dining room was a woman that Jayden recognized as Kitten, one of Kayden's longtime slides. She was at the table with a friend in nothing but their underwear smoking a blunt and doing lines.

"Hey, Jay," Kitten greeted with a smile. "You trying to hit this?"

She tried to pass the blunt to him, but he shook his head. He wasn't even fazed by how voluptuous she or her friend looked in their black lace underwear. Jayden was more focused on why there were four bricks of cocaine out on the coffee table in front of his brother.

"Kayden, what the fuck, yo?"

"Chill, bro. I can't have you coming up in my place of business wilding."

"Wilding?" Jayden made a face. "Nigga, you sitting up in a ghetto with the work and guns like it's nothing. You real hot right now."

"I ain't hot," Kayden laughed. "Ain't no better place to hide out than in plain sight, you feel me?"

He reached and dapped up the man sitting beside him. Jayden shook his head and sighed. His brother always had a thing for moving recklessly, and he thought that Kay had learned his lesson when he almost got bumped up in Chicago. Their father, Greyson, had given him the task of being the face of his business on an expansion deal. Instead of doing things Greyson's way, Kayden decided to throw in a few of his own ideas in the mix. He didn't know how to keep it business, but he did know how to keep it hood. He opened up five trap houses around the city and hunted down all of the competition on some "get down or lay down" type stuff. In turn, he got the turf but almost lost his freedom. If it weren't for Greyson's connections in law enforcement, Kayden would have been looking at a fifty-year bid. Instead, he just had to leave the city. Greyson replaced him with another young cat, Casanova, who he trusted to hold things down in the Chi. Things had been quiet the year Kayden was gone, and Jayden finally had things moving smoothly the way he needed them to. Eventually, their father would step aside as the king of New York, and when he did, Jayden wanted the transition to be without issue. But there Kayden was, trapping out of an apartment complex that looked to host the police at least five times a week.

"Just sit down, Jay. Let's talk."

"First tell me what Dad's work is doing just sitting in the open like this."

Kayden looked from his brother, and then back to the glass coffee table. He made a face like he couldn't see why Jayden didn't understand what was going on.

"That ain't Pop's work. Look at the packaging."

He threw one of the kilos to his brother, and Jayden caught it with one hand. At first, he was going to call his twin a fool because the special wrapping looked just like their father's, but the closer he looked, he could see the difference.

"His seal ain't on here," he said out loud.

The seal he spoke of was the one that his father put on every kilo package. It was how he kept track of his work and how everyone who did business with him knew if the package was legit or not.

"Bingo," Kayden said. "I got a call from Miguel—"

"The head of the Mexican Mafia?"

"Yea, him," Kayden confirmed.

"Why he call you?"

"You mean why did he call me and not you? He did, but you was too busy crying over a bitch to answer a business phone call."

Jayden didn't say anything. He could have come at Kayden with a verbal blow of his own, but instead, he chose to stand down.

"You buggin', yo. What Miguel say?"

"No, *you* buggin', nigga. Anyway, he said that he placed an order with Pops and some niggas brought him this shit."

"The Mexicans are some of Dad's most loyal customers. Ain't no way he would try to snake them." Jayden was suddenly intrigued by what Kayden was telling him.

"Exactly. That's why I had my mans, Dino, here," the man beside Kayden nodded his head, "do some research."

"Word? What he find out."

"We tracked down where the fake dope is coming from. Some out-of-town niggas been out here on the move right under our noses."

"Nah," Jayden shook his head. "Don't nobody enter this city without me knowing about it. Especially doing no shit like this."

"They can enter if they have a key."

"Ain't no key."

"You sure about that?" Kayden asked, sending Jayden into a whirl of his own thoughts.

"Does Dad know?" Jayden asked in a low tone after a few moments.

"Hell, nah, but we need to dead the issue."

"Word. Straight like that. So what's the move? Do you know anything about these niggas?"

"I had Dino scope out the niggas last night after Miguel brought me this bullshit. After a few shots of Patrón, they got real lippy. We found out who their key is," Kayden said and looked Jayden dead in his eyes. "It's Slime."

"Slime? That man has been working for Dad since he was fifteen."

Roderick "Slime" Davis started off working as a street runner for Greyson back when the movement was just taking off. Slowly, he worked his way up in the ranks until finally he became the head of distribution. Only a few people knew the location of the warehouse used to package up all of the work orders. Greyson used a decorative type of wrap for all of his work, and once each kilo was wrapped up, his seal was placed on it. It was his stamp in the game. No one else was doing it, and it set him apart from the competition. However, whereas Slime had access to the wrapping papers, he did not have access to the seal. Only Greyson's right-hand man, Tip, had the ability to place Greyson's seal.

Jayden just didn't understand why Slime would do anything to cross Greyson. When he had literally nothing, Greyson gave him the means to get everything. He was considered family to them all, so if what Kayden was saying was the truth, it was a greasy double cross.

"Niggas always want more than what's in the hand that's feeding them," Kayden said, reading Jayden's mind. "Word is, one of the niggas is his people."

"Cousin," Dino said.

"I don't know what's gotten into this nigga, but we've been waiting for you to get here so that we can go and find out. You tryin'a ride out or what?"

"It's business. Of course, I'm gon' ride."

Chapter 5

Jayden

When they left the apartment building, Jayden half-hoped that he would see the girl sitting on the steps, but, of course, she was long gone. For some reason, her smile lingered in his mind in a way that he honestly didn't want any woman's to in a while.

He followed behind his brother's G-Wagen on the highway, already knowing where they were headed. The secret warehouse was located underneath Greyson's dry-cleaning business, Pleasantly Clean, and the majority of the customers were regulars and had been going there for years.

When they arrived, they pulled to the back and parked in the alley behind the dry cleaners. Kayden hopped out first with a duffle bag over his shoulder; then Jayden followed suit. The only entrance to the warehouse was through a door in the back of the large building that led to a set of stairs. Jayden reached into the pocket of his coat to find the key to the door, but Kayden beat him to it.

"What, you think you the only one with a key?" he asked when he saw Jayden's eyebrow raise. "Pops gave it to me a few weeks ago."

"After the shit you pulled in Chicago?" Jayden asked, walking through the doorway first.

"That 'shit' I pulled in Chicago brought in more business than even Pop's predicted."

"Nigga, you went out there on some Rah-Rah Beanie Sigel shit," Jayden said, going down the stairs.

It was cold outside, and it honestly didn't feel any better in that stairwell. The blue concrete walls didn't do any good at holding heat inside, but once they were off of the stairs, there was a hallway that led to their destination. Jayden could feel the air around him growing warmer by the second.

"It got the job done."

"Your ego almost brought down the entire empire."

"But it didn't. Pops handled that for me."

"Like always," Jayden said when they got to the five-inch thick door.

He reached to open it, but Kayden caught his arm. He whipped to face his twin and saw a look that he didn't recognize. It was a look that he didn't think he had ever made.

"Yo, what's that supposed to mean, Jay?" Kayden challenged.

Jayden heard his brother's menacing tone and saw that the look in his eyes matched, but he had never been one to back down from a challenge.

"It means we aren't kids anymore, bro. The shit you do doesn't just affect you. If you go down; we all go down. Now, you're back moving like a rookie."

"I told you that work in the apartment wasn't mine. I showed you proof."

"A'ight, I can accept that. But if you think for one second I believe that you aren't trapping out of that bitch, you're crazy. You can't tell me that all of those upgrades just came with the place. And you had that big nigga at the door with the big chopper. You wildin', G."

"So what?" Kayden put his hands in his pocket. "You're trying to tell me how to move now?"

"When it's jeopardizing my shit, yea. It looks like I might have to. The stunts you pulled in Chicago ain't gon' fly here, Kay. You gon' have to chill out."

"Your shit? Did you forget that we're twins, brother? You aren't better than me. What's yours is mine, and vice versa. We shared a womb, and I'm six minutes older. Never forget that."

"Duly noted, but apparently that extra six minutes when I was baking gave me the common sense that you don't have. This ain't about me being better than you; this is about me knowing what's best for the business. We deaded the way of trap houses years ago. The only niggas that trap Dad's work out of traps are the niggas that buy wholesale, and that's not our problem. When you were gone, Dad trusted me with a lot of tasks, and I'm not about to have you here undoing my hard work, understand? I want that fucking trap closed down by the end of the day, or you gon' force my hand."

"Or else what? You gon' tell Dad on me or something?" Kayden chuckled.

"Nah," Jayden said. "I'm a grown-ass man. I can handle my own light work."

Kayden looked like there was more he wanted to say, and Jayden knew it was just sitting at the tip of his tongue. He must have known that it was a battle that he wasn't going to win. He gave one nod and let Jayden's arm go.

The steel door did not have a doorknob. The only way to open it was a little console on the wall. Jayden flipped the top open, input in the eight-digit code, and on the last number, there was a loud clicking sound as the door swung open. The door was completely soundproof, but once open, they heard the sounds of loud music and somebody yelling over it.

"Bitch! That ain't how you bag the coke! Get yo' high ass off the production floor and come back in thirty minutes."

Jayden would recognize Slime's deep baritone voice anywhere. He was a dark-skinned bald man. He was only a few years older than the twins but looked to be in his midthirties. He was tall and slim but had a muscular build. He didn't need them, but he always had on a pair of designer spectacles.

"Bitches love a nigga with glasses," he would always say when somebody asked.

The warehouse was the size of an average basement. There wasn't much furniture, just tables and chairs for the women bagging up the product. They wore masks over their faces and white robes over their bra and panties. One of them sat in the far corner pouting with her arms crossed. From the looks of it, everything was running smoothly. Jayden saw piled up work stacked neatly in the corner ready to be stamped with Greyson's seal and then delivered. Slime didn't notice the twins enter his work area until he finally looked up.

"Well, if it ain't my favorite people!" he said, throwing his hands in the air.

The smile on his face showed that he was genuinely happy to see them. That raised a few hairs for Jayden. If he were moving foul, then he should have been alarmed by their sudden presence. Slime walked up and dapped them up and greeted. His eyebrow lifted when Kayden was hesitant to shake his hand.

"Damn, son, why you always so uptight? Smile a little. Shit, I'm used to Jayden being all tight about shit, but, damn. I thought twins were opposites of each other. Looks like neither one of you got a happy bone."

Under any other circumstance, Jayden might have smiled. He may have even laughed, but right then, he needed to get down to the bottom of the fake dope lobbing around his city.

"As much fun as it would be, we aren't here to see how you're doing, Slime," Jayden said, and then nodded at Kayden to hand Slime the bad on his shoulders. "We're here to find out some information. We have reason to believe you can give it to us."

"What's this, you brought me a gift?" Slime asked, taking the bag from Kayden.

He looked into it and pulled out one of the bricks of cocaine. At first glance, the expression on his face was alarmed, like a kid caught with his hand in the candy jar. Jayden's hand slowly went to his waist, preparing to do away with the problem.

"Somebody wasn't happy with their product?" Slime asked and threw Jayden completely for a loop.

"What?"

"That's what this is, right? Why else would you bring the product back to me? Oh shit . . . Greyson isn't going to like this. Yo, who was it? Those damn Haitians, I bet. They were talking all that shit about how the work in Florida is ten times better than it is here. They must be trying to start some shit!"

"Slime—Slime!" Jayden put his hands up to silence the man. "Ain't nobody trying to return no product. Take a good look at the shit in your hands. That's *not* my father's cocaine."

Slime did as he was told, and the moment he saw what was missing, the seal, his eyes widened; then he looked up at the twins. An understanding look crossed his face, and suddenly he knew why the twins had come there to show it to him.

"The seal is missing," he said. "This is a copycat. You—you can't possibly think that I have anything to do with this shit."

"You're the only one with access to the wrapping paper. It's not easily duplicated, so that means it can only come from one place," Jayden pointed to where the special paper was on one of the tables. "Here. So is there anything that you would like to tell us?"

Jayden didn't notice until then that his brother's old Desert Eagle was already pointed at Slime's face. Slime swallowed hard as he looked down the butt of the gun. He shook his head, and although scared, stood his ground.

"You think I'm out here pushing fake work? After everything Greyson has done for me? I would never cross him or his family like that. It would be like crossing my own!"

Jayden studied him for a few seconds before turning to his brother's angry face.

"What was it them hounds of yours found out, Kayden?"

"Man! It don't matter. Can't you see this nigga is playing us?"

"Fuck you mean it don't matter?" Jayden asked, surprised at his brother's statement. "You got a gun in this nigga's face. Produce the facts that he's guilty so we can handle our shit and be out."

Kayden had enough of his twin acting as if he was the more superior one out of the two. When he saw that his brother wasn't going to let up, he did what he had to do.

Bang! Bang!

Kayden released two bullets from his weapon. The close range did more than just snap Slime's head back. It made it explode. The women bagging up product jumped and sucked their breath, but none of them screamed. It was not their first time being in the midst of violence, but a wave of shock filled the entire room.

"Yo, man, what the fuck!" Jayden exclaimed when Slime's body collapsed to the ground. "What the fuck!"

"He was talking too much," Kayden said, tucking his weapon away.

"You ain't even let him speak!"

"Fuck did he need to speak for? I gave you all the information and showed you all the proof you needed. Pops was right. It's a good thing I'm back. You done got soft out here."

"What?"

"You heard me, Jay. Why you think he gave me these keys and even asked me to come back to New York in the first place? You ain't moving the way a boss move. The ice done melted around your heart or something, my G. What's up, you gon' hit me again? The way you did over a bitch and some pussy? Try it, and I bet you this time, we both gon' leave here bloody."

He saw the way Jayden had flexed through his coat. He didn't miss a beat, and he balled his hands into fists as well just in case times called for him to use them. Jayden reached in his pocket and pulled out his phone. He took a few steps away from Kayden as he dialed a number and placed the phone to his ear.

"Aye, yo, Mags, we're going to need a cleanup at the warehouse. Yea, Slime had an accident," he paused. "Yup, fifteen minutes is good."

Jayden turned back to his brother, but his eyes fell on Slime's dead body. The blood from his head was leaking on the concrete floor and was running every which way. Despite the dead body on the ground, the women never stopped doing their jobs. They avoided eye contact with the two brothers, probably fearful that they would become the next victims. Jayden let out a breath of air and shook his head before he turned his back on the scene.

"Since you made the mess, you stay here until it's cleaned up," he threw over his shoulder as he walked out. "And until every last order is ready to be moved out."

He'd had it up to here with Kayden's stunts. He didn't understand it because most twins were close. Most siblings, for that matter, but it seemed like the two of them couldn't get on the same page if their lives depended on it. All Kayden had been doing was showing him how much he didn't respect Jayden. However, Jayden didn't know why he was even surprised at that. Kayden had been trying to show him up ever since they were kids. He knew there was only one person who could get Kayden in check. Their father. He made a mental note to have a sit-down with Greyson soon as he got back into his vehicle and pulled away from the building. Something had to give, even if it meant putting Kayden on the bench for a while.

Chapter 6

Faye

There were only a few boxes in the apartment left to take down to the moving truck, and Faye was in the living room out of breath. She was fully dressed in a pair of her thickest high-waist jeans, a pair of old, all-black Uggs, her winter coat, and a hat over her head. It was almost noon, and she'd been hard at work trying to get everything out of there since eight o'clock. Minus the help of the movers she'd hired to do the heavy lifting, it was just her. She didn't mind it, though. The constant moving around kept her mind off of the face that she was really leaving. She just had to. The constant reminder of the way things were weeks before was becoming too much to stand. She was sitting on one of the boxes, taking a swig of water, when she heard a knock on the slightly open apartment door.

"Can I come in—Jaymar!"

Before the sweet voice could finish asking permission to enter, the cutest toddler boy pushed the door open and ran inside. Faye smiled when she saw his familiar dimples and copper-colored eyes. She opened her arms just in time to receive his hug and placed a kiss on his forehead.

"Baby boy!" she said with a smile. "I was wondering when you were going to make your way over to see me!"

"Auntie Faye! Where all your stuff go?" His high-pitched voice was so cute it was almost too much to take.

"Auntie Faye is moving, baby, but you can come visit me whenever you want!"

"Girl, why didn't you say anything? You know I would have helped you move!"

Faye grinned sheepishly at her friend, Lee Lee, as she came into the apartment. She was wearing a cute black leather jacket over a cute blouse and a pair of jeans made perfectly to fit over her wide hips. The high-knee Michael Kors boots she wore matched perfectly the jacket she was wearing. The two had known each other for a while but only had just become close friends in the past two years. Lee Lee was the only one who had been there for Faye in the midst of everything going on around her. Still, somehow along the line, Faye had managed to shut her out too.

"Lee Lee, you know I'm an independent black woman," she joked.

"You're so stupid," Lee Lee smirked and rolled her eyes and took a seat on the other box in the living room.

"For real. Plus, I just needed the time to clear my head."

"How have you been? I feel like I haven't seen you in forever."

"I'm sorry. This is just really . . . a big adjustment for me. I never thought that this was the way I'd say good-bye, you know?"

"Yea, me and my mom aren't even close like that, but if something happened to her, I think I'd go crazy. I've been praying for you and your healing every night, though, friend."

"And I appreciate it. I need every prayer that I can get right about now. But enough about me. What have you and my li'l man been up to?" Faye tickled Jaymar, who was leaned up against her legs, sending him into a fit of giggles.

"Just the same old bullshit. The only thing that's changing is the day."

"His d-a-d-d-y still on bullshit?" Faye asked, spelling out the word so Jaymar wouldn't know who they were talking about.

"Yes. He's still upset that I don't want to be with him."

"Be with him while he's out here in every ho's bed? I don't think so, and he's a fool to think that you would ever come back and deal with that mess."

"Exactly. Plus, it's been almost a year. Let go of that hurt and be a damn daddy. Jaymar didn't do anything."

"Please don't tell me he's acting crazy to this baby."

"Girl! Just last week he wasn't trying to buy Jaymar's inhaler! You know all that mess I was going through with his insurance? In the midst of all of that, my baby had gotten sick, so I'm like, nigga, your child needs his medicine."

"Why didn't you just ask me? You know I would have come through for you."

"You were just dealing with so much, Faye, or I would have."

"I understand. So Damien didn't get it?"

"Hell, nah," Lee Lee shook her head in disgust. "But get this. Some nosy nigga standing at the bottom of the steps outside heard me cursing him out. Boy gave me five bands to handle my business."

"For real?" Faye's eyebrows shot up. "Somebody in *this* neighborhood had *that* kind of money to give?"

"Yes, girl. The crazy thing is, the next day, everything got settled with his insurance so now I just have all of this money."

"You haven't spent any of it?"

"Nope," Lee Lee said. "I'm trying to figure out what I want to do with it. Since you're leaving, I was thinking about buying out of my lease. I don't want these to be the only walls that Jaymar sees. I want my baby to grow up in a nice neighborhood. Speaking of that, what place did you settle on?"

"The three-bedroom condo on the other side of Brook-lyn."

"Look at you! Out here popping," Lee Lee smiled genuinely. "I don't think I'll be able to get anything that nice, but honestly, anything is better than here."

"I heard that," Faye said, thinking about the second life insurance policy she found out her mother had. That one was for $500,000, and the money had just hit her account the day before. "I'll help you, wherever you decide to go."

"Thanks, friend. So what about Carmen? I saw her sniffing around here not too long ago, but I don't remember if I saw her at the funeral."

"Girl, because that trifling bitch wasn't there. She came here and pulled the plug on my mama and didn't even stay to say her last good-bye."

"Money hungry." Lee Lee shook her head.

"I swear, that shit had me mad tight. Because as soon as she found out that there was no insurance money for her, she bounced like it wasn't nothing. I can't stand her ass."

"How could you do that to your own mother? Mm-mm-mm. What Detective Sell-Out have to say about how it all happened in the first place?"

"The same thing. Every time, it's the same shit. That they don't have any new leads, but they're 'working on it.'"

"Working on it? It's been almost a month!"

"My thoughts exactly. They ain't doing nothing to solve the case, but I knew a long time ago they wouldn't. That's why I'm taking matters into my own hands."

"Own hands?" Lee Lee raised her eyebrow up at Faye. "Bitch, what you talking about? 'Cause if you're talking about playing cops and robbers, you're bugging."

"Nah," Faye shook her head. "I'm not. Somebody murdered her, Lee Lee. This wasn't some 'accident,' and that's the main reason why I'm so unsettled. Whatever happened that night outside of that nightclub was because of me. I can't let it go until I have some answers."

"Hold up, slow down, and rewind. Because of you? I must have missed a turn or something, because I'm lost."

Faye didn't say anything, she just kissed Jaymar on his forehead again and moved him gently out of her way. She disappeared for a second, going into her mother's room to grab a folder from the closet. When she came back, she resumed her seat. Jaymar didn't come back to her. He'd gone to the corner to play with a couple of toy dinosaurs he'd produced from his pocket. Faye scooted her box closer and focused all of her attention on Lee Lee.

"I found this stuff in my mom's room. Remember when I told you that I was adopted and that my mom didn't know who my real parents were? Well, that was a lie."

"That you were adopted?"

"No, that she didn't know who my real parents were." Faye handed Lee Lee the red folder. "She knew the whole time, but she kept it a secret from me."

"Why does this birth certificate say 'Regret'?" Lee Lee asked, examining the piece of paper.

"That was my name when I entered this world. Mama changed it not too long after I came to live with her."

"They named you Regret? Yo, that's some fucked-up shit. But wait, it says here that your birth father is—"

Her eyes bulged.

"Greyson Vincent," Faye finished for her. "That's not the craziest part. Match my date of birth with the date of birth of his sons and their mother's name."

"Oh my God," Lee Lee's eyes got even wider, if that was possible, as she went back and forth between the birth certificate and the Internet article that Faye had printed. "Whoa. This is mad crazy, Faye. I-if they're twins, and y'all were all born on the same day, to the same woman . . . Y'all are triplets. And wait!" She held the article closer to her face. "This is the guy that gave me the five thousand! Well, shit, one of them, anyway."

"What?" It was Faye's turn to be wide eyed. "They were here?"

"I think only one of them," Lee Lee said. "And now a lot of shit is making sense to me if these are Greyson's sons. Ain't no secret that they're moving around what they're moving around. You've been shut away in here, but that apartment down the hall has been seeing a lot of traffic lately. I wouldn't be surprised if they're trapping outta that bitch."

"So, you don't think he was here for me?"

"For you? Why would they be here for you?"

"You didn't read the letter in that folder, but my mama was trying to blackmail Greyson into giving her money for us. She said in the letter that if he gave it to her, she would stay quiet about my existence. I did some digging and found some information about the club they found her body outside of. Including who the owner is."

She pulled out the piece of paper at the bottom. On it was listed the name of the club, Shooters, how much it cost, also the year it was built. She slid her finger across the page from the word "Owner" to where it listed Greyson Vincent's name.

"Faye . . ." Lee Lee whispered.

"He got the copy of the letter that Mama sent him. I think he had her meet him there, and he killed her. And you know what else? Everybody talks about the cops Greyson has on payroll like it's a joke, but I believe it. It makes sense why Detective Winthrop hasn't made any breaks in the case—because he doesn't even plan to. I have to find out the truth on my own. Lee Lee . . . I have to get inside of that club."

Chapter 7

Faye

"I'ma throw this money like a free throw. You just keep dancing like a freak, ho. Arch your back, put your hands on your knees, ho!"

The voice of the late Speaker Knockerz filled the entire club, and all of the women on the crowded dance floor did as he said. Shooters was packed that night, and everyone was dressed to impress. The lights were dimmed down low, but the colorful strobe lights made the whole party look lit. Faye and Lee Lee stood at the bar sipping on their drinks. In her glass, Faye had Hen and Coke to calm her nerves. Although she was dressed to have a good time, she was not there do so.

"Are you sure you want to be here?" she asked Lee Lee.

When Faye had told her the plan, Lee Lee didn't hesitate to tell her that she would be tagging along. Faye tried to talk her out of it, but Lee Lee wasn't having it.

"Girl, there wasn't no way I was letting you do this alone! Plus, I needed to get out of the house, shit."

"OK," Faye nodded scanning the club. "Tell me if you see one of the twins."

"You mean triplets?" Lee Lee said. "Because they are your brothers."

"By blood, but that doesn't mean they're my family."

"Now that I think about it," Lee Lee said, studying Faye's face, "you do look a lot like them. That's crazy."

"No, what's crazy is that we still need to figure out a way to get upstairs. I think that's where they keep the camera."

"Do you ladies need another drink?" the sexy bartender interrupted their conversation. He was a chocolate dream, and Faye's eyes lingered on his lips. They were full and looked like they worked wonders at whatever they chose to do. "I'll even only charge you half the price, because y'all are looking mighty fine tonight."

It was true. Lee Lee wore a red strapless dress, while Faye had settled for a black cutout back dress. Their hips were popping, and their asses looked absolutely luscious. Of course, their heels did nothing but make everything sit up and stand out even more. Faye smiled at the bartender and shook her head.

"I'm not even done with my first glass yet."

"What are your names?"

"I'm Faye, and this is my girl, Lee Lee."

"Well, Faye and Lee Lee, y'all aren't done with your drinks 'cause y'all over here babysitting them. Y'all are too busy gossiping about your baby daddy drama."

His last sentence came out like a question instead of a statement. He locked eyes with Faye and gave her a small sexy smile.

"Well, I don't have a baby daddy, for one," she told him and found herself sexily slurping her Hennessey in his direction. "And for two, if I did, why would that be your business?"

"My bad, shorty, I shouldn't have assumed," he said, licking his lips in a sexy "LL Cool J" manner.

"Shit, I got one," Lee Lee butted in. "And if I see that slimy-ass nigga in here, I'ma need to borrow one of those bottles, Mr. Bartender. 'Cause I'm going right upside his head with it!"

"Whoa!" he said, laughing. "Chill, shorty. This ain't even that kind of party. Don't ever let no nigga fuck up your groove. If a fuck nigga is a fuck nigga, let him be that. You can't turn a chicken into a rooster, remember that."

"Giving more advice to the ladies, I see, Quez?" a deep voice countered their entire conversation.

"Chill, Jay," Quez said, showing off his pearly whites. "You know a nigga always has to keep it real."

Lee Lee and Faye turned to see who it was coming from . . . and were face-to-face with Jayden Vincent. Faye turned quickly back around as he reached and dapped Quez up. Lee Lee stepped slightly to the side so she and Faye were back to back. Faye was thankful because now Jayden had no choice but to focus all of his attention on Lee Lee. She had butterflies in her stomach, and when she heard them talking behind her, they turned into knots.

It was Faye's first time ever seeing him up close in person. She realized if she had met him before then, she would have known. They were identical strangers. When she looked into his face, she'd seen all of her own features. She thanked God that their eyes didn't lock because then, her cover would have been blown. Their eyes . . . She wondered if they were their mother's or their father's . . .

"You OK?"

"Huh?" Faye asked, snapping out of her thoughts.

"I said are you OK? You look like that hen finally done got to you. Lightweight."

"Did you . . . Did you just call me a lightweight?"

"Yea, unless I'm wrong?"

Faye looked down at the drink in her hand and took the straw out so she could down the rest of it. It burned her throat going down, but she welcomed the sizzling feeling.

"Damn, shorty."

"Now who's a lightweight?" she asked when she felt a nudge in her rib.

"Hey, are you good?" Lee Lee asked when she leaned back. When Faye nodded, Lee Lee gave her a look and said, "OK, cool. Jayden is about to show me the upstairs of the club. I shouldn't be gone too long."

"She can come too if she wants," Faye heard Jayden say behind her, but still, she never turned her head.

"Nah, y'all go ahead." Faye was grateful for Quez's voice at that moment. "She's cool right where she's at."

Faye crinkled her eyebrows at Lee Lee, but couldn't say to her what was really on her mind right then. She wanted to know what the hell her friend was doing. Lee Lee walked off with Jayden, leaving her with Quez.

"How old are you?"

Faye turned back to Quez and made a face at his question.

"Nobody ever told you that it was rude to ask a woman her age?"

"Yea, but they also said a closed mouth doesn't learn anything. Confusing, right?"

Faye tried to purse her lips, but she ended up looking silly because the smile spread across her lips anyway. There was something about him that she couldn't help but to like. It probably had something to do with his handsome face and nice body. He put her in the mind of a mix between Lance Gross and Kofi Siriboe.

"I'm twenty-five," she answered reluctantly.

"Well, isn't that a coincidence. Me too. That wasn't so hard now, was it?"

"Do you flirt like this with all of the women who come up to the bar?"

"Only if they're as fine as you," he responded, and she rolled her eyes, making to walk away. He caught her hand and flashed her another pearly white smile. "And I have never met anyone as fine as you."

"You're funny," Faye shook her head at him.

Why am I flashing my dimple at this man like he's some sort of comedian? she thought to herself. *Why do my nipples keep tingling whenever he smiles at me? I need to stay focused.*

"How am I funny? I'm just being honest." At that moment, another young bartender, a woman, made an appearance behind the bar. "Welp, looks like I'm off work for the night."

"But the night isn't even over yet," Faye said, checking the watch on her wrist. "There are still a few hours until the club lets out."

"I said I was off work, not that I was leaving." Quez came from around the bar and grabbed her hand again. "Dance with me."

"Oh no," she shook her head. "I didn't really come here to dance."

"Then what did you come to do? Watch everybody else dance? If you're worried about your girl, don't be. Jayden is a cool dude. He's going to make sure she's straight. So why don't you just let loose a little and," he pulled her close to him, "dance with me?"

"OK," was all she could get out.

He smelled so good, and his body felt heavenly pressed against hers. He walked backward all the way to the dance floor, slowly grinding his body on hers to the music. SZA's song "The Weekend" was bouncing off of the walls in the club, and once on the dance floor, Faye realized that her body was already dancing to the beat. They wound and grinded together for the duration of the song, catching each other's vibe and energy. Although they were surrounded by people, Faye didn't see anyone else but him. Before she knew it, they had danced together for five songs, and she felt the one glass of Hennessey sneaking up on her.

"You need to sit down?" Quez asked, noticing a change in her energy.

When Faye nodded, he gently grabbed her hand and led her to one of the tables on the side. He pulled her chair out for her before taking a seat himself and smiled at her.

"What are you smiling about?"

"You," he said. "Where did you come from? I've been working here for almost a year now, and I don't think I've ever seen you in here before."

"Because you haven't. I haven't really been out much lately."

"What, are you one those stay-at-the-house-and-read types?"

"No . . . My mother just died last month," she said and wished she hadn't. Why had she told him that? "This is the first time since then that I really even allowed myself to have a good time."

"I'm sorry to hear that," he said tenderly, caressing her hand with his thumb. "Loss, especially of that kind, is never easy to deal with. But I'm glad you're trying to come back to yourself. That's always the first step in healing."

"You're good at this kind of thing, aren't you?" Faye didn't want him to ask her how Chrishelle died, so she switched gears.

"And this *thing* would be?"

"Giving good advice."

"I mean, I guess you can say that. My parents had three kids, and well, as the middle child, I guess becoming a mediator became a job. It didn't pay very well, but, hey, I always got the job done."

"Nothing wrong with a man that always knows the right thing to say at the right time," Faye said. "We all need someone like that in our lives."

"Well, hopefully, we can exchange numbers so that I can stay in your life for a while."

"That was so smooth!" Faye exclaimed, and they both laughed.

"Whaaaat?" He dragged out the question pretending like he didn't know what she was talking about.

"You know what! Oh my goodness, you might be too smooth for me, I don't know."

"Or you might just be too smooth for me. We'll never know unless we talk tomorrow, and the day after that too."

Faye couldn't remember the last time a smile stayed on her face for as long as it did when she was talking to Quez. He was smooth all right and spoke like a man who knew what he wanted out of life. She could tell that he was intelligent, but had just enough thug in him to make him appealing to her. And his eyes . . . She could tell that they had things hidden behind them. Things that she would love to explore if she just—

"Faye! Girl, I've been looking all over for you!"

Faye's head snapped up, and she noticed Lee Lee standing there. Alone. Faye's eyes searched around, but she didn't see Jayden in sight. When she focused back on Lee Lee, she did, however, notice that her girl's edges had sweated out.

"I've been with Quez this whole time."

"Oh well, I hate to cut your night short, but my sitter just called me and said that Jaymar won't stop crying. I need to go get him." Lee Lee seemed to be in a rush, and she opened her eyes and jerked her neck slightly at Faye.

Faye, suddenly catching the drift that something might have happened, jumped up from her seat. Quez, who still had her hand, didn't let her go until she looked back at him.

"I'm sorry, Quez, I have to go. I'm her ride."

"Give me your phone," he told her, and she grabbed it out of her clutch. He put his number in it and smiled when he saved it and handed it back to her. "I just called myself and saved your number. You'll be hearing from me, Miss Faye."

Faye gave him one last smile before following Lee Lee and walking fast. Faye maneuvered the best she could through the crowd to keep up, but it seemed as if her friend was almost running to get out of there. When finally they reached the outside parking lot and were out of earshot, Faye had to know what was going on.

"Lee Lee, what the hell happened in there? You were gone with that man for hours—and why is your hair sweated out?" she asked once they were inside of the cold car.

"I did what I had to do," Lee Lee said. "Now, please, can you turn some heat on and drive off before Jayden tries to find me?"

"Not until you tell me what you did!"

Lee Lee reached into her chain link purse and pulled out a disk. Holding it up so Faye could see it, she could make out something scribbled on the front of it. On top it read: *Outside camera 4,* and under that was a date. The same day that her mother was murdered. Lee Lee had gotten the video footage. Faye gasped once she realized what it was.

"Fuck, Lee Lee . . ."

"Drive."

Chapter 8

Lee Lee

"So, we meet again."

His voice sent shivers down her spine, but then again, that could have been the Crown Royal she just swallowed. She sidestepped so that she could be between him and Faye.

Damn, he's even finer than I remember, she thought.

Jayden Vincent stood before her wearing a silk burgundy button-up with a pair of tan pants and pair of burgundy loafers. He smelled so heavenly that Lee Lee almost put her neck in his neck just to inhale him. She slowly batted her eyes at him seductively. Although she'd only had one drink, she had drunk it on an empty stomach, and she felt her tip come faster than usual. He wasn't just looking like a snack. He was the fried chicken, macaroni, greens, *and* the corn bread.

"I guess we do," she said. "You stalking me or something?"

"I mean," Jayden looked her up and down, allowing his eyes to linger on her thighs before they settled on her full lips, "you're looking fine enough to stalk. Who did you come in here to meet? That nigga you were on the phone with the other day?"

"Ha-ha, very funny," she said. "But I'm actually just out with my girl for the night. We decided to step out, get our dance thing popping."

"Is that right?" Jayden's eyes twinkled slightly as he stared at her.

"That's right."

"Is this your first time here?" he asked.

"No, I've been here once or twice before. Now that I think about it, I've seen you around before."

"Either me or my brother. Our father owns the place, and we just help run it."

"Oh really?" Lee Lee acted as if she didn't know. "That's dope. Kind of like this Gucci shirt you're rocking. I like it."

"How do you know this is Gucci? Did I leave the tag on or something?"

She laughed as he patted himself down and shook her head.

"No, I just have an eye for nice things. I used to be a booster," she said and shrugged her shoulders. "And I don't care if you judge me because, shit, I had to eat. But when I was doing that, I discovered I have a knack for being able to eye a piece of clothing and know instantly who the designer is."

"One thing you should know about me is that I don't judge anyone," he told her, moving a little closer. "Least of all someone as beautiful as you. The world we're living in today isn't easy for anybody."

"Yea, some people have it easier than others." Lee Lee looked around the club and then winked at him.

"Oh, you taking shots now?"

"Not really a shot, just stating a fact."

"I don't judge you, but you judge me. Ain't that some shit?" he said, and she giggled again. "Contrary to what you may believe, being the son to a man as powerful as my father is, nothing is easy. Just because I have some money in my pocket doesn't mean that other parts in my life aren't lacking."

"Enlighten me," Lee Lee said, leaning into him so he knew she was not intimidated by him.

She stared up into his eyes intensely, opening herself up to him. She didn't know what it was that he saw in her eyes. Whatever it was made him place his hand on her face and stroke it gently with his thumb.

"Another time," he said. "Right now, how about I take you on a tour of the club?"

"Well, I've already seen everything down here."

"What about the upstairs? I bet you didn't know that there is a restaurant up there, right?"

"Really? Is it open?"

"For you? Always. Come on."

"Okay. Let me make sure my girl is all right with that. Hey, are you good?" Lee Lee asked when she leaned back and set her glass down on the bar. When Faye nodded, Lee Lee gave her a look and said, "OK, cool. Jayden is about to show me the upstairs of the club. I shouldn't be gone too long."

"She can come too if she wants," Jayden offered.

"Nah, y'all go ahead," Quez said. "She's cool right where she's at."

Jayden shrugged and offered Lee Lee his arm. She gladly took it, and they walked away. Faye had looked at her as though she was crazy, but they'd come there to get the security footage of the night her mother had been murdered. There was no way that her look-alike ass would have been able to even get past Jayden's security upstairs without questions being asked. Lee Lee just hoped that by going wherever Jayden went would lead her to where she needed to be. She also hoped that his charm wouldn't distract her from what she needed to do.

"So how old is your son?"

"Huh?"

"Your son, how old is he?"

"Oh, I'm sorry," Lee Lee said. As they walked through the crowds of people, she noticed many curious eyes on the pair. "He's three."

"That's a good age. What's his name?"

"Jaymar. That's my little man right there," Lee Lee said, smiling fondly, thinking about her son.

Jayden led her through a door on the side of the club where two big men were standing in front of. They nodded at him and stepped out of his way so that he and Lee Lee could get through. The door led them to a hallway, and at the end of it, there was an elevator to take them to the upper level.

"There actually is a door on the outside where you can get in directly to the restaurant, but we can take a shortcut," he told her when the elevator doors shut. "Did you ever handle your business the other day?"

"Yes, I did," Lee Lee told him. "Thank you, again, by the way. You must be balling out of control if you can afford to give me five bands like it's nothing."

"No man can afford to give any dollar amount away. I looked at it as an investment."

The elevator doors opened, and he stepped out, but Lee Lee's feet stayed planted where they were at. She put her hand on her hip and popped it out.

"What do you mean an 'investment'? I ain't no ho."

"I never said you were," Jayden said, but when he saw that she still wasn't going to budge he elaborated. "I invested in your life. Everybody needs some help, and the vibe I get from you is that you're a good mother. If I can contribute to a black kid growing up into a healthy black man, then I'm going to do it. Now, will you come on? I have a taste for some hot wings."

Satisfied with his answer, Lee Lee stepped out of the elevator.

"Whoa," she said when she took in her surroundings.

It was like a blast from the past. She was in the jazziest, snazziest restaurant that she'd ever seen. Along the black and red walls were framed portraits of famous black musicians, and in the far left corner, there were three long steps that led to a piano on a stage. The tables and booths were black on the red-carpeted floor, and every seat had a menu in front of it. Playing softly from the speakers was a beautiful jazz melody, and Lee Lee felt her body swaying as she walked.

"This is so nice," she breathed.

"Thanks," Jayden said, looking around. "It was my idea to put this up here. I like the old-school vibe."

"Really? I thought the party downstairs was more your scene."

"Why so?" Jayden pulled out a chair for her.

"I mean, I don't know," Lee Lee shrugged after she sat down. "You're young and fine. I guess I figured you were like the rest of the niggas your age. All about the turnup and partying."

"That shit is cool. Don't get me wrong, I'm more of a chill type of nigga, though. I just like to vibe and enjoy my time, honestly."

"Old soul, I like that."

"What you're really gon' like is these wings. I'll be right back, shorty. Let me go put them in the oil."

"Where's the chef?" she asked curiously.

She leaned back and looked around him at the kitchen. The lights were off, and it seemed as they were the only ones up there. Jayden put his arms out and smiled.

"You're looking at him."

"Uhhh . . ."

"No faith!" Jayden laughed and backed away from the table. "I'll be right back."

He went into the kitchen, and Lee Lee watched him navigate smoothly around it through a rectangular opening in the wall. A man that could cook was always a turn-on, and from what she could see, it seemed as though he knew what he was doing. Shortly after she heard the grease popping from chicken being dropped in it, he returned. The sleeves to his button-up were rolled up to his elbows, and he sat down across from her. He grabbed his phone from his pocket and slid it over to her, and she looked at it, wondering what she was supposed to do with it.

"I know how you women act at the end of the night, so I'm asking for your number now."

"That doesn't sound like a question to me."

"Please, will you put your number in my phone, Lee Lee Badass?" he tried again, and she smiled.

"That's what my name is going to be in your phone, too, since you want to be smart. All your little girlfriends are going to wonder who I am."

She opened his phone, surprised that he didn't have a locked code, and went to his contacts. In his phone, there were only a handful of numbers saved, all of them men. She wanted to say something about it but figured it wasn't her place to dig into his personal life like that. When she slid his phone back across the table, he put it away and clasped his hands together. He had a thick scar on his right hand, like he'd been sliced with something sharp, like glass. She liked it; it gave him character. His eyes stared at her as if he was looking for something that he didn't want to find if it meant that he had to look away. His gaze made her squirm in her seat. She couldn't read his expression, and she wondered what thoughts were going through his mind.

"You're looking at me like you want to bite me."

"I do."

His response shocked her, and when he licked his lips, she had to suck her teeth.

Damn, Faye. Why does your brother have to be so fine? I'm not even gon' front like I'm tryin'a hold this pussy from him. Yup . . . He can get it right on this table if he wants to.

Her chest rose up and down slowly as she grew warm between her legs. She felt herself grow wetter with each nasty thought that entered her mind. She imagined how his stroke game was, and if he liked it slow or fast. Probably both, yeah . . . Baby looked like he could put it down. And those lips? They would be so beautiful wrapped around her swollen clit. See, Lee Lee didn't just like to be licked on. She liked for her lover to suck on her pussy like a Jolly Rancher, the blue kind. The two of them fucked each other with their eyes for minutes, and she wondered what he was imagining doing to her. She wouldn't know unless she asked.

"Are you thinking about how well you'd fuck me, or how well you'd kiss all over my pussy?" Her voice came out as a purr.

"Mmm . . . bold. I like that."

"We can play 'Get to Know You' later," Lee Lee told him. "Right now, I want you to tell me what you're thinking at this very moment."

"Right now?"

"Yes. Right now."

"I'm thinking about how beautiful you are. And how much more beautiful you'd be with your face scrunched up."

"Is that right? And what's going to have my face scrunched up, Jayden?"

"Come here and find out."

Lee Lee's legs responded before the statement even completely registered in her mind. Before she knew it, she had straddled him and could feel his hard erection pressed against her engorged clit. While she was walking over to him, he must have undone his belt and slid his pants down. She reached her hand down and stroked him slowly through the hole in the front of his boxers. She moaned at the size of him.

I knew he was going to have a big dick.

Her lips found his, and she kissed him deeply, sucking on his tongue for as long as she could. His lips were so soft, and he kissed her back tenderly. He pulled her dress down, and when released, her breasts bounced freely. He broke the kiss with her lips so that he could wrap his lips around her dark brown nipples. As he sucked and nibbled, his hands made their way to her ass.

"Damn, shorty, you're so thick!" He palmed her cheeks and made them jiggle in his hands.

In her hand, she felt his dick jump from excitement. He was ready, and so was she.

"You want this pussy?"

"Mmm-hmm."

"OK," she said, pulling his manhood through his boxer's slit. "But listen—"

"I'm not gon' judge you for this, shorty. Don't trip," Jayden said.

"That's sweet, but that's not what I was going to say." She licked his bottom lip. "I was going to tell you that I'm a nasty bitch who likes to do nasty shit. So don't be hiding in my bushes after this."

On the last word, she pushed her panties to the side and slid him inside of her. His dick had to be ten inches at least, and its thickness awakened senses that had never been touched before. Her face twisted up in pleasure as she slid all the way down. She went to bounce back up, but Jayden held her still.

"Nah, let me fuck you, ma. Let me fuck this pussy," he said to her.

He held her so she wouldn't fall and stood up. Softly, he laid her on the table, pulling himself out of her so he could position himself on top of her.

"Ooouu!" she moaned. "Put it back. Please . . ."

"This what you want?" he asked, sliding it back in. "Hmm?"

"Yes, baby," Lee Lee moaned.

It had been a little over a month since the last time she'd had sex, so it felt like a long time coming. He felt so good inside of her, and the only way to describe it was pure bliss. He worked his love muscle in and out of her and kept telling her to just take it.

"Just let me fuck you," he breathily whispered in her ear as he plowed deep into her. "Let me treat this pussy."

He hit her with a mixture of slow and fast strokes that had Lee Lee's eyes rolling in the back of her head. Her hands went from rubbing his six-pack to scratching up his defined back. Her legs were shaky, but she kept them up and wide open for him.

"That's right," he said. "Take this dick. Take it."

His thrusts grew so powerful that Lee Lee was forced to wrap her legs around his waist. Her arms flew around his shoulders, and she put her face in his neck.

"Ooouu, baby. Ooouu, baby," she kept moaning over and over while shaking her head.

She could hear how wet she was whenever he pulled out and went back in. She was so gushy, and it turned her on even more that he was not afraid to moan in her ear. He gripped her thighs, and she felt his nails dig into her skin as he pumped.

"Damn, this is some good pussy. Baby girl, you got some good-ass pussy. Can I hurt this pussy?"

"Yes . . ."

"I said, can I hurt this pussy?"

"Unhh!" Lee Lee squealed at the powerful thrust he gave her. "Yessss!"

"OK," he breathed and then proceeded to beat her cat up ferociously.

He was pounding into her so mercilessly that the table began to squeak, but neither one of them seemed to care. Lee Lee felt her walls throb and her clit jump.

"Ahhhh! Jayden!" She arched her back and jerked due to the explosion between her legs.

He pulled out suddenly and held the tip of his dick in his hands as he grunted over her. Some of his nut trickled through his fingers and fell on her leg. A loud beeping noise sounded from the kitchen, and he got off of her.

"That's the food," Jayden said, standing up. "Let me go check on it."

"Is there a place in here for me to clean up?"

"Yea," he said, buckling his belt. "To the far right of the elevator, there's a hallway that leads to my office. I have a full bathroom in it."

"You must do this often," she raised her eyebrow at him.

"Nah, I'm just always working and barely home," he shrugged. "But look, shorty, go get cleaned up and when you come back, be prepared to have the hot wings of your lifetime."

She climbed off of the table and fixed her dress the best she could. He went into the kitchen, and she followed his directions to his office. When she got to the big room, the doorknob turned easily. Her heart began to beat fast when she flicked on the light. Inside, on top of the desk, was a monitor that showed the sightings of every camera in the building. The view kept switching from camera to camera, but every inch of the club was being covered. She looked behind her to make sure she wasn't being watched before she shut the door and locked it.

"Hurry up, Lee Lee. Hurry up," she coached herself. "Where does he keep his security footage copies?"

She walked right past the bathroom and rummaged through all the drawers on the desk. Nothing. She spun around the room until her eyes fell on a tall file cabinet. The only problem was that you needed a key to open it.

"Shit," she said, putting her hands on her head. Then, she suddenly remembered who she was and where she was from. "A paper clip."

Her father, Marley, had taught her how to pick a lock when she was just eight years old. He told her it was a skill that she needed to have since they lived in a world where anything could happen. She quickly located a large paper clip and hurried over to the file cabinet. It took her all of thirty seconds to hear the click that she was aiming for. The first two drawers had nothing in them but paperwork, but the last one was gold.

"Bingo!" She smiled, looking at all of the skinny disk cases.

Her hand sifted through them. They all had writing on them; not just writing, dates. She didn't stop until she found the date she was looking for. November twenty-ninth. She took the disk from its case and slid it under her dress. It was tight enough to hold it in place. She closed the drawers back and tried to put everything back to the way it was before she had entered. She exited the room faster than what she hoped Jayden expected. Stepping as silently as she could, Lee Lee went to grab her clutch from the table, and then made her way back to the elevator. Just as she hoped, Jayden was still busy in the kitchen and didn't even notice her resurface. She held her breath when she pressed the elevator button, happy that it did not make a noise when the doors opened. She rushed inside, and once the doors were shut, she took the disk from inside her dress and put it in her clutch. Her chest hurt because she didn't take another breath until she was back on the first floor.

Trying her best to walk normal, Lee Lee walked through the doors and avoided the eye contact of the bouncers guarding the door. But that didn't mean that she didn't hear their snickers. They probably thought Jayden had slept with her and told her to get ghost.

Fuck what they think. Find Faye!

She hurriedly searched the entire club, feverishly looking for her friend when finally she spotted her in the distance sitting down at the table with the bartender from earlier. She had a big smile on her face and looked like she was actually enjoying herself. It was almost as if she forgot why they were really there.

"Faye! Girl, I've been looking all over for you!"

Faye's head snapped in the direction of her voice. At first, Faye's eyes fished around her, but when they didn't find what they were looking for, they went back to Lee Lee.

"I've been with Quez this whole time."

"Oh well, I hate to cut your night short, but my sitter just called me and said that Jaymar won't stop crying. I need to go get him."

Lee Lee just wanted to get out of there before Jayden realized that she was gone. There were no words to explain why she had left so quickly. They had to get out of there before they were caught red-handed, and she hoped Faye was catching her drift.

"I'm sorry, Quez, I have to go. I'm her ride."

Lee Lee waited for the two of them to exchange numbers, and as soon as Faye was on her feet, she took off toward the exit.

"Lee Lee, what the hell happened in there? You were gone with that man for hours—and why is your hair sweated out?" Faye asked once they were inside of her cold car.

"I did what I had to do," Lee Lee said. Her heart was pounding so loudly that she swore she heard it in her ears. "Now, please, can you turn some heat on and drive off before Jayden tries to find me?"

"Not until you tell me what you did!"

Lee Lee reached into her chain link purse and pulled out a disk. Holding it up so Faye could see it, she could make out something scribbled on the front of it. It was a date, the same day that her mother was murdered. Lee Lee had gotten the video footage. She gasped once she realized what it was.

"Fuck, Lee Lee . . ."

"Drive."

That time, Faye did as she was told and turned the key in the ignition of her brand-new white Chrysler 300. She sped away from the club and headed back to Lee Lee's apartment complex. Lee Lee could see Faye's hands shaking, and when they were finally safely inside of her home, her friend could hardly wait to put the disk in the DVD player.

Jaymar was staying over at her sister's house for the night, so they had the entire two bedrooms to themselves. Faye flicked the TV on with Lee Lee's remote, and the two of them sat on the queen-sized bed watching the screen.

Faye had to fast-forward through a lot of footage to get to the part where Chrishelle could be seen. The video didn't have any sound, but Chrishelle's face was visible as she waited outside of the club. She was at one of the side doors, and they watched her knock a few times before the door finally opened. If the camera had been angled a little more to the right, they would have been able to see who opened the door, but unless that person stepped outside, he would forever be a mystery.

When Chrishelle disappeared inside, Faye fast-forwarded it again and saw that her mom was inside for a little over fifteen minutes before she came back out. The difference between her when she walked in versus when she walked out was that now she had a briefcase in her hands. She turned her head behind her to say something to the person in the doorway, but what happened next was almost too much to watch. As she stood with her face turned to the door, she didn't even see the man in the hoodie behind her sneak up.

The man had something in his hands that looked like
a bat, a metal bat. He struck her one time in the back of
her head, and she dropped instantly. Tears welled up
in Lee Lee's eyes as she watched Chrishelle lying on the
ground with blood leaking from her head. Her body was
still jerking when the person who had been standing in
the doorway finally stepped outside. Lee Lee and Faye
gasped because he was somebody they both recognized.

In the video, he said something to the man with the bat
before reaching into his pocket to hand him a big wad of
cash. After snatching the money, the man ran off screen,
leaving the dying woman alone with the person who had
set her up.

He just stood there for a second, watching her twitch
and jerk. It was almost as if he was getting . . . pleasure
by seeing her that way. He did not help her, and he was
not going to. Instead, he spit on her body and kicked her
hard in the ribs.

"Oh, Mama." Faye's voice shook, and she stopped the
video as the man went to kick her again. She couldn't
watch anymore. "Her last real feeling was pain. They
killed her. They killed my mama. All because of me. I'm
going to kill them all. She didn't deserve to die like that."

"That c-can't be Jayden," Lee Lee heard herself say. "It
can't be. It has to be the other one."

She was referring to the man in the video who had
opened the side door. It was obvious that Chrishelle
had been set up, but Lee Lee couldn't see Jayden doing
that sort of thing. It didn't seem like his character . . . but
then again, she didn't really know anything about him.

"And you know that how? They're identical, and for all
we know, the other one could have been in the doorway
out of camera shot."

"It just doesn't seem like something he would do. That
was a setup."

"Just because you let him run all up in you doesn't mean you know him," Faye exclaimed. "Think with your head and not your pussy! Just because he gave you some money doesn't mean he cares about you. Niggas like that throw money away like it's garbage."

She popped the DVD out of the player and stormed out of the apartment.

Chapter 9

Faye

"Ahhhhhhhhhh!"

Faye's high-pitched scream filled her car, and she banged on the steering wheel with her fists. She hadn't driven off yet because she couldn't see clearly. Tears covered her whole face, and she sobbed uncontrollably. She had finally gotten what she was looking for, but she had not been prepared to see what was on the disk. She couldn't get the image of her mother's body twitching on the ground out of her mind. Nor could she remove the face of the person who'd done it to Chrishelle. It was her face, well, almost her face. She couldn't tell which brother it was just by the video, but just like she told Lee Lee, they both had to go down now.

"Mama, you didn't deserve this," she said, putting her hands over her face and dropping her forehead to the steering wheel. "Why did they take you away from me? You should have just left me where you found me; then none of this would have ever happened."

No regret.

The thought that came to her was in her mother's voice. It was a phrase that she often used, but it meant the most one particular time. As she sniffled and rocked back and forth, Faye spiraled into a sea of her own memories.

"It's not much, but it's my home."

Chrishelle had just unlocked the door to her apartment and swung the door open so that Regret could walk through. For Chrishelle, it might have been "not much," but to Regret, the quaint two-bedroom apartment was everything. It was fully furnished and even had a china cabinet in the living room.

"Your room is down the hallway," Chrishelle pointed. "Go on and look. I'll bring your bag back."

Regret didn't need to be told twice. She zoomed down the hallway and stopped abruptly when she got to the room down the hall. She spun in a circle, taking in the sight. It was amazing. She had a big bed, bigger than the one at the orphanage. There was a desk with many new note-books stacked up awaiting someone to make the first mark, and a cup of writing utensils next to it. On the ground was a colorful rug that matched the comforter on the bed, and when she turned her head to the closet, she saw that it was full of clothes. New clothes, not hand-me-downs, and she only knew that because everything still had the tags on them.

"Do you like it?"

Chrishelle's voice snuck up on her, but Regret didn't jump. Chrishelle set the suitcase she had lugged in on the ground and put her hands on her hips. Regret had a look of wonder on her face, and she waited for the girl to speak. She didn't; she was silent as a mime.

"Honey, is something wrong? I knew I shouldn't have gotten this dang rug. It's too bright, isn't it? We can go back tomorrow and pick one out that you like."

"No," Regret shook her head and looked up at Chrishelle. "No, everything is fine. I-I've never had a room that I've liked so much."

"Well, then, what's wrong?"

"Are you sure that you want me to live with you? Are you going to take me back?"

Her question weighed down on Chrishelle's heart.
That explained why Regret had been so quiet on the
drive home. She was afraid to get too comfortable.
Everybody else had taken her back, so what would
make Chrishelle any different? Chrishelle took Regret by
the hand and motioned for her to have a seat on the bed.
When she spoke, her voice was soft, because her words
were coming straight from her heart.

"Look, honey, since the first day I met you, I knew you
were special. You are smart, kind, and beautiful in every
way. There is no way that I would ever take you back
so somebody else can have all of your goodness. Never."

"What about your own daughter? What if she wants to
come back?"

"Carmen? Please. That girl is eighteen now. I love her
with all my might, but sometimes that still isn't enough
to make someone love you back the way you wished
they did."

"What does that mean?"

"It means that Carmen always blamed me for the fact
that her daddy left us."

"Well, was it your fault?"

"No," Chrishelle sighed. "I don't think so, anyway. He
was just always on the move. There was always some
fun he'd rather be having. There were always other
women. I mean, maybe we could have worked it out if
I wasn't so prudish back then. The woman I am now he
would love, but back then, I guess I just wasn't enough."

"No," Regret squeezed Chrishelle's hand in hers. "You
were enough, but a rib can't fit into the body of the
wrong man. It doesn't matter what you could have done
or would have done differently; if he didn't see you, then
he doesn't deserve you at any time."

Chrishelle was speechless at the wisdom spewing
from the mouth of a child. She blinked her eyes when she
felt them moisten and pulled Regret closer to her.

"I'm never taking you back. I love you, do you know that?"

"I mean you have to; looks like you're stuck with me!"

"You're right! You give me faith in this world," she laughed, and then stopped as if something had just dawned on her. "That's it. Faith!"

"Huh?" Regret asked and leaned back to look at Chrishelle. She wore a confused look on her face. "Faith?"

"Yes, Faith. Look, Regret, I was thinking about your name the other night. And, well . . . How would you feel about changing it?"

"To Faith?"

"Yes, or whatever you like. But from now on out, we are going to live life with no regrets, and the first step is getting rid of that name. You are not a regret to me or anyone else around you."

"I was to my real parents."

"And that is their loss. You will never be a regret to me. So what do you say?"

Regret pondered over Chrishelle's words for a few moments. She, of course, wanted to change her name; she'd always wanted to. However, she did not like the name Faith. It didn't fit her, at least not at that time.

"What's your middle name, Chrishelle?"

"Mine? It's Tamia."

"OK, well, I don't like the name Faith," Regret said and put her hands up when Chrishelle made a face. "I'm sorry! It's just not for me. But I do like the name Faye Tamia . . . Jackson."

Chrishelle's entire face softened when she heard what Regret wanted to change her name to. She knew after the first day that she spent with the girl that she filled a piece in her heart that had been void for so long. It only took three visits for her to sign up as her foster parent. But in that moment, she knew she would be looking to sign official adoption papers.

"All right, then," she approved. "Faye it is. From here on out, that is your name. Now, do me a favor and try on the clothes in that closet. I need to know if they fit because if not, I need to exchange them. How do you feel about starting public school?"

Faye sniffled herself back to reality. She wiped all of the tears from her face, but she could feel how puffy her eyes had gotten. The memories she had of Chrishelle were so vivid it felt like she could run up to their old apartment and see her in the kitchen making dinner.

After she began staying with Chrishelle, it took some time to adjust to the change of having the life of a normal kid. She started public school and got into many scuffles with other kids, but Chrishelle was always there for her. Even when she was wrong, Chrishelle would be in the principal's office defending her. She was there to take care of all of Faye's bruises, even when the bruise was inside. When Faye began to call her "Mom," it was natural, because that's who she was. The love Faye had for her was unconditional, and when she entered her life, Faye couldn't imagine living without her.

Now she had to.

She sighed and swallowed hard. Her thoughts went back to Lee Lee, and her teeth clenched. Maybe she had been too hard on her. None of what was going on was her fault, and Faye shouldn't have yelled at her and stormed out like that. She'd risked her life to get Faye the information that was needed, and, although it was an unpleasant viewing, Faye had expected it. She still didn't even know what Lee Lee did to get the disk or ask her if she made sure there were no—

"Cameras. Shit!"

Before she knew it, Faye was out of the car and back in the building outside of Lee Lee's apartment. She knocked on the chipped brown door until Lee Lee came to it. In the time that Faye was gone, Lee Lee had completely changed clothes. She was in a comfortable Victoria's Secret sweat set and had a scarf over her braids. Faye noticed that her shoes were on, and so was her coat.

"Were you going somewhere?"

"Yea," Lee Lee said, cocking her head. "Outside to check on your ass. I've was watching you through my window. I wanted to make sure you were oka—"

Before she finished, Faye threw her arms around her, and Lee Lee didn't hesitate to give her some love back.

"I'm sorry, girl. This shit just ain't easy. I still have so many questions."

"I know. This shit is just sick."

When they pulled away from each other, Lee Lee stepped back to grant Faye access, and she walked back into the apartment. That time, the two women posted up in the living room.

"I just want to know why," Faye said. "Why not just give her the money? Does Greyson hate me that much?"

"You gon' call the detective?"

"No," Faye said, feeling her anger start to boil. "He could have easily gotten the video if he was really trying. I don't trust him."

"He probably is crooked."

"Exactly," Faye agreed. "Greyson is a powerful man."

"So what are you going to do?"

"Exactly what my mama wanted to do, plus tax. I don't want to be here anymore, Lee Lee. I bought a house, and whenever I'm in it, I feel so empty. So alone. I have a nice new car, but whenever I drive it, I feel like I don't have a real destination. So, I'm going to finish the task, get the money, and get ghost. But before I leave, I'm going to burn Greyson Vincent's entire operation to the ground."

"How?"

"What apartment number did you say you think his sons are trapping out of?"

"Apartment 205."

Faye pulled her phone out of the clutch she hadn't set down. It was the first time the whole night that she'd checked her phone. She saw that the time read just after three in the morning and that she had a few missed calls from Carmen. She knew she was not going to return them, so she erased all three messages that were left for her.

"What are you about to do?" Lee Lee asked, but Faye had already dialed the three digits.

"Nine-one-one, please state your emergency," a young woman's voice answered the phone.

"Hi, yes, my name is Mable." Faye tried her best to make her voice sound meek like an elderly woman's. "Yea. I live over here in the Kings Court apartments in Bed-Stuy, and I can't sleep. Them boys is upstairs making all that damn noise again, and I just heard a gun go off! I'm frightened for my life. They have been bringing drugs and all kinds of ungodly things into that apartment."

"You said the Kings Court apartment?"

"Yes, ma'am. They're in apartment 205—Ahh! They shooting! They shooting! Please hurry!"

Click!

She put her phone back in her clutch.

"Genius!" Lee Lee said.

"This is only the beginning," Faye said, standing to her feet. "I need to ask you something before they get here."

"What's up?"

"When you did what you did to get the disk, did you check for cameras?"

Lee Lee's eyes widened, and she inhaled sharply. She opened her mouth to apologize, but Faye shook her head.

"It's OK. Everything happened so fast. But I don't think you can stay here anymore. Go grab as much shit of yours and Jaymar's that you can. Y'all may have to come and live with me. I'm sorry for bringing you into this, Lee Lee. You got shit to lose."

"Yea," Lee Lee said and stood up, embracing Faye. "You. Where I'm from, we ride for our friends. Jaymar will be OK with my sister for a few more days. Shit, I've kept her son for weeks at a time. I'll be right back."

Faye waited for Lee Lee as she rummaged around her house trying to throw as many things as she could into a suitcase. Every once in a while Faye would look out the window in the living room to make sure the police hadn't arrived yet. She didn't want to be there when they did.

"Lee Lee, we need to go!" she called.

"I'm ready!" Lee Lee ran from the back rooms with a large duffle bag over her shoulder and pulling two suitcases.

"OK, we're out," Faye said, taking one of the suitcases. "No regrets."

Chapter 10

Kayden

The vein on his right temple always bulged when he was worried. Mentally, he was flooded, and it showed all over his face. From the moment he woke up that morning he received nothing but bad news. Sunday was supposed to be the Lord's Day, but for him, it had the devil written all over it.

"What the fuck?" he said out loud to himself as he stood in the kitchen of his condo watching the news.

He had been leaning up against the marble island in the center of his large, modern-styled kitchen, eating a bowl of Cap'n Crunch when the breaking news story hit the big screen. Supposedly, an anonymous drug bust had happened the night before that had led to several arrests. He didn't become alarmed until the cameraman showed a shot of the King's Court apartments, and the news lady said that was where the bust had gone down.

"We don't know the names of all who were involved in last night's arrest," the blond woman said, "but we do know that officials recovered at least $20,000 in drugs and money. More on this story when we come back."

Kayden was in shock. He was so stunned that his mouth was open, and the spoon in his hand was frozen a centimeter away from his lips. He couldn't believe it. The spoon dropped back into the bowl with a loud clank, and his hands balled into fists. Making his way back into his

room, he snatched his phone from off of the nightstand
by his bed and dialed the first person that came to mind.

"Yo, no heads-up?" his voice came out gruff and angry.

"There was no time," Detective Winthrop said in a
hushed tone. "They've been on me like white on rice all
morning. I haven't had time to call anyone."

"That's bullshit, and you know it!"

"It's the truth!"

Kayden took a deep breath and began to pace the floor
in his room. He, of course, had lied when he told Jayden
that he hadn't been trapping out of Kitten's apartment.
And, of course, Jayden had seen right through the bullshit. What Kayden hadn't done was shut down the operation when Jayden had asked him to. After all, the only
man that he answered to was their father, and the last
time he checked, Jayden wasn't him. However, right
then, he was regretting that situation. If the dope and
money were tracked back to him, it would be a bad thing
for them all. As much as he hated to admit it, Jayden had
been right.

"What all do they know?" he asked.

"Nothing yet. None of the men arrested are saying
anything. And that girl you got seems pretty solid. But . . ."

"But what?"

"You know how shit goes once the interrogation really
starts. Do you think they're going to hold up when they
realize how much time they're facing?"

Kayden wanted to say yes, but in actuality, he did not
know. Dino, Flex, and Tony had been riding with him
since he left Chicago. He'd met them while he was there,
and they were the most solid and thoroughbred niggas
around. But then again, everybody was that way when he
was up up. What about when he was down? Would they
talk to the feds once they got hit with them years? His
paranoia told him no, and to get rid of the problem.

"I'ma handle it. I got some people. This shit can't touch my dad's front door, do you understand that?"

"Kayden—"

"What am I paying you for?" Kayden barked. "My involvement in this shit needs to be nonexistent. And what's this shit about an anonymous call?"

"That's what I was trying to tell you."

"What?"

"That apartment complex . . ."

"What about it?"

"Remember that little 'situation' we had awhile back?"

"You gotta be more specific than that, Winthrop."

"With the letter that you intercepted. The one that was supposed to go to your father."

"Yea. I handled that."

"Maybe not. The woman and her daughter lived in the King's Court apartment complex before the mom was— died." The detective caught himself. "So, are you sure nobody knew what you were doing up there? We tracked the number of the anonymous caller from last night."

"And?"

"The phone number is registered to a Faye Jackson. The same name as the daughter."

Kayden's jaw flexed again, and he disconnected the phone. It took him all of five minutes to get completely dressed and be out the door. Knowing it might not have been a good idea, his anger had the best of him, and he drove by the King's Court apartment complex. All he saw was yellow tape and squad cars. There was no way that he was going to make it into that building.

"Shit!" he said and hit the steering wheel of his Mercedes hard with his palms. "Shit shit shit!"

On the way down there, he'd called in a favor to someone, so he knew that the situation with his people in jail would be handled. Even Kitten. Yea, shorty had some good top and could fuck him good, but so could the next slide. She had to go. No loose ends. She would be handled the same way Chrishelle had been.

Without trying to, his mind went back to the day he found the unopened letter on his father's desk. He had been outside of Greyson's office, waiting for the cleaning lady to do her thing. Her name was Tami, and she'd been cleaning the building for almost a year. She was young and had a pretty, innocent face. Her hair was usually in a pulled back ponytail, and whenever Kayden saw her, she was in her work attire. She didn't know that he was there, and he almost missed it, but when she pulled out the envelope slyly from her pocket and set it on the desk, it was the most curious thing. When she left, Kayden made like he'd just gotten there so she wouldn't be alarmed.

"You always do the best job with my father's office. Thank you, Tami," Kayden flashed her his charming smile. "Take the rest of the day off, why don't you?"

"Oh no," Tami shook her head. "Mr. Vincent likes me to clean every office in this building the same way I do his, and his is the first stop of the day! Thank you, though, Mr. Kayden. Have a good one."

With that, she bustled away. It was obvious that she did not want to stay around there for too long. What was more obvious was that, even when he wasn't around, Greyson's power was. Kayden watched Tami swish away down the hallway of his father's Fortune 500 marketing company before he entered the big office space. He had to admit it, his father was living every boy in the hood's dream. He'd figured out the perfect way to blend the street life that was embedded in his DNA and the corporate life that everyone wanted him to live. The marketing company that was, of course, named

Greyson Enterprises, was his biggest accomplishment. When he first started, it was worth about $100 million. Since then, it had grown to five times that.

Curiosity got the best of him, and he picked up the envelope that Tami had snuck in there. The two words on the outside of the envelope had been written with a fine hand. They said simply "From Chrishelle."

"Chrishelle? Who is Chrishelle?"

At first, he didn't open the letter, thinking that she was one of his father's ladies of the night. Then again, why would she feel the need to pay a maid to sneak in a letter if that was the case? Why not just send it in an edible arrangement or something to flatter the old man? His finger acted before his mind told it to, and soon enough, he had the typed up letter in his hands and was reading out loud.

"Dear Greyson,

As you know, I have been caring for your child since she was ten years old. You know, the child that you threw to the side as if she was nothing? The third child that nobody knows about. I'm sure there are many blogs and magazines that would love to get their hands on a story about how their dear Mr. Vincent left his child for dead in an orphanage when he had more than enough means to take care of her. What kind of dent would that put in your pockets, huh? But for a price, I am willing to keep my mouth shut. I want $5 million. Faye, who you know as Regret, is a good woman. She is smart, beautiful, and compassionate. She has deserved much more than what life has thrown her way. The least that you can do as her father is give her a decent future, and you will never have to hear from us again. My

*number is at the bottom of this letter. Please contact
me at your earliest convenience."*

He had to read the letter two more times to get a real
grip on the words. Third child? But when? Had Greyson
stepped out on their mother a long time ago? Is that
why this Chrishelle woman was trying to get money?

He looked in the envelope and saw that there was
another folded up piece of paper inside of it. When he
pulled it out and saw what it was, he had to take a seat
in his father's chair. It was a birth certificate certifying
the birth of a woman named "Regret You Vincent." A
woman who had the same date of birth as he and his
brother, and it wasn't fake. He saw both his mother and
father's signatures at the bottom of the certificate. He
checked the time of her birth and saw that she was born
two minutes after Jayden. He knew that his mother
had died shortly after child birth, and it was always
something that Greyson refused to talk about. Now he
knew why. He and Jayden weren't twins.

He spent the rest of the afternoon doing his best
research on Chrishelle and Regret. Money talked, and
his connections went a long way in New York. In an
hour's time, he found out that Regret had lived in St.
Peter's orphanage since the time she was born and until
Chrishelle Jackson officially adopted her and changed
her name to Faye Jackson. When his informant was
giving him their living arrangements, Kayden cut him
off and asked for her phone number instead. He wanted
a sit-down meeting with her. For once, he might have
found some sort of leverage over his father. He didn't
hesitate to call the number he was given as soon as he
could.

"Hello?" a voice sweeter than honey answered on the
first ring.

"Chrishelle."

"Greyson?" she asked, and Kayden paused.

"Yes," he lied. "I got your letter."

"And?"

"And we need to meet."

"For what? You read what I want. We both know that what I say is true."

"We need to meet so that I can give you what you want. I don't need for this type of thing to resurface. Not now."

Chrishelle was silent on the other end. He knew she was still on the line because he could still hear her breathing. She was pondering what her next move would be, he could tell, so he helped her make a decision.

"No funny business. If you are worried about your safety, meet me at my nightclub, tomorrow night. As I'm sure you know, it is busy every night, so there will be eyes everywhere."

"OK. Tomorrow night at eight."

"Perfect."

His father had bailed him out of a sticky situation; now, it was his turn to return the favor. After he told her the address, he went to his own home and removed all of the money from the safe in the floor under his California king bed. The next night came faster than what he would have liked, but he was at the club where he said he would be. It was busting, like it normally was, and everybody seemed to be having a good time. There was a fine shorty on the dance floor that he wanted to holler at, but before he took a step, one of his bouncers patted his shoulder.

"You have company. Side door," the bouncer told him.

Kayden fixed the collar on his suit as he walked through the crowd of people and to the door. He'd told Chrishelle to knock on the side door because he didn't want her coming through the front. It was too crowded, and she most likely wouldn't have even gotten a chance to speak to the bouncer up there.

"Come in," he said to the casually dressed older woman.

She was beautiful and wore her hair curly on the top of her head. She put him in the mind of Jada Pinkett back in the day, and it was clear to see that she'd held on to her youth without issue.

"You look nice," he complimented her, and she cut her eyes at him.

"I'm not here for compliments," she said and looked around. "Kayden . . . Jayden, whichever one you are, where is your father?"

"Kayden," he informed her. "And my father wasn't able to make it tonight, so he sent me instead."

"You?"

"Yes, me. And if you follow me upstairs, I have your payment ready. My father doesn't need something like this leaking into the media. He just opened another business in California. That's actually where he's at tonight. Come with me."

He held out his arm, and reluctantly, after looking around a few more times, she took it. Kayden had always had a special charm with the ladies. They trusted him, even when they knew that they shouldn't.

"So, you know about your sister?" Chrishelle asked as they headed down the hall toward an elevator.

"Yes."

"For how long?"

"I found out when you sent my father that letter," Kayden told her honestly. "It makes sense now why he never talks about my mother."

"Because he blames her for your mother's death."

"He told you?" Kayden raised his eyebrow at her when they stepped into the elevator, and he pressed the number two.

"No, I have never had the pleasure to sit down and talk to him about it, unfortunately. I was hoping I would get the chance to tonight, but you'll do, I guess." She looked him up and down. "I put two and two together at first and recently found out more information. When he was up and coming, all of New York knew how much he adored Taylor. I went to school with her back in the day. She was a sweetheart. I see why he loved her. He let everyone know it too. When she got pregnant, it was widely known that she was having twins. She never knew about the third child. Her body couldn't handle the stress that came with having Faye. She lived long enough to sign the birth certificate. I truly don't believe that she even saw the name that Greyson chose for the child. She had to have been so weak . . ."

"Damn," Kayden said when the elevator doors opened again and they were on the second floor. "That's deep. I guess I've never really thought to think about how I felt about not having a mother. Pops always kept us busy."

"Too busy to think?"

"No. Too busy to ask questions," he said and pulled his arm away from her. "After you."

Chrishelle, whose eyes swooped the room before she did, stepped off of the elevator. They were now in a restaurant above the club, and it was completely vacant. Kayden stepped out after her and took her to a table that had a briefcase sitting on top of it.

"Nice place," Chrishelle complimented the restaurant's setup. "I get an old-school vibe up here."

"I would say thank you, but this was my brother's idea. It's not open to the public yet, and I don't understand why. It looks done to me."

"He came up with all of this by himself?"

"Our father and me are usually too busy dealing with real business to meddle in these types of things. I would *have hired somebody to design the place, but, Jayden . . . well, Jayden—"*

"Has an old soul. Like my Faye," Chrishelle's tone held a drip of fondness in it. "That's why he hasn't opened it yet. Just because it looks right to our eyes doesn't mean that it's ready to his."

"I feel you. But we didn't come here to talk about the opening of this restaurant, did we?" Kayden asked and opened the briefcase and showed her all of the Benjamins inside.

"How much is it?"

"Half."

"Half as in only two point five million?"

"Yes, you will get the rest once you sign a nondisclosure agreement that I will type up myself. Unfortunately, this family cannot just go solely based off of your word."

"Family? Faye is your family. Five million is nothing to you. In your whole life, I've sure you have all seen fifty times that. She has not. It took me a long time to get her to the point where she could even smile genuinely. I won't sit around another second while we play a game of the princes and the pauper! She deserves the full five. Now. Or I'm on the phone with every blogger and magazine before the sun comes up. Now, you can have my word that I will never tell a soul. I haven't in twenty years. But I'm not signing any paper."

Kayden studied her, trying to catch her bluff. However, if they were playing a game of cards, her poker face was foolproof. She was dead serious, and Kayden sighed.

"I will get it to you first thing in the morning, but only if you agree to not make those phone calls."

"Deal," Chrishelle said, snapping the briefcase closed. "I'll let you know when and where to meet me, and you and your family won't ever hear from us again." She started toward the elevator doors, but paused in the

middle of her stroll and turned to face him. "You would really rather give me this money than get to know your family? Your sister? A person with the same eyes and face as you?"

"You make it sound all mystical and shit," Kayden chuckled and leaned against the table behind him. He crossed his arms and shrugged his shoulders. "She may be related to me by blood, but that doesn't make her my family. I already have one person to split the pie with. I'm not trying to turn it into thirds. Now you have what you want, please make sure that neither me nor my father sees you again. Or her. He named her Regret for a reason."

He watched her jaw clench and saw that his words hit her somewhere unseen to his eyes. She pursed her lips and scoffed.

"I see that it is true what they say. A selfish man breeds selfish-ass children. Maybe it was a good thing that she wasn't brought up with you and your brother, because that girl has a heart of gold. But I will tell you something. Greyson Vincent is not the first kingpin to touch this city, and he won't be the last. Everybody knows that the game has an agenda, and the final page in every book is written the same way every time. He is going to meet the same sticky end as all of the rest. Either in jail or dead. Same with you. So enjoy the half of pie that you want so bad while you can." She patted the briefcase and held it up. "We'll settle for the crumbs like we've been doing. Have a good night, Kayden."

Turning her back to him she got on the elevator and pressed the button to take her back to the place she'd originally come from. As the doors shut, Kayden locked eyes with her, sending an eerie smile right when they touched. When he saw the number light up above the closed doors telling him that she'd made it to the main floor, he pulled out his phone and dialed a number.

"Yo. What's up, Boss?"

"Dino," Kayden said, standing up straight. "She's heading your way."

"Got it."

The phone clicked, and the call ended. He had given Chrishelle a head start, and even an empowering moment. Little did she know, it would be her last moment. He hoped that she felt fulfilled with the millions she had in her possession, because she would only have them for about five more minutes. He went back down to the lower level and saw that the commotion hadn't let up. It was still busting, and everyone was having a good time. A few people called his name, but he was too focused on making it to the side door.

He was mentally timing everything. Chrishelle should have already made it outside by that time, and when he didn't see her in sight, he knew he must have been right. He reached the side door and, as he had informed, the bouncers were no longer there. He told them before Chrishelle even showed up to be gone by the time she made it back downstairs. The less witnesses, the better. He opened the door, expecting to see her already laid out at the side of the building, but saw that he had opened the door a few seconds too early.

Chrishelle had only taken a few steps away from the building, but when she heard the door open behind her, she turned her head.

"What, did you come up with the rest of the money?" she asked when she saw that it was Kayden.

"No, I came to get mine back."

On the last word, Dino, who was wearing an all-black hoodie and jeans, brought a metal bat down hard on the back of her head. The force from the hit was so powerful, Kayden heard the cracking of her skull. She didn't even know what had hit her as she fell to the ground. Her *body began to twitch violently, and it seemed as though she was having a seizure. The back of her head was gushing blood onto the concrete next to her, and Dino went to hit her again, but Kayden stopped him.*

"Nah, fam. She good. Ain't no way she'll survive that," *he said, digging into his pocket and handing him a roll of hundreds.* "Get ghost. I'll take it from here."

When Dino ran off, Kayden stepped toward Chrishelle's body. He watched her for a few moments, wondering when she would take her last breath. He wondered if she would do it while he watched her. There was something about death that intrigued him, especially when he was the cause of it. It made him feel powerful and in control.

"What a waste of a beautiful woman," *he said, spitting on her.* "You just couldn't leave well enough . . . alone!"

He kicked her savagely in her rib cage, causing her to gasp in pain.

"We don't care about your little Regret, but I'll make sure I find her and do her just like I did you!"

He kicked her again, harder, before he placed his last call for the night.

"Detective Winthrop," *a masculine voice answered.*

"It's me."

"Look, man," *the detective said once he heard Kayden's voice. Kayden heard some movement and some background talking before Detective Winthrop got back on the phone. He spoke in a hushed and quick tone.* "The last time you called me, I had to cover up the murders of three teenage boys."

"I paid you well that time, didn't I?"

"Yes, but—"

"But nothing. I paid you well then, and I'm going to pay you better this time. You see, Detective, you're just like me. An opportunist. It could be the smallest crack, but you'd still try to slip through it. Fifty thousand dollars, cash. Right now."

There was a pause.

"What do you need me to do?"

"You're about to get an anonymous tip," Kayden said, feeding him the story. "There is a woman who was mugged on the side of the building. She's lying here dying right now. I need you to be the lead on the case."

"Why don't you just clean it up yourself?"

"That's what I'm doing," Kayden said. "Cleaning it up the legal way. This isn't the first dead body that has been found outside of this club. It won't be the last, either. Handle it."

He hung up the phone before the detective could say another word. Like he'd said on the phone, Detective Winthrop would do anything for the sake of a dollar. That was why Kayden had recruited him awhile back. He had pull, power, and most of all, the drive to do whatever was necessary to make his name look good . . . even if that entailed getting his hands a little dirty in the process. Kayden took one last look at Chrishelle before disappearing back into the club. He was so high off of the fact that he'd just gotten rid of a major problem for his father that he didn't for one second think about the tiny security camera on the side of the wall . . .

He had to get that recording and destroy it. He had been green and placed too much trust in Detective Winthrop. The detective had slipped up, but then again, he didn't know the true nature of why Chrishelle was murdered. He wasn't sure that anybody else did, and he wanted to make sure nobody found out either. He had just gotten his father's trust back and was on his last leg.

The real reason why Kayden was so hell-bent on proving himself to Greyson was because it was no secret that the man was thinking about stepping down for a while.

In the meantime, only one of his sons would take his seat and oversee all of his business operations. He didn't want anything to come between his chances of being the king of it all; he couldn't risk it. He would wipe out anyone and anything that got in his way—just like he did Slime.

When he got back to New York, he saw all of the things that Jayden was in charge of. A year made one hell of a difference, and his brother was the man on top in the streets when Greyson wasn't around. Before he left, when he moved around, people would ask which twin he was. But when he came back, everyone just assumed he was Jayden. It was the most irritating feeling in the world, and when Jayden told him to lie low for a while, Kayden wasn't having it. He wasn't in the business of being in anyone's shadow. He went to his father to pitch himself for a new opportunity, like manning the warehouse, but Greyson shut him down, telling him that Slime had that on lock, but told Kayden that he could "help out" if he wanted to. He then gave Kayden a set of keys and told him the code to get in the warehouse. Greyson told Kayden to prove himself by making sure that all of the work was distributed correctly, like he was some sort of street runner or something. In other words, Kayden wasn't happy with the arrangement, but he made do with it until he figured out his next move. He almost felt bad that Slime got the short end of the stick in his plan, but if it was ever a choice between himself and another, so be it.

He began to rob his father blind, replacing the good cocaine with some stuff he'd brought back with him from Chicago. He originally was going to trap out of Kitten's apartment for a few months, just until he had enough clientele to really set up shop. Dino and the rest of them were in on everything, and when finally he made the choice to off Slime, he called Jayden to make everything normal. His first mistake was letting his twin meet him at the spot. His second mistake was moving so hastily and forgetting about the other problem on his hand. He was supposed to be searching for the sister he had so that he could get rid of her. However, it looked like she was doing his job so he didn't have to.

She was coming to him.

Chapter 11

Jayden

The small squeak in the spinning chair didn't bother Jayden as he spun in it. He was so deep in his thoughts that he barely saw any of his surroundings. His mind was on the night before and trying to decipher exactly what had happened between him and Lee Lee. It was only sex, he kept trying to tell himself, but a part of him didn't feel that way. Since he'd met her, something about the way she held herself sparked a flame inside of him. And when he was inside and swimming in her sea, he was sure that she had felt it too.

He had waited for her like a fool, not knowing that she'd already run out on him. But why? He couldn't figure it out. Why did she leave without saying good-bye? Did she have second thoughts about letting him sex her on top of the table? Was she embarrassed? Or maybe she had to get back to her friend. The shy friend that didn't want to turn around. Or maybe . . . Maybe she didn't want to show her face. But why would she be scared for Jayden to see her?

His thoughts were what led him to watch the security footage from when Lee Lee was in his office. He saw that she never even went to the bathroom. He watched her go through his things and pick the lock to his tall file cabinet. She rummaged through there for a few seconds before she found what she was looking for. She was smooth, sliding the disk under her dress. It was even smoother how she was able to get on the elevator without him seeing or hearing a thing. The power of her pussy had him on cloud nine, in the kitchen cooking for her like a sucker.

Now there he was, spinning in his chair the next afternoon with the empty disk case in his hands. He had no idea what was on the disk, but that wasn't what had him so distraught. Whereas he didn't have the footage to the outside camera, he still had the footage to the inside. It took him awhile to find anything, but before he knew it, he was watching his brother bring a woman, an older woman, up to the restaurant. Now, Jayden knew that Kayden couldn't stand being up there. He was upset that his father hadn't allowed him to decorate it or choose the menu, so Jayden was curious about what he was doing.

At first he thought that maybe his brother had a thing for older chicks and just wanted some privacy. But when Jayden saw the briefcase of money, his attention spiked. What was he doing? And why did Lee Lee want the disk that had the footage from the side camera of the building? No one ever even went over there except the bouncers when they wanted to smoke their weed on breaks. The most that ever happened over there was a month ago when a woman was mugged. But what did that have to do with Lee Lee?

A knock on the door interrupted his thoughts, and when he finally stopped spinning, he saw Kayden standing there.

"Damn, man, you look like shit," Jayden told him.

"I could say the same thing about you," Kayden said, commenting on Jayden's unbuttoned shirt.

It was true, Jayden hadn't gotten a wink of sleep. He also hadn't had time to shower, so he was still in the same getup as the night before. He subconsciously tried to smooth the wrinkles out of his shirt.

"Touché," he said.

"You watch the news?" Kayden asked, but then looked and saw that the TV was off.

"No," Jayden answered, and then raised his eyebrow at his brother's face. He looked unsettled, and that was an expression Kayden never liked to show. "I've been up here all day. What's up? What did you do?"

Before Kayden could stop him, Jayden already had the remote in his hand. He flicked the TV on and turned to one of the news channels. The drug bust was still the main topic of the day, and Jayden was quiet when he turned to another news station. It was the same thing there.

"Nigga . . ."

"I know, bro. It's all bad. But I have it handled. It ain't even gon' touch Pop's front door."

"Handled? I told yo' ass days ago to dead that fucking operation."

"I told you I got the shit handled! I'm tired of you treating me like I'm some type of little boy or something. Don't forget we're the same person, nigga!"

"We aren't," Jayden growled. "Not even close. You may look like me, but we are nothing alike."

"Man, whatever," Kayden waved a hand at Jayden and went to the file cabinet. "I'm just here to grab one thing; then I'm out."

"You looking for this?" He held up the disk case so Kayden could see it.

"How did you—"

"What's on this disk, Kay?"

"Man, nothing."

"Yo, you lying, son," Jayden said. "Nigga, I always know when a lie comes from your mouth. What the fuck is on this tape, man?"

"Look," Kayden sighed and balled his fists in frustration, "just give me the damn disk, and I'll handle it, a'ight?"

"Yea, since you've been so good at handling everything else. I must look like a fool to you." Although the case was empty, Jayden could see in Kayden's eyes how much he wanted the disk that was supposed to be in it. He used that as leverage. "I ain't giving you shit until you tell me what's on here."

Kayden's fists tightened, and he looked at Jayden like he wanted a piece of him. He let out a loud shout before punching the file cabinet, leaving a dent in the top drawer.

"A'ight, fuck it," Kayden said. "I had to tie up some loose ends for Pops."

"Loose ends that I don't know about?"

"Loose ends that he doesn't even know about. Or that he tried to forget."

"What do you mean?"

"Do you even wonder why he don't never talk about our mother?"

"Because who the fuck wants to talk about their dead wife all the time?" Jayden said, wondering what that had to do with anything.

"But he don't never say shit about it. It's uncharted territory, and I know why. He's been hiding a secret from us all these years. We aren't twins, my nigga."

"What? Nigga . . . get out," Jayden had enough and was starting to think that maybe his brother was getting high off of his own supply.

"I'm dead ass. We aren't twins," he said, pulling a folded up white envelope from his pocket. "We're triplets."

He tossed the envelope to Jayden who looked down and saw the words *From Chrishelle* written on the outside of it. He opened it and pulled the contents out. Jayden was about to open his mouth and tell his brother how crazy he sounded until he read the birth certificate in his hands. Dropping that to his lap he read the letter out loud, and as he read, all of the dots began to connect.

"We have a sister?"

"Apparently."

"How could Dad not tell us about this?"

"Look at her name, nigga. She's the reason that our mom died. Her body couldn't handle the third birth. No one even knew she was in there."

"But that's not her fault," Jayden said. "Why would he hate her? That doesn't even sound like Dad."

"That sounds like him now. Dad was a savage back then. One thing never changed, though: his ego and his pride. He let her grow up with a name like Regret and never tried to find her." Jayden looked at the name on the envelope, at his sister's adoptive mother's handwriting, and his brother's words suddenly dawned on him. He slowly rose to his feet. "That woman I saw you with on the surveillance . . . If Dad never got this letter, then . . . Then you met her. That woman on the video was Chrishelle, wasn't it?"

"What are you doing watching footage of me?"

"I was just trying to figure out why anyone would want to steal this disk that you want so badly." He opened the case and showed Kayden that it was empty. "Now I know why. You murdered that woman. What the fuck are you on, my nigga?"

"She was threatening to ruin us!"

"She was trying to get what our sister deserves! And you killed her, man?"

"Yes," Kayden answered without hesitation. "And I'm going to kill Regret or Faye—whatever she's calling herself. I'm going to kill her too."

"Our sister?" Jayden asked, thinking back to Lee Lee's friend. Could she have been right under his nose, and he didn't even realize it. "You're trying to kill our sister?"

"Just tying up all loose ends."

"Yo, you're bugging." Jayden became fully aware that he didn't recognize his brother anymore.

"See?" Kayden shook his head, "I knew you done went soft on me. Look at the bigger picture, brother."

"What bigger picture? That you're going around killing people that you have no reason to kill? These women aren't our enemies! And our sister is family, whether we know her or not! You moving around like a maniac searching for his chance to shine. I bet . . . I bet Slime ain't even do that shit. I bet you set that shit up!"

He was just speaking out of anger, but when he saw the smile spread across Kayden's face, he knew he was right.

"Slime was in the way," Kayden shrugged. "I'm trying to make my way up in the ranks, brother. And you and I both know there is only room for one of us at the top."

Jayden didn't know what had happened until he heard the gunshots and felt the burning sensations multiple times in his chest. It was a pain that he'd never felt before because he'd never been shot before. That's what the goons around him were for, to take and make shots for him. He fell out of the chair and slumped into the corner, clutching his chest. His vision blurred, but he could see Kayden putting his gun back on his waist and walking toward him.

"It was going to come to this eventually, Jay," Kayden told him. "No hard feelings, and it will always be love, brother. But I already have had to share everything with you, and there isn't room for the three of us. I love money more than I care about what twins are supposed to be. We have never been brothers. Pops pit us against each other the day we could walk. It is what it is. Now let me look and see what made you even think about that empty disk case."

Jayden's wind had been knocked completely out of him, and he was going in and out of consciousness. Blood was seeping through his button-up and dripping on the floor while Kayden was calmly looking at the computer screen on the desk.

"Damn, shorty is a freak," Kayden commented as he watched Jayden getting it on with her on the table. "But I'm not trying to see this. Let me fast-forward—oh wait. There we go. So, shorty is the one who got the disk. Ookay. Like I said, brother, you were going soft. You let a bitch get one up on you. I'll take that." Kayden bent down and searched through his brother's pockets for his phone. His finger slid across the screen until he found what he needed. "Let's call shorty for a meet up, shall we?"

Jayden's mind was screaming, but he was too weak to move or speak. When he heard Lee Lee's muffled voice answer the phone, he wanted to tell her it was a setup, but he couldn't.

"You ran out on me last night." Pause. "It's all good. I know things ended on a weird note. I understand why you jetted, and I'm not tripping. But I would love to see you sometime today, if possible." Kayden paused. "You gon' make me beg? Pleaseee. I haven't been able to get you off my mind, and you left before you could eat, so technically, I still owe you a meal." He paused again and smiled big at Jayden. "Perfect. I'll meet you there in one hour. I have the perfect place for us to go."

He disconnected the phone and pocketed it. He bent back over the computer and clicked around a few times. When he was done, he stood up straight and shook his head at his brother, who was barely breathing.

"That Desert Eagle does some damage, boyyy. But I'll catch you at your funeral, Jay, and don't worry. I just erased all the footage from the entire building today and shut off all cameras from your computer. Do you know you've had the same passwords since high school? I gotta go, brother. Looks like I have a date."

With that, he exited the room without a regret in the world to, in his mind, finish cutting all loose ends.

Chapter 12

Lee Lee

She knew she shouldn't have left. She knew the safest place was with Faye, but when he called and she heard his voice, all of that went out of the window. She had been trying her best not the think about the incidents that had taken place the night before, but she couldn't. She couldn't get the feeling of Jayden stroking between her legs out of her mind. She hadn't been able to stop wanting him to call her, and when he did, the butterflies in her stomach went crazy.

"Hello?"

"You ran out on me last night," she heard Jayden say.

"I'm sorry," Lee Lee said.

She got up from the bed she'd been lying on and tiptoed to the open door of the room she'd chosen in Faye's house. She peeked out and looked down the hall and saw that Faye's door was shut. Still, she closed hers, just in case.

"I'm sorry," she said again. "My girl, um, my girl ended up texting me and telling me that she was ready to go."

"It's all good. I understand why you jetted, and I'm not tripping. But I would love to see you sometime today, if possible."

"Ummm . . . I don't know. I don't think I can today."

In her heart, she felt that it was not Jayden on that video, but she knew that Faye would not understand.

They were both her enemies, and there was no changing her mind. The last thing Lee Lee wanted to do was choose between her friend and a man she barely even knew.

"You gon' make me beg?" Jayden's sensual voice sent shivers down her spine again. "Pleaseee. I haven't been able to get you off my mind, and you left before you could eat, so technically, I still owe you a meal."

"I know." Lee Lee couldn't help but to giggle. She bit her lip and thought about her next course of action. She felt that what Faye didn't know wouldn't hurt her. She could just tell her she went to her sister's house to visit Jaymar, which she planned on doing that day anyway. "All right. Meet me in front of my apartment in an hour."

"Perfect. I'll meet you there in one hour. I have the perfect place for us to go."

"OK. See you soon."

Lee Lee disconnected the call and went to the closet to put her tan Ugg boots on. She was fully dressed in a pair of light-colored jeans, a long sleeved white shirt, and a tan puffer vest. She made sure her edges were slicked and her braids were still on point before she used her phone to request an Uber.

She assumed that Faye was sleeping, because she didn't even hear the chime of the alarm when Lee Lee opened and closed the front door. It seemed like the drive took forever, and her Uber driver kept trying to make conversation. She was happy once she saw the familiar cobblestone building, but she was even happier when she saw the familiar SL Benz parked in front of the building.

"What's up?" she said when she got in the car and got comfortable in the passenger seat.

"You," Jayden said, flashing her his most charming smile. "You're looking nice."

"Thank you," she said, and he licked his lips sexily at her. "Where are we going?"

"It's a surprise," he said and rubbed her thigh gently before he pulled away from the curb.

Faye is wrong about him, she thought to herself as she stared at the side of his face.

She couldn't wait for him to wine and dine her. She'd never really had that before. Most men just ordered takeout instead of just taking her out. She knew she was worth more than that, but around there, she just took what she could get. Most men of Jayden's stature looked at women like her as hood rats, so, even though she tried not to show it, she was geeked that he was even giving her the time of day. Before she turned them back to the highway, her eyes fell on a mole on his cheek. She didn't remember seeing that the night before, but maybe she had overlooked it. No . . . She was sure he didn't have a mole on his face. She wasn't that drunk. Instantly, her eyes went to his hand, and she swallowed hard when she did not see the scar there. She sucked in her breath and quickly turned her head to face the front.

"Jayden?" she asked softly.

"What's good, shorty?"

"How much money did you give me the other day? I can't remember."

He must have felt her leg get tense under his hand because he glanced over at her and saw her solemn face. He clenched his jaw when he saw her swallow; then he smirked.

"Damn, this nigga is out here tricking to hoes too? My brother is wilding."

Lee Lee gasped, and tears filled her eyes. She'd walked right into a deadly trap.

"I knew you weren't Jayden!"

"Nah, I'm flyer than that nigga. My name is Kayden. And you? Lee Lee, you are going to lead the person I really want right to me."

"Never!" Lee Lee would never sell out her friend.

She reached over and grabbed the steering wheel and made the car swerve right. The red soccer mom van driving next to them blared her horn loudly when the Mercedes barely missed it. Lee Lee tried to do it again, but Kayden pushed her back in her seat. She figured her next bet would be to try to signal to the other cars for help, but the tint on the car was too dark. She wouldn't have gotten the chance to, even if the passing cars could see her anyway. Kayden hit her so hard in the temple with his fist that her last sight was of the glove compartment as her body slumped forward.

Chapter 13

Faye

"How the hell did this girl end up here?" Faye parked her vehicle in the parking lot on the side of the dry cleaners.

She had come to pick up Lee Lee after receiving a distressed text. Looking around, Faye didn't see her friend anywhere, and when she called, the phone kept going straight to voice mail. Faye rolled her eyes and checked the text message again.

Girl, this damn Uber driver dead ass just kicked me out of the car! He was trying to flirt with me, and I cursed his ass clean smooth the fuck out! I'm over here at Pleasantly Clean, in the back. Please come get me!

Faye groaned because she had told Lee Lee that she was on the way. She didn't know why she wouldn't be out front waiting for her, but Faye went to the back of the building where Lee Lee said she was. She put her hands as deep as they could go in her pockets and put her head down so the bitter wind wouldn't bring tears to her eyes. When she reached the back, she found that she was standing in a wide alley, but Lee Lee was still nowhere in sight. There was a door in the back of the building that was slightly ajar. Faye figured that her friend had gone inside to stay warm.

"Lee Lee?" Faye called when she was inside. "Leeee Leeee!"

Shit! This girl is going to make me look for her ass when she's the one who asked me to come!

"In here!"

She heard a woman's voice call back. Faye was so ready to get in and get out, that she didn't even pay attention to the fact that the voice didn't even belong to Lee Lee. She made her way down a hallway toward an open door, huffing and puffing.

"Bitch, when you ask for a ride you're supposed to be outside and ready! Why did I have to come down here just to fin—Oh my God. Lee Lee!"

She walked through the doorway and into what looked like a hostage situation. Hog-tied and along the concrete wall in the room were eight women, not including Lee Lee. They were in some type of dope shop. Faye saw the powdery substance on the tables in the room. The half-naked women must have been the workers because they still had their gloves on. All of their mouths were taped shut, but Lee Lee's eyes had tears in them when she saw Faye come through the door. Faye rushed to her friend and gently pulled the tape from her lips.

"Lee Lee, what's going on?"

"H-him," she responded.

Her voice was raspy, like she had been screaming, and her eyes looked past Faye. Before Faye could turn around, she heard the sound of a heavy door shut.

"Nice of you to join the show, Regret. Or is it Faye, now?"

She turned her head to face the owner of the voice and found herself looking at a male version of herself. Except his eyes had so much hate in them. Slowly standing to her feet, she swallowed the little liquid she had in her throat and felt her heart freeze over. The plan had been for her to plot on them, not the other way around. She should have known that if they had killed her mother, then it would only be a matter of time before they found her too.

"It's Kayden," Lee Lee said from the ground. "He's behind all of it. He killed your mom, Faye."

"Guilty," Kayden put his hands up like a child caught red-handed. "That bitch was going to destroy the empire my father built. But now I'm getting rid of the problem."

Faye felt her knees become weak, but she tried her best to hold her ground. "You killed an innocent woman. She would have never spoke a word about me."

"I don't trust anybody," Kayden said and began to walk circles around her. He must have seen Faye's eyes go the door because he chuckled. "You need to know the code to get in and out of here, sweetheart. You and your friend aren't going anywhere. Now, tell me, how do you want to die?"

"You're sick," Faye whispered.

She could feel him behind her, but she was frozen in place. There was nowhere to run, and when he placed his lips by her ear, she jumped.

"You think so?"

"I'm your sister." She figured it wouldn't move him, but it was worth a try.

"Sister?" He laughed. "You tried that on the wrong brother. I don't even know you. You aren't my sister. You call me sick, but, no, I'm just a man who's on his way to having it all, and I won't stop until I get it. One sibling down, one to go."

"Y-you killed Jayden?"

"Shot him right in the chest."

"But he's your brother. You've known him your whole life."

"Can you imagine, growing up with a twin brother and having everyone treat you like you're the outcast? The screwup?" Kayden stepped back from her. "It was always Jayden this, Jayden that! Or, Kayden, why don't you act more like Jayden? Kayden, you're being a bad influence on Jayden. Well, I'm sick of it! I've *been* sick of it! And if you think for one second I'm going to deal with two of you, then you're sadly mistaken!"

Faye finally got the courage to turn around to face his madness. His expression was pure rage, and Fay knew it would have to be an act of God if she made it out of there alive. She understood that he didn't hate her; he hated Jayden. And since she was a part of them, she reminded Kayden of him.

"So . . . So you're upset because Jayden was better than you at everything?"

"Yo, bitch!" Kayden got in her face and snatched her up by her neck. "You don't know what the fuck you're talking about."

"You're mad," Faye struggled to speak as her hands clawed at his, "that you are a shadow. A shadow of the better brother. You're reckless."

"Shut up!" Kayden threw her forcefully to the cold ground, and she gasped for air. "Your smart mouth just cost you a life." He pulled a gun from his waist and aimed it at the first girl along the wall. Her eyes grew wide, and she shook her head feverishly, squealing through the tape on her mouth. "How's this for reckless?"

Boom!

Faye looked on in horror when he shot the girl close range in the head. The girl's head bounced back, and the wall behind her was splattered with blood and brains.

"What about this?"

Boom!

"Or this?"

Boom!

"Stop!" Faye screamed when the third girl dropped.

"Fuck you."

Boom! Boom! Boom!

He didn't stop until all of the girls except for Lee Lee were dead. Lee Lee was sobbing. She had been sprayed with the blood and brains of the women who had just been murdered beside her. Faye crawled over to her friend and wrapped her arms around her. She was crying too when she saw the dead women. It only took a split second for their lives to be taken, and the crazed look in Kayden's eyes showed that he had no regrets about it.

"Please, she doesn't have anything to do with it." Faye gripped Lee Lee as tightly as she could. "Please, she has a son."

"I'm sure all these bitches have kids," Kayden said, reloading his weapon. "You think I give a fuck about that?"

"Please. It's me that you want. Not her. Just kill me."

"When I leave here today, I will be the sole heir to my father's empire."

"How are you going to explain it all?"

"I'm a good liar." Kayden shrugged his shoulders and aimed the gun at Faye. "I'll wing it."

Boom!

"Ahh!" Faye called out in agony when the bullet opened her arm up.

"Eat it!" Kayden shouted. "Eat the pain the way I have had to eat it for the past twenty-five years!"

He was so busy yelling that he didn't hear the click of the steel door opening behind him. Kayden aimed the gun at Lee Lee's head.

"You would die for the bitch that led you to your death? You are a fool, shorty."

"I'm sorry," Faye winced and applied pressure to her arm, "that you never felt love. All my life I thought I was an outcast, but I realize that maybe that was the wrong triplet. It was you. Because I have felt nothing but love for as long as I can remember." She moved her body in front of her friend the same way Lee Lee had that night at the club. "I won't let you kill her."

"And I won't let him kill you."

Boom!

Kayden felt the burning sensation in the back of his knee. He fell to the ground. Faye snatched the gun from him with her good hand and jumped to her feet. Her left arm hung limp at her side, and she looked to where the gunshot had come from. Standing there, in an unbuttoned bloodstained shirt with a bulletproof vest under it was Jayden Vincent. There looked to be a few bullets in the chest of his vest, but one must have hit him in the shoulder. He was still bleeding, and the pain from his wound showed on his sweat-riddled face.

"H-he said you were dead," Faye breathed.

"Vest," Jayden grinned sheepishly but flinched from the pain in his shoulder. He turned first to the dead workers on the ground, and then back to where his brother was grimacing on the ground. "I knew you would come here, Kay. I don't know who you are anymore, man."

"You never did!" Kayden sucked his teeth and looked as if he was trying to stomach the pain. "Go on, do it! Kill me!"

Jayden raised the gun up and aimed it in Kayden's direction. His finger applied pressure to the trigger of his pistol.

"*Do it!* I tried to off you—return the favor."

Faye looked at Jayden, and she saw that with every fiber in his being that he wanted to pull the trigger. She saw something in his eyes that she had seen in hers too many times in the mirror when she was younger. Regret. She had already untied Lee Lee, and the two of them made their way to where Jayden was standing. Faye's good arm went to the gun, and she pushed it down gently.

"Don't do anything that you will regret later," she told him. "He's not worth it. Too many people have died already."

"She's right," he said with his eyes still on Kayden. "You're not worth shit, nigga. I'll let Dad handle you. This time, I'm sure he won't be so lenient."

"Come on, y'all," Lee Lee said with a shaky voice. "Let's get out of here."

She began walking to the door, but Faye and Jayden stayed where they were.

"All this time I had a sister," Jayden said, staring into Faye's eyes. "I'm so s—"

"Don't apologize for things that you had no control over," Faye told him, shaking her head at the words that had almost come from his mouth. "Just please take me to the hospital. I've never been shot before, and this shit is painful."

He grinned again and winced, reminding him that he needed to go to the hospital too. But neither the pain in his shoulder nor the pain in her arm could stop the inevitable embrace. She clung to him, and she felt all of the love that she'd been missing since her mother was killed seep through him and into her. She opened her mouth to say something, but as she pulled back, she saw a movement behind Jayden's back. While the two of them had been having their moment, Kayden had reached in his sock and pulled out a small firearm. He pointed it at the back center of Jayden's head, and Faye's reflexes reacted before her mind.

"No!" she shouted and aimed the gun that she'd taken from him.

She fired one time, and the power from the gun jerked her shoulder back, but she still hit her target. Right in the neck. He fell to the side with a shocked expression on his face, and his hands around his own throat that time. He choked and gurgled on his own blood. His last vision was of Jayden and Faye, watching his soul leave his body. He reached a hand out to them, but instead of helping him, Jayden took Fay's good hand, and they turned their backs on their brother forever.

When they reached the steel door, Lee Lee had come running frantically back down the hallway.

"I heard a gunshot and . . ." She looked behind them at Kayden's body. "Oh, he's dead."

"It's over," Faye said. "It's all finally over."

Lee Lee offered support to both of them as they made their way up the stairs. When they got outside, the bitter cold hit Faye in the face, but that time, she welcomed it. She realized that there was so much she'd taken for granted, especially while she was on her revenge binge. As they walked to Kayden's Mercedes G-Wagen, since Jayden had driven it there, she let go of the rest of the malice eating away at her heart. That was not how Chrishelle had raised her to be, and it would not be how she remained.

"So, what now?" Lee Lee asked her. "Are you going to go after Greyson?"

"Yes," Faye replied. "But not to kill him. For closure."

"I'll go with you," Jayden told her. "I can use this golden child shit for something good this time. Where's your car at?"

"In the front, but I don't think I can drive it right now," she told him motioning to her arm.

"Are you good? You need me to carry you?"

"I can't feel it anymore. And you don't look to be in good shape to be carrying anybody. Here, lean on my good side and I'll help you walk to the car."

"It hit the top of my shoulder." Jayden tried to downplay his pain. "I'll be all right."

"I can tell y'all are related already!" Lee Lee said, looking back and forth between them. "Trying to act all tough knowing damn well that shit hurts! Y'all better hurry up and get to this damn car. I just had a gun to my head! I'm trying to go and get to my baby and love on him, but first, I'ma drop your look-alike asses off at the hospital. Come on!"

Lee Lee took the keys from Jayden and went to open the doors. Jayden helped Faye into the passenger's seat, and she touched his arm before he shut the door.

"Thank you for saving us. Why did you do it?"

"Because she got some bomb-ass pussy," Jayden said, looking at Lee Lee, and then back to Faye. "And because you're my sister. Maybe you were the sibling I was supposed to have."

"Only time will tell."

"We have nothing but that, and I know one thing is for sure."

"What's that?"

"You gon' always have family."

He shut her door before he saw the smile spread on her face and hopped in the backseat. For the first time in a long time, despite the blood leaking from her arm and the fact that they had all almost been killed . . . Faye felt happiness. It was radiating through her like the blood in her veins, and that time when the tears fell from her eyes, they weren't from being sad. The only thing left to do was face her biological father. That was inevitable, and the last step to mend her heart.

"No regrets," she whispered as Lee Lee drove out of the alley and toward the nearest hospital. "Not now, not ever."

Love Seldom. Trust Never.

by

Ty Marshall

Prologue

On the last day of his life, Old Man Al relaxed on the deck of his yacht, enjoying the sunset. He was a true vet in the Miami drug game, if there ever was one. He had seen it all and done a lot more. Al was once the person you had to come see. The plug, the gatekeeper to the streets, and he controlled who was able to go through those gates. There was a time when if Al blessed you, you were on in a major way. That was before his gambling problems derailed him. He lost his connect due to short and late payments. Only because of years of doing good business with the cartel had they spared his life. They just cut him off, dried him out. That didn't stop him from gambling, though. Al eventually swindled away most of his possessions. Except for the fifty-foot yacht that he used to cruise the waters of the Florida Keys. Al had a glass of cognac in one hand and a cigar in the other as he relaxed in a chair on the deck, enjoying the view.

Miami really could give a person a false sense of security. The sunny weather, moderate temperatures, and clear blue water gave most people the feeling that they were safer than they really were. It was just an illusion, a beautiful distraction from the dangers that were always close by. Old Man Al knew that better than most. He had experienced both triumph and tragedy here. He loved living on the water and spent most of his time as close to it as possible. It was his tranquil place, but just like the rest of Miami, there were always a million things brewing right under its serene surface.

He finished the drink in his glass and placed it down in front of him. Then he picked up the gun next to the empty glass and tears began to cloud his vision. The shame he felt was eating him alive and made him not want to go on living. His gambling addiction had made him a poor excuse for a man, and he decided that the world would be better off without him in it.

Suddenly, the sound of a single gunshot pierced the air, disturbing the calm and peacefulness, causing a flock of seagulls to fly away. The chirping of birds over-head was immediately followed by the thud of the gun falling from Al's dead hand.

Chapter One

The Early Years

Li'l East stared at the open casket as he sat on the edge of the wooden church pew, his hands resting on his legs. He wore a white dress shirt that was buttoned uncomfortably tight around his neck, a black tie, and an oversized blazer that had been hand-me-downed from one of his older cousins. His slacks were high water, barely long enough to cover the thick pair of white sweat socks and cheap dress shoes he wore. Still, his eyes never strayed from the face of the man lying in the casket. Although he was only eleven years old, East had already been to several funerals at such an early age. Still, he had never seen a dead body up close until today. He had always managed to keep his distance from the front of the church; instead, allowing others to grieve over the dead bodies of their loved ones. But this was a body he couldn't avoid. This time, he was required to sit on the front row, right beside his mother, in between her best friend who offered him comfort by continually rubbing the middle of his back. This time, the body wasn't a family friend or some upstanding member of the community who required that respect be paid to them.

The body in the casket belonged to his father.

The church was crowded. Crying faces filling every row, most of them attractive women his father had been in some form of a relationship with. One woman sat in an adjacent pew, dressed in all-black, holding a small baby that East was sure belonged to his father, her eyes hidden behind dark shades to conceal her pain. The deceased man taking with him a piece of her heart.

The walls of the church were lined with men dressed in dark clothes, their heads bowed, their talking restricted to muffled hisses; their eyes glued to the floor, unable to look up at the man many had known since childhood.

East paid little attention to those around him. Instead, his eyes remained on the waxy glaze of his father's face. The caked-on makeup gave him an artificial gleam. Strangers would always stop East and tell him how much they looked alike. He could never see what they saw. Maybe his hatred for the man wouldn't allow him to. As the pastor began to read from the scripture, East's thoughts were floating far from this place. He was no longer in some stale church with tidal waves of sadness all around him. His mind was in another place, which allowed his expression to be free of worry or emotion. That lasted for as long as it took for the pastor to finish his eulogy. Then East took a deep breath and rose to his feet.

Releasing his mother's hand, he walked slowly toward the casket. He could feel the church grow quieter behind him, then go completely silent. Truthfully, he would have preferred to be alone. Allowed to spend time with his father in private without all the crying and screaming of strangers. He wanted to speak words only meant for his father's ears. It was something he had never had the chance to do while he was alive, and now he would forever be denied the opportunity to do so. The man lying in front of him had been mostly absent from his life since the time he was born. All East had was neighborhood stories, street tales, but he had so many questions that only his father could answer. Now he was forced to say his final good-byes to a man he knew very little about.

The heavy odor of the undertaker's fluids and powders made East's nostrils burn as he stood over the casket, studying his father. For a moment, he allowed himself to see their resemblance. His father was a handsome man. The dark suit he wore did little to hide his muscular build. However, it did cover the bullet holes that had sapped the life from his body. Six shots fired from a gun by a person who would never be arrested. Even at his young age, East understood the world he lived in. It was a world a child his age should have feared; yet, he was strangely drawn to it. Both consciously and subconsciously, he learned that murder was a natural by-product of the streets. The "kill or be killed" mindset was as intricate a part of Miami as the beaches and palm trees. Shootings were not unusual in his neighborhood, which was one of the poorest. Neither were the people who looked the other way, and the secrets that were kept for decades. In ghettos like Liberty City, Overtown, Opa-Locka, Little River, and Carol City, those who ran their mouths received a harsh and brutal punishment. East didn't know why his father had been killed, but like everyone else, he had heard the rumors.

For most of his life, East hated the mere thought of his father, but now he found himself with a bunch of what-ifs. A lump began to form in his throat. The thought of an unfulfilled relationship between the two of them the cause. At that moment, East didn't know who he felt more sorrow for, himself or his father. He lowered his head, closing his eyelids tight, refusing to let a tear fall from his watery eyes. He felt confused by the sudden surge of emotions. He was used to burying his feelings deep inside. He had to be tough. That's what his mother always preached. "You're a young black boy from the ghetto of Miami. Nobody in this world is gonna feel sorry for you, boy," she would say. He was all his mother had, and vice versa. They were each other's protector. Although they didn't have a lot, they always had each other.

So where is this compassion for my father coming from? Why do I feel an ounce of love for a man who never showed me any? he questioned himself, but his young mind had no answer, only more confusion.

East pulled a folded note from his pocket, then leaned closer and slid it into the inside pocket of his father's suit. He had written the note the night before. It was filled with all the things he had ever wanted to say to him—good and bad. He made a silent vow that all the ill feelings he felt toward his father would go in the ground with him on that day, but that was easier said than done. East patted the note in place, looked at his father in the casket one last time, then turned and walked out of the church.

"Are you okay?" his mother, Ebony, asked after the funeral as people filled the community center in the projects for the repast. She was a devoted mother. Although money was always tight, she made sure to spoil her child with attention, teaching him about love, respect, and loyalty. She was grooming a young, black man and knew those life lessons were important for him to have. In a way, she had grown up with him.

Allen Iverson Eastwood was the only child of his young mother. Twenty-five-year-old Ebony Jones was a very attractive woman. She had the kind of alluring features that drew attention to her wherever she went. She was a short redbone with green eyes and perfectly proportioned curves. Her hair was dyed honey-blond and flowed down to her shoulders. Not only was she blessed with looks, she had a heart of gold and loved her son with all of it.

At the tender age of fourteen, she had hooked up with a handsome, smooth-talking hustler named Derek

Eastwood. Six years older than her and much wiser to the ways of the world, his charm proven irresistible. It didn't take long before he became the first man she had sex with.

Deliberate and skillfully, Derek made passionate love to her that first night, educating young Ebony about her virgin body, exploring parts of her that she never knew existed. His ability to please her sexually was unlike anything she had ever felt and better than she could have ever imagined. The sex between them was so enjoyable that she found herself becoming addicted to it. Every time exceeded the last time. With every orgasm, she cried tears of pleasure and pain, both with pure satisfaction. And she always needed more. Derek unleashed the sexual beast within her. She wanted as much sex as he could give her. She craved the kind of lovemaking only he could give to her. Ebony wasn't sure if it was love, lust, or just some misguided teenager obsession that made it all so mind-blowing. There was only one thing she was sure of; she wanted the feeling to last forever. But forever is a mighty long time and apparently, it was too long for Derek. After a tearful phone call in which Ebony explained that she had missed her period for the second straight month, it would be four long years before she saw or heard from him again. By then, their son was walking, talking, and looking just like him. Derek would be in but mostly out of East's life until the day he died, leaving Ebony with the sole responsibility of raising their son.

"I love you, baby," her voice cracked and lips trembled as she looked at her son.

East looked into her eyes and noticed that they were becoming moist. He watched as the tears formed and slowly fell on her cheeks. He hated to see his mother cry. Sometimes he wondered if he was the reason that she was always so sad and stressed. Maybe it was his fault that she struggled to make ends meet. Maybe he was the cause of her pain.

The ugly truth was that she was struggling to keep it together. What East didn't know was that it had nothing to do with him or the funeral. It had everything to do with the fact that she hadn't been able to pop a pill all day. Ebony had been diagnosed with depression and anxiety and had a growing dependence on her prescription medication. She had started to overuse them, especially during stressful times in her life. This was one of those times. The need of the magic little pill to take the edge off was slowly getting the best of her. The only problem was . . . She didn't have any left.

"Please, don't cry, Ma. I love you too," East embraced her tightly. He already stood as tall as her, something he had inherited from his father's side.

Ebony felt his hand delicately wipe the tears from her cheek. She forged a smile, and they stood quietly staring at each other for a moment. When she looked in his face, she saw a smaller version of the man that lay dead in the casket back at the church. After all these years, Ebony had never loved another man the way she had loved Derek. The good and the bad—no other man would ever compare to him. Ebony attempted to break eye contact by looking away, but East grabbed her hand, his expression becoming very serious.

"What's wrong, baby?" she asked.

East took a long breath and sighed, "Ma, you still loved my father, didn't you?"

Ebony was caught off guard for a second. It was like he had read her mind. She thought about how to explain something so complex as love to an eleven-year-old. She reached out and grabbed both of his hands. "Yes. Yes, I did. I loved your father very much," she answered honestly. She could tell East wasn't pleased with her reply.

"Why? He ain't never did nothing for us. Ever," he declared, his anger much more apparent now. He treasured the ground Ebony walked on. It had been a struggle for her raising him alone. As a teenage dropout in the projects, on welfare, with nothing but a tenth-grade education, she was doing the best she could. She busted her ass to get her GED and completed ten months of courses at Everest Institute to become a medical assistant. East never saw her flaws when he looked at her, only her triumphs and her strength. She was godly in his eyes. He vowed to always do whatever was necessary to protect her and change their poor living conditions.

Ebony smiled. She was amazed at how much East had grown. He was quickly becoming a young man. It made her proud.

"Baby, I'll always love him because he gave me you," she confessed, caressing the side of his face and looking in his eyes. "I want you to remember what I'm about to tell you. You were made out of love. And despite what you might hear, your daddy was a good man. I want you to always know and believe that. You hear me?" she said.

East admired her attempt to cast his father in a good light, but he knew better. He would forever see him as a man more concerned with chasing pretty women and money than anything else. East chose not to respond to his mother. He kissed her on the cheek again and offered a halfhearted smile before walking out of the front door of the community center. He was content to avoid the flood of visitors bearing food, sympathy, and fake well wishes.

Outside of the community center, East stood alone, watching a group of teenagers playing basketball in the park across the street. Cars zoomed up and down the street, and people were going about their day like everything was normal. That's because to them it was. Nothing had changed in their world. Death only affected those connected to the deceased. Life went on for the living. In that moment, East found peace in his thoughts. After all, nothing had really changed in his life either.

"Hey," a voice called out to him from behind, grabbing his attention.

East turned around. He immediately recognized the man in the dark blue suit and white shirt with no tie. It was hard not to; Ricardo Wheeler was the man in Liberty City. A local legend, revered by the entire community. The former middleweight boxer was an alternate on the '96 Olympic Team in Atlanta and was a middle-of-the-road contender as a pro. He had done well for himself after his career ended, owning a boxing gym and a grocery store in the neighborhood. He was known to rub shoulders with a lot of important people around the city of Miami.

Ricardo removed the dark shades from his face. "What's your last name, li'l man?" he questioned.

East hesitated, unsure if he wanted to divulge that type of information.

"Is it Eastwood?" Ricardo asked, sensing the boy's apprehension.

"Yeah. Why?" East asked reluctantly.

Ricardo began to nod in confirmation. "I knew it," he said calmly as he flashed a perfect smile. It was a disarming grin, letting East know he didn't have to worry. There was no danger in talking to him. "Derek Eastwood was yo' daddy?"

"I guess you can say that," East acknowledged. "Why, you knew him?"

"I wouldn't be alive if I didn't," Ricardo recalled. He looked over his shoulder back at the street before finishing his story. "Me and yo' daddy go way back. He helped me out of a bad situation, one time . . . back in the day," he admitted, continuing to eye the young man in front of him. If Ricardo didn't know any better, he would have sworn Derek had spit the little nigga out himself. "Damn, you look just like him," Ricardo shook his head in astonishment. "Who's yo' momma?" he wondered aloud in a cool Southern drawl.

East hated for someone to say that he resembled his father. Even more so now that there were rumors swirling about Derek being a snitch. Word on the street was that's what got him killed. Although he didn't know if the gossip was true or not, East felt a great bit of shame about it. Nobody wants to be the son of a snitch. That was a lifetime scar he didn't want to wear. Still, he was surprised to see Ricardo there to pay his respects. He had no idea the two men knew each other or even ran in the same circles. Truth was, he didn't know much about what his father did or who he knew. "Tweet," he answered, calling his mother by the name she was most known by.

"Tweet yo' momma? Get the hell outta here." Ricardo couldn't believe it. His voice was unable to hide his surprise.

That nigga D. His ass was fuckin' pretty li'l Tweet back in the day. He had to be the first nigga to crack the seal on that pussy. Ricardo shook his head. The thought caused a slight grin to crease his lips as he reminisced. East picked up on it.

"You know my mother?"

"Shit, I know yo' whole family. They good people," Ricardo said. He hadn't lied. Tweet had always been a respectable female with a good reputation from a solid family. When she dropped out of high school and popped up pregnant, it was like it came out of nowhere. Nobody even knew she was having sex or with whom. For Ricardo, it had stayed that way until that very moment. "You should have yo' momma bring you by my gym sometime," he offered. "Maybe I can tell you some stories about me and yo' daddy back in the day. Nothing like the shit being said about him now." Ricardo rubbed his hand over his beard.

"I don't care about what niggas saying." East hid his lie well, pretending that the rumors didn't bother him.

"That's good. That's real good. Never worry about what niggas gotta say, especially if they ain't putting no money in your pocket," Ricardo schooled. East didn't know what he admired more, the jewel from Ricardo or the gold Rolex on his left wrist. Ricardo reached into his pocket and pulled out a knot of money. He peeled off a few hundred-dollar bills and walked toward East. "Here, make sure yo' momma get that and tell her I said sorry," he said, placing the crisp bills into the young boy's hand. "And make sure you stop by my gym one of these days. I'll keep an eye out for you."

A white Bentley Continental Flying Spur bending the corner pulled East's eyes away from Ricardo, capturing his attention. The luxury vehicle pulled to a stop at the curb. A medium-built man got out of the passenger side and opened the back door. He had butterscotch skin, a low cut with faint waves, and wore gold-framed glasses. He wore no gaudy jewelry, just a gold Rolex similar to the one Ricardo had on. As Ricardo passed, he whispered something to the man. East couldn't hear what was said, but whatever it was made the two men look his way and stare for a moment. Ricardo got in the car; then the man closed the door behind him. It was the flyest shit East had ever seen in his eleven years on earth. He smiled, and the car pulled off, disappearing around the corner.

Later that night, East lay in his bed staring up at the ceiling thinking about Ricardo's words. He could hear them clearly as if he had just spoken them. The words danced around in his head until they found a perfect resting spot in his brain. East's astute mind allowed him to figure things out quicker than other kids his age. As time passed, his thoughts calmed, and he began to drift off to sleep. He was almost in Dreamville when Ebony knocked gently on his bedroom door and it slowly opened.

Making her way to the edge of his bed, she noticed that he was still awake. "Boy, why are you still up at this time of night?" she asked, taking a seat next to him.

East shrugged. "I don't know. I couldn't go to sleep."

"Why?" she reached out and ran her fingers through his curly hair.

"I was just thinking." His voice was pure, and his eyes were filled with a child's innocence.

"Thinking about what?" Ebony questioned.

"Stuff," he replied hoping to avoid having to tell her actually what was on his mind.

"What kinda stuff?"

"Boy stuff . . . No, important man stuff. You wouldn't understand it," he chuckled.

"Oh yeah?" Ebony laughed with him.

"Yup," he said, puffing out his chest and smiling from ear to ear.

"Boy, please. You ain't no man yet," she said, tickling him, causing East to scream in laughter. "Now . . . take . . . your . . . butt . . . to . . . sleep . . . before . . . I . . . whip . . . that . . . ass," she teased, tickling him with every word.

"OK. OK. OK," East couldn't stop laughing as he pleaded for it to be over.

"Good night, baby." Ebony kissed her son before getting up. She fixed his covers, tucking him comfortably back into bed. Then she walked toward the door but paused when East called out to her.

"Ma," he blurted out, then leaped out of the bed. East raced over to his dresser and retrieved the money Ricardo had given him earlier that day. "I almost forgot. Here, this is for you." He handed the money to his mother.

Ebony looked down at the large bills, then back up at her son with raised eyebrows. She turned her head to the side. Her motherly instincts kicked in, telling her something wasn't right. "Boy, where'd you get this money from?" she demanded.

"From the boxer dude, Ricardo Wheeler. He said he knew my father," East explained.

"Yeah, I know who he is," Ebony said. "I didn't know he knew your father, though."

"He said, he wouldn't be alive if he didn't. Something about my father helping him back in the day," East recalled.

"Oh . . . OK. That was nice of him," Ebony smiled.

"He wants me to come by his boxing gym. Can I go?" East pleaded.

"No, I don't like you fighting as it is," she quickly dismissed.

"Please, Ma."

"I'll think about it."

"Pleeeease," he begged some more.

Ebony saw the seriousness in his face. She couldn't deny that face. "OK, boy, you can go," she caved in to his request. "Now, go to bed." Then she walked out of the room.

Chapter Two

It didn't take East long to give in to his youthful curiosity. Only forty-eight hours passed before he found himself standing in front of Ricardo's boxing gym. The allure was too much for him to ignore. Outside the gym, he noticed the white Bentley from the other day parked out front. Spotting the beautiful vehicle made his heart rate speed up a bit. Anxiety surged through his body, making him question the real reason why he was there.

Do I want to know more about my father? Or more about Ricardo Wheeler? Truthfully, it was a little of both that had led him there. Ricardo's magnetic aura and East's intrigue had created the perfect storm.

Once inside, East played the cut, fading into a corner and watching everything from afar. He felt nervous and excited at the same time. He leaned against a wall, taking in his surroundings and listening to the unfamiliar sounds of the gym. The grunts of the fighters, the thuds from the gloves hitting punching bags, and the hiss of the rope being skipped. It was all new to him. Even the scent of the gym was unlike anything he had smelled before. It was a distinct odor of sweat and leather, spit and blood.

As time passed, he felt more comfortable. East began to make his way around the gym until he found himself standing in front of a vacant heavy bag. He threw a couple of punches causing the bag to sway back and forth slightly. He threw a few more before grabbing the bag with both hands, stopping it again. Peeking around the

bag, he saw a group of teenagers, around his age, standing near the ring. They were admiring the young fighter
inside throwing combinations as his trainer called out
numbers and doted over him. East recognized the trainer.
He was the man that had opened the door of the Bentley
for Ricardo the day of his father's funeral. East studied
the two in the ring, then soon found himself mirroring
their routine, throwing the punches as they were called
out. He was mesmerized not by the fighters but by the
atmosphere. Unbeknownst to him, there had been a
set of eyes watching him from the moment he entered
the gym. Ricardo had been paying close attention from
his normal seat in the corner of the gym. Suddenly, the
trainer lowered his puncher's mitts and turned toward
the group of teenagers gathered around the ring.

"Any of y'all wanna get some rounds in today?" he
asked. His hoarse voice overpowering every other sound
in the gym without having to scream.

The teenagers became silent and filled with tension.
East could feel their apprehension thicken the air.

Why ain't nobody raising their hand? he asked himself, eagerly scanning the boys' faces for a would-be
challenger. Now the whole gym grew quiet. You could
hear the tick of the clock on the wall, but still, no one
answered the challenge. When no one volunteered to
spar with the young fighter, East stepped forward and
raised his hand. "I do," he declared, walking toward the
ring. Every eye in the gym fell on him.

A smile spread across the face of the man inside the
ring. He looked over at Ricardo who was sitting in a corner of the gym, pretending to read the newspaper. He
nodded his head, giving his approval. The boy in the
ring was his son, Ricardo Jr., affectionately known as
Dos. He was the best young prospect in the gym. There
would be no better way to see what East was made of
than to throw him right into the hottest of fires.

"Yo, Tez, that's my li'l man Eastwood," Ricardo declared. "Get 'em some gear. Let's see what he got," he said smoothly, rising to his feet. His words caused a complete frenzy. Kids began gathering around the ring clapping their hands and chanting, wanting to see a fight.

"Dawg, fight! Dawg, fight!" the boys cheered.

"Man, that kid is crazy . . ."

"No one can beat Dos . . ."

"Yeah, Dos 'bout to fuck li'l homie up," a chorus of voices said throughout the gym.

Still, East never wavered. He climbed into the ring, and Tez began fitting him with the proper equipment as the chanting grew louder. East had never worn headgear, a mouthpiece, or gloves before. The equipment felt heavy on him.

How can you fight with all this on? his young mind contemplated.

He had never been inside a ring either, but he had more than his share of fistfights in the neighborhood. He wasn't scared of anyone. There was no bitch in him or fear in his eyes as he looked across the ring, where Dos wore a look of overconfidence on his face. The buzz in the gym was like the Colosseum in Rome. Two young gladiators preparing for battle.

East walked to the middle of the ring, still adjusting the mouthpiece comfortably in his mouth. They touched gloves, signaling the start of the fight. Before he knew it, he was eating two quick jabs that bloodied his lip instantly. The overconfident smirk returned to Dos's face before he threw another one. East slipped it and fired a punch of his own but missed badly. Dos chuckled. Showing his ring experience, he feinted with a jab, then landed a hard right hand that staggered East back into the ropes. With catlike quickness, Dos was right up on him again, smothering him with punches, sending East into a protective shell. Purely off of instinct, East sprang off the ropes with a hard right hook that connected to Dos's head, causing the smirk to disappear from his face. He shot a quick left hook that Dos dipped and returned a left hook to East's rib cage. He faked a right jab that made East throw up his guard to block his face, leaving himself open to a crushing kidney shot.

"Uhhh," East let out a grunt. He was barely able to take the painful blow, staggering against the ropes. Dos moved in for the kill, throwing a quick combo to the body and head, dropping East to one knee, gasping for breath.

Tez stepped between them, but Ricardo intervened. "Nah, don't stop it. Let them dawgs fight. You know the rules. Only the strong survive. The weak gonna fold first." He knew pressure busted pipes. If East had any quit in him, it was bound to show itself inside the ring.

East caught his breath. He looked over at Ricardo, then up at Tez before rising to his feet.

"You good?" Tez asked.

East nodded his head, dying for the chance to get back in the action. As soon as Tez moved out of the way, East shot a lazy jab that Dos slipped easily, then caught him with another combo. Two to the head and one to the body. This time, East took it like a champ and came back with a vicious hook to the body and an uppercut that snapped Dos's head back, sitting him on his ass. The punch drew *oohs* and *aahs* from the other kids around the ring.

Dos banged his gloves on the canvas in frustration, then got back up. Now, East was the one with the smirk on his face. The two of them circled and feinted at each other, this time with more respect and more fatigue. Dos was the quicker of the two, but East clearly hit harder. They stood in the middle of the ring going toe to toe, trading blows even after Tez called time. Finally, when neither could throw another blow, they stopped, both bending over with their hands on their knees, breathing heavily through their mouths.

"Y'all finished?" Tez asked.

"Yeah . . . They're done," Ricardo declared, stepping inside the ring. Both boys were exhausted and battered. "That was a good fight. Give it up for them," he told the group around the ring. They all clapped. Ricardo was impressed by what he saw from the new kid. He already knew what his son was made out of, but East had gained his respect. What the young kid lacked in skill, he more than made up for it with toughness and heart, a trait Ricardo was very fond of.

"Li'l man got crazy heart," Tez spoke in his low, raspy tone to Ricardo as they stood side by side.

"Yeah. I want you to keep him close. Take him under your wing, show him the ropes. I want to be able to keep my eye on him," Ricardo instructed.

"Say no more," Tez replied. He was Ricardo's right-hand man. They had been running together since they were teenagers. Ricardo felt confident with Tez by his side.

For his part, Dos would never admit it, but that had been the toughest fight of his young life. East had gained his respect also. After catching his breath, he walked over with a smile and extended his hand to East. "Good work," he said with childlike enthusiasm.

East hadn't decided how he felt about Dos yet, so he remained guarded. He wasn't used to fighting someone, then talking to them immediately after. It felt weird that Dos was standing in his face smiling, wanting to talk. "Yeah," he replied dryly.

"What's your name?" Dos questioned, curious to know more about the new face.

"East."

"East? That's not a name. That's a direction," Dos laughed. "What kinda name is that?"

"It's my name," East challenged, glaring at him.

Dos could see the new kid wasn't much for jokes. "Anyway, I'm Dos—"

"Dos?" East interrupted, shaking his head. "And you think *my* name is funny?"

"It's because I'm the second," Dos explained.

"I ain't the second nobody. I'm the *first* me," East said proudly and smirked.

Dos sucked his teeth; he had just been one-upped in the verbal game of chess. "Your dad and my dad were friends," he said, switching the subject.

"How'd you know that?" East's brow wrinkled a bit.

"My dad told me. He said you would be coming by the gym."

East looked over at Ricardo who was talking with Tez, then back at Dos and nodded his head.

"How come I ain't never seen you around before?" Dos asked.

East shrugged his shoulders. "I ain't never seen you before either."

"True," he agreed. "Well, if your dad and my dad were friends, we should be too."

"A'ight," East replied.

"My dad about to take me to get pizza. You wanna come?"

"Yeah," East answered, not wanting to miss the chance to take a ride in Ricardo's Bentley.

Over the course of the next few months, he and Dos would become close friends. Had a thing or two gone differently in life, they might have stayed that way.

Ten-year-old Shaun stood in the front of the apartments with his friend Ques, dribbling a basketball, while his twin sister, Shantelle, sat on the steps watching them play. Although they were twins, they had extremely different personalities. Shaun, who everyone called Screw, was hyperactive. He had earned his nickname from people in the neighborhood who said he had a screw missing in his head for some of the crazy things he would do. Shantelle, on the other hand, was more reserved than her brother. A bit of a nerd, she was one of the top students in her sixth-grade class.

"C'mon, Screw, let's go to the park and shoot some hoops," Ques pleaded as he tried to take the ball away from his friend.

"Uh-uh!" Shantelle said immediately. "Momma said we have to stay right here," she asserted.

"Man, shut up!" Screw barked. "He ain't even talking to you. Mind ya business."

"I'ma tell Momma if you go," she promised.

Screw walked over to the steps, looking his sister straight in the eyes, and said, "Snitches get stitches."

Before she could counter, a white car pulling up in front of the apartments drew all of their attention.

"Whose car is that?" Ques wondered out loud.

"I don't know, but I'm 'bouta see," Screw said, sprinting toward the sidewalk with Ques on his heels. When the car came to a complete stop, both boys were shocked to see East get out of the backseat.

"Oh shiiit," Screw said, approaching East and giving him five. Although he was a year younger, the two were best friends, just like their mothers were. "That's a Bentley?" he asked, amazed by the luxury vehicle.

"Yeah," East said with a smile on his face.

"What happened to your lip?" Screw asked, seeing the dried blood.

"Long story," East shrugged.

That's when Screw noticed the other kid emerge from the backseat of the Bentley. They locked eyes at the same time and glared at each other for several seconds.

"What you looking at?" Screw tested. He didn't like his position as East's best friend being threatened. He immediately felt like the other kid was trying to trespass on his territory.

"I'm looking at you. What's up?" Dos replied.

They started walking toward each other, until they met in the middle. They began shoving, but no punches were thrown before East stepped between them.

"Be easy," he said, pushing them apart. "This is Dos." He introduced his new friend. "Dos, this my best friend Screw. And that's Ques," he said, pointing to the short, chubby, brown-skinned one.

"Yeah, *best* friend," Screw repeated.

At that moment, Angela walked out of the front door of her apartment and on to the porch, just in time to see Ricardo get out of the car. "Whose pretty car is that?" she asked but really wanted to ask about the handsome man getting out of it. "And what's your brother and them up too?" she questioned Shantelle.

"I don't know, Momma" she answered. "But East just got out of that car and Shaun tryin'a fight that boy," Shantelle filled her mother in like she always did. Angela stood there with her arms folded, watching the boys until Ricardo and his son pulled off in that pretty car.

"Hey, Ms. Angela," East smiled as he walked up to the steps of the apartment.

"Hey, baby," she smiled back. "Who was that?"

"My friend Dos and his dad."

Is Dos's mother in the picture? she thought to herself but knew better than to ask a child that. "Your mother has to work late tonight, so she asked if you could spend the night here," she told him.

"OK," he answered.

"Momma, since East's spending the night, can we go to the park and play basketball for a little while?" Screw asked, standing in place, dribbling his ball.

"How you know he wanna go?" Shantelle asked, frowning her face.

"How you know he don't?" Screw retorted. "You wanna go, right? Tell her," he looked over at East trying to persuade him with his eyes.

"Cut it out before I slapped both of y'all," Angela chastised her children. "Y'all can go to the playground but be back here before it gets dark. You hear me?"

"Yes," the boys all said in unison, then turned and walked off.

"Can I go?" Shantelle asked.

"No. I need you to help me with dinner," Angela replied.

Shantelle stood up, grabbed her book, and went into the house, her little feelings hurt. As soon as she got in the house, Shantelle sat in the chair by the window. From there, she watched East, her brother, and Ques walking to the park.

Angela watched her daughter stare out the window from the couch. She knew Shantelle had a little crush on East, and she thought it was cute. "C'mere," she patted her hand on the couch. "Come sit next to me." Shantelle got up, walked over to her mother, and sat down. Angela put her arm around her. "I see the way you look at that boy. You like him, don't you?"

"Who?" Shantelle replied, pretending not to know what she was talking about.

"Girl, don't play with me," Angela said, now smiling. "You know I'm talking about East."

"Ill. No, I don't like him," Shantelle uttered.

"Good," Angela said, knowing her daughter was lying. "Because you know, Auntie Tweet is like my sister. Which makes you and East family."

Shantelle remained quiet for a moment, then looked up at her mother, "Momma, you and Auntie Tweet ain't really sisters. So that means me and East ain't really family."

Angela couldn't contain herself. She burst out laughing. "You always was my smartest child," she joked, pulling Shantelle into her warm embrace. The two of them shared a good laugh for a few minutes.

"I do like him, Momma," Shantelle admitted. "But he doesn't pay me any attention. He just wants to hang out with Shaun and Ques all the time," she said with such sadness.

Angela shook her head. Her baby girl had it bad. "Listen, baby, be it East or some other boy, you're too young to have boys on the brain. Don't worry about that. You're a very pretty girl, and you're smart. When the time comes, boys will be lining up to get with you. For now, just keep your head in them books and keep bringing home those good grades I love. OK?"

"Yes, ma'am," she replied, then rested her head on her mother's shoulder. The two of them watched TV until dinner was ready.

Chapter Three

2010

Thirteen-year-old East was growing up fast. Not only in height but also in knowledge. He thirsted for it. Every day he would go to the gym to soak up game from the old-timers that hung around. He also realized that although he admired Ricardo's brazen style, Tez's laid-back temperament appealed to him more. With Tez, his brain always got more of a workout than his body did. They would have long conversations about important things in life. Tez schooled him through boxing lessons while passing down jewels and codes of the street. East was receiving a duel education like none other. As Tez spoke, East absorbed everything with a grasp that exceeded his age.

"You have to be able to put things out of your mind quickly," Tez explained one night as he drove East home in his Mercedes. "You might get hit with a punch that shakes you a little bit. You might lose a round here and there. Bad things are going to happen. You have to get over it quick, or you'll be a sitting duck. It's all about how you react."

Tez had noticed East's down demeanor all day and learned that his mother had lost her job recently. The young man was wearing the stress on his heart and the burden on his shoulders and face. Tez was once again using boxing to teach a life lesson.

East sat in the passenger seat soaking it all in like a sponge. Cruising the city with Tez, he noticed all the pretty women breaking their necks to speak and all the street niggas showing love when they rode by. East always knew the respect Tez had but witnessing it first-hand was something else. Ricardo had love in the streets too, but what the streets showed Tez felt deep-rooted.

Tez had become his mentor, like the father that he needed in his life, and East had become the son that Tez never knew he wanted. There was just something about the li'l nigga that Tez loved. He was smart for his age, very attentive, but most importantly, he was fearless. East was a special breed, whether he knew it or not.

"Tell me what you see," Tez said.

"Whatchu mean?"

"Look around you. What do you see?" he repeated, pointing out the window.

East stared out at the city as it passed by. He was still a little perplexed by the question. "People," he said, causing Tez to laugh.

"Nah, you see opportunity. The world is filled with it. If you can't make money on an earth this big, you deserve to stay broke," Tez explained.

"I'm not tryin'a be broke," East assured him, and he meant every word.

"I already know," Tez smiled. "Look, this shit with your mother is gonna be all right. I don't want you to worry about it," he declared, pulling up in front of East's apartment and parking. He reached into his pocket to pull out a wad of money and noticed East staring at the gun on his lap.

"Why you always ride with your gun on your lap?" he inquired.

"Things can come at you fast, without warning. You never have to get ready if you stay ready," Tez schooled while counting out money from his knot. "Here," he extended the bills toward East. "This should help with the bills for a minute, until ya mother's able to get back on her feet. I know you been stressing. You ain't gotta do that no more. If you need something, come to me." East hesitated to take the money. "What's wrong?"

"I ain't no charity case," East bucked.

Tez chuckled but not in a funny way. He admired the young boy's defiance, but it was misguided on this occasion. He cut the engine off. "You think I look at you like that?" he asked aggressively, turning his body to face East. His tone rose slightly. "If you think I look at you like that, you don't understand shit, and I know you smarter than that." The words spilled out with the hurt of a father's disappointment. He had too much love for East to look at him as anything less than a son.

East nodded his understanding. He could feel the hurt overpowering the anger in Tez's words. "I didn't mean it like that. I just rather earn mines."

"I understand, but . . ." Tez paused to calm himself. His voice was low when he spoke again. "Sometimes you earn things through respect, a'ight? I got nothing but love and respect for you, li'l homie. So take it," He once again extended the stack of bills.

"A'ight, but I owe you," East said before taking the money.

"Real friends don't count favors. That's ho shit."

East nodded and gave Tez a pound. "Thanks."

"A'ight. I'll see you tomorrow."

Ebony saw the Mercedes pull up and knew it was her son being dropped off. She never complained about all the time East spent at the gym. She knew as long as he was there, he would be out of the streets and out of trouble. She also understood that in order for him to grow into the man she wanted him to be, he had to be around strong men like Ricardo and Tez.

Since being let go from her job, Ebony had spent most days sitting in the window watching all the people hanging out in front of the apartment building. She sat and studied them for hours at a time until she got to know them and their roles in the neighborhood. She had never paid much attention to what others were into, but by observing, she quickly learned who was who and what was what.

"Hey, Ma," East greeted upon entering the apartment. "You been sitting there since I left?" he asked. Ebony forged a halfhearted smile, but it didn't fool him. He could see the sadness in her eyes and could tell she was stressed. He reached out his arms and pulled his mother into his tight embrace. He loved her more than life itself. She was his queen. He promised himself that one day he would make everything right in her world and give her everything she wanted in life.

East's loving embrace only made her feel worse. Ebony had lost her job and hadn't been completely honest with her son about why. She had been caught forging the doctor's signature in order to get pills to feed her dependence. Only by the grace of God and the kindness in the doctor's heart, he hadn't decided to involve the police. Instead, he terminated her employment. She hadn't told anybody the truth, not even Angela.

"I know you stressed out about your job, but everything is gonna be all right," East said.

"I hope so." Ebony sounded so deflated.

It hurt to hear and see his mother in such a depressed state. It seemed to be getting worse by the day. "I know so," East replied, pulling the money Tez gave him out of his pocket.

"Boy, give me that! What da hell you do to get all this money?" Ebony snatched it out of his hand.

"Nothing," East assured. "I won it in a boxing tournament."

"Why I'm just hearing about this tournament?" Ebony eyed him up and down.

He shrugged his shoulders. "It wasn't nothing planned. Just happened today at the gym," he lied. Not to be deceitful, he didn't want his mother to feel like she was accepting handouts. He knew she had too much pride for that.

"How much is this?" she asked, beginning to count it.

"It's $2,500. That should be enough to take care of things until you get a new job," East said proudly, filled with excitement.

"No, baby, this is yours. You keep it." She handed the money back to him.

He pushed it away. "Nah, Ma, what's mine is yours."

Ebony nodded slowly but didn't reply. She couldn't believe her eyes. East never ceased to amaze her. But as she finished counting the money, her mind was already in another place.

"Ma, you okay?" East asked, noticing the change in her behavior. He had never seen a look like that before on her face.

"Yeah, baby, I'm good. You hungry?" she asked, quickly pocketing her emotions in front of him.

"No, I ate already. I'm just tired."

"OK, well, take a shower before you go to bed," she instructed.

"I know. I love you," he replied, wrapping his arms around her and kissing her cheek.

That brought a smile back to Ebony's face. She stared at her son. No matter how bad she felt on the inside, with just one look or one word, he could make her feel whole again. "I love you too." Ebony watched him walk down the hallway into the bathroom and close the door.

About an hour later, she found herself sitting alone on the couch with her cell phone in her hand. All kinds of thoughts were racing in and out of her confused mind. She felt ashamed. She couldn't believe what she was about to do. A lone tear rested in the corner of her eye, waiting to fall at any second. The weight of guilt fell upon her, causing the tear she tried to suppress to roll down her cheek, followed by another and another. When she heard the sound of a car pulling up out front, she wiped away the tears and stood up from the couch. Ebony tightened her robe, making sure to cover the silk bra and panties she wore underneath. Hearing the car's engine shut off, then the door open, she took a long, deep breath to calm her nerves. From the window, she could see a handsome man with milk chocolate skin get out and close the door. Ebony walked to the front door to meet him and opened it.

"What's up, beautiful?" he said, entering the apartment bringing with him a manly scent of Calvin Klein cologne.

Ebony inhaled his scent as he passed, then closed the door behind him. She turned to face him with a big grin on her face. "Hey, Lance."

"Is your son asleep?" he asked respectfully looking toward the hallway that led to the bedrooms.

"Yeah. He went to bed a little while ago," she whispered.

Lance reached into his jacket pocket, pulled out a bottle of prescription pills, and handed it to her. Ebony took it and slipped it into her robe. She took one of the $100 bills East had given her and placed it into the palm of Lance's hand. She let her fingernails dance gently over his fingers as she pulled her hand from his.

"Thank you," she said sensually.

"You know you can call me for whatever, whenever, right? It don't have to be just for that," Lance said smoothly like he had said the line a thousand times before. He licked his full lips and put his arms around her waist. His eyes lustfully scanned her entire body. He wanted her, this she knew.

"I know, baby. But maybe some other time," Ebony forced herself to say. Lance was still fine, she had to admit. They had fucked a few times, years ago, but nothing serious ever came from it. Ebony knew from then that Lance was the go-to man for the pills. He moved discreetly, so she didn't worry about her business getting out in the street.

Lance pulled her closer, kissing her on the neck, first softly, then more passionately. She tasted like French vanilla and honey. "You sure, ma?" he whispered between kisses.

"Yeah. I just needed these until I get some more insurance—"

Lance cut her off with a kiss on the lips. "I understand." He continued kissing her. "I just want to taste your pussy." He pulled at the tie on her robe, revealing the silk bra and panties underneath. His dick was swelling in his jeans.

Ebony's clit began to pulsate. The puddle forming in her panties had her ready to submit to his request. She wanted to lead him to the bedroom and sit her juicy vagina on his face. She could use the release, and Lance knew how to work his tongue.

Hearing the sound of movement behind her, Ebony quickly turned to see East standing in the hallway. Still half-asleep, his head was cocked to the side like a confused puppy trying to understand what he was seeing.

"Ma, you all right?" he asked.

Ebony's heart sank to her stomach. She felt so embarrassed, quickly snatching her robe closed. She raced over to him and hugged him tightly. "Yes, baby. I'm all right." She looked back at Lance and swore she could see him blushing through his chocolate skin. His face was filled with awkwardness, and he was at a loss for words. "My friend just came to check on us, that's all."

"Yeah, well, we okay. You can leave now." East could feel his heart swell in his chest. He balled his fist tight, scowling at Lance. He knew right then that he didn't like the handsome stranger.

"He was just leaving, baby," Ebony motioned with her eyes to Lance, who tried to hide the smirk on his face.

Li'l man ain't playing, he thought to himself. He said his good nights, then exited the apartment as smooth as he entered. "Call me," he put his hand to his ear, walking down the steps of the apartment.

Ebony locked the door behind him, then walked East back to his room. She felt horrible. "I'm sorry you had to see that," she apologized, not knowing what else to say. East didn't respond. He just got back in his bed and turned his back. Ebony sighed deeply as she lingered in his doorway.

Minutes later, she stood in front of the mirror in her bedroom, disappointed in herself, a glass of water in one hand and a Xanax in the palm of the other. She placed the pill in her mouth and quickly washed it down with the water. It had been a long day. She couldn't wait for the pill to kick in. She strolled over to her bed and lay down, clicking off the lamp next to her bed, waiting for the euphoric feeling to take over her body.

"Girl, he did *what?*" Angela shouted on the other end of the phone, unable to contain her laughter.

"Yes, had his little fists balled up and everything," Ebony explained from the comfort of her couch as she talked to her best friend.

"That East is gonna be hell when he get older. That's one helluva li'l boy you raising, Tweet," Angela said.

"Who you telling, Angie? I already know." Ebony had filled her friend in on the events of the past night, sparing her the details about buying illegal pills from Lance.

"So you gonna see him again?" Angela's voice lowered to a whisper as she was filled with excitement and anticipation.

"I . . . I don't know, girl," Ebony was unsure. Her body wanted to, but after what had happened with East, she didn't know if it was worth the trouble.

"What you mean, you don't know? When the last time you got some dick? You better let that man knock the dust off that pussy," she joked like Chris Tucker in *Friday*.

"Whatever," Ebony laughed out loud. "I don't need nobody to knock the dust off of nothing over here. Speak for yourself."

"Humph. Don't worry about me. I'm doing just fine," Angela snapped back.

"Hmm-mm. That's why you got arthritis in your fingers now."

They both broke out into laughter.

"Momma . . ."

"Momma, I'm hungry . . ."

Ebony could hear the voices of Angela's twins coming through the phone. She knew that was her friend's cue.

"Girl, these kids working my last nerve," Angela huffed. "Let me get up and fix them something to eat before I get a DFCS case," she joked.

"Tell my babies I said hi," Ebony cooed. "I'll call you later."

Ebony relaxed back into the comfortable cushions of her sofa and laughed to herself. Angela was right. It had been awhile since she had some *good* dick. "Maybe I should give Lance a call," she mumbled under her breath. "His stroke game ain't all that, but that nigga know he can eat some pussy." She smiled at the recollection.

Chapter Four

"Damn, I wish I could go," Screw complained, walking next to East.

"Me too," Ques added.

"Don't worry about it," East tried soothing their disappointment. "One day it'll be my house y'all coming to. And we'll have pool parties every day," he said.

"Yeah, but that's a long time from now," Ques said.

"Man, shut up," Screw punched Ques in the shoulder. "Don't be a hater. One day, I'm gonna have a big mansion like Ricardo too . . . with a club inside . . . with stripper poles," he was thinking out loud. "And I'm gonna fly different strippers in, every week."

Ques looked off into the distance like he suddenly could see everything Screw was saying. East shook his head and laughed at his friends. "Y'all stupid."

"Here comes ya boy," Screw suddenly said, seeing a tinted SUV round the corner, his smile melting into a sneer that traveled to his eyes, causing his face to crumple.

When the vehicle came to a stop, Dos leaped from the backseat before the driver could make it all the way around to open the door for him. "What up?" he said to Screw and Ques.

"What's up?" they both replied. They were friendly with Dos but not friends. The only thing they all had in common was East.

"You ready to roll?" Dos asked East as his driver stood behind him holding the door open. It was his birthday, and his father was throwing him a pool party at their house. Dos didn't have time to chill and talk. He was ready to celebrate.

"Yeah, I'm ready." East slapped five with his friends before leaving them behind.

"I don't know why East hang with that nigga," Screw said as the SUV pulled away.

"'Cause he rich," Ques said with a smile that quickly melted when Screw glared at him. "Yeah . . . Me either." He usually just went along with whatever Screw had to say. Truthfully, he really had no beef with Dos. He actually thought he was cool, but he would never tell Screw that.

"Tweet, what you up to?" Angela side eyed her best friend as they stood in the middle of her living room. Ebony was all dressed up and looked breathtaking. She definitely wasn't planning on spending the evening home or alone.

"East is spending the night out with Dos. So, I'm getting up with Lance tonight," she bragged, twerking in a playful manner.

"Heeeey." Angela joined in on the fun, slapping her friend on the ass while she danced.

"Yeah, girl, I need me some baaad," she confessed. "I didn't know how much until the other night. That man kissed my neck and had me leaking like a faucet." It had been so long since she had allowed herself to even think about sex, but Lance had awakened a burning desire within her body.

Ebony and Angela had a sisterlike relationship. Whenever Ebony needed someone to talk to, she could always count on Angie. Beside East, she was the only person Ebony ever confided in. She could tell her about anything and knew she would never hear it repeated. They had each other's back.

"Just don't put it on that nigga too much. You don't need no more stalkers," Angela said.

"I know, right?" They both broke out into laughter, reminiscing about someone from her past. "I'll go easy on him." Ebony moved her hips in a circle.

"Girl, you something else."

Before Ebony could respond, the sound of a car interrupted them. She walked over to the window and saw Lance's BMW 750 parked outside. "That's him." She glanced back at her friend. "I'll call you later to give you the details. Hopefully it's tomorrow when I do." She stuck her tongue out and laughed her way out the door.

As she entered Lance's car, he couldn't help but stare. Ebony looked like she had walked out of the pages of a magazine. Her long, black lashes and green eyes had him hypnotized. She was gorgeous, and this time around, Lance was determined to make her his.

Ebony slid her body into the leather seats of his BMW. Seeing the lustful look in his eyes, she smiled, knowing exactly what was on his mind. "It's been so long since I've been out," she said, relaxing in her seat and watching the city pass by out the window.

Lance looked over at her as he drove. "A woman as beautiful as you shouldn't be cooped up in the house. You should be able to do whatever your heart desires," he said. "I'm still trying to figure out why some nigga ain't wife you up yet."

She looked over at him. "Why? That's what you trying to do?"

Lance licked his lips. "Most definitely."

"Is that right?" Ebony smiled.

"You hungry?" he asked smoothly.

"Nope."

"You wanna catch a movie?"

"Nope." A seductive smile creased her lips.

"What you trying to do then?" he asked but already knew the answer from the look in her eyes.

Saying nothing, Ebony slowly rubbed her hand on his leg. Lance could already feel his dick getting hard in his pants. He reached over, placing his hand on the inside of her thigh and finessed his hand up her skirt. Ebony went with it and didn't stop him. She moved her seat back and held her breath as he moved her panties to the side. When she felt his fingers enter her, she released a passionate moan. The car was quiet. The only sound was her wetness as he moved his fingers in and out of her. With her eyes closed and her head resting on the headrest, she softly bit down on her lip and moaned. Lance was making her drip with ecstasy. Ebony opened her eyes and noticed the bulge in his pants. She smiled again, her body surging with desire. Lance's eyes were filled with sexual hunger. He craved her. Ebony turned her hips toward him to make it easier for him to reach her G-spot. Lance couldn't control himself. All he could think about was digging deep inside of her, deeper than anyone had ever gone before.

"Oh shit," Ebony moaned as he began to move his fingers faster. "I'm coming, baby . . . I'm coming," she cried out.

"Give me that shit. Come all over my fingers," Lance said, and soon after, Ebony's body surrendered to his demands.

The scene at Ricardo's house was straight out of a rap video. It was unlike any kid's birthday party East had been to before. There were half-naked women in skimpy bathing suits all around him. In the hallways, in the kitchen—everywhere he turned. And there were naked women in the pool out back. East could only imagine that this was what Uncle Luke's house looked like. Still, he remained his normal calm self, not wanting to appear overwhelmed by his surroundings. After all, he and Dos were the underage kids in attendance.

Ricardo made it known to all the women that it was his son's birthday, and they were to give him extra special attention. Titties and asses were being flashed at Dos all night, and he loved it more and more each time it happened.

"You see that?" he asked, tapping East annoyingly. "That's the phattest one so far," he pointed to the female twerking on all fours in front of them. He tossed a few of the singles in his hand on her like he had done it plenty of times before. Dos was in heaven. His father couldn't take him to the strip club yet, so he brought the strip club to him.

East admired the woman as well, tossing a few singles on her. She had the biggest ass he had ever seen in his life, and he felt himself beginning to swell.

The curvy woman glanced over her shoulder at him, her eyes drawn to the growing bulge in his pants. She rose to her feet, walked over, and rubbed up against him, leaving her scent and body shimmer on his shirt. She was pleasantly surprised by what she felt. "I see you gonna be a problem in a few years, cutie," she whispered in his ear, then kissed his cheek.

East played it cool outwardly, though she had fed his ego until it was full. He slipped a stack of singles into the thong bottoms of her bathing suit and smiled.

"Hold up. Hold up. I'm the birthday boy. I need a kiss too," Dos announced brashly with a bright smile on his handsome face. He pointed a finger at each side of his face. The woman's smiled widened. She ran her manicured fingers through his curly top, then planted kisses on both cheeks.

For some strange reason, East's mind drifted to thoughts of his mother. He saw her getting all dressed up to go out. He left before her but wanted to make sure she was safe.

"Where you going?" Dos asked, seeing his friend walking away.

"To call my mother. I need to check on her," East replied like he was the parent, and she was the child.

"Momma's boy," Dos sucked his teeth and uttered under his breath, shaking his head as East disappeared into one of the rooms.

Dos didn't have that problem. His mother had moved to California, and she rarely came to visit him and vice versa. She wasn't really the motherly type and preferred the freedom of having her child live with his father. It didn't bother Dos at all. It was normal to him. Given a choice, he would rather live with Ricardo anyway. He mirrored everything about his father, from his walk to his talk. The name Dos truly fit.

Outside, Ricardo and Tez sat poolside, enjoying the view of two naked women tongue kissing and sucking on each other's breasts in the pool. They were discussing business when the conversation turned to the two boys they were molding for the future.

"I think tonight's the night," Ricardo announced, blowing a ring of cigar smoke into the air. "Time for them li'l niggas to bust their cherry," he said, looking across the pool into the house at them.

Tez laughed and leaned back in his chair. "You think they ready?"

"Hell muthafuckin' yeah. We were around their age when Old Man Al got us our first piece of pussy," Ricardo stated.

"After we got our first taste, we was on a pussy chase that whole summer," Tez recalled the fond memory with a smile.

"Especially that nigga D," Ricardo remembered, speaking of East's father.

They both went silent for a minute at the mention of his name. It was like they were thinking about the exact same thing. Tez bit the inside of his cheek and flared his nose.

"By the way," Ricardo switched the subject, "Old Man Al on his way out. He been fucking up like crazy," he revealed.

"How you know?" Tez inquired.

"I got ears. I hear shit," Ricardo stated. "I'm gonna try to link with the plug myself. I know I can make that happen." He eyed Tez, looking for a reaction but got none.

Silence once again washed over them. It remained that way for a little while until Ricardo broke it. "Fuck all that, though, I'm getting Dos some pussy tonight," he boasted. "Two bitch. It's his birthday." He put up two fingers in Tez's face. "What you think, should we let li'l Eastwood get his dick wet too?"

"Yeah. I got him," Tez's raspy laugh sounded like he needed to clear his throat.

"Sic one of these bitches on that cool-ass li'l nigga. If he anything like his daddy was, he gonna know exactly what to do," Ricardo declared. "I'm picking those two kissing in the pool for Dos," he said, grabbing his crotch. "I might have to give them a test run first, though." Ricardo turned to one of the guys sitting close by. "Go in the house and get my son and li'l Eastwood for me."

The man got up from his seat and moments later, he emerged from the house with the boys in tow. By the time they returned, Ricardo had the two girls from the pool waiting next to him. They knew what they were there to do.

Ricardo said nothing, only giving them a nod. They walked over to Dos, each grabbing one of his hands and leading him away. Dos looked back over his shoulder and smiled with his eyes at East, just as he disappeared into the house. East laughed. Ricardo beamed with pride knowing his son was about to cross over from being a boy into manhood.

The whole time, Tez remained quiet. He was studying the scene and reading faces. Finally, he rose to his feet and slapped five with Ricardo. "I'm out, fam," he declared.

"You out?" Ricardo questioned with a confusion etched on his face.

"Yeah. I'm gonna head to the crib. We'll link up tomorrow," Tez said. He rubbed East on the top of his head. "I'll see you later, a'ight? Have fun."

East took the seat that Tez had vacated next to Ricardo. When Tez neared the back of the house, he paused to whisper something in the ear of a cocoa-brown female with a sexy, well-toned body. The way she wore her hair long on one side and cut short on the other brought out the splendor in her alluring features. Her eyes locked on East like a target as Tez spoke intimately in her ear. When they were finished, Tez continued on his way.

The woman slowly sashayed her beautiful, young body around the pool and over to East, who watched her closely as she approached. "Are you East?" her sultry voice spilled from her lips into his ear.

"Yes," he answered, looking up at her in awe.

"I'm Candice. Come with me, cutie. I want to show you something," she said, waving him to her by curling her index finger. Ricardo laughed and patted him on the back. East rose to his feet. Candice held him by the hand, leading the way into the house and up the steps. As they climbed the stairs, she looked back at him and smiled softly. "Don't be afraid. I got you."

After entering the bedroom, Candice closed the door silently behind them. Nervousness was flowing through East's whole body. He scanned the room, from the floor to the ceiling. His attention was instantly drawn back to Candice when she began to remove her pink bathing suit. He watched it slide off her body and drop around her feet. East felt his heart leap in his chest and his dick pulse in his pants. His heart began to pound in his chest as he soaked in her flawless hourglass figure. Candice's round ass swished back and forth as she walked to the bed. She climbed in the middle of it, leaning back against a pile of pillows.

East felt his eyes widen and his eyebrows rise, along with his manhood. His erection grew as he watched her spread her legs and began to rub herself.

"Take off your clothes, baby, and come get in the bed with me," she said in a seductive voice that made his throbbing manhood pound harder.

He slowly removed his shirt, feeling a little shy, knowing she was watching him. He wondered if his dick was big enough and hoped she wouldn't laugh when he dropped his pants.

Candice sat up on the bed, her eyes widened with surprise when she saw him remove his pants and boxers. She swiveled her way to the edge of the bed to get closer. East walked toward the bed, eager to join her. Candice looked forward to introducing her handsome young student to the joys of sex. She intended to educate him properly.

"Thanks for dinner," Lance smirked, relaxing his head comfortably on Ebony's inner thigh. He could still feel her body shivering as they lay in the plush hotel bed. Ebony was the type of woman Lance dreamed about. She had the looks of a model and the body of a goddess. The combination was breathtaking. He had never been more turned on in his life. He sat up, scanning her body from head to toe.

I could make love to this woman forever, he thought to himself.

Ebony hadn't had sex in a long time, and Lance's oral skills had left her moaning, groaning, and calling for the Lord. She was hot, horny, and exhausted but yearned for more pleasure. She sat up and pushed him on his back. She leaned forward and gave him a passionate kiss. While their mouths were intertwined together, her hand moved down his body and grabbed his dick. She began to caress it until it was hard again; then she swung her leg over him like a ballerina. Straddling him, she began to feed inch after inch of him into her wetness until she had it all inside her. She let out a gasp of satisfaction and began to rock her hips back and forth.

Lance could only lie back and enjoy the ride. His eyes rolled back into his head. The sound of her phat ass slapping against him filled the room.

"Give me that dick, nigga," she shouted. "Give . . . me . . . all . . . that . . . fuckin' . . . dick." She was dominant and controlling, continuing to aggressively bounce up and down on him without stopping.

Lance couldn't take it much longer. He felt his climax approaching like a runaway train. Beads of sweat covered his forehead and began to run down his face. He gripped Ebony's ass cheeks and thrust his hips, trying to match, pump for pump. She accepted the challenge, but he was no match for her. She rode him faster and faster.

"Oh shit! I'm 'bout to come," Lance groaned, pulling out of her and exploding on her ass.

Ebony exhaled deeply, collapsing on his chest. She felt his thick, warm come dripping down her ass. She looked at him. He was exhausted, breathing heavily with his eyes closed. She smiled, basking in the moment. "That was good."

"Hell yeah," he sighed.

An hour later, they climbed back into his BMW and headed for Ebony's apartment. As he drove, a satisfied grin came across his face. He could still smell the sweet scent of her on his lips. It was a gratifying feeling. He felt himself getting harder at the memory of being face deep in her warm, wet vagina. Halfway to Ebony's apartment, his phone buzzed, and he looked at the number. "Fuck!"

"What's wrong, daddy?" Ebony asked in a sweet tone.

Hearing her call him daddy brought a smile to his face. He knew he had put it down. "I need to make a stop and take care of some business real quick. You don't mind, do you?" he asked.

Ebony hesitated briefly before speaking. "I . . . I don't know about that, Lance. I really just wanna go home and get in my bed. It's late."

"You got a curfew or something?" he joked. "Nah, seriously, it'll be real quick. I promise," he assured her with charming eyes.

Ebony folded her arms across her chest. "OK," she pouted playfully. "Go handle your business."

"Thank you," he smiled, then made a U-turn.

Fifteen minutes passed before Lance pulled up in front of a pool hall and wing spot. Expensive cars were parked all around the popular hangout. Lance opened his glove compartment, and Ebony's eyes lit up, seeing bottles of pills inside. She made sure to conceal her excitement, not wanting to alarm him. He took out one of the bottles and slammed it shut.

"I'll be right back," he promised, then opened the door and got out.

The moment he vanished from her sight, Ebony began wondering if she could slip a few pills into her purse without him noticing they were missing. She looked out the window nervously, thinking he could come back at any time. Before she opened the glove compartment, she began to have second thoughts. Taking pills from the doctor's office was one thing but taking from Lance felt like stealing. It felt wrong.

Nah, I ain't no thief, she told herself and aborted the mission. Instead, she switched her attention to her surroundings. There were several men standing in front of the pool hall talking. Ebony could tell they were in the game. Their loud jewelry and expensive clothes told their story immediately. That's what she appreciated about Lance. He moved discreetly and didn't advertise his occupation to the world.

The entire lot was filled with luxury vehicles. Ebony knew she was in the midst of real hustlers and street niggas. The scene made her a little uncomfortable, and she started to get impatient. As she scanned the parking lot, a specific car held her interest a little longer than the rest. She was certain that she recognized the black Mercedes. Just then, Lance walked out the front door of the pool hall and got in.

"That didn't take long, right?" he looked at her and said. "I told you it would be quick." He smiled, turning the key in the ignition.

Boom! Boom! Boom!

The sound of gunshots sent everyone scattering and stunned Ebony, causing a loud ringing in her ears, the bright flashes lighting up the inside of the car. The powerful blast entered Lance's head just behind his left ear. The bullet burst through his head before exiting through his face. The force of the shot blew the back of his head off, along with a portion of his brain. Blood and brains splattered all over the dashboard.

Ebony looked over in time to see Lance's body slump over into her lap, blood spilling from the back of his head. She began screaming hysterically at the top of her lungs, looking down at the gruesome sight. She was ready for a straitjacket. She could feel her skirt absorbing his warm blood. Her heart was hammering in her chest. She was forced to swallow her next scream, or maybe it got caught in her throat when she found herself staring down the barrel of the same gun that had just killed Lance. Ebony closed her eyes, throwing her hands up in surrender like they were bulletproof and prayed that no more shots came. Surprisingly, they didn't, but when she opened her eyes, she wished she hadn't. Ebony was staring Lance's killer right in the face and couldn't believe her eyes. Before she could find her voice, he walked away from the car.

"Oh my God . . . Oh my God . . . Oh my God," Ebony repeated, flying into a frenzied state of panic. She struggled to get Lance off her lap, tussling with his body but couldn't budge him. He was too heavy. Her legs felt trapped underneath his weight, pinning her to the leather seat. Her heart raced uncontrollably, tears running down her face ruining what was left of her eye makeup. She continued to push and squirm, wiggle and twist until she freed herself, clearing her escape from the car. Ebony took off running, snatching her shoes off in the first few steps, then stopping in her tracks. She turned on a dime and scurried back to the open car door. Reaching inside, she popped open the glove compartment, grabbing the remaining bottles of pills and threw them into her handbag as she fled the scene.

A short time later, Ebony stood in front of her apartment, trembling, trying to get the key in the door. She was a nervous wreck, turning something so routine into an unmanageable task. She had hailed a taxi home but didn't say a word the whole ride. She couldn't get the image of Lance's bullet-riddled head out of her mind.

One minute we were fucking, and then . . . She couldn't even bring herself to finish the thought.

"Fuck," she complained about her shaky hands, frustration getting the best of her.

Already stressed out and skittish, the sound of footsteps at her rear rattled her completely. She fumbled everything in her grasp, sending her shoes, handbag, and keys tumbling to the ground. She yelped as the man appeared from the shadows. It was him. Lance's killer.

"Sshh." Tez put his finger to his lips, holding a gun in his other hand. "Pick up the keys and open the door," he instructed her. Knowing that East wasn't at home, he'd rather continue their conversation inside her apartment.

"Please," she begged, her face wrinkling into an ugly cry. "I won't say anything. I promise."

Tez hushed her again. "Open the door."

"Please," she continued to beg. "I got East," she cried, hoping by mentioning her son's name, it would somehow save her from Tez's wrath.

"Open the door." This time he repeated himself with irritation in his command. Ebony didn't say another word; she just did what she was told. "Sit down," Tez demanded, closing the door behind them and locking it.

Ebony took a seat on the couch. Burying her face into her hands, she began crying harder. She couldn't believe how her night out had gone so wrong.

Tez stood there watching her cry, wondering, what were the odds? He had been searching for Lance for weeks. He owed Tez money and hadn't been answering his phone calls. Lance moved so stealthily, he was hard to catch up to. And just like that, he pulled into the wrong parking lot at the right time. It was like he fell right into Tez's lap. Lance never saw it coming, but Tez never imagined Ebony being in the passenger seat. He almost killed her purely off of reflex. Truthfully, he was still wrestling with the thought. It went against everything he believed to leave a witness to a murder. But his love for East trumped what he knew needed to be done, and that's what had him torn. If Ebony was anybody else, she would've already been dead, but he had already taken enough from East.

Tez walked over and took a seat next to Ebony on the couch. "Look, Tweet, I'm not here to hurt you," his raspy voice always made him sound like a lifetime smoker, although he never was. "I just wanted to make sure we have a clear understanding about tonight."

"Why'd you kill Lance?" she cried out. She was so distraught.

"That's none of your business. You should just be more careful about the company you keep," he informed her. There was no need for details, and there wasn't any emotion in his expression. At least not the type Ebony expected from a man who had just murdered someone. "What you seen tonight can never be talked about again. Not to your homegirls. Not to your family. Not even to East. You understand me?" he declared. "If you do, we gonna have to go down a road I'd really hate to travel with you. I love East, and I never want to do anything to hurt him. . . ." He stopped himself from talking, feeling a bit choked up. He began shaking his head, grasping the depth of his love for East.

Ebony looked up, and for the first time, she saw emotion in his face. His eyes were watery. The expression had only appeared when Tez spoke about hurting East. She could see the deep affection he had for her child, and it touched her soul. Although he may not have known it, Tez had just endeared himself to her, not in a romantic way but like family. She would hold his secret for eternity and never speak on it again.

"I gotchu, Tez. I promise. My lips are sealed forever. You have nothing to worry about," she assured him through her sniffles.

He stared into her eyes and couldn't find the lie. With most people, that wouldn't be enough for them to live, but tonight, it sufficed. He stood up, tucked his gun into his waist, and walked to the door. Ebony got up and followed him.

"Thank you, Tez. Thank you so much," she whispered softly. She was grateful to him for sparing her life, but strangely, she was thankful for him being in East's life too. He may not have been the clean-cut role model she once envisioned him to be. That was kind of a fantasy anyway. Everybody from the neighborhood had some type of dirt with them; it came with the territory. But Tez loved her son, this she was sure of. She was also certain that a time would come when East might have to get a little dirty. Tez could teach him things she never could. Vital things a boy growing up in the slums of Miami needed to know.

Ebony closed the door behind him. She was still a bundle of nerves. As soon as she locked the door, she exhaled deeply and broke down crying again. The reality of it all hit her at once. She had come so close to losing her own life. Although her tears were mostly for herself, she mourned for Lance as well. Her tears rained down her face. She needed something to cope. Her eyes darted to her handbag on the couch. She snatched it up and removed the bottles of pills she had taken from the glove compartment. Still crying, she spun the bottles around to read the label. To her dismay, they weren't Xanax.

Instead, they were Percocet. She quickly removed the top and put two in her hand. Ebony was so emotional, at that moment, she didn't care. Her only desire was to not feel anything for a while. No stress, no fear, no anxiety, no sadness. She hated being at the mercy of her feelings. She dreaded the roller coaster of emotions that was sure to haunt her. She wanted to be numb to it all.

Chapter Five

For East, it started like any other day. Sitting in the living room trying to spend time with Ebony before he headed to the gym. Recently, he noticed that his mother had become withdrawn and a bit antisocial. She didn't call or visit her best friend Angela as much as she used to and spent most of her time lying around on the couch or sleeping. Ebony wasn't her normally affectionate self when it came to her son either. She was moody, easily irritated, and tended to forget things or just didn't care about them. East understood the pressure she was under and figured she was down from not being able to find a job during the past few months. Like a loving son, he tried his best to help her get through it. He wouldn't ask for things he knew she couldn't get. Instead, he became self-reliant in order to ease the burden.

"Ma, you really need to get out of this house today," he said, opening the blinds. "Look how nice it is outside."

"Boy, this Miami. It's always nice outside. I don't care about that," she dismissed. "I'ma be right here watching this marathon of *First 48*," she said.

Suddenly, like it had come out of nowhere, Ebony started breathing really hard. First, she reached for her neck, feeling as though someone had their hand wrapped around her throat. Then she grabbed her chest, feeling a searing pain. She kept breathing harder and harder. At first, East cracked a smile, thinking that she was joking around. Ebony would do all kinds of stuff to make him laugh.

"Ma, stop playing," he chuckled. But Ebony didn't stop; she just kept gasping for air. "Ma," East said. This time there was no laughter in his voice. He knew she wasn't joking. He froze momentarily, in shock and disbelief. Unbeknownst to him, she was going into cardiac arrest from all the Percocet pills she had been taking.

Call 911, he thought to himself; then he shouted it.

"Call 911!" It was like he was telling someone else in the room to do it. But there was no one else. Just him and her, like it always had been. East raced to the phone and dialed. "Hold on, Ma," he pleaded as tears filled his young eyes. "They said they're on the way," he told her.

Minutes later, East opened the door for the paramedics, and they rushed over to Ebony who lay unconscious on the floor. They ripped her shirt open and began working on her. Soon after, she was being put on a stretcher, taken out of the house, and put into the back of the ambulance.

East followed the paramedics out of the house. Outside, all the neighbors were on the stoops and porches looking on in. They had expressions of sadness, anxiousness, and fear on their faces.

Ms. Angela came racing out of her house just as they were putting her in the ambulance. There were tears running down her face, and she was screaming frantically. Screw and Shantelle looked on in shock.

For East, it all seemed like a blur. He couldn't even remember the ride to the hospital. Tez met them when they got there. Angela sat directly across from him, crying and praying with her twins at her side. Shantelle rubbed her mother's hand, but deep down, she wished she was sitting next to East. It broke her little heart to see him so hurt. Tez sat right by East's side for hours and hours, until eventually, one of the doctors came out to the waiting room. Spotting him, Tez and Ms. Angela rose to their feet to greet him. East remained seated, but he would never forget the words that came out of the doctor's mouth. "She didn't make it. Your mom . . . didn't make it. I'm sorry."

East felt like he had a huge knot in his stomach. He began to cry hysterically, experiencing all kinds of emotions that he had never felt before. Tez had tears in his eyes but showed strength, not letting one fall until East got up and hugged him. He buried his head in Tez's chest and cried like a baby.

Chapter Six

Five Years Later

The beautiful, long stemmed rose in Lauryn's trembling hand paled in comparison to the flawless diamond on the same hand she clutched it in. Her heart was heavy and aching as she stood in front of the beautifully sculpted statue of a weeping angel, hugging the headstone. Lauryn had been to her father's grave site hundreds of times in the past few years. She came dressed in black like always. The same way she had on the day of his funeral. Every time she made him the same promise. Every time it felt like it was the first time she had been to visit. It was like picking the scab off a wound. The initial pain would return as soon as she pulled up in front of the cemetery gates.

After losing her father, there was something inside of her that would never heal. The memory of his death would start playing in her mind before she could even get out of the car. Up until then, it had been the worst day of her life and the most pain she had ever felt. Even now, it was still a crippling feeling. She felt sick just being there. She placed her hand over her midsection as she felt it lurch. Her chest threatened to cave in as she fought back tears, trying to find the words to say, even though they were always the same.

"I miss you so much, Daddy," a mournful cry escaped her lips, grief consuming her. She keeled over, falling to her knees, hugging the headstone tightly before tracing her fingers over it.

East stood a few feet away, silent, dressed in all black as well. His young features were stoic, his baby face remaining in a hard expression. His hand close to the gun on his waist. He was there to do a job. The woman he was guarding was the boss's new, young wife, Lauryn Wheeler. Ricardo had entrusted him to keep his most prized possession safe. He was close enough to protect her if needed, but not close enough to invade her privacy. His natural instinct was to offer her comfort. It bothered him to see her broken and in such pain, but he knew better. He knew to keep his distance. Still, East found himself staring at her in admiration. Even in such sadness, her beauty was rare. It delighted the eyes. Her glow was radiant. It was like the sun lived in the lining of her skin. Her full lips and doelike eyes had put men twice his age in a trance. She could have any nigga in the city if she wanted. She had always appeared regal to East. Putting on a brave face for the world to see. But in that moment, her willingness to be vulnerable in front of him allowed him to see how delicate she really was. He turned his face away, ashamed that he was witnessing such a private emotional moment. He thought it better if he waited for her by the car. She didn't even notice him walk away.

"Ain't you supposed to be her shadow?" the driver asked East. "You a li'l too far away, if you ask me."

"Ain't nobody ask you, though," East countered.

"Ricardo'll kill your li'l ass if anything happens to her," the driver chuckled, then blew out a cloud of cigarette smoke. Everybody knew how serious Ricardo was about Lauryn. She didn't go anywhere without protection.

"She deserves to grieve in private," East responded.

"Yeah, a'ight. I'm just saying—"

"That's your problem. You talk too fucking much. What you doing out of the car anyway?" East's cold stare put an end to their conversation. The driver tossed his cigarette to the ground, circled the truck, and got behind the wheel. Despite his young age, East was well respected within the organization. He was like Tez's son and a second son to Ricardo. Both men were equal partners. He leaned against the hood of the SUV and waited patiently for Lauryn to finish.

There was a time when Lauryn felt like she had the world on a string. Her whole life was in front of her then. She had been so confident, so full of cheer. That seemed so long ago. She hadn't even entered womanhood when her father died. She hadn't known the rules. Now at twenty-five years old, she was no longer a bright-eyed teenage girl. She was well versed in the workings of the underworld. Her youthful innocence had been violently snatched away, leaving behind a woman hardened by grief and anger, nothing but collateral damage of the drug game. She rested her head against the headstone and whispered to her father, words only meant for his ears.

Until then, the sky had been perfect, but it was quickly changing. Miami weather was funny like that. The beautiful blue shade was turning into a hard grey. Large pillows of cloud beginning to form blocked out the sun. A gust of wind blew, stirring the trees; then Lauryn heard a pitter-patter as the first pearls of rain dropped on the leaves. The rainfall suddenly became more intense, mixing with the trail of tears streaming down her face. She laid the rose in her hand on top of the headstone, then walked away. East raced over, meeting her more than halfway, providing her shelter from the rain underneath an umbrella. The drops were drumming against the ground nonstop as they made it to her car. East reached out, opening the door for her and helping her in. Once she was safely inside, he slammed the door shut behind her, closed the umbrella, and got into the front passenger seat of the black Lincoln Navigator.

Lauryn sat in the back composing herself, wiping away the remaining tears while looking at her reflection in a compact mirror. Her beautiful face hid the hurt well behind designer labels and foreign cars. She forged a smile as her eyes met East's, and he told the driver to start the engine. Suddenly, the sun came out again, casting slanted beams of light across the cemetery. Steam rose slowly from the grass. It rose up eerily and drifted mistlike toward the golden sun. The image was so vivid that it stayed with Lauryn for the rest of the day. She took it as a sign that things would get better. "After the rain, the sun will shine again," she mumbled to herself.

"Huh?" East asked, looking over his shoulder at her.

"Nothing," she quickly dismissed. "We can go now," she instructed. After visiting her father's grave, there was only one thing in the world that could brighten Lauryn's spirits. A little retail therapy.

For East, pulling up to Ricardo's new home felt like he was in another world. Palm Island was only a fifteen-minute drive from where he grew up in Liberty City, but despite the short distance, the places couldn't have been farther apart. The exclusive waterfront neighborhood was home to the stars. There was lush landscaping throughout the entire island and beautiful water features that connect the properties to their natural environment fronting Biscayne Bay. Ricardo had recently purchased a 6,800-square foot, island-style home with a pool and boat dock attached at the rear.

Arriving through the gate, the circular courtyard had stone pavers, grouted with lawn and a fountain in the middle, creating a striking scenery. A few foreign vehicles adorned the driveway, along with tinted out SUVs. Two large palm trees stood like pillars near the front of the mansion, adding to the appeal of the property. Ricardo, Tez, and Dos stood out front engaged in a conversation. To East, it felt like a scene out of a movie. He got out of the truck and opened the back door for Lauryn.

"Thank you," she said in a sweet tone as he helped her out of the car. She smiled, but her eyes didn't. There was so much pain laying behind her exterior, right there in the windows to her soul.

"You all right?" East inquired. His nature wouldn't let him ignore what he saw.

"I'll be fine, East. Thanks for asking," she replied in a somber tone. It was rare that any of her husband's workers said a word to her. Most were afraid to even make eye contact with the boss's new, young wife. Not East. He always said, "Good morning" or "Good night" and acknowledged her when she passed. Lauryn appreciated his humbleness and enjoyed his presence when he accompanied her places. Ricardo's other workers were like robots in suits. East had a youthful innocence that hadn't been hardened by the world yet. She admired it, but at the same time, was a bit envious, recalling when she saw the world like he did. Lauryn spotted Ricardo's observant eyes on her. She cut her eyes evilly at her husband and quickly walked in the house. East retrieved the bags from her shopping spree and followed her into the mansion.

"Wifey look pissed. Whatchu do now?" Tez questioned.

Ricardo shrugged, barely acknowledged her behavior, and refused to entertain the conversation. He knew Lauryn was spoiled and because of that, she wasn't going anywhere. Not in a million years. She always returned from her father's grave site with a cloud of sadness surrounding her. It was nothing a shopping spree or expensive gifts couldn't clear up. The two continued to talk and walk, leaving Dos behind.

"Look at you, nigga," Dos laughed as East appeared from the front door. "You look like the Secret Service," he quipped, brushing imaginary lint from East's suit. "When you gonna stop with all that Alfred shit," referring to the character famous for being Batman's butler, "and come get some real money with ya boy?" Dos was draped up and dripped out. Gucci down with a big Cuban link chain hanging from his neck and diamonds in his ear. He was getting street money, and it showed.

East ignored the jab. That was Dos. Always talking big, always bragging. The two were polar opposites, but they were friends. East moved at his own pace. He knew his time would come to get in the game, but like everything else he did, he was being strategic. "I see you, playboy," East replied, dapping him up.

"Let's go get something to eat. I'm hungry as shit," Dos said, walking over to his brand-new Mercedes S-Class Coupe, a graduation gift from his father.

"Bet."

"Yo, you really need to step ya car game up," Dos declared. The difference between the two could be seen in the cars they drove. While Dos preferred luxury and the status that came with the Benz, East drove an old school.

"This a classic," East reminded him, then slammed his door.

Ricardo and Tez watched the two of them drive away like proud fathers. "Eastwood been doing a good job keeping Lauryn safe, but I think it's time for a promotion," Ricardo stated. He, like everyone else, saw the potential in East and thought it was time for him to get on the front line.

"I don't think he ready yet," Tez replied.

"Fuck you mean he not ready?" Ricardo shot back. "He more ready than any of these li'l niggas."

"I don't know," Tez shrugged.

Ricardo eyed him with suspicion. "You act like you his daddy," he said. Tez had become a little too attached to East. He was being overprotective. "You *killed* his daddy. You *ain't* his daddy," Ricardo reminded him.

"I did that for you." Tez gritted his teeth.

"And?" Ricardo remained indifferent. "If you got issues, you need to see a therapist. Otherwise, get over that shit. 'Cause I ain't a therapist, and I ain't running a day care. I'm in the drug business, and I got thorough young niggas on our team. I breed 'em that way. I've bred them to be loyal. And I'm gonna put them to work, *all* of them. Shit, these houses and cars ain't gonna pay for themselves."

"That's easy for you to say," Tez replied. When shit hits the fan, it would be him on the front line, not Ricardo. Tez knew in his heart East was ready. He was more ready than even Ricardo knew. He just wanted to protect him from the life and keep him away from the game as long as he could. Tez had been in the streets long enough to know that it changes people. Some in worse ways than others. He witnessed it firsthand. He had killed plenty of men, including East's father, many on the word of Ricardo, and their ghosts haunted him, especially Derek Eastwood's. He had gotten used to not sleeping peacefully at night. He was a hustler, but he was also a killer, and killers killed. It was what he had signed up for once he took his first life. Maybe he had gotten too attached to East, but so what? He loved him. Tez had seen and done so much, he didn't wish his life on anyone—certainly not East.

"What the fuck that mean?" Ricardo barked.

"Forget it," Tez answered.

"Nah, say what's on ya mind. You feeling a way?" Ricardo could read Tez's eyes. He didn't like the fact that his authority was being questioned.

"I just don't think East is ready, that's all," Tez repeated.

"He ready 'cause I said he ready," Ricardo asserted with a finality that ended the conversation.

"I can't believe you got your cousin hustlin' with you," East said surprisingly after hearing Dos's story. He leaned back in his seat and shook his head. He and Dos were enjoying breakfast in the middle of the day at IHOP. "You crazy. That li'l nigga gonna get you locked up or killed. Plus, I don't trust his ass. His eyes be looking all beady and shit."

"He's my family. I trust him," Dos said.

"Good luck with that," East replied.

Dos shrugged nonchalantly and continued eating his pancakes. "It should be me and you, bro, but you bullshittin'. So, it is what it is," he replied calmly.

At that moment the waitress arrived at their table. "How's the food? Can I get you anything else?" she asked.

East calmly looked up and was pleasantly surprised. "Jasmine?"

"Hey, East. What's up?" she replied cheerfully with a strong New York accent.

He had arrived after Dos, who had ordered for him, so he hadn't seen the waitress yet. "I didn't know you worked here," he said.

"Part time," she replied with a smile. "I bartend at a club at night too."

"I see. I'm gonna have to start coming here a li'l more," Dos interrupted with a smile. East shot him a look, but he either didn't catch it or ignored it. He had been flirting with Jasmine since he arrived. She was gorgeous. She had a flawless mocha skin tone with full, pouty lips and deep-dish dimples. Her ass still looked round and curvy despite the loose-fitting uniform she wore. Dos had to have her.

"Anyway, it's good to see you again, East." She smiled hard.

"You too," he replied.

Dos felt like a third wheel in their energy. Still, he couldn't stop staring at her ass as she walked away. "You know her?" he whispered. "I know you fuckin' that bitch," he said but secretly was hoping East said no.

"Nah, it ain't like that. I used to holla at her friend. Tell you the truth, I didn't know she was back in town. Last I heard, she moved back to New York or some shit," East explained.

"Put me on, nigga. I always wanted to fuck a bitch from New York, son," he imitated a New Yorker's accent.

East chuckled. "Put yourself on, B," he mocked, downing his orange juice.

Dos smirked. He suddenly got up and walked across the restaurant toward Jasmine, who was in the midst of taking down another table's orders. When she turned around, she was startled at his presence in her face.

"Excuse you," she sassed.

"You should let me take you out," Dos proclaimed with a handsome smile.

"And why would I do that?" she rolled her eyes and walked around him.

Dos followed behind her. "Why wouldn't you?" he countered.

"Dos, please," she replied and rolled her eyes again.

"Oh, so you know a nigga's name."

"Boy, who don't know your name . . . with your ho ass,"
Jasmine stated and walked into the kitchen. Dos followed. "What are you doing?" she asked, looking around
in a panic and laughed nervously. "You can't be in here."

"First of all, I go wherever I want. Second, I ain't a ho.
I just ain't found nothing worth giving my undivided
attention to. Until now," he said seriously.

"Excuse me, young man. You're not supposed to be in
here," the manager walked in and said.

Dos ignored her. "You gonna let me take you out?" he
asked Jasmine.

"Young man," the manager said again, this time more
aggressively.

"C'mon, at least give me your number."

"Ms. Pollard, please let your friend know that if he
doesn't leave now, I will fire you!" the manager scolded.

"C'mon, Dos, go," Jasmine pleaded with him.

"Nope. I'm not leaving until you either give me your
number or agree to go out with me," he poked out his lips
and pouted like a little child.

Jasmine giggled. She knew what kind of person Dos
was, but he was sexy and charming. She was feeling him,
and word was, his dick game was crazy.

"OK, take my number." She couldn't contain her smile.

"What is it?" he said, pulling out his phone.

She gave him the number.

Dos smiled as he typed the numbers in his phone.
"I'ma call you later, a'ight?"

"Yes. Now go before you get me fired," she said, pushing him out of the kitchen.

Chapter Seven

It was after midnight when Ricardo Wheeler decided to summon East to meet with him. After entering the office of his boxing gym, Ricardo sat behind a desk preparing to make the call. The walls of the office were covered with old fight posters, Sonny Liston versus Cassius Clay, Durán versus Leonard, to name a few. Ricardo picked up his cell phone and dialed. He had no contacts stored, just a knack for remembering numbers. He would have called from the office phone, except it was tapped. So was the other line in the gym. He knew it but kept them that way to mislead cops and any other unwanted listeners.

Across town, inside his bedroom, East lay awake in the bed with a cloud of weed smoke dancing above him. The only light in the room came from the TV. A rerun episode of *Martin* was playing, but he wasn't paying it any mind. Suddenly, his phone rang on the nightstand, grabbing his attention. He ashed the weed. "What's up?" he said answering on the third ring.

"Eastwood." Ricardo was still the only person that had ever called East by his whole last name, so instantly he knew who the voice on the phone belonged to. "I need to see you."

"Can it wait?" East asked, uninterested in getting out of his bed. It had already been a long day having to run around with Lauryn.

"Nah, it can't. I need to see you right now," Ricardo's tone was serious and firm. "It's important. My guys are waiting outside for you," he declared.

East sat up in the bed. It was almost one in the morning.

What is so important that Ricardo sent his men to my apartment? he thought to himself. Something didn't feel right. He got out of the bed and went into the living room with his gun in his hand. East walked over to the window and looked outside. He spotted Ricardo's men exactly where he said they would be. In front of his apartment, standing in front of two black Mercedes.

"You still there?" Ricardo broke the long pause.

"Yeah, I'm here," East answered in a low voice. "You wanna give me a heads-up on what's this about?"

"Nah. You'll find out when you get here," Ricardo replied with finality. Then the line went dead.

East let the phone linger by his ear for a moment before he lowered it. He wasn't sure what the fuck was happening. All he knew was something wasn't right. He was caught off guard by the phone call and the tone of the conversation. Ricardo had always preferred to avoid the phone altogether. He usually handed down orders two men deep, to ensure that nothing could be traced back to him. He was old school, but the fact that he had made the call himself had East's mind racing. He got dressed in a hurry and went outside where Ricardo's stone-faced goons awaited him. An awkward silence came over them as he approached. Before he could get closer, they halted his progress by surrounding him. One of the henchmen stepped forward and patted him down, removing the gun from underneath his hoodie.

"I'm gonna hold on to this," he said, tucking East's gun into his own waist.

"What's going on?" East asked, but the henchmen didn't respond before making him get in one of the cars. East remained calm as he rode in the backseat next to one of the goons. He didn't say a word. Peering out the back window, he could see the other car, filled with more of Ricardo's men, following them as well. He had no idea what was going on, but if they were trying to scare him, it wasn't working. He didn't scare easily.

The driver rolled to a stop in an alley behind the gym. East got out, and so did everyone else. When he turned and saw them all, an electric bolt of energy surged through his body. Hostile looks on the faces of each man fueled the tension in the air. He had come up with a few of them in Ricardo's gym. Now they were all dressed in black, the color of death. East stared in each of their eyes, looking for the one who would be bold enough to step up and kill him. He was ready for whatever, trying to guess how it would happen, but to his surprise, no one made a move on him. He couldn't understand why they were standing there, passively watching, but he noticed there was one face conspicuous in its absence.

"Where's Tez?" East called out to no one in particular.

"Don't worry about that," one of the henchmen replied before nudging him forward, toward the back entrance.

The gym was dimly lit and eerily silent when East entered. It felt like the temperature had suddenly dipped, a cold chill sweeping over him. At first, there was only the sound of his own footsteps, then floating in from the back of the gym, the faint murmur of voices. In the distance, East spotted more of Ricardo's men. They appeared to be enjoying a laugh. As he came into the light, East spotted Tez on a stool in the middle of the gym, hunched over, staring at his shoes like an athlete removed from a game that was hopelessly lost. His face was bloodied and battered. His jaw looked grotesque, swelling a great deal from the beating he had suffered. His lips were moving but whatever he was saying East couldn't understand it.

Next to Tez, Ricardo leaned against the ring's apron with both hands in the pockets of the Adidas tracksuit he wore. His sleeves were rolled up, his diamond-faced, gold Rolex on full display. Although his attire was understated, his piercing eyes exuded power, and his strong presence could be felt by all in the gym. Now in his forties, Ricardo sported a freshly shaved bald head and a thick, full beard. He had gained a small potbelly since his fighting days. In a weird way, it enhanced his bosslike appearance, representing the way he was eating off the streets. A "money gut," he called it.

East could never forget the first time he walked into the gym. He was just a kid, eleven or maybe twelve, he thought. He had a similar feeling that day as he did right now.

Back then, the community saw Ricardo as a positive influence on the neighborhood kids. Little did any of them know, the gym was his own personal breeding ground. He had spawned the next generation of cocaine cowboys. His own personal army of killers and dealers, who had pledged their undying loyalty to him.

But that was then; this was now. Ricardo, flanked closely by Dos, slowly began to circle Tez on the stool. He took his time, wanting to choose his words carefully. Everyone held their breath waiting for him to speak. When he finally did, his husky Southern accent was cold and calculated.

"I knew dis nigga here since we were kids. That's longer than any of you been alive. But I got a feeling you're going to outlive our man, Tez," Ricardo said while never taking his eyes off of East. "My momma had a saying, *scratch a lie, find a thief.* Meaning if a nigga'll lie to you, he'll steal from you, and if he'd steal from you, he'd kill you," he explained, circling Tez with his hands still in his pocket.

Tez never looked up. Even when Ricardo placed a hand on his shoulder and smiled. A gesture of twisted reassurance that he was going to be dead very soon. Like a sledgehammer to the chest, it hit East what was happening. Tez had somehow crossed Ricardo, and now he was going to kill him, and maybe anybody close to him. East cursed under his breath, knowing that meant his fate was probably sealed too. Tez was not only his mentor, but he had become like a father figure to him. He held him in higher regards than he did Ricardo himself.

Ricardo walked over and stood directly in front of him. The two of them, toe to toe and eye to eye. "You know what I hate worse than a liar and a thief?" he asked rhetorically. "A disloyal-ass rat!" Ricardo's voice echoed through the gym.

There was complete silence. Ricardo was so close that East could hear him breathing.

A rat? East thought to himself.

"Yeah, a rat. A fuckin' snitch," Ricardo said like he had read East's thoughts.

Hell no, East thought to himself. In all the years he had been around him, he had never heard Tez say a negative word about Ricardo. He strongly doubted what was being said about his mentor although he had to admit, Tez had to be angered by the nepotism that was soon to make Dos second-in-command over him within the organization. After all, Tez had helped build Ricardo into a powerful man on the streets of Miami when Dos was still a little boy. During war times, the threat of letting Tez off the leash became a major part of Ricardo's mystique, and intimidation, sometimes, was a better weapon than a gun. Even with all that, East could never see Tez pulling a move like that.

Kill Ricardo and take over, maybe . . . but snitch? . . . Nah, he thought to himself.

"You wouldn't happen to know anything about that, would you?" If Ricardo asked a question, he most likely already knew the answer.

East had always been good at tests, and his gut feeling was telling him to be honest. So, he did. "Nah."

"You sure about that?" Ricardo pressed, clearly trying to read him.

"Very sure," East answered strongly. There was no change in his demeanor or dent in his conviction. He had already accepted there was a chance he wouldn't make it out of there alive. He had nothing to lose, so he spoke his mind. "I don't think Tez would do—"

Ricardo cut him off with a look. He could be a very intimidating person, but as he searched East's eyes, he found no fear or deception; only the truth. "You always been a solid li'l nigga," he said, putting his hand on East's shoulder. Ricardo saw him as likeable and shrewd for his age, with tons of heart. He was as tough as Dos but with none of the recklessness.

"I wanna see what you really made of," Ricardo declared, removing a Glock .40 from his waist. "Kill Tez." Ricardo ordered murder effortlessly, like it was a number three on a fast-food menu, his eyes piecing through East as he handed him the gun.

Ricardo's words lingered in the air for a moment. He knew how close East was to Tez. He wanted to break that bond. *He* was the boss, the *only* voice that really counted. He had made a mistake letting Tez mentor East. Now he was going to fix it. If East showed any hesitation to follow his orders, Ricardo would know he could never fully trust him. It didn't matter how much he liked him, East would have to die along with Tez.

East took a deep breath. His stomach sank, although his outer appearance remained unchanged. He had never killed anybody before, and now Ricardo was going to make him kill Tez as a test of his loyalty. He locked eyes with Dos hoping to find some type of support but found none. Dos refused to hold his gaze, turning his eyes away.

East had always followed his head and not his heart. The heart was just a motor. The head was meant to drive. Although just eighteen years old, East always envisioned there would come a time when he was set financially, that he could retire from the game. Now looking at Tez, a man twenty-plus years his senior, he realized that would never happen. You didn't retire from the game; the game retired you—most times with a bullet. Tez had lived his life governed by the same rules and honored the same codes he taught East, and where had it gotten him? Here. A young man who genuinely loved him was being forced to end his life. It was then that East realized what Tez had been mumbling under his breath the whole time. . . . *It wasn't me.* East wondered how long Tez had tried to explain his side of the story to Ricardo. He also knew better to think Tez would ever beg for his life. He wasn't built like that. He was a gangster in every sense of the word. Right or wrong.

East took the gun out of Ricardo's hand and slowly walked behind Tez. He was stopped by the sound of Ricardo's commanding voice.

"Nah, not like that. In front. Look a man in the eyes when you send him to God," he instructed. Ricardo didn't have a gun in his hand, but East knew he wouldn't leave the gym alive if he shot anyone besides Tez. That still didn't stop the thought from crossing his mind.

Just then, Dos walked over, gun in hand. "Look up, fuck nigga," he taunted Tez. "Be a man about it."

East cocked his head and glared at Dos. He felt that no matter what Tez was being accused of, he deserved more respect than he was being shown. Still, Tez didn't say anything and did as he was told. He looked up with not a tear in sight, staring directly at East.

When their eyes met, East could feel his heart wrench. He was consumed with emotions, causing him to hesitate for a moment. Ricardo was having none of it. He quickly nodded at Dos, who raised his gun, aiming it at East's head.

"It's him or you, Eastwood," Ricardo stated, letting East know that if he didn't kill Tez, he would die also.

East eyed Dos intensely. He couldn't believe he was pointing a gun at him. Dos unsympathetically shrugged his shoulders, fully prepared to follow through on his father's orders. No matter what happened, after tonight, their friendship would never be the same. East remained unfazed and unafraid by what he was facing. His biggest flaw was his lack of fear. Whatever was coming his way, he would be a G about it.

"I'm sorry," Tez suddenly uttered. No one in the gym knew who his apology was meant for. Ricardo, East, or God. Maybe it was meant for all three. East didn't want to know which, but in his heart, he knew it was for him.

East raised the gun pointing it at Tez's head. Both of them were sickened but grateful for the sight of each other on the opposite ends of the gun. If it had to be any-body, Tez was glad it was East. He had groomed him to be unflappable. Even now, his protégé's hand was steady as he felt the barrel of the gun press against his forehead. In a strange way, he found pride in that. He would be his first kill. Tez didn't move, blink, or flinch. "Love seldom. Trust never," he stated. The words caught East by sur-prise. Even in death, Tez offered a lesson. It was the last he would teach East but probably the most important.

East squeezed the trigger. Tez's body flew backward off the stool, so hard that his knees made a cracking sound and his body made a thud as it hit the ground. Blood splatter smacked East in the face. The scent of Tez's blood in the air mixed with the smell of his shit. East felt a wave of calm wash over him, erasing the hesitation he had felt. Strangely, he felt nothing . . . no fear, no disgust, no anger. He had been trained to put bad things that happened out of his mind quickly.

Ricardo nodded to Dos who lowered his gun. He rubbed his beard as he approached. East had passed the test with flying colors. He was exactly who Ricardo thought he was, a no-nonsense young nigga, all about his business with the heart to kill. He had a star pupil on his hands. "You did good, Eastwood," he said like a proud parent, grabbing East by the shoulders and shaking him. There was a joy in his voice that wasn't there before. "Your future is bright, believe that," he proclaimed. Dos wasn't so happy. He didn't like his father openly doting on East all of a sudden.

East forced a smile and passed the gun back to Ricardo, sure he was no longer in danger of being killed. He sneered at Dos. "You put a gun to my head. You should've pulled the trigger, pussy."

"Fuck you. Next time, I will," Dos boasted.

"Won't be a next time," East assured him. Then with a final glance down at Tez's dead body, he walked out the back door of the gym. He got into a waiting car, and Ricardo's men drove him home. East wasn't sad or even angry. For now, he was only numb, staring straight-ahead the whole ride.

Chapter Eight

2017

East pulled his black '66 Chevy Impala into the Annie Coleman housing projects in Liberty City. Since the night of Tez's murder, the dynamics of his relationship with Ricardo had changed. He was no longer hired muscle, protecting Lauryn. Now, Ricardo was supplying him with bricks, and he was flourishing. East and Dos was another story. They remained at odds, their relationship permanently damaged by the events of that night.

Still, East was doing well for himself, controlling a few spots of his own. This one was inside the projects, known as The Rockies, that was making about $7,500 a day. He needed a two-man team to run the spot, making sure everything went smoothly. East was big on loyalty, so naturally, he chose Screw and Ques. They had all come up together like a family. The two of them had no problem playing their position. They all understood that gunplay was part of the game. East made sure his team stayed fully loaded and instilled in them to play no games whatsoever. On more than one occasion, they had to put in gun work to defend the turf.

East grabbed the shopping bag from under his seat, then slid the Glock .40 in his waist. He checked his surroundings before getting out of the car. There was a lot of foot traffic moving up and down the street. The courtyard was lined with junkies. East made his way through them all, his chain swinging back and forth on his shirt, walking up to the apartment on the second floor. Things seemed to be moving the way he liked it, and he made sure his spots never ran out of work. He knocked on the door and immediately heard barking coming from the other side. A few seconds later, Screw let him in.

"What's up, whoa?" Screw said, slapping five with his comrade, then shutting the door. He was holding a vicious pit bull at bay on a leash. "Sit," he instructed the dog, and it did. Screw, being mixed with black, Jamaican, and Puerto Rican, had a very light complexion and a slim build with long, matted dreads. He had gold slugs in his mouth and was unmistakably Dade County raised. His pants sagged off his ass, exposing a gun on his waistline. At nineteen, he was a year younger than East but a few inches taller and a lot wilder.

"What up, nigga? You always stuffing your fuckin' face," East joked to Ques, who was sitting on a fold up chair feasting on some jerk chicken, rice, and peas. Ques nodded in agreement and smiled, his boyish good looks and dimples on full display.

The small apartment that they were hustling out of had nothing more in it than a couch, a TV with a PS4 hooked to it, a table with drugs on it, and a chopper laying across the couch where Screw had been sitting.

"How's this shit movin'?" East asked, setting the shopping bag on the table.

"Faster than a muthafucka. We'll probably be done with dat dere in a few hours," Screw said confidently.

"Yeah, money coming through here faster than we can count the shit," Ques added while licking the tips of his fingers.

"Yeah?" East questioned like he didn't believe what he was hearing, although he knew he was getting the best coke in the city from Ricardo.

"This shit is butter. The junkies loving it. We just made fifteen hundid in a half hour," Screw boasted. A knock on the door grabbed their attention and made the dog start barking again. It was a sell and another one followed right behind it.

The sound of the toilet flushing grabbed East's attention. He turned in the direction of the bathroom. "I know y'all niggas ain't got no hoes in here?" he barked, clearly not feeling the fact that Screw and Ques probably had some young freak from the projects in the trap spot.

"Nigga, that's Twin," Screw dismissed. "She brought niggas some food. We ain't ate shit all day," he continued to explain. "Twin," as he referred to her, was his twin sister, Shantelle.

Seconds later, a short, light-skinned female wearing a tied-up wife beater and cut up jeans emerged from behind the bathroom door. She had a pretty face with long, black hair and almond-shaped eyes. Her eyebrows were perfectly arched, and her nails freshly manicured.

The fact that she was a familiar face did nothing to melt the icy stare on East's face. "I don't want *nobody* in the spot. I'on care *who* it is."

"Hello to you too, East," she said. "I just had to use the bathroom. I wasn't staying long," she spoke up before her brother could explain further. "Just give me my money for the food so I can go," she huffed, sucking her teeth and sticking out her hand.

East didn't say another word, but all in the room could see he was still angry. Screw dug in his pocket and pulled out a knot of money. "Thanks for the food, sis," he said. "Here, this is for Momma. She called and said she needed some money." He passed his sister two crisp hundred-dollar bills.

"You need to take it to her yourself," Shantelle said, stuffing the money in her handbag.

"Yeah, I know," he admitted, then kissed her on the cheek. Shantelle left without saying good-bye to anyone else. Screw turned to East after shutting the door behind her. "My fault, whoa. Moms needed—"

East lifted his hand and cut him off. "You ain't gotta explain that shit to me. Moms always come first. I understand." It had been more than five years since he had lost his mother. Not a day went by that she didn't cross his mind. Ms. Angela had become like a second mother to him in Ebony's absence. Just the mention of her made East's angry stare disappear. "Y'all got that bread for me?" he asked, rubbing his hands together, getting right back to the business at hand.

"Don't we always," Ques answered and rose from the chair. He set his food on the counter before entering the kitchen. Reaching inside one of the cabinets, he pulled out a plastic shopping bag that was full of rubber banded stacks of money. He walked over to East and handed it to him. "We gon' sell out before the morning, though, I'm tellin' you."

"Y'all should be good with that," East assured him, pointing to the bag on the table. It contained enough coke for the spot to run for at least another 24 hours. He never kept more dope in the spot than needed. That way, if police raided or the spot got robbed, he wouldn't take a big loss.

He looked down at his phone. He had a text message. He read it to himself, then looked back up at Screw. "I'll be back tomorrow. I got some shit I need to take care of right now. I'm gonna need you to ride with me to go see Ricardo tomorrow."

"Bet," Screw said. He knew that meant East was going to re-up and needed an extra set of eyes and gun with him. Screw was East's right hand. The one he trusted more than anybody because he never hesitated to swing his iron in a tight spot.

East gave both his comrades five, then left the spot. He headed a few blocks away to an apartment he used as a stash house. Once inside, he put up the money he had collected. Minutes later, he was back in his car, on the move again, heading straight to Miami Gardens.

Pulling into the parking lot of Miami Finga Licking, East parked next to a car with the engine running. He rolled his window down and simultaneously, the passenger-side window of the other car did as well.

"What took you so long?" Shantelle said as she looked over at him.

"I had to make a stop first."

"You act like somebody got all night to be waiting on you," she sassed.

"Why you ain't leave then?" he said confidently, then flashed a charming smile. His pearly white teeth only enhanced his handsome face and made her smile back. "You got some food?" When she lifted the bag of takeout, he nodded for her to get in with him, and she did.

As they pulled away, East stared in the rearview mirror back at the car she had gotten out of. There was a female in the driver's seat. Shantelle saw the look on his face and tried to put his mind at ease. "Don't worry. That's my homegirl from school. She ain't gonna run her mouth. She don't know you or my brother," she explained.

East ran his hand over the light beard on his face. "What makes you think I'm worried?" Then they both laughed. "When you came home?" he asked her.

"Yesterday," she replied.

"How long you here for?"

"Two weeks," she informed him.

"How's school? You like it up there?" he asked. "You meet any interesting people?"

"Are you asking if I've met any guys?"

"Nah, that ain't none of my business," he said. "But since you brought it up . . ."

Shantelle laughed. "I've been on a date or two. Nothing serious," she admitted. Although she was old enough to make her own decisions, she was his closest friend's twin sister. Out of respect, they kept their thing a secret.

They had grown up either next door to each other or under the same roof for most of their lives. East had been to all her family functions. Attended all her graduations since elementary school. He had driven her to college on her first day. Her own mother called him "nephew." Shantelle knew if Angela or Screw found out about them, they would be highly upset. She didn't care. He was too sexy to deny herself the pleasure.

A girl has needs, she told herself. East knew exactly how to fulfil them. The sexual chemistry between them was unmatched.

By the time they reached the hotel, the lust between them was on full display. East sat on the edge of the bed with no shirt and a pair of basketball shorts on. He had the build of an athlete, standing six foot four, solid without being overly muscular. His arms, neck, back, and chest were covered with tattoos that popped off his honey-dipped skin.

Shantelle approached and stood between his legs, wearing nothing but a red bra and panties. She had a body that was out of this world. Superthick in all the right places. She was pretty and smart with a rough edge to her that was hidden beneath the surface. Her tattoos were only visible when she was nearly naked. East ran his hand over the tattoo on her thigh. It was a gun surrounded by bouquet of thorn-stemmed roses. The artwork was beautiful . . . and dangerous, sort of like her. East knew he was crossing the line every time he entered her body. He fought against their attraction at first, explaining to her how wrong it would be for them to hook up. He told her she should find someone at her school like a lawyer or a doctor, maybe even an athlete, anybody but him. He was a street nigga. That came with a lifestyle she didn't have to subject herself to. She had options unlike him or her brother. She was attending Florida State University on a scholarship, studying sociology. None of what he said mattered to her, though. Shantelle wanted what she wanted.

She had a smile on her face as she caressed his head, rubbing her hand over his waves. East's naturally slanted eyes were even lower from the weed they were smoking. He took a pull off the blunt. Shantelle leaned in, and he blew the smoke into her mouth. Their lips met as he palmed her ass. She could feel the wetness between her thighs building as he slid her thong panties to the side and began rubbing her clit. He passed her the weed. She hit it, then passed it back. Shantelle got down on her knees, pulling East's manhood out of his shorts. He had length and girth. His dick felt heavy in her hand as she began to stroke it. Looking seductively into his eyes, she circled her tongue around the mushroom-shaped tip, then slid his full erection into her warm, wet mouth. East hit the weed and watched as her head bobbed up and down, making his dick disappear, then reappear. His head fell back as she took him deeper into her throat, wet sounds and slurps filling the room. He blew a cloud of smoke from his lungs, then ashed the weed.

"Damn, ma," he grunted. He couldn't take it any longer. When Shantelle came up for air, he pulled her up to her feet, then down on top of him aggressively. She straddled him, sliding down on him, letting out a soft moan as she took him deep inside her wetness. Her eyes rolled into the back of her head as his thickness filled her insides completely.

"Oh shit," Shantelle moaned as she held on to his broad shoulders and bounced up and down. He gripped her ass cheeks, digging deep in her pussy with long strokes. She could feel the pressure in her stomach. They were both breathing heavily, kissing each other passionately as their bodies became one. "I missed you," she called out as her mouth fell open in orgasmic bliss.

"I missed you too," he replied.

"I fuckin' love you," she whispered softly.

"You too," he said.

They were lying to each other, and they knew it, but the sex was so good and being high only enhanced the feeling. Their love was purely physical. He just wanted her pleasure, and she just wanted his pain. It was a mutually beneficial arrangement between friends.

Dos stood on the balcony of his luxury condo overlooking Biscayne Bay with his phone to his ear. From his high perch, he had a perfect view of the water and American Airlines Arena in the distance. His night had been going similar to his view—until it was interrupted by a phone call.

"I ain't tryin'a hear that shit right now, Jaz," he barked into the phone. "It ain't like I ain't tell you from day one what it was. I told you I wasn't shit. I told you not to fall in love with me. You chose not to listen. Now, here we are."

"That's not fair," Jasmine sobbed on the other end of the phone.

"Life's not always fair," Dos said coldly.

"What about our son?" She tried using the one thing she knew he cared about. She had given him what every man dreamed of: a male heir. Someone to carry on his legacy after he was gone. The only thing was, Dos was still building his legacy. In his mind, he had only just begun.

"I love my son," he proclaimed truthfully.

"Just not me . . . right?" she asked as the phone went silent. She truly loved Dos, despite all the shit he had put her through. The different women. The constant cheating. She had stayed through it all. He was the father of her child, and she just wanted them to be a family.

Dos was the sky to her, a respected dope boy with a dope dick and money to burn. She was hooked. There was only one problem. Dos wasn't trying to be tied down to one woman, baby mother or not. He was the prince of the city, and he couldn't wait to be king. He changed women like he did his underwear, and he showered twice a day. His heart was filled with ambition; that's it. There wasn't any room for love. By the time Jasmine realized it, she was already too deeply in love, with a baby on the way.

"I ain't tryin'a go back and forth about this all night. I got shit to do," he declared.

"I love you, Dos. Just come home so we can talk," she pleaded with him.

"Home?" He laughed into the phone, then hung up.

Jasmine lay in bed, holding her son on her chest. She was a thousand miles away from her entire family back in Queens. She felt more alone than ever. Her son was all she had left. She closed her eyes, feeling the tears escape out of the sides of them. Her heartbeat increased as she cried in silence, not wanting her son to hear her grief. She kissed him on the forehead as he slept peacefully in her arms. Jasmine made a promise to herself that she would raise him to be nothing like the man that had helped make him. She kissed him again, then placed him down on the bed next to her as tears continued to spill down her cheeks.

She rose from the bed, grabbing the rolled up weed off the nightstand in one motion. Jasmine needed to smoke one to calm her nerves. She walked out on the balcony of her luxury apartment with nothing on but a small T-shirt and high-waist thong panties. Her brown, round ass cheeks hung out of the bottom of her panties as she strutted across the room.

Dos had her living in the heart of the Brickell District in downtown Miami, surrounded by fine dining and boutiques, where she could shop as much as she wanted to. He had provided her with the best of everything, from fashion to jewelry. She could have anything her heart desired, but it didn't matter. The material things meant nothing now. What her heart desired the most was him, the one thing she couldn't have the way she wanted. She would trade all the luxuries afforded to her just to be with the man she loved. She would give anything to have Dos sleeping next to her every night. Making love to her body in the way only he could. The thought of Dos touching her body made Jasmine shut her eyes and briefly relive one of their nights of passionate sex. With her looks, she could bed any man she wanted, but she only wanted Dos and wouldn't dare give his pussy away. Even if he didn't believe her when she told him so. He would just laugh in her face. Instead of believing and appreciating her, Dos would keep his distance for weeks at a time, pop in to fuck, and then he would be gone again.

As Jasmine stood overlooking downtown Miami, she felt like she was mourning death. That's how much it hurt. She was devastated, heartbroken, and confused, unable to grasp any of her thoughts. Her heart was so heavy in her chest, she could barely breathe. The weight of her emotions seemed too much to bear on her body. She looked over her shoulder, back at her son lying on the bed. Her heart nearly broke in two. What was she supposed to do now? How did she go forward? Without Dos, she had no idea of what would become of her and her child. The thought alone caused her to lose what was left of her composure. Her heart wrenched. She began crying hysterically, snot and tears making a mess of her pretty face. Jasmine was in the midst of a storm. One she didn't know if she could weather. "Everything is falling apart," she whispered. "But that's okay. I'm gonna be all right. . . . We're gonna to be all right," she told herself, looking back at her son who was the splitting image of Dos. She had to muster the strength to survive for him, even if she couldn't do it for herself.

Jasmine lit the backwood in her hand, took a long pull, then exhaled deeply. She began wiping away the tears on her face. Dos had committed one of the deadliest sins known to a woman: betrayal. There was nothing more dangerous than a woman scorned. "This nigga done broke my heart for the last time," she seethed. Jasmine spoke out loud, trying to convince herself. Hatred burned in her soul. Suddenly, those watery eyes became steely ones, and her broken heart became black as it beat violently in her chest. She wanted Dos to hurt like she did.

Back inside Dos's condo, a thick redbone stripper with blond hair was ass naked and hunched over the table sniffing lines of cocaine through a hundred-dollar bill. Coke wasn't Dos's thing. He only smoked weed, but he didn't have a problem providing the party favors. Another badass Cubana stripper was lying across the couch ass naked as well. She was high off coke too and was feeling hot and horny. They had all just finished fucking, and she was ready for round two.

"*Ven aqui, papi,*" she said with a cute Spanish accent. "Let me suck that big dick." She licked her lips.

Dos smiled and walked toward the couch. He was already hard. He stood in front of her as she slid to the edge of the couch and grabbed his dick aggressively. Dos rubbed his hand through her long, silky hair as she smacked herself in the face with his manhood. She began to suck on his balls as the redbone with the blond hair joined in, playing with the tip of his dick with her tongue. They alternated, one sucking his dick, the other licking his balls. Dos put both hands behind her head and leaned his head back with his eyes closed. All he could hear was wet and popping sounds as they went to work. Finally, the redbone looked up at him and said, "Fuck me, daddy."

"You want this dick, bitch?" he said, then bent her over the arm of the couch with her ass up in the air.

"Fuck this pussy," she purred, looking over her shoulder at him and licking her lips.

Dos smacked her phat ass and grabbed her hips as he entered her from the back.

"Oh shit," she moaned, throwing her ass back at him. "Deeper, daddy, deeper."

Dos began punishing her, digging in her guts harder. Her ass jiggled and rippled like waves in the ocean as she received every thrust. "Oh my God," she began to scream at the top of her lungs from the intense orgasm. Dos continued pounding until the other stripper became jealous.

"Bring that dick over here, papi," she moaned out to him. Her legs were spread open, up in the air like a peace sign, and she was rubbing her clit.

Dos walked over and plunged his rock-hard manhood into her waiting wetness. She started to come instantly, biting down on her lip and caressing her own breasts. "Oh yes, like that. I feel it in my stomach," she cried out from the pleasure.

"I know you do," he bragged.

"Fuck that tight little pussy," the redbone shouted instructions as she rubbed her clit and looked on.

Dos's stroke became more powerful and deliberate as he felt his climax nearing. He clenched his teeth and pumped harder and harder.

"Yeah, baby, give me that nut," the redbone called out to him.

Dos pulled out of the Cuban stripper and released his seed all over the redbone beauty's face. "Aaaahhhh," he moaned, then collapsed on the couch breathing heavily.

Chapter Nine

Watching from the ground as his shooter fled on foot, Ricardo could feel the warmth of his own blood beneath him. He felt a searing pain in his body like he had never felt before. It had all happened so fast. The assassin appeared out of thin air. Ricardo hadn't even heard the first shot, but he felt it and the slugs that followed. The fact that he was in so much pain was the only thing that let him know that he was still alive. But for how long? He needed medical attention immediately.

Searching the parking lot, he couldn't understand why his bodyguard hadn't come to his aid yet. Then he spotted his dead body stretched out a few feet away. Ricardo tried to move, but he couldn't find the strength to drag his body across the parking lot and into his gym. He lay there staring up at the cloudy grey sky, clinging to life with thoughts of his past playing in his mind. With every breath he took, another ghost would appear to him, friends and foes alike. There were so many faces that they started to blur together, and so did his vision.

The black Ford F150 pulled alongside the beat-up Honda in the secluded spot behind an abandoned church. Kev quickly jumped out and got into Rio's truck.

"Put the gun in there," he said, immediately passing Kev a small, black lockbox. "I gotta make that shit disappear ASAP."

Kev placed the gun in the box. He still was breathing heavily from the rush of adrenaline.

"You got him?" Rio asked.

"Hell yeah," Kev answered like he had been offended. "You ain't deal wit' a amateur," he bragged. "I hit him, and the nigga with 'em four times each. Left 'em both slumped in the parking lot."

"So you sure he's dead?" Rio pressed. He was dead serious. He turned his body to face Kev, wanting to see his eyes as he answered.

"Yeah, nigga. He dead as shit," Kev assured him. The fact the Rio was pressing him so hard made him a little annoyed and anxious. Kev was ready to get paid and get gone.

Rio could sense the urgency within the truck too. "The rest of your bread in the glove box," he said, pointing.

That's all Kev wanted to hear. His eyes lit up as he reached for the glove compartment. His expression quickly changed when he didn't see anything inside. "Ain't shit in here—"

With a noise no louder than a whisper, Rio filled Kev's body with five shots from a gun with a silencer that he gripped in his hand. Kev's body slowly leaned against the door of the truck. Rio reached across his body and opened it, letting Kev's body fall to the ground. Rio had never planned on letting Kev live. He was just a means to an end. He knew too much, and Rio didn't trust him enough to believe he could keep a secret. The less people that knew the truth about Ricardo's murder, the better.

The only thing was . . . Ricardo wasn't dead, at least not yet.

The ambulance's siren pierced the air like the wail of a woman in agony as it raced along the rain-slicked streets. Pedestrians and drivers alike watched as it whizzed by with looks of apprehension on their faces. It was like they could feel the impending drama building in the air, because many of them already knew who was inside. The shooting had only occurred a short time ago, but the streets were already abuzz with what had gone down. Ricardo Wheeler, the man among men, had been shot outside his boxing gym. His trusted bodyguard had been killed in the process. Talk was rampant in the streets about who was responsible. No one knew, but they knew the response would be swift and brutal. In the streets, some dudes were respected, some were feared, and some were loved. Ricardo was all three.

Inside the ambulance, a female EMT worker sat beside him, gripping his hand. She held it tightly as if she were trying to will the life back into him. "Sir, can you hear me?" she questioned. "Just hold on, sir, we're almost there." Ricardo's breathing was shallow. His eyes were closed, but he indeed heard her.

"I think we might be losing him," another male worker proclaimed. "The police said to see if he knows who did this to him," he told his coworker.

"Sir, can you hear me?" she asked again. Seeing Ricardo's eyes move under his eyelids, she took it as a yes. "We're almost at the hospital," she assured him before asking, "Do you know the person who did this?"

Ricardo didn't know who was behind it, but even if he did and could speak, he wouldn't have said a thing. He just wanted them to hurry and get him to the hospital. He was in a fight for his life, and at the moment, he was struggling to survive. He could feel his strength waning; then darkness and silence engulfed him.

Lying awake in the bed next to a still sleeping Shantelle, East tried to force himself not to think about his mother or Tez. Not a day had passed that he didn't miss them both or regret killing Tez. East had been taught to quickly put things out of his mind. It was a skill that had served him well up until now. But killing Tez was the one thing he couldn't shake. It had continued to bother him. The pain hadn't faded over the years; it only seemed to increase. Nothing had felt the same since he lost both Ebony and Tez. A piece of him had died along with them.

His phone ringing on the nightstand broke him from his thoughts. "Yeah," he quickly answered, thankful for the distraction.

"You see the news?" Screw asked.

"Nah, what's up?"

"Nigga, turn on the news right now," Screw told him.

East grabbed the remote and turned on the TV. There was breaking news. A deadly shooting. A dead body covered with sheets, in front of Ricardo's boxing gym.

"Somebody tried to kill Ricardo," Screw said.

East sat up in the bed with such urgency that it woke Shantelle.

"What's wrong?" she said in a fog of sleepiness, her heart pounding from being startled.

"Let me call you back." East quickly rushed to hang up the phone, not wanting Screw to recognize Shantelle's voice. He told himself that this would be the last time they hooked up. He needed to be the one to put a stop to it because he knew she never would. Shit could go real bad if Screw found out.

"What's going on?" she asked, her naked body peeking from under the sheet.

East didn't respond immediately, not out of rudeness, but he didn't have an answer. He used the remote to increase the volume, and they both listened to the female reporter on the TV. She hadn't even finished her report before he was out of the bed and getting dressed.

"What's happening?" the concern in Shantelle's voice was evident.

It served as another reminder to East why he needed to end things with her. She needed to be as far away from shit like this as possible.

"Isn't that Ricardo's gym on—"

East interrupted her before she could finish her sentence. "Yeah. Get dressed. I gotta take you . . . home." The last words came out a bit awkward.

"You can drop me at my girl's house. I have a key," Shantelle told him, then smirked at the look of relief his face showed.

The loud banging at the door startled Dos from his sleep. He removed the legs of the naked women in his bed from across his body, grabbed his gun from under his pillow, and got out of the bed.

"Dos, get up! We gotta go! It's your pops," the voice screamed on a continuous loop from the other side of the door.

Dos looked through the peephole. His cousin was on the other side with a frantic look on his face. Dos snatched the door open and stood in the doorway naked with his gun in his hand. "What the fuck you talkin' 'bout? What about my pops?" he asked with a scowl on his face.

"He got shot outside the gym this morning," Rio told him. "He still alive but—" Dos raced to grab some clothes before he could finish his sentence.

The doors of the emergency room opened. East turned in time to see Dos rushing through them, dressed in a Nike jogging suit with Rio following close behind. His chest heaved up and down as he marched over to the nurse's station. "Where's my father?" he barked, banging his hands down on the desk. He was full of adrenaline and could barely contain his anger. Dos always operated purely off emotions.

The security guard on duty quickly approached. "Sir, you're gonna have to calm down or I'ma have to ask you to leave," his voice boomed through the ER.

Dos pinched the tip of his nose and looked up at the ceiling. "My father was just shot. If you don't wanna be next, you'll get the fuck outta my face," he threatened the security guard. The cold stare made the man take a step back. Dos was heated that the security guard would have the audacity to press him.

"Sir, please calm down so I can help you," one of the older nurses spoke up, trying to defuse the situation. She had a soothing voice and seemed to be the one in charge.

"I'm calm," Dos replied. His chest was still heaving up and down.

"Now what is your father's name, young man? And when was he brought—"

Before the nurse could finish her questions, Dos turned and saw East quickly approaching them from across the lobby. He met him halfway. Without a greeting, he asked, "Where's my father?"

East shrugged his shoulders. "I don't know. They wouldn't tell me nothing either."

Dos sighed in frustration. "Whatchu doing here anyway?" he scoffed. There was distaste in his tone.

"Same thing you're doing here," East retorted.

Dos chuckled inwardly. They had once been close. But that no longer was the case. Dos viewed East as beneath him. Truth was, East wasn't born to follow. He had boss potential. Ricardo knew it, and so did Dos, deep down inside.

"Excuse me, Nurse," the sultry sound of a woman's voice called out. "I'm Mrs. Wheeler. Can you tell me where my husband is?"

East and Dos turned toward Lauryn, who was standing at the nurse's station, flanked by her bodyguard. Nearly fifteen years younger than her husband, Lauryn mesmerized any man that looked at her. She had unmatched beauty with flawless bronze skin and a tight body. Her hair was pulled up in a top bun, and she was draped in designer clothes from head to toe. The spoils of being the trophy wife of a boss. She had dry tear lines on her face. Her eyes were red and swollen from crying the whole ride to the hospital.

"Here comes the doctor now, ma'am. He will be able to tell you everything you need to know." The nurse pointed in the direction of a tall, slender white man in a white lab coat.

Lauryn rushed over to him with Dos, East, and Rio right behind her. "Doctor, I'm Mrs. Wheeler. Is my husband okay?" She didn't realize that she was holding her breath, bracing for his answer.

The doctor was caught off guard by the sight of the beautiful woman standing in front of him. She looked more like his patient's daughter than his wife. He cleared his throat to regain his professionalism, preparing to deliver the news. "Well, ma'am, Mr. Wheeler's condition is still very much touch and go at this moment. He was shot multiple times. We are doing everything we can for him."

Tears clouded Lauryn's eyes as they ran down her face. She shook uncontrollably. Her legs felt weak. Her emotions were all over the place. She grabbed the doctor's arm. "Can I see him, please? Just for a minute." She eyed the doctor with her soft brown eyes that made men melt. The doctor was no exception.

He cleared his throat once again as his face became a blushing red. "I'm sorry, Mrs. Wheeler, did you say it was? I wish I could, but I have to say no. It's too early," he answered before trying to walk away.

Dos grabbed the doctor's arm, stopping him in his tracks. He squeezed so tight the doctor could feel the circulation stop. Dos stepped closer, so now their faces were only inches apart. "My father better live or you won't, understand me?" he assured the doctor. The crazed look in his eyes struck fear in the poor man.

"Dos, chill," Rio said, grabbing his arm, trying to calm the escalating tension. "That ain't helping the situation. Let the man do his job."

Dos released the doctor's arm, then shot Rio a menacing look. Rio let his arm go. Dos eyed East for a moment, then walked away in anger. The bodyguard that had accompanied Lauryn escorted her to the waiting room. Suddenly, Dos stopped midstride and marched back over to East. "Let me talk to you outside for a minute." East nodded, and with that, they headed for the front door.

Once they were outside, Rio stayed back while Dos and East walked side by side. Dos lit a Newport and took a long drag. He was on edge. "Where you was this morning?"

"What?" East snapped back.

"You hard of hearing? I said, where were you this morning when my father got shot? Cuz you been acting different ever since the shit with Tez. Now you up here at the hospital, acting all concerned and shit. It don't add up." Dos's anger was at a rolling boil.

"Nigga, you don't even believe that shit you're saying," East quickly dismissed him. "What's wrong wit' you?" he questioned Dos's thinking.

"What's wrong wit' me?" Dos snapped, gesturing with his hands toward the hospital. "Nigga, my father lying shot up in the hospital is what the fuck is wrong with me."

"And you should be in there, praying he make it instead of out here talking reckless to me."

"Who is you to tell me what I should be doing? I ain't ask for your advice," he seethed.

"So, what's there to talk about then?" East replied becoming aggravated with the back and forth. He knew Dos was too hot tempered to ever think sensibly anyway.

"You was always good at being the help," Dos asserted in a condescending tone. He eyed East up and down. "So help."

"What the fuck you say?" East pressed him, so they were face-to-face.

Dos smirked. "You ain't deaf, nigga." He blew smoke from his mouth, then tossed his cigarette to the ground. Neither of them was willing to back down. "My pops been spoon-feeding you. If my plug got shot, I'd be out here in the daytime with a flashlight trying to find who did it. 'Cause that's fucking with my money. Unless you had something to do with it," Dos wondered aloud, eyeing East suspiciously. "I'm calling the shots for now, and I say, there's a green light on any and everybody. No exceptions." Dos made sure to emphasize his last statement so East knew that included him as well.

East chuckled. "Only because your father is in there right now," he said, pointing toward the hospital. "And I know you ain't thinking straight. I'm gonna forget you just said that." East swallowed hard, maintaining his composure. "You always wanted to be the boss, right, *Junior?*" He called Dos by the name he hated. "Here's your big chance," he countered, then walked away.

"Tell me something, East, 'cause I'm really starting to wonder about you." Dos's words floated through the air stopping East in his tracks. His muscles flexed and twitched as he walked back toward Dos.

"What?"

"Since when you turned into a jellyfish? 'Cause I can remember one time in particular when you used to have that killer instinct. Remember? *Pow!*" Dos made a gun with his finger and pulled the trigger, referring to East murdering his mentor, Tez. He was now questioning if East no longer had a backbone or the heart for the streets.

"Fuck you," East shot back. "You and I both know better than that, but go handle your business, nigga. You the boss now, right? King of Miami," he shouted while sarcastically clapping his hands. "If and when you decide you really wanna do something, you know where to find me." East shook his head, then walked to his car. He decided that coming to the hospital today was a bad idea. He would check on Ricardo another time.

Rio approached Dos as East hopped in his car and drove off. "What's up wit' that nigga?"

"Fuck him." Dos was dismissive.

"He ain't really family, anyway," Rio said.

"Exactly," Dos agreed, then headed back inside the hospital.

Chapter Ten

East stood quietly in front of his mother's grave. He had come to replace the flowers, something he did often. He knew she would want and appreciate that. He didn't say much when he came, choosing, instead, just to enjoy the peacefulness of sitting with his mother. He remembered doing the same thing the night she died.

After the doctor delivered the devastating news that Ebony had passed, another doctor entered the waiting room minutes later. He offered East the opportunity to see his mother's body. Even then, East was brave behind his years. He showed no hesitation in doing so. With tears in his eyes, he followed the doctor. Entering the room where his mother's body was, East climbed in the bed with her and rubbed her hair. As he stood in the cemetery years later, he could still recall how soft it felt. He traced his hand across her face, slow and gently like a blind person would to log someone's appearance into their brain. East lay there for hours, just looking at her, staying with her, not wanting to leave. It was the one thing he could do to make himself feel better . . . not leave. Because leaving her would mean she was really gone, and he wasn't ready to accept that. So he stayed there, rubbing her hair and kissing her face for hours until Tez finally took him home.

East was startled from his thoughts by the sound of grass crunching under someone's feet. He looked away from his mother's headstone, expecting to see a groundskeeper. Instead, Lauryn was standing there, looking flawless like usual, although he could tell she was using sunglasses as a veil, probably to hide her red-rimmed eyes. Not a hair on her head was out of place. She wore a white tank top, skintight jeans, pink Christian Louboutin pumps, and held a pink Chanel bag in one hand and a Starbucks cup in the other. She was always put together. Her way of distracting from the hurt she felt. That might have fooled everyone else, but East recognized the look. He had seen it before, during his younger days as her bodyguard.

"I didn't mean to interrupt," she said softly. "I wasn't even sure if it was you." East remained silent momentarily. She could see he was thrown off by her presence. "I'm here visiting my father. He's over there," she pointed.

"That's right," East said, quickly remembering as he looked in that direction.

"I'm sorry I didn't speak the other night at the hospital."

"I understand," he assured her that he hadn't taken offense. "How is he?" he inquired about Ricardo.

Lauryn lowered her head. "Nothing has changed . . . yet." East nodded. "It's nice seeing you again," she said. He had matured nicely since his days as one of her many bodyguards.

"It's nice to see you too." East noticed there was nobody shadowing her. "If you don't mind me asking, shouldn't there be someone with you?"

"I gave them the day off," she revealed.

East smiled. He had always gotten the impression Lauryn didn't like her every move being shadowed. With Ricardo in the hospital, she had taken the opportunity to move more freely. After a long pause, he said, "Well . . . be safe," and turned to walk away.

"Don't go," she blurted out surprisingly. "If you don't mind. It would be nice to have you here . . . like old times." And for the first time, a smile creased her face.

"I can do that." East smiled too.

Lauryn was thankful he decided to stay and keep her company. Having East there wouldn't take away the pain, but it strangely gave her some comfort. When he stepped away to allow her privacy to grieve, she grabbed his hand to stop him, then pulled him closer for support.

He smells so good, she thought to herself, then let the thought *good* turn her attention to her father. East kept her company until she finished her visit. When she was ready to leave, he escorted her to the parking lot. He opened her car door for her.

"Old habits dead hard," she quipped.

East laughed. "Oh, you got jokes."

"I'm just kidding," she chuckled. "I can see that ain't your thing no more." She too recognized what everyone saw in East. He was a different breed. A charismatic street nigga that was a goon and a hustler, all in one. He was destined for greatness. He had too much potential not to.

"It good to see you not dressed in black," he said seriously.

"You noticed." Lauryn appreciated that he had. She removed her shades and took him in completely. She studied his handsome face, and her eyes zoomed in to the tattoos on his neck. She couldn't help but notice how he had matured into a sexy piece of eye candy. Although he was forbidden fruit, it didn't hurt to look. She smiled.

"I always did." East returned the gesture. It was impossible not to. Lauryn did this thing with her eyes when she spoke. It was like a magnetic pull that drew people in. She had a captivating aura and could cast a spell with her alluring eyes.

"It feels good to be seen. You know . . . like a person and not a trophy sometimes," she explained, then laughed nervously, pushing back tears. She had so much pent-up emotions, she felt like she would explode.

"You've been through a lot," East said. "No one expects you to be Superwoman all the time."

"This is so embarrassing," she sighed and attempted to wipe her tears, only to be stopped by East.

"No apologies needed. If you need to cry . . . cry. It's like taking your soul to the Laundromat."

"What you know about some Lyfe Jennings?" she asked, cracking a smirk through her tears.

"You'd be surprised what I know," East said.

"You'd be more surprised what you don't," Lauryn said. The tone of her voice suddenly changed.

"What don't I know? Tell me," East searched her eyes intensely. Despite Lauryn's calm exterior, there was now a different look in her eyes. The look of a woman who knew more than she was willing to say. It had appeared out of nowhere, almost involuntary. Her eyes seemed to hold secrets that were buried deep inside but dying to reveal themselves.

"There's always a few missing parts to everyone's story," she explained. Lauryn stared at East. For some reason, she felt comfortable. That wasn't always the case for Lauryn being around men that worked for her husband. Most never said a word to her and were afraid to even make eye contact. They made her feel like a thing and not a person. East was different. He didn't treat her like that. He made her feel normal, like she did before she was the boss's wife. Secretly, Lauryn despised that title. It put her in a bubble. She wasn't allowed to be herself. But in his presence, she felt free. Even if it was only for the brief moment that they stood alone in the parking lot of a cemetery. It was a feeling she hadn't experienced in a long time.

"What's that supposed to mean?" he asked.

"Nobody is who they seem, but everybody is exactly who they are," she replied.

"Then who are you? The *real* you." His mouth asked the question, but the look in his eyes said so much more. It said he wanted to know the deepest parts of her. Not just the beautiful surface. No man had ever looked at her the way he did. It was so mesmerizing that it momentarily took her breath away.

"I'm just regular ol' me," she said softly.

East stepped closer to her. The smell of his cologne invaded her nostrils again. She inhaled deeply. She didn't want to move. She just wanted to be still and enjoy his energy. It was refreshing.

"Believe me, ma, there is nothing regular about you. Any man who thinks that is a fool." His boldness shocked her, but it spoke to her soul.

"Stop, East. You can't be looking at me like that. We shouldn't be—"

Before she could finish, East kissed her. Something in his kiss shot through her body. It was electric. She wanted to pull away, but she didn't. She just couldn't. Instead, she leaned in toward him and kept kissing him, more passionately.

Suddenly, she pulled back, breathless. "This is wrong," she said. When he tried to reply, she quickly cut him off. "No, East, this is wrong. This is so wrong. We can't do this. We shouldn't be doing this," she said, getting into her car in a feverish haste. "You need to forget this ever happened." She slammed the door and pulled off.

East stood frozen for a moment, unsure of what had just happened. He had gotten caught up in the moment and crossed the line. "Fuck," he scolded himself. He had just made a move on Ricardo's wife. He hadn't thought about the consequences of his actions until it was too late. That wasn't like him. A mistake like that could cost him his life, and rightfully so, he thought to himself. He knew better. He might have just signed his death certificate. He only hoped Lauryn stayed true to her word and forgot it ever happened.

Lauryn rushed into the house. Closing the door, she leaned her back against it. "Woo," she exhaled, trying to calm her raging heart. Kissing East had given her a feeling that wasn't easily forgotten. After taking a few seconds to gather her thoughts, she headed straight upstairs to shower. A little while later, she descended the stairs into the kitchen and searched the cabinets for the biggest wineglass she could find. When she located it, she poured herself a glass of wine and took a few sips. She set the glass on the marble countertop and enjoyed her view. The floor-to-ceiling glass patio doors in the kitchen made the room feel like it extended outdoors to where the ocean was her backyard. From her position, she had a perfect view across the water to South Beach. At night, the strip would come alive with people. The buildings would light up with vibrant colors. The lights reflecting off the water created an amazing optic she enjoyed. Suddenly, a noise disturbed her from the calm and peacefulness she had found within her thoughts. Before she could turn to see what it was, someone grabbed her from behind and placed their hand over her mouth. She was easily overpowered and felt paralyzed with fear.

"Do what I say and you won't get hurt," the intruder barked out instructions. "You understand?" Lauryn nodded her head. "Good girl," he said, caressing her hair and the side of her face.

Lauryn gasped as the man's hands began exploring her body. She could feel him becoming aroused as he pressed his body against hers. She felt like her heart would leap from her chest at any moment as his hand made its way down to her waist. He easily untied her silk robe, exposing her naked breasts and lace panties. When the air hit the beads of water that remained from her shower, her Hershey Kiss nipples became erect. The intruder rubbed her breasts, then squeezed them aggressively. Lauryn fought back tears as he had his way with her. Her next breath got stuck in her throat, feeling his hand over her crotch area. He began rubbing her clit through her panties. It was all happening so fast. She wanted to scream, but no one would hear her. She was alone with the intruder and at his mercy. He yanked at her panties, forcefully ripping them away, giving himself a clear path to her shaved pussy. Lauryn grunted in pain as he plunged his two fingers into her. To both of their surprise, Lauryn was wet, something she couldn't help. It seemed to turn him on more, make his breathing become heavier in her ear.

"You like that shit, don't you, bitch?" he taunted as he roughly worked his fingers in and out of her. "You up in this big house by yourself. No one to guard you or help you."

Lauryn began to grunt and groan from the pain. She tried to speak, but his hand was still covering her mouth, muffling her speech.

"What, bitch?" he asked harshly in her ear while continuing to stroke her with his fingers. Finally, he removed his hand from her mouth.

Lauryn felt like she had just emerged from the deepest waters. She took in a deep breath of air, then in a loud whisper, she cried out, "Oh my God, that feels so good."

She spun around, and when her lips met Dos's lips, they melted into each other. Their tongues danced with each other. Dos stuck his fingers in her mouth, allowing her to taste her own juices. Lauryn licked his fingers clean. They began tearing at each other's clothes, stripping down until they were both naked in the middle of the kitchen.

"Did you remember to turn off the cameras?" she asked.

"Yeah." Dos pressed her back against the kitchen's island, then dropped to his knees. Lauryn lifted her leg and rested it on his shoulder, grabbing the back of his head and guiding his face into her pulsating lotus flower. Dos worked his tongue like a helicopter propeller inside her pussy. Lauryn held on to anything she could grab, first the counter, then his head, and eventually his ears as he sucked and slurped on her swollen clit. Lauryn's moans grew louder. She had given all her security detail the day off for this reason. Her legs became weak and began to shake, and her muscles tensed up as Dos took her body to its own personal nirvana.

"Oh, baby, right there. Yessss," she cried out as her mouth fell open from the orgasm surging through her body.

Dos stroked himself as he rose to his feet. Lauryn turned around and bent over the counter. Using both her hands to spread her ass cheeks, she gave him easy access to her pink wetness. He eased his rock-hard dick into her moist pussy and quickly found his rhythm. Lauryn moved her hips, taking all of him inside of her. Their bodies made loud noises as their flesh slapped together. Lauryn call his name while she climaxed again. Dos gripped her ass and thrust harder, digging deeper inside of her with every powerful stroke. He began to moan, feeling his climax building. She could feel him throbbing inside of her walls. She began to throw her ass back at him in short, circular movements until she heard him let out a primal scream. Dos pulled out of her pussy, stroking himself until he spilled his seed on her round ass.

He lay on top of her back as she rested her body on the counter, their chests heaving up and down, trying to catch their breaths. A few minutes passed before Lauryn moved, walking out of the kitchen and up the stairs to the bedroom. Dos followed behind her, and they picked up right where they left off.

Chapter Eleven

Early the next morning, a knock on the door woke Rio from his sleep on the couch. He had been too tired to make it to his bedroom the night before and crashed on his sofa. He stretched his arms toward the ceiling and rubbed his nose while yawning. He got up as the knocking continued and walked over to the door. Looking through peephole, he saw an old head junkie named Freddy, wearing a worn-out "Made in Dade" T-shirt. He always came around to wash Rio's car for money or drugs.

"It's too early for this shit," Rio sighed and mumbled to himself. He was still half-asleep. "Freddy, I should beat ya muthafuckin' ass, coming to my crib this early in the morning," he ranted as he snatched the door open. Rio stuttered his next words, caught by surprise. A dark-skinned gunman with huge jail muscles had Freddy by the back of his shirt with a big gun to the back of his head. The gunman forced his way inside the apartment, followed by another gunman that quickly stuck his gun in Rio's face.

"What the fuck is going on?" Rio uttered, no longer asleep. He had been caught slipping. His gun was still sitting on the coffee table next to a duffle bag.

"Get the fuck on the floor, fuck nigga," the dark-skinned gunman told Rio as he slammed Freddy to the floor and put his foot on his back. The other gunman did the same to Rio. "Watch them niggas," the dark-skinned one told his partner. "If they move, pop they muthafuckin' ass, you hear me?" Then he began searching the apartment. He didn't have to search long. Rio had left money and two bricks of coke in the open duffle bag on the table. With all the goods already neatly stuffed inside the bag, the gunman walked back over to Rio and began brutally pistol-whipping him, over and over. Rio's face became a bloody mess; so did his shirt. "I should kill you right now," he threatened with his gun to Rio's head. He pulled his phone from his pocket and dropped it on the floor next to Rio. "Call him," he barked.

"Call who?" Rio groaned.

"Don't play with me, nigga. You know who," the gun-man shouted. "Pick it up and call Dos, right now."

"I can't see," Rio whimpered. There was blood pouring into his eyes, and his face continued to leak.

The gunman looked over to his partner that was standing over Freddy. He nodded and without hesitating, the man fired two shots into Freddy's head. The dark-skinned gunman calmly squatted down next to Rio with his gun aimed at him and said, "Dial the fuckin' number." Struggling with his vision, Rio did his best to do just that.

Dos sat at the foot of the bed that Lauryn shared with his father, getting dressed. She lay there studying his every move. To her, Dos was everything Ricardo wasn't: young and aggressive. He just wasn't the boss yet. That was something they were both hoping to change in the very near future. Dos felt like a god. He saw the world as his and everything in it he should have, including his father's beautiful wife.

"What happened, Dos? Why is he still alive?" Lauryn complained. "You promised to take care of it. Take care of it. Instead of burying him, I'm having to visit him in the hospital and fake tears for them nosy-ass nurses."

Lauryn folded her arms across her chest frustrated and disappointed. "I don't know why you just didn't do it yourself."

Since Dos lacked the patience it took to wait his turn, he had tried to speed up the process. Things hadn't gone exactly as planned, and Ricardo wasn't dead. His excessive amount of ambition made him believe that any rule could be broken except for one.

"How many times do I have to tell you, I'm not about to shoot my own father." He quickly grew angry at the suggestion. "I'm not doing that," he insisted. Dos wanted Ricardo out dead, but he didn't have the guts to do it himself.

Lauryn crawled up behind him like a temptress and wrapped her arms around him. "If you did it, you'd know it would be done right," she said softly in his ear.

"What did I just say?" he barked, breaking free from her embrace and standing up. "I'll figure out another way. Don't worry about it. You keep doing your part, and I'll do mine," he reassured her, shaking his head as he admired her naked body. The phone rang, grabbing his attention away from Lauryn. He walked over to the nightstand and picked it up. "Yeah," he huffed.

"Dos—"

The gunman snatched the phone away before Rio could finish. He placed it to his ear.

"Rio?" Dos called out into the phone.

"This Dos?" a voice asked aggressively from the other end of the phone.

"Who this?"

"This Zo, nigga."

Dos's eyes widened, and his face looked like he saw a ghost.

"What's wrong?" Lauryn whispered with concern, seeing the worried look on his face.

Dos knew the name Zo well. He was Kev's older brother. He was a straight menace on the streets; a jack boy and a killer. Up until recently, he had been locked up, but he was home now and out for vengeance. "What's up?" Dos challenged. "The fuck we got to talk about?"

"You killed my brother!"

"I don't know what the fuck you talking about. And from the sound of it, neither do you."

"Before he died, my brother told me about a job he was supposed to do for you," Zo said. Dos thought his heart stopped when he heard that. "Don't worry, though. When I catch you, I'm putting you, your faggot-ass father, and anybody else you love in a body bag. For free . . . starting with ya man right here," Zo declared.

Dos heard Rio scream through the phone, followed by gunshots. There was a brief moment of silence before the phone went dead. Dos was so angry he tossed his phone across the room.

"What just happened, Dos?" Lauryn asked in a panic after seeing his reaction. She had heard the conversation and the gunshots.

He pinched the bridge of his nose, then gave her a menacing look. "Nothing! I got it under control."

"Under control? Really?" she shouted before hushing her tone. "Your father's not dead, and somebody besides us knows we're behind it. Seems to me, all you did was make the shit worse. What if someone else finds out?" She knew the consequences if anyone was to find out about her and Dos's betrayal. They would both be dead. The thought alone gave her the bubble guts. Ricardo was not a man of mercy. Whoever he deemed responsible would pay with their lives.

Lauryn stood up from the bed and grabbed her silk Versace robe to cover her naked body. She headed over toward the balcony door in her bedroom and pulled the drapes back slightly, giving her a view of the pool and allowing the sunlight to beam into the bedroom.

Dos marched over and spun her around forcefully. He gripped her face firmly, squeezing it with his hand. "Let me tell you something. Ain't nobody gonna find out shit, unless you open your fuckin' mouth," he said. His eyes were threatening. He let her face go. "I said I'll take care of it, and I will." His overflowing confidence was on full display. "Get dressed and take your ass to see my pops. What kind of wife ain't by her husband's side around the clock after he's been shot anyway? Focus on that," he seethed, then walked out of the room.

Lauryn sighed deeply, fear surging all through her body. She had no other choice but to trust in Dos. They weren't soul mates by any stretch of the imagination. They weren't even in love, although the sex between them was otherworldly. Dos took her body to unimaginable places and hit spots Ricardo couldn't reach. They were just two souls with an ax to grind against a common enemy. Lauryn wanted to be free from Ricardo's control, and Dos wanted to be king. As the saying goes, *The enemy of my enemy is my friend.*

Chapter Twelve

The next night, Dos's phone rang as he drove around the city looking for Zo. He sighed deeply seeing Jasmine's name flashing across his screen. It was at least the twentieth time she had called. He had too much going on to deal with her bullshit, but he knew if he didn't answer she wouldn't stop calling anytime soon. He decided to answer it, in case it had something to do with his son. "What! Damn," he shouted into the phone.

"You can't just ignore my calls, Dos. We have a son—in case you forgot," Jasmine said.

"Yeah. I can't forget that," he said sarcastically.

"Why would you ever want to?" she questioned.

"Never want to forget my son, just wish I could forget his momma," he shot back. "What do you want? I got lots of shit going on right now."

"Yeah, I heard. The streets been talking," she replied.

"That's your fuckin' problem now," he snapped. "You always got an open ear for someone to say some shit about me. Told you before you need to stop listening to them hoes at your job."

"Whatever, you just need to be safe. You got people out here that love and care about you," Jasmine confessed her feelings. The phone went silent for a moment, Dos refusing to respond to her last statement. After a long pause, she continued. "Anyway, I need money for Tre's day care."

"I'll bring it to you in a couple of days. Shit is crazy right now."

"It can't wait 'til then," she whined. "I've been calling you, and you haven't been answering. It has to be paid in the morning or they're gonna put him out of school," she complained. "If they put him out, I have to reapply just to get him on the list again. And then, ain't no telling how long it will be before he could go back. You remember how long it took him to get him in there the first time—"

"Yeah. Yeah. Okay." Dos sighed into the phone, then cut her off. "Where you at now?"

"I'm at work," she said with an attitude, stating the obvious. Jasmine knew Dos could hear the loud music bumping in the background.

"A'ight, I'm on my way."

A short while later, Dos pulled up and parked a block away from the club. If Zo knew he was responsible for killing Kev, there was no telling who else knew. He had to be on point, not just from Zo, but the police too. He got out and tucked his gun into his waist. Then he headed inside the club. Once inside, he bumped into a dude that bought bricks from him. He looked at Dos like he had seen a ghost.

"What the fuck you doing in here, my nigga?" the dude yelled over the music, dapping Dos.

"I'm lookin' for somebody," Dos said, unwilling to give any more information than that. He didn't need everyone knowing that Jasmine was his baby mother and that she worked in there.

"I heard about you. I heard niggas looking for you, for killing Kev. That shit fucked up," the dude said, shaking his head.

"I'on know nothin' 'bout that," Dos said, quickly putting an end to the conversation, moving past him and heading for the bar where Jasmine was.

When Jasmine spotted Dos coming through the crowd of people, her insides began to bubble. She was filled with nervous energy. She turned her head, making eye contact with Zo. He was posted in the cut at the end of the bar with a hat pulled low over his face. He followed her eyes in Dos's direction.

Dos approached the bar, squeezing between two female waitresses waiting for their orders. He admired their bodies, looking them up and down and smiling. They smiled back, appreciating the fine-looking stranger in their midst.

"Hey, daddy, you need some help?" one of them flirted with him.

"I'm good. Maybe another time, another place, though," he said and smirked. "Jasmine!" he yelled over the music trying to get her attention.

She glanced over her shoulder at him from the other end of the bar. Her heart was pounding in her chest as she watched Zo get up from his seat and began to circle around to where Dos was standing.

Dos called out to Jasmine again, this time waving her to him. "I don't have all night, c'mon," he shouted. She hesitated to move. Dos noticed her weird behavior. Something was off about her. He could tell by the look on her face. Her eyes looked away from him, and when he followed them, he saw what she was looking at.

Suddenly, gunfire erupted inside the club. Panic ensued within seconds, people scrambling in every direction. Dos ducked to the floor and pulled out his gun as the gunshots continued to fly his way. Zo was relentlessly firing. Dos searched through the crowd until he spotted Zo's exact position. He popped up from the floor and started returning fire.

It was raining bullets inside the club, both men shooting at each other through the crowd of running people. Zo emptied his clip, then slipped out the back of the club in the chaos of all the screaming, panicked people.

Quickly, Dos slipped out the front of the club, hitting the front door with everyone else, and headed straight for his car. When he got outside, police were coming down the streets. He jumped into his Benz and sped away.

Dos's phone rang as he was driving. He was already planning how he was going to move on Zo when he saw Rio's name come across the scene. That meant it could only be one person since Rio was dead.

"Bitch-ass nigga. You a dead man," Dos barked in the phone. His voice was filled with emotion and adrenaline.

"Fuck you. Suck my dick. You living on borrowed time," Zo laughed and banged on him.

Dos gritted his teeth as the phone call ended. "I'ma kill that nigga!" he shouted, banging his fist on the steering wheel. Now Jasmine's face appeared in his mind. He noticed how she was acting funny back at the club and also how she hadn't called to check on him. "Foul-ass bitch. I'ma kill her too," he seethed. His phone began ringing again. This time it was Lauryn. He ignored the call, but she called right back, then again, and again. Finally, he answered. "What's up? What you want?" his adrenaline mixing with anger as he spoke.

"What's up, son? It's good to hear your voice."

Dos's heart skipped a beat hearing his father's voice on the phone. "Hey . . . Hey, Pops." His voice was unsteady from shock and surprise. "When you wake up?" he asked.

"Not 'how you feeling' or 'good to hear your voice'?" Ricardo questioned with a hoarse laugh.

"You know what I meant, Pops," Dos calmed his nervousness. "Something crazy just happened. I ain't thinking straight right now."

"Come up to the hospital in the morning and you can tell me all about it. For now, I'm gonna get some more rest. I just wanted to hear your voice," Ricardo said.

"You do that," Dos said. "Oh, and Pops?"

"What?" Ricardo replied.

"I love you. It's good to have you back from the dead."

"It's good to be back," Ricardo said, then hung up.

Dos let the phone linger next to his ear for a second, then let it fall to the seat.

Dos sat in his car in front of Jasmine's building with his gun on his lap. He had been downstairs for over an hour, contemplating killing her. Every time he convinced himself to get out of the car and do it, his son's face would flash before his eyes. He was so conflicted. He had never been so sure—and unsure—of anything before in his life. Jasmine's betrayal should be dealt with one way—death. She had earned it, but had he pushed her to that point? He questioned himself. And if he was being truthful with himself, the answer would be yes. He knew it. She had never done anything but tried to love him. He, in return, gave her his ass to kiss. He had turned a good girl bad, and it had almost cost him his life. But should it cost her hers was the question. Jasmine deserved to die. But his son, Tre, didn't deserve to grow up without a mother like he had. When it boiled down to it, Dos loved his son more than he hated his baby's mother.

He took the clip out of the gun and tossed it on the passenger seat. He didn't trust himself. Then he got out of the car and walked inside Jasmine's building. He put his key in the front door of her apartment and walked in.

Jasmine was sitting in the living room, holding their son in her arms. It was like she was waiting for him. Her heart felt like it leaped into her throat when Dos walked into the house. He had a crazed look in his eyes. Tre called out for his da-da, as soon as he spotted Dos, but he ignored him. Tears began falling from Jasmine's eyes, noticing the black latex gloves on his hands. She knew what he was capable of. She wasn't naïve to the type of man he was.

Dos walked over and sat down next to her. He knew being so close to her made her uncomfortable. He took his son out of her arms and sat him on his lap and began playing with him. Never once did he make eye contact with Jasmine. Finally, he spoke, but when he did, his voice was eerily calm. "I know what you did."

Jasmine started to cry harder. "I'm sorry, Dos."

"No, you're not," he replied.

"I swear," Jasmine pleaded. "He threatened to kill me and Tre, if—"

Dos stopped the words from coming out of her mouth by wrapping his hand around her throat. "Don't use my son as an excuse, bitch," he gritted his teeth as he squeezed. "I want you to take Tre and move back to New York. You got forty-eight hours to leave. You understand me? If I ever see your fucking face again, I'm gonna kill you. I promise. When I wanna see my son, I'll send for him." Finally, Dos released his grip on her neck. Jasmine gasped for air. Dos kissed his son on the cheek, then sat him next to her. He rose to his feet and tossed a stack of hundreds on the coffee table, then looked back at her. She had tears racing down her face as she sat deathly still. "When I come through here in two days, you better be gone," he said, then walked out of the house, not bothering to close the door behind him.

Lauryn sat by the window in the hospital, watching her husband sleep. She felt like her world was falling apart in front of her eyes. It made her sadder than it did angry; still, tears filled her eyes as she thought about it. She had been under Ricardo's thumb long enough. She needed out. She felt like his hostage. He monitored her every waking moment. Her bodyguards were not there for protection but more to keep her captive. They reported everything about her back to Ricardo. There were cameras all throughout her home. Ricardo said they were for their safety, but she knew he used them to keep an eye on her when he wasn't around. He had only trusted her to be alone with Dos and before that, East. That was how she and Dos eventually became intimate. Spending time together, they realized they shared a similar hatred for Ricardo. They hatched a plan that benefitted both of them, but now, it was falling apart quickly. Ricardo would be coming home any day now, which meant, back to her dreaded routine life. She enjoyed him being in the hospital, honestly. It gave her a bit of freedom. She sent the guards away on some days and enjoyed just being a normal person. That was surely over now. Tears danced down her face as she recalled how she had gotten to this place in her life.

The fifty-foot, state-of-the-art yacht smoothly cruised the waters of the Florida Keys, somewhere between the Atlantic Ocean and the Gulf of Mexico. Al Biggs had a glass of cognac in one hand and a cigar in the other as he relaxed in a chair on the deck, enjoying the view. This was his second yacht, and he spared no expense this time around. It was lavishly decorated with gold faucets and sinks, mink rugs, and high-end entertainment.

"What do you think? Beautiful, ain't it?" he asked the man sitting across from him.

"Yes, it is," Ricardo said. He wasn't talking about the boat or the water, however. His eyes were locked on Old Man Al's twenty-year-old daughter, as she navigated the boat through the sea. She was gorgeous. More beautiful than any woman Ricardo had seen before. Her skin looked like it had been kissed by the sun, and her eyes looked like he could see heaven in them.

"How 'bout I let you use my boat anytime you want until I'm able to pay you back the money I owe you?" Al said.

Ricardo leaned back in his chair and looked out at the water. "I'm not really into boats, Al."

"This is not any ol' boat," Al explained. "I paid top dollar for this yacht. This is top-shelf shit you cruising on," he bragged and laughed.

"That's the thing. I'm trying to get paid in dollars too. I loaned you cash. I want cash in return," Ricardo commanded. "I've been more patient with you than most, out of respect, but I can't guarantee you how much longer that's gonna last."

"I know. I know. I appreciate you. I just need a little more time, Rico." By calling Ricardo by his childhood nickname, Al was banking on the history between the two of them. Before Ricardo was a street dude on the come up with dreams of being a boss, he was a boxer, and before that, he was a local kid with a dream of becoming world champ one day. That's where Al Biggs knew him from. Al was the biggest drug dealer in Liberty City at that time. He used to look out for Ricardo, big time. Keeping money in his pocket, giving him cars to drive, even getting him his first piece of pussy. Anything to keep him out of trouble, out of the streets and on the right path. When his boxing career didn't turn out like everyone thought, he turned to Al then too. And like always, Old Man Al took care of him. He put Ricardo in the game, and before he knew it, he was living larger than he ever had as a boxer. After his first taste of street money, there was no turning back for Ricardo. He dove into the streets headfirst. Now he had outgrown his teacher, like a fish that outgrew the pond.

"Just hold on to my boat until I can pay you back," Al pleaded.

"I told you, this ain't my thing. I wouldn't know the first thing to do with it," Ricardo said.

"C'mon, Rico, it gotta be something we can work out."

Ricardo grew quiet; then his eyes turned toward Al's daughter Lauryn again. He wanted her more than he wanted the money he was owed. "I think I got a way we can clear your tab," Ricardo smiled.

"What's that?" Old Man Al asked.

"What if you gave me you daughter's hand in marriage?" Ricardo sat back in his seat and waited for an answer.

"Lauryn?" Al laughed, thinking Ricardo had to be joking. But when he found himself the only one laughing, he became serious as well. "My daughter is only twenty. She's a little girl," he said angrily.

"I don't mean you no disrespect, but she ain't no little girl. She all woman," Ricardo explained.

"In looks only but not in the mind. Not for a man like you," Al replied.

"C'mon, Al, it's not like I'm trying to make her part of my harem or anything. I'm offering marriage, my last name. A lifetime commitment. You've raised her and gave her nothing but the best. I can continue to do that. You know me and what I'm about. You know she will be well taken care of. The cartel has cut you off. You're drowning in gambling debts. How long you think your lifestyle gonna last?" he questioned, giving the old man something to think about.

As they pulled the boat back into the harbor, Ricardo approached Lauryn and winked at her. She smiled, and he returned the gesture. "How you doing? I'm Ricardo," he introduced himself.

"I know who you are," she smiled. "I'm Lauryn."

"I already know," he told her. "You're a very beautiful woman," he complimented, causing her to blush. She *was flattered by the attention. She was raised by a hustler, and she knew a boss when she saw one. Ricardo was definitely that. "Your future bright, baby. From now on, you gonna be mine."*

Lauryn giggled. She thought he was joking, but he wasn't.

"I'm serious," Ricardo explained to her. "Do you love your father?" he smoothly asked.

"Of course."

"So, you would do anything for him, right?" Ricardo questioned.

"Yes," she replied once again.

"Your father owes me a lot of money, baby girl. A whole lotta money. He can't afford to pay. In our line of business, that's not good for business. I've killed men for far less," he said with such seriousness that Lauryn felt it in her chest. "I respect your father to the upmost. So, we worked out another way for him to pay off his debt. Ain't that right, Al?"

"Daddy?" Lauryn called out to him, confused.

"I don't want to force you. I'm not into that. I'm not trying to pimp you or nothing like that. I want you to be my wife," Ricardo declared. "But I must tell you that if you deny my request and your father can't pay me what he owes, I'm going to kill him."

Tears were now building in the wells of Lauryn's eyes. She knew about her father's gambling problem. She watched as all their possessions slowly disappeared over the years. "Daddy?" she cried out to him again, her eyes pleading with fear.

Al was so ashamed he couldn't even look his daughter in the eye. "Baby, you don't have to do anything you don't want to." The strings of his heart were being pulled from every which way. He saw the fright and confusion in Lauryn's eyes. But what crushed him even more was he knew she would do anything to spare him. *Love sacrifices.*

"I'm gonna treat you like a queen. You won't want for nothing," Ricardo told her. "But I need an answer . . . right now. Time is money, and your father can't afford to waste another second of mine," he said, pulling the gun from his waist, showing her how serious he was about killing her father.

"OK," she said. It was almost as if the word slipped out involuntarily. There was no thought, no apprehension. It was a gun and her father's life or a marriage. The choice was easy.

"Thank you," Al sighed in relief.

"You're the real winner in the family," Ricardo said sarcastically to Lauryn. "You gained a husband and didn't lose ya father. Sound like good math to me," he shrugged.

Lauryn was silent, and her body was stiff. The back of her throat became dry, and she tried her hardest to swallow the knot that formed in it. She couldn't believe or understand why this was happening to her. Why this man just came and changed the whole course of her life and destroyed her father's existence for what she knew it to be. Lauryn looked toward her dad and decided against calling out for him again. He was defeated, and she felt it. She could feel his weakness and failure oozing from his pores. She let out a tear and decided she will now be his strength.

A few hours later, Al relaxed on the deck of the yacht enjoying the sunset. He finished the drink in his glass and placed it down in front of him. He picked up the gun at his side as tears began to cloud his vision. He thought by handing over his daughter, he had saved his own life. But the shame he felt was eating him alive and made him not want to go on living. His gambling addiction *had made him a poor excuse for a man and an even worse father. Lauryn was truly better off without him. His only joy was knowing she would be taken care of in a way he could no longer provide for her. After all, he had groomed Ricardo himself.*

Suddenly, the sound of a single gunshot pierced the air, disturbing the calm and peacefulness, causing a flock of seagulls to fly away. The chirping of birds overhead was immediately followed by the thud of the gun falling from Al's dead hand.

Lauryn wiped the tears running down her cheeks as she thought about her father. He would have moved heaven and earth for her. All these years later, the pain still remained. Ricardo kept his word. She wanted for nothing. He had given her the best that life had to offer. But he treated her like a possession and not his wife. She felt like a prisoner. She was convinced Ricardo would never see her as anything more than a payoff for a debt. She was his beautiful trophy. She was there to be seen and not heard. Lauryn wasn't an evil woman; she just wanted out and knew he would never let her be free. Watching him sleep, the thought of killing him crossed her mind. She walked over to the bed and stood over him. It would be so easy to put a pillow over his face and rid herself of him. She reached for the pillow at the foot of the bed. At first her hands trembled, but soon they steadied as she contemplated murder. Then she heard the door to the room open and looked up to see the night nurse entering. She placed the pillow down on the bed and smiled, stepping aside to allow the woman to check on Ricardo.

Chapter Thirteen

The mild summer air flowed with ease through East's bedroom window. He sat rolling up some weed when his phone rang. He looked at the screen. It was a number he hadn't seen in a long time. He frowned his brow, wondering why the person was calling him. He started not to answer, but his curiosity got the better of him. "Hello," he said and was immediately bombarded with tearful cries and words. "Calm down. What? You're where?" East said. Jasmine was so distraught on the other end of the phone he could barely understand her. "Slow down. Slow down. You said what now?"

Jasmine proceeded to tell him everything that happened the other night at the club between Dos and Zo. East had already heard about it on the streets, but he played dumb, allowing her to fill in all the blanks for him. Jasmine was more than happy to. She was pissed about being exiled to New York. Honestly, East thought she was lucky that was all she got, but he never mentioned it. He just listened, and when she was finished, he wished her the best and hung up. He sat back on his couch and lit up some weed as he digested all that Jasmine had told him. He had an idea. He called Screw and Ques and told them to meet him in front of the projects in an hour.

The next day, East pulled up to Ricardo's home. When Lauryn opened the door, her words got caught in her throat. She hadn't seen him since they had kissed at the cemetery weeks earlier. She had tried her best to put the kiss out of her mind but seeing him brought it all back. Her hands became clammy as butterflies fluttered in her stomach. She normally was the one to have that effect on men, but the tables had been turned on her. She felt nervous in his presence and looked away from his gaze. She led him out to the back of the house where Ricardo sat at a table poolside.

Ricardo, with the help of his cane, slowly rose to his feet to shake East's hand and give him a hug, then returned to his seat.

"How you feeling?" East asked.

"I've been better, but I've been worse too," Ricardo laughed.

"I got something that I think will make you feel a lot better," East said.

"What's that? I like surprises as long as they are the good kind." Ricardo's face brightened with anticipation.

"I can show you better than I can tell you," East explained, then helped Ricardo to his feet.

He guided Ricardo out to the front of the house, where his car was parked. East went to the rear of the car and opened the trunk. Inside, there was a dark-skinned man in his late twenties. His wrists and ankles had been hog-tied, his mouth duct taped. He was squirming around trying to free himself. When Zo saw Ricardo and East standing over him, his face turned ashen white, and his eyes grew as wide as an eight-lane highway.

"I think this is the man who shot you," East announced.

"It wasn't him. It was his brother," Ricardo said, and up until then, he had not revealed that he had seen who shot him. "But he will do for now," he said with a devilish grin. He was going to enjoy killing Zo. Finally, he would have a taste of vengeance. His adrenaline seemed to give him the strength he needed to complete his mission. Three weeks ago, there had been an attempt made on his life. He had been shot four times outside the boxing gym he owned, but luckily, he survived. Although there were still two bullets lodged in his back, Ricardo was starting to get used to dealing with the constant pain that radiated through his body from the remaining slugs. He no longer could move with the same graceful fluidity he once had. That was still taking some time to get used to, along with the fact that his body felt like it had aged a full decade overnight. Four bullets ripping through you would do that to anybody. He was still a little paranoid, wearing a bulletproof vest under his grey Nike tracksuit as he stood in his driveway. Ricardo's dark eyes were cold and filled with murderous intent, his mind playing over the savage physical violence he planned to inflict on Zo. Twisted scenarios of torture slowly moved through his head, like hungry sharks circling a bleeding man. Until he exacted revenge, Ricardo would not be healed physically or mentally, just a broken shell of the man he once was. His eyes widened with excitement and anticipation. He had to refrain from killing Zo right there.

"I got a place where we can take him." He looked over at East and smirked. East nodded and slammed the trunk closed.

Lauryn watched from the bedroom window in a panic as she listened to their conversation. When she saw them drive away in East's car, she quickly dialed Dos's number. She paced back and forth in the middle of the bedroom. His phone seemed to ring forever before he picked up.

"What's good, ma," he answered calmly.

"Nothing is good. Nothing at all!" she cried into the phone.

"Wow, hold up. What's going on?"

"East just came here with somebody tied up in his trunk. I think it was that guy Zo." She whispered the last part like someone was listening in on their conversation.

"What!" Dos was now in a slight panic, but he tried masking it to keep her calm. "You sure?"

"Yes. They just left together. Oh shit, we're dead, Dos." She wanted to throw up; instead, she began to cry harder.

"Calm down. I'm gonna figure this shit out."

"No," she screamed, "there's nothing 'to figure out.' We have to leave."

"Leave?"

"Yes. We have to get out of town, or your father is going to kill us. Ahh!" she shouted. She should have never gotten in cahoots with Dos.

Although he hated to admit it, the safest place to be for both of them was out of town. At least, until he could find a way to fix things. "OK. OK. Let me think," he said.

He was taking too long for her liking. She was the one in immediate danger. Ricardo could come back at any moment and kill her. "I'm leaving, Dos—with or without you," she stated.

"You right, ma. You should get the fuck out of there right now," Dos admitted. "Grab what you can and get in your car. I'll meet you somewhere."

Lauryn was already packing, stuffing a few important things into her designer carry-on bag. "There's a motel by the airport. You know the one."

"Yeah," he said. "I'll meet you there in half an hour," he promised.

"Dos, if you don't show—" she started, but he cut her off.

"I'll be there," he assured her.

"If you don't, I'm leaving without you," she said, then hung up the phone. She raced frantically around the room grabbing things, then headed for her car.

***

From the spot in the middle of the floor where he lay writhing in pain, Zo could hear someone walking across the floor in the darkness. Suddenly, Ricardo Wheeler emerged from the shadows of the warehouse carrying something in his hand that Zo could not quite make out. He walked with a heavy limp. His eyes were dark and cold when he reached Zo. Then he set the bright red gas can down. He knelt down beside him and pulled the duct tape from his mouth. Zo immediately spit in his face, hoping it would anger Ricardo enough to put him out of his misery quickly. There was no such chance of that happening.

Ricardo merely took out a handkerchief from his pocket and wiped his face clean. He rose to his feet and swung his head side to side, cracking his neck. He pulled the gun from his waist. He looked at the black .45 in his hand, but gripping a loaded pistol had long lost its excitement. He wasn't there for thrills today. He was there for revenge. His blood warmed at the thought of that. Every muscle in his body began to tingle. He was a pro, at the top of his game. Standing over Zo, he felt at the height of his power.

How dare someone test my position! he thought to himself, then he kicked Zo in the stomach.

Ricardo looked at his victim's grimacing face. The smell of fear hung in the air. "What made you niggas think you could come for my crown?" The high that came from having power was like a drug. It sent a euphoric feeling through his body, numbing his own pain from head to toe. "Now look at you." He put the gun next to Zo's ear and pulled the trigger. The loud noise echoed through the warehouse.

"Ahhh!" Zo screamed in excruciating pain. His eardrum had been busted and blood leaked from his ear. The

loud ringing in his head went on for minutes. Zo began
to struggle to free himself, to no avail. He looked like an
animal trying to break its restraints. His constant moans
and pleas fell on deaf ears. Ricardo planned to make an
example out of him. The next person would think twice
before making a move on him. He had to restore order
in the streets. Reestablish the pecking order in Miami's
underworld. He picked up the gas can that sat at his feet
and began pouring gasoline over Zo's body and head.

"Not like this—please!" Zo wailed in terror.

"No, I think this is perfect," Ricardo replied. "What you
think, East?" he asked, looking off to the side where he
was standing.

East nodded.

"Tells everyone who's still in charge. I think my message will be very clear," Ricardo continued. He reached
in his pocket and removed a cigar. He put it in his mouth
and lit it.

Zo shouted, "No! Not like this!" as Ricardo began to
puff on the cigar. "This wasn't me or my brother's idea.
My brother was hired to kill you."

That statement intrigued Ricardo, causing him to hesitate before tossing the cigar on Zo. "Hired by who?" he
commanded to know.

"Your son," Zo revealed.

"Dos?" Ricardo's hearty laugh filled the spacious warehouse. "No way my son had anything to do with this."

"I have no reason to lie to you. I know I'm going to die. I
have nothing to gain. Just thought you should know."

"Bullshit," Ricardo challenged.

"How do you think my brother knew exactly where
you'd be that early in the morning?" Zo asked. "Who
were you supposed to be meeting with?"

The question was so heavy it felt as though Ricardo's
chest would collapse from absorbing it into his heart.

Because he knew the answer. It was one he didn't want to accept. The rage that burned in his eyes for Zo began to dim quickly before it faded completely, doused by the hurt and betrayal he suddenly felt. His soul was crushed into broken shards of glass. This was something he would have never expected. No man could fathom that his own seed—his flesh and blood, his one true heir—could be capable of such disloyalty. He had been betrayed in the most painful way. Ricardo always had his eye on everyone within his organization . . . except the one person he should've been watching. The person he would've never thought to keep under close observation. The person closest to him, closest to his heart. Dos had done the unthinkable. In return, Ricardo was left with the hardest choice he would ever have to make in his life. He knew in his heart there really was no other choice, but what hurt the most was knowing he didn't have the heart to do it himself. Ricardo let a single tear fall from his eye. Then he tossed the lit cigar on Zo, instantly sending him up in flames. As he watched him burn, Ricardo felt East's comforting hand on his shoulder.

"You believe him?" East asked somberly.

Ricardo slowly nodded his head in confirmation. "I was supposed to meet Dos that morning, but he never showed," he admitted reluctantly, every word drenched in sadness.

"Where'd he say he was?" East inquired.

"He said he had overslept. Something about fucking two bitches the night before."

"C'mon, let's get out of here," East said, helping Ricardo to the car. Ricardo's adrenaline had worn off, and he was feeling the pain.

Physically and emotionally.

Chapter Fourteen

Ricardo sat alone at the desk in his home office, feeling sick to his stomach. He couldn't watch any longer. He pointed the remote at the TV and cut it off. He now knew the reason for his son's betrayal. The love and affection of a woman—his woman.

After returning home with East, he found Lauryn gone, along with many of her things. He also found his safe wide open. She had cleaned him out, taking all the money and bricks she could find. He was sure then that she was in on everything with Dos. He checked the tapes from the security cameras, and there she was, taking everything she could before vanishing.

Ricardo's thoughts were in shambles. He had been betrayed by two of the people he loved the most. He wondered if they had been intimate in his home. He checked the hidden camera no one knew about, and what he saw broke him. Dos and Lauryn fucking in his bed while he lay in a coma in the hospital. Lauryn's ass propped up in the air, on their bed as his son pounded her relentlessly from behind. Ricardo tossed the half-empty glass of Cognac across the room. The tiny hairs on his neck stood up. Fury took over his entire body. His breathing pattern quickened, and he became hot, beads of sweat forming on his forehead. "I'm going to enjoy killing that little bitch. I should've fed her and her father to the sharks," he reminisced about that fateful day on the yacht, years ago.

He had other plans for his son. Ricardo knew he could never curl the trigger on his own seed, even after all the disloyalty. He got up from behind the desk and walked slowly in the living room, where East was on the phone pacing back and forth. He was trying to locate Dos and Lauryn's whereabouts.

"OK, thanks. I owe you, my nigga," East said as he ended the phone call. He looked at Ricardo and could see the pain in his face. He could only imagine what he must have been feeling inside. "I know where they are," he told Ricardo. "My man said he seen both of their cars at some low-budget, crackhead motel by the airport."

"They trying to lie low and get out of town."

"Where would they go?" East asked.

"California, probably," Ricardo said. "Dos's mother lives out there," he revealed. "C'mon, let's go take care of this." Ricardo didn't sound excited at all by what he had to do. He turned to East as they made it to the door. "You know, you're my only son now," Ricardo said, grabbing him by the shoulders.

Ricardo sat in silence as they drove. He couldn't help but to compare Dos and East and think about how they had turned out. He was truly amazed at what East had become. He was even sharper than he thought. Plus, he was honorable. At that moment, Ricardo wished that East was his own son. From the day he walked into the boxing gym, Ricardo knew he was destined for greatness. Ricardo had an eye for talent. He could spot a kid and know exactly how to use him within his organization for his own benefit. He truly couldn't bring himself to murder his own son, but East had proved before that he could do what most couldn't. He could kill despite emotion.

"Some things might need to be done tonight that I might not necessarily be comfortable with doing," Ricardo confessed.

"I understand," East replied. "Don't worry, I got you," he assured Ricardo. The look in his eyes matched his words.

Ricardo was relieved. His hands would remain clean, although his heart would forever be dirty.

Ungrateful bastard, he thought to himself about Dos right as they turned in the motel parking lot.

It didn't take long to spot the cars. They were the most expensive ones in the parking lot and stuck out like an ink spot in milk.

"Look, there they are," East said, pointing to the two vehicles. "They gotta be in that room right there."

They parked and got out. They didn't say a word to each other as they walked toward the door, each man filled with so many thoughts and emotions. Everything was right. It was a perfect night for murder. Above the rustling trees, thick grey clouds hung over the city as an occasional streak of lightning flashed in the night sky. Although it was almost midnight, the stifling humidity hadn't diminished nor faded. The air was thick, hot, and still. The steady hum of air conditioners echoed outside the motel rooms, mixing with Ricardo and East's footsteps. They were there to kill. They both knew it, but it didn't make it any easier. Both had performed the task of murder plenty of times before, but tonight, there was an unfamiliar heaviness in their hearts. A weight on their shoulders that made the concrete seem to buckle underneath each step they took.

Ricardo removed the gun from his waist. East already had his out. From outside the door, they could hear the TV blaring. It sounded like *SportsCenter*. Ricardo took a deep breath as East knocked heavily on the door. After a moment, it opened slowly, but Ricardo didn't wait. He pushed himself into the room, gun raised, followed closely by East.

What Ricardo saw made him hesitate to shoot. Dos was tied to a chair, wearing only a bloody wife beater and boxer briefs. His face was swollen and bruised from the tremendous beating he had suffered. He was bleeding from a gash in his head, and his mouth was duct taped.

"What the fuck is this?" Ricardo said . . . before he felt a thud to the back of his head and the world faded to black.

When Ricardo came to, he was still inside the motel room. For a moment, it was still spinning as he tried to focus. His blurry vision slowly cleared; then his heart sank. East stood with his gun at his side, next to a tied up Dos, while Screw and Ques had their guns trained on Ricardo himself.

"You know, before Tez died, he told me the story about how you played him and my father against each other. He confessed to killing him. I respected him for telling me the truth," East recalled. "I barely knew my father, so it didn't bother me, but I loved Tez," East said.

Ricardo was starting to get an idea of what this was about. Confidence could be a weakness if it exceeds its limit. Ricardo had first underestimated Dos, and now he had done the same with East. This time, it would prove to be a fatal mistake.

"You did the same thing to me and Dos, all these years. Playing us against each other. Even tonight, with all the, 'You my only real son now, East' shit." He shook his head putting his hand on Dos's shoulder. A sympathetic gesture, even if he truly had none for him.

"Eastwood, let me explain," Ricardo tried speaking, but East would have none of it. He was in control.

"Ain't nothing to explain. You can't talk your way out of this one," East promised. Then he walked over to him. "You made me kill Tez. Now, kill Dos," he said, handing

Ricardo his own gun back. "And before you even think about it, there's only shot in there."

Ricardo began to cry like a child at the choice he had been given. When he didn't move fast enough for East's liking, Screw walked over and put a gun to his head.

"It's him or you," East reminded him of the words he had once told him.

Ricardo had ordered him to kill so effortlessly that night, but now, he would do the deed himself. He walked over to Dos and lifted the gun. His hand was unsteady, trembling uncontrollably. Tears ran down his face as his finger remained paralyzed, unable to curl on the trigger. "Please, Eastwood. Don't make me do this. He's my son," he pleaded.

Dos looked up into his father's eyes. The man he had tried to have killed only a few weeks prior and now present with the same opportunity to kill him. He felt like the lowest of lows. Seeing the agony on his father's face made Dos hurt more for him than he did himself. He began to sob equally as hard as Ricardo.

"A father shouldn't have to watch his son die," East declared. Then he nodded to Ques who turned up the volume of the TV, just as East shot Ricardo in the head. His body collapsed to the floor with a heavy thud.

Screw then shot Dos in the back of the head. The force slumped his whole body over in the chair.

East looked around at the bodies of father and son. He had finally got his revenge, but he didn't feel the need to celebrate. Surprisingly, he felt nothing . . . no joy, no happiness, or sadness. He face remained expressionless. He nodded to Screw, then exited the room, leaving him and Ques to take care of the bodies. Ricardo's run was over, and Dos's was too, before it even got started.

East walked into his apartment and was met by Lauryn sitting in the living room staring at him with a worried look on her face. There was so much that needed to be said, but neither could find their voice. Just the fact that he was there and safe was enough for Lauryn. Their plan had worked. Nothing beat a double cross like a triple cross. They had played both Ricardo and Dos perfectly.

East found himself lost in her eyes. Since he was seventeen years old and tasked with being her bodyguard, she had been his weakness. Now he was hers. Lauryn wanted him off her mind and on her body. Something in her soul was drawn to his energy. She had watched East mature from a humble young boy to an honorable man, and a man he was indeed. He stood staring back at her like he saw heaven in her eyes.

Lauryn felt nervous, even though for the first time everything felt right in her heart. She stood to her feet. She wore black tights and a hoodie. Her hair was pulled back in a ponytail with her soft curls hanging down the middle of her back. She was the epitome of beauty in his eyes. Even with no makeup on, she was still the prettiest woman he had ever seen. Her flawless bronze skin and doe eyes were all she ever needed to impress him. East admired her and took notice of all her attributes down to the mole underneath her right eye. He ran his hand over her hair and down her face. "What's in the bag?" he asked, looking around her at the duffel on the coffee table.

"Everything he owed us," she said softly.

Lauryn walked over and unzipped it. There were a dozen sparkling white bricks and at least two hundred thousand in cash inside. "Ricardo took from me. So, I took from him," she began to cry.

East engulfed her in his arms. He held on to her with everything he had in him, like he was trying to absorb her pain into his body. He wished he could take away her suffering. "I'm sorry you went through all that, but it's over now," he apologized. Ricardo was Lauryn's boogie monster. But she melted in East's embrace. His strong arms around her, comforting her, made her feel safe. When she looked at East, she saw a king, one she didn't mind standing beside or behind.

He ran his hand over the top of her head, smoothing out her ponytail in the most affectionate way. Lauryn's body ached in pleasure when he touched her. Both of their foreheads were together as he spoke to her. She kept her eyes closed as she just took in his words and intoxicating smell. The hint of tequila on his breath was inviting, and she wanted to taste him. His aura commanded her attention and awakened her body. East licked his lips as he looked lustfully at her. He kissed her lips. She welcomed his kiss by grabbing his face. She pressed her face against his and slipped her tongue into his mouth. Her peach lip gloss mixed with her tears tasted like heaven on earth to him. In one swift motion, East lifted Lauryn off her feet and sat on the couch, allowing her to straddle him. Lauryn gasped, slowly opening her mouth. She felt as light as a feather on a natural high. She wrapped her arms around his neck and grazed her French manicured tips across his neck. Jolts of electricity ran up East's spine. He inhaled her scent into his being, and she did the same. Every sexual experience Lauryn had before now was either done unwillingly or with an ulterior motive. For the very first time, it all felt right. East was good for her soul. He was different. He was willing to love and protect her the way Ricardo should have, and the way Dos couldn't. Lauryn could feel his hard dick pressing against her pelvic area. She needed this; she wanted to be touched by him. East pulled her hoodie over her head and admired her perky C-cup breasts in her La Perla bra.

"You sure I'm who you want?" he uttered while nibbling on her shoulder. His hands were calloused but felt magnificent as he rubbed up and down, from her neck down to her arms.

"Yes," she whispered in a sexy tone. She wanted to submit to him. That was all East wanted to hear. After all that she had been through, he didn't want her to do anything against her will.

Lauryn stood up and removed her tights slowly. East's dick jumped in anticipation when he took in a full view of her body. She was perfect. The seductive look on her face turned him on more. She sought his approval. He nodded his head, more in admiration than acceptance. She straddled him again, now with his dick fully exposed and at attention. She climbed on top and held her breath when his girth entered her. At first, she couldn't sit all the way down on top of it. He filled her vaginal walls completely. East understood her apprehension and quickly turned her over on her back. He began giving her slow, steady strokes in and out of her pussy. Lauryn moaned with every entry, panting every time he exited her. East wanted her for so long, he was trying to convey his feelings for her with his strokes. Lauryn's body could tell. His sex felt so good, better than she ever had before. Her clit would pulsate every time he moved past her hymen. Every stroke East delivered to her was precise and intense, his mouth slightly ajar, loving the tightness of her pussy. Lauryn tried to control her moans, but East would have none of it.

"Let it out, ma. Tell me how you feel," he commanded in a whisper. Her juices poured over his dick effortlessly. East sped up his pace, taking her to another level of ecstasy. When he lifted her leg on his shoulder, Lauryn's mouth fell open in an O of pleasure, and she called out to him. East was hitting spots she never knew existed.

She thought her stomach shifted every time he entered her deeper. Lauryn clawed at his tattooed back and invited the pleasurable pain even more. East welcomed every part of her into him. He put every care or worry to the back of his head and solely focused on bringing her body to new heights. Lauryn's body began to quiver as she crossed the threshold into an orgasmic state. East took pride in pleasing her. He felt his climax and started stroking her harder and deeper until he could no longer contain his eruption. As they lay next to each other, Lauryn gave a sigh of bliss, her heart pounding in her chest. East ran his fingers through her hair as his chest heaved up and down. Their bodies tingled all over. He smiled inwardly. He had got revenge *and* the girl.

The End

The Bag Is In

by

Marlon PS White

Chapter One

"One day I'ma get tired of this same routine. Day in and day out, it's the exact same thing; never any excitement. One day I'ma find me another man, a rich man, one who wants to eat tacos, apple pie, and watch all the shows I watch."

Marisa, divorced, was fifty-seven years young. Although gray-haired, she had convinced herself she was still in her prime. Now living alone, with the exception of her two cats, she'd watched hundreds of movies. That also included thousands of episodes of crime shows. A thirst for the wild side and a master's degree in television crime shows led her to believe she was a hood detective. Marisa was always on a case. Keeping late hours posted watching reruns of *Law and Order,* the grandmother of five was always on time for work. Catching three different buses to work, her eyes felt weary.

Once arriving, Marisa punched the clock. Reaching inside her locker, she took out, opened, and downed an energy drink. Immediately after, she fell into her regular routine, getting straight to cleaning rooms she was assigned. With an abnormal amount of them still occupied on this Thursday morning, the middle-aged woman rearranged the usual order. She'd skipped the ones that were filled. Eagerly, she then cleaned the ones that weren't or at least didn't have a do-not-disturb sign on them. Deep in her own zone, she was quicker than normal finishing the rooms that had definitely checked out.

Marisa was ahead of schedule in a short amount of time. Her arthritis wasn't acting up, so she was good.

Checking her watch, she knew to pump her brakes. Slowly, she then pushed her cart while in deep-rooted thought about the last episode of her favorite show. Mentally distracted, she sloppily got done with room 212. Checking her list, she proceeded down the hallway. Stopping at room 217, Marisa glanced downward. Quickly observing no do-not disturb sign on the door, she did what she was trained to do.

"Housekeeping," she announced as loudly as her old vocal cords would allow. Tapping on the door, she repeated it once more.

With no one responding, she reached on her side. Raising her arm, she swiped her master key card in the lock. A green light flashed. Marisa turned the handle to the left. Using her hip, she pushed the door open. With towels in arm, she crossed the threshold. Peeking around the door, Marisa announced housekeeping once again. She didn't want to alarm any guests if they were asleep or just didn't hear her.

The housekeeper eased farther into the double room, seeing if it needed cleaning for sure. Off the rip, she easily took notice the bed was unmade. A large black, oversized duffle bag sat in the center of the messy blanket and sheet. Marisa found it to be odd.

I wonder who would leave something this big right on the bed, and it looks dirty. She looked around the room. It was empty. Then in the bathroom, which still had shower moisture on the walls and the closet. Once again, she found nothing. No clothing, no suitcases. Some empty cans lay on the floor, and a few candy wrappers were thrown about. Then a few rubber bands and a small writing pad were on the desk. To Marisa, it appeared like whoever had rented the room had left in a rush.

Now caught up in her feelings, she felt a chill. It felt eerie, as if something was strange. Paranoid along with being gone off watching a late-night TV crime show, her mind started playing tricks on her. Playing detective, she got closer, seeing a huge red spot forming on the side of the bag and leaking onto the sheet.

Oh my God! Oh my God! It can't be. She started backing up. *I know my eyes must be playing tricks on me. Oh God! It's big enough to put a body inside. Well, at least a cut up one. Oh my God, it looks lumpy.* Marisa started to shake uncontrollably. She clutched at her now-racing heart with her frail old hand.

Terrified, the grandmother slowly eased her way toward the door. She kept a keen eye focused on the duffle bag, which she believed had moved some.

Maybe they are still alive? No, they're dead. They have to be, zipped up like that. Praying whoever killed the poor person stuffed in the duffle bag wouldn't catch her in the room and cut her up too, she felt dizzy. Holding on to the wall to balance herself, she took several deep breaths. Once in the hallway, she used her master key card to open an empty room. Wasting no time, Marisa ducked inside. Rushing over to the nightstand, she used the phone to dial for help.

"This is 911. What is your emergency?" the woman said flatly, not interested.

"Yes, yes! Oh my God, there's a dead body in a bag."

"I'm sorry, miss, you said what?"

"Yes." Marisa's lips quivered as she spoke. "The body is stuffed in a huge duffle bag on the bed. There's blood everywhere. I think the dead person moved. Please send the police, please!" Marisa pleaded with the operator as her voice cracked.

The operator could tell that although the woman's story seemed off, especially a dead body moving, she had a job to do. She was trained to ask pertinent questions and keep all callers calm. Quickly, she asked Marisa her location. In response, Marisa rambled off the name and place where she and the dead body could be found to the now-amused operator. She assured the panicked woman the police were en route and should be arriving shortly.

Juan and Karen were leaving Denny's. They had just finished a hearty breakfast. With full stomachs, the pair headed back to their room. It had been a long night. They had put in some serious work while in town. Now it was time for them to get ghost, load up their belongings, and get on the road back to Arizona. They had a lot of multiple hours' drive in front of them and wanted to get going. Unfortunately, neither of them had any idea the housekeeper had been in their room. There was no way the pair could know she'd discovered the duffle bag, let alone had reported it for the resting place of a mutilated body.

When they arrived back at the hotel, everything seemed to be normal. Karen circled the parking lot twice as she was taught to do. Then she found a spot to park. Juan and Karen always tried not to look suspicious as they walked quickly to the room. The notorious duo had been extracareful as always, but yet and still, were seconds away from getting knocked by the local authorities on the humble. Standing outside the door, Juan fumbled with the key. With the lock light finally signaling green, the two entered. When they got into the room, he went straight over to the bed. Satisfied he'd completed the task he and Karen were assigned, he smirked. He up-zipped and checked the duffle bag once more. Karen started to pick up any random trash left, putting it in a small bag so it could be thrown away down the road. They wanted to cover their tracks if the police, FBI, ATF, Homeland

Security, or anyone else that would interrupt their ongoing illegal dealings ever surfaced and wanted to investigate.

Juan and Karen simultaneously noticed one side of the bag was damp. It had a still-growing red stain. The bright red moisture was on the bedding as well as on the duffle bag. Not caring about the ruined sheets on the bed, Juan lifted the huge bag up, slipping the straps over his shoulder. He made sure the red damp part was not touching his shirt. Just to make sure, he stood in front of the mirror adjusting it a few more times while he waited for his partner in crime to use the bathroom. He knew they could just stop at one of the local stores and purchase another duffle bag to transfer the valuable contents. There was no need to run the risk of getting pulled over and questioned about the ever-growing redness.

Making sure her hair looked good, Karen was taking her own sweet time. Although she knew they had to get on the road, the mere thought of hearing Juan's mouth for all those hours made her temples throb in pain. After looking around the room one final time, she moved toward the door.

Juan had just about enough of her uppity ways. He repositioned the duffle bag as he yelled at her in Spanish. "You stupid white trash, this fucking duffle bag ain't light. Hurry up and open the damn door before I really start to bugging! Then you really gonna have a problem!"

Karen had spent days, and even weeks, with him on the road, yet had no idea what he'd just said. However, by the tone of his voice, she figured it was nothing good. Catching an immediate attitude, she huffed and puffed and snatched the door open, granting Juan his wish.

Chapter Two

The police quickly arrived at the hotel's front entrance. Driving in an unmarked vehicle, they parked in the check-in area. After going into the lobby, they were met by not only a hysterical Marisa, but the day manager as well. As she rattled on her detailed account of what she saw in room 217, the day manager shook his head in disbelief. He'd seen a lot of things take place since he started working there, but nothing as bizarre as what he was hearing described. The housekeeper swore she saw the seemingly deceased cut up body not just move, but also beg for help.

While the veteran female cop stood with the manager believing the woman to be no more than a loon, the other cop, a rookie, was young and gung ho. He was living for everything Marisa had claimed. He had the manager pull the check-in records and ran the plate Karen had left on file. After running her out-of-state driver's license as well, he persuaded his partner to investigate further.

As the makeshift posse of four made their way down the hallway, the officers advised Marisa and the manager to stay a short distance back, just in case. The rookie was merely seconds away from knocking on room 217 when he heard a man yelling in Spanish from the other side of the door. He'd taken Spanish in high school and could make out some of what had been said. His heart raced, and adrenalin kicked into total overdrive. He quickly signaled his partner to get ready. It was about to go down.

Things from that point went from zero to a hundred, and pandemonium ensued. The female officer barely had time to call for backup just as the hotel room door swung wide open.

With Marisa and the manager taking cover in one of the empty rooms, they peeked out. Both of the cops stood just outside of room 217 with guns drawn. What could have been no more than a simple question-and-answer incident had escalated to a full-blown one. The housekeeper's imagination was about to spark a possible murder involving two of the hotel's guests.

The male officer barked out orders. It was easily apparent he meant business. "All right, freeze! Put your hands up, both of y'all! Drop that damn duffle bag and get down on the floor now!"

Karen was in utter shock. Having a gun shoved directly in her face was just about the last thing she was expecting to jump off this morning. Motionless, she stood as if she were doing the mannequin challenge. Her throat grew dry. She couldn't swallow. She couldn't think, let alone speak. As the cop's voice grew louder with his demands, Karen felt warm piss run down her leg, although she had just come out of the bathroom. Now beet red, her otherwise pale skin tone had rapidly turned colors. The female officer rushed from behind her partner, also ordering Karen to the ground. Seeing that she was not voluntarily complying, the officer roughly snatched her by the collar. Karen was then cuffed on the floor in the hallway with a knee roughly pressed in her lower spine area. Finally able to speak, Karen called the police woman all kinds of stinking hoes and nasty bitches as Marisa and the manager looked on.

Juan's reaction was nothing like that of his counterpart. He was not new to the game of the police showing up abruptly. So, hood raised, instinctively, he spun around. Seemingly in one swift motion, he dropped the duffle bag from his shoulders. As the oversized bag fell to the carpeted floor right behind Karen's feet, Juan was about his business. She would have to solely deal with the aftermath about whatever was coming next.

Wasting no time, he bolted full speed into the bathroom. Slamming the flimsy door behind him, he turned the lock. Juan realized it would only be a matter of seconds before the eager cop would force his way in. The only thing that would surely slow Joe Law up was if they thought he also had a weapon. "Don't fuck around and get shot fucking with me," he stalled for time in English, then started mumbling in Spanish. Juan's eyes widened. They darted around as he paced the floor. Searching the small bathroom, he grabbed a small metal trash can from underneath the sink. Briefly closing his eyes, he then smashed the window out. As the glass shattered, he heard the young cop kicking at the door as he yelled for him to come out with his hands up.

Knowing that the policeman didn't care one bit about his threat of gunfire, Juan stood up on the toilet. With ease, he managed to climb through the window. On the way jumping down, he cut himself deeply on the upper arm across one of his many tattoos and lower leg. Leaving a trail of blood, the now-criminal on the run limped along the back of the hotel. Met by an eight-foot chain-linked fence, he hesitated only for a split second to catch his breath. Juan looked over his shoulder to see if anyone was on his trail. Like a teenager, he scaled the fence as quickly as he possibly could. Landing in the parking lot of Family Dollar, he could hear police sirens close by. The glaring sounds seemed to be coming from all over the place. Momentarily, Juan had a flashback to Border Patrol on his ass when he first crossed from Mexico into America well over ten years ago.

Juan was almost out of breath. Feeling as if he were invisible, he ducked behind a parked Ford Explorer for temporary refuge. It was broad daylight so he knew that bit would play itself out as soon as the owner returned to the vehicle. Juan saw a wooded area on the other side of the street from the parking lot. Feeling as if certain freedom was in sight, he made a run for it, sore cut leg and all. He had no choice unless he wanted to get knocked. It was definitely do or die, so to speak. Making it three yards, maybe no more than four, ironically, the unimaginable happened. Out of nowhere, a speeding police car with sirens blaring hit him. The already-injured Juan went airborne. Strange as it may seem, he clearly saw everything in slow motion while his body twirled from the impact. He knew he was cooked before he could hit the ground good and stop bouncing. The driver that'd struck him jumped from the patrol car, along with his partner. Each had their gun drawn and pointed at his head. Before long, two more unmarked vehicles came to a stop, screeching tires. The next thing next, the original gung ho cop was on his back. He socked Juan in the rear of his head, going ham about him attempting to still get away. As if he could run anywhere, with blood leaking from his head, an obvious broken leg and arm.

"Don't fucking move, you wetback son of a bitch. Put your hands behind your back now," the overzealous cop yelled, not in the mood for any more rise-and-fly-type bullshit.

Juan blacked out once the officer's fist made contact with his head. Like his counterpart Karen, he was finally handcuffed. Juan's unconscious shell of a body was callously picked up off the pavement. With no great

regard for his visible injuries, he was tossed in the back
of a squad car. The normal procedure would be to call
an ambulance for any injured perpetrator before moving
them, but like today and any other day for these uni-
formed gladiators, the law simply doesn't apply.

Hog-tied, handcuffed in the rear of the squad car,
Juan's entire body was numb. He struggled to catch his
breath as he regained consciousness. It felt like his chest
was caving in. The street soldier knew at least one of his
legs was broken, if not both. Leaking from the huge gash
across his forehead, he was soon tasting his own blood.
His mind raced. He was in denial over what'd just jumped
off. Closing his eyes, he quickly went over every moment
of the past twenty-four hours since getting into town. He
couldn't figure out what exactly made the police get on to
him and Karen. Was it one of the many small-time dealers they'd delivered product to? Or was it Greedy and his
girl he'd trusted and just bragged about so much?

In the midst of him questioning the means of him and
Karen being apprehended, Juan wondered where all the
rest of the fanfare was that usually came with this sort of
arrest. Sure, the news reporters and cameras were slowly
pulling up, but where were the swarms of ATF officers?
Where were the feds and the Special Task Force and
Tactical Teams? Throughout the thick blood that now
covered his entire face, all Juan could make out were
some local mom-and-pop small-town police not sure
what to do or say next. This double arrest was obviously
above their pay grade. Following up on a strange 911
call, this was not what they'd expected to find. They had
a high-ranking team member of a drug cartel, a white
woman, and a duffle bag full of money.

*How did these clown cops get on? What the fuck
just happened? Damn! How?* Juan clenched his teeth,
knowing he would have to face a fate worse than the

judge or jail—the cartel. He racked his scattered brain trying to figure out which one of the many teams he'd dealt with on this trip had ratted him and Karen out. Juan even thought about his niece's estranged family members that supposedly still lived in Detroit, but quickly shot that scenario down. It had to be a leak, but the question was . . . who?

Chapter Three

Room 217 was paid up in cash for two days. Although their stay was traditionally brief, it would serve to be on the safe side if things didn't go as planned. Soda cans, chips, and a few random candy bar wrappers covered the nightstand. A dark-colored empty duffle bag was the only visible sign of luggage. Surrounded by dirty money, the ill matched pair had been at it seemingly for hours. Every hour of every day they were on the time clock of the devil. Their schedule was tight. They'd been down this road numerous times before. Veterans in transport, each had a position to play. The organization Juan and Karen worked for didn't play games. When it came to business, it was zero tolerance—no excuses, no fuckups. The two of them knew what they'd signed up for. Each understood the risks they took every go-around. The "man" had made that clear early on. Deliver—or die trying; no in-between.

"It is what it is and can't be no other way. I swear on my dead mother's grave. May her sweet soul rest in peace," Juan grinned, quickly crossing his heart. Looking upward, he then kissed the red stone rosary hanging around his neck. "I ain't gonna lie. That dude Greedy is turning out to be better than expected. I wasn't sure at first, considering it was a family pass. But look at all of this we working with."

Why don't he just shut up and let me do what I'm doing in damn peace? Karen tried blocking Juan out.

She had no such luck. He was consumed with corrupt power and definitely on one.

"Yeah, they about they hustle. Him and ole girl keep showing up and showing out on this bread. They remind me of my family, my bloodline. You see this here," he pulled up his shirt sleeve so Karen could see, yet again, the huge detailed tat that appeared to be somehow burned into his skin. "You can't just go around and get this. This is my family brand. You have this, it means you come from a long line of killers, hustlers, and money-makers. We known state to state, legendary in this game."

Oh my God, not that story about his family again. I'll be glad when we finish this run. This guy working on my last nerve. I don't know how much more I can take. Soon, the days became months on the road with Juan, and the months, years.

Juan strutted around the room as if he'd discovered the reincarnation of Bonnie and Clyde. Moving back the room-darkening curtains, he scanned the parking lot. Seeing no signs of early-morning movement, he shut the curtain. Not missing a beat, his verbal recess was over. He went right back at it. "Yeah, like I was saying, the ticket always be straight, you feel me? No bullshit in the game. And that shit fucking is rare. I mean, damn, you feel me?"

Karen was posted at the desk. She didn't bother looking up. In her mind, there was no great need to acknowledge her cohort's words of praise for Greedy and his bitch. She had a job to do that didn't detail giving a fuck about two niggas' buying-product skills, let alone Juan's dead mother. As long as the count was good, she was good. Concentrating, Karen continued counting the multitudes of twenties by hand. Ensuring the street-weathered bills were all facing the same direction, she finally glanced his way. Briefly locking eyes with Juan, she simply nodded before placing each small stack into the electronic counter.

Juan took that blank expression gesture as affirmation he'd been heard. In his feelings of being a road boss, he continued to hold motel court. Abruptly, the subject changed, as it always did with him. After years of dealing with the law, Juan felt he was an expert. He believed he knew it all. "Yeah, when you doing wrong, you gotta be all on it. Get your ass in, get your ass out. And if you get caught up, don't say jack shit. Not even your name."

"I know, Juan. I know. You done told me this before." Karen rolled her eyes to the ceiling, wishing he'd just be quiet. His behavior had her suffering from a severe migraine. She was exhausted, not to mention hungry. There was only so much soda and junk food she could take. Stepping away from the desk, she stretched her arms. She felt a cramp in her left lower leg but shook it off. Thankfully, Karen had counted and wrapped the last banded bundle of cash. Jotting down her final figures, the blond-haired beauty took a deep breath. Rubbing what she believed to be sleep out of the corner of each eye, she exhaled with relief. The count was on point. It was all there. The bag was secure.

"So, yeah, okay, mommy, we good or not? What's the word?" Juan waited for her response.

Karen rolled her eyes knowing that he'd dropped the ball in counting well over an hour ago. Now, here he stood, having the nerve to rush her answer. Glancing over her shoulder, she sarcastically reassured him that all was good. "Yeah, everything is everything. I mean, like, you think that Greedy's girl Gigi is the only one that can handle business?"

Juan followed her to the bathroom door. Easily, he felt her female attitude trait fill the air. Yet, it didn't matter. He overlooked her backhanded comment. He was still hell-bent on slow schooling her on not helping the police do their job. "Yeah, Karen, whatever on all that. And shit, I'm glad that count is good. But remember what I was saying. Motherfuckers be sitting all up on social media running off at the mouth. They snitching about this and that, and the damn cops be posted on that bitch. They be taking notes and building cases on niggas off of hearsay."

"Damn, Juan, oh my freaking God. Just please let me take a shower. Then we can eat something before we hit the road," Karen insisted, shutting the door in his face. Turning on the hot water, she was relieved to be finally out of ear range of Juan's loudmouthed street code rants. They'd been on the road for close to seventy-three hours straight before arriving in Detroit. Combine the travel time with the song-and-dance bullshit their clientele put them through, Karen was spent. She'd used her remaining bit of energy counting up. The last thing she needed— or wanted—was her male counterpart being on some wild brain ego trip, at least not on an empty stomach.

Juan stepped back. He knew Karen needed a break. It was obvious the trip from Arizona had taken its toll. Throughout the many times they'd traveled the highways together, he'd grown to read her like a book. Besides being a stripper when funds got low, Karen was the perfect mule. She was white, well-spoken, and most of all, a great driver. However, when it came to talking shit and really being about that hood life, that wasn't her. Karen Collette James wasn't cut like a sista from around the way or even one of Juan's bloodline Mexican mommies. The once-good-girl-turned-semibad never could be. Karen was who and what she was.

Outside the city limits of Southwest Detroit, Juan himself was drained. Yet, the adrenalin rush he felt from handling business was enough to keep him going. Like Karen, he'd also been up for hours counting. Leaving

Karen to get herself together, Juan walked away from the door and over to the far side of the room. Standing in front of the desk, he folded his arms. Nodding his head, he grinned with sheer satisfaction. After a few seconds of gloating, he checked his watch. With the oversized duffle bag now lying in the middle of the bed, it was time to go back to work, back to the hustle and grind.

Reaching down, the over-the-road mastermind grabbed several bundles of money. Using a bright red bold marker, Juan started putting his unique mark on all of the bundles of hundred-dollar bills first. Tossing them into the duffle bag, he then marked the fifties with the color blue. After doing the same color coding on the remaining cash, he threw the markers in the now fully stuffed bag as well before zipping it closed. Juan boxed up the money counter. Gathering up the empty Saran Wrap packaging the ticket money had been bundled in, he then floor based. Like a hood detective on the search for clues, he collected any other signs that could possibly point to illegal activity having had taken place in room 217.

The loyal lieutenant was thorough. It was understood he allowed no discrepancies when it came to handling the organization's ill-gotten funds. He rose up in the ranks of the treacherous team when his boss failed to dot all the i's and cross all the t's. That slipup cost him and two generations of his bloodline their lives. Juan had moved with caution for the last four years. However, this morning's brazen decision could possibly place him on the endangered list. One that could turn his already-crazy world upside down.

Karen emerged from the bathroom, and Juan took her place, needing to take a piss. Her stringy hair was slightly damp. Not taking the time to dry it all the way, she slipped on a baseball cap she'd purchased from one of the many rest areas along the highway. Relieved Juan had finished packing up all the money, she got her purse off the side of the bed. Grabbing the handles of the now-filled duffle bag, a frail Karen struggled to lift it. After two attempts, she managed to throw it against the backboard of the bed. She frowned when it rolled back into the middle of the mattress.

Now nearing seven in the morning, the couple finally left in search of food before hitting the road back to Arizona. The only thing they had to do is swing back by the room, snatch up the cash, and be out. Juan closed the brown wooden door. Out of habit, he pulled and pushed on it several times, ensuring it was locked. He had an uneasy feeling come over him as he walked away, like he'd forgotten something. Not wanting to read something into nothing that was probably nothing more than hunger and lack of sleep, he shook it off.

Now out in the parking lot, Karen pressed the unlock button on the single Cadillac Escalade key she held in her hand. The organization gave it to her as a gift, fully loaded with hidden compartments in the floor boards and interior panels, although it was more of an investment. They wanted her to feel as comfortable and worry-free as possible. Karen climbed behind the wheel and drove out of the parking lot. Juan played his role as just the passenger, not a ranking member of a well-orchestrated, drug-trafficking operation.

Chapter Four

Juan was in excruciating pain. His right leg was cut, busted, and definitely broke. His arm was twisted, and the bone was visible. The fierce impact with the squad car had him delirious. As luck would have it, a team of reporters was having breakfast at the exact same place he and Karen had just left. Of course, what the men were firsthand witnesses to was aired out live, although at a distance, for all of social media to see. Seconds before the menace was rushed away in a police car, an official news truck swerved up. The tires of the truck screeched to a halt in the parking lot. The side door slid open. The cameraman hopped out of the vehicle. Both boots on the ground, he ran over to the police car. His main goal was to get footage of the bloody Hispanic man before the cops pulled off. Not wanting to have their newly arrested perp on display, an officer stepped in. Quickly, he blocked the camera with his hand. Raising his voice, he ordered the cameraman to step away from the squad car. The officer let him know in no uncertain terms he'd take a ride to lockup for interfering with police business. Doing as he was told, the cameraman took a few steps backward near the group of other gathering reporters. By then, a reporter from the truck, a black man with a receding hairline and a cheap two-piece blue suit, rambled into a microphone.

"Today, we are following a still-unfolding story. In this breaking news, local police were called by an employee

of this hotel," he made reference to the building a few yards behind him. "They were called in to investigate a possible homicide. Although there was no body discovered, our sources tell us something else was found. Upon entering one of the many rooms at the hotel, the police discovered a large undisclosed amount of cash. Of course, as I said, it's extremely early on in what has happened, but once again, our sources tell us the currency may indeed be linked to a major drug operation. Right now, the DEA is being called on the scene. I'm sure they will be conducting interviews with the person that placed the original call, along with other hotel staff. At this time, two suspects are in cuffs, a white woman in her midthirties and a Hispanic male also in his thirties. Apparently, he's being taken to the hospital for injuries he sustained while trying to flee from the police. Anyway, as I stated, they are both in custody. Their names have not been released as of yet. This is Robert McCall reporting live from the Holiday Inn Express. We'll have more information tonight at eleven."

Life was crazy real. And in Detroit, times were definitely hard. People all over did what they needed to do to survive. Sometimes if you were from around the way, you were blessed if that grind was legal. You never felt handcuffs or had to call collect and pray your peoples accepted the charges. Borrowing bond money was never an issue. But more often, that money hustle had the supreme curse of being against the white man's laws. For out of towners Juan and his front girl Karen, as much as they tried to fly underneath the radar, sometimes they couldn't. But when out and about on a mission, they lived under the strict street laws. The only one that mattered if you wanted to stay alive in the game: keep your mouth

shut and lawyer up. After watching the early-morning
breaking news report, each and every mid-level drug
dealer that'd benefited from the bag being dropped the
night prior prayed. They hoped the two unidentified people the reporter spoke of would live by that code, especially if it was 100 percent proven to be Karen and Juan.

In Southwest Detroit, those same exact sentiments
were shared. Greedy, also known as Donnie Green,
and Gigi, aka Gina Dotson, were labeled the notorious
Southwest Detroit's Bonnie and Clyde of the dope game.
They were at one of their many traps they held down with
an iron fist. Today, this one on Fourth Street was in rota-
tion to be used to hand the work out. It wasn't hot like
the other traps, so it would do. The bag was in, so all was
good in the hood. Last night, they'd hooked up with their
plug from Arizona, Juan. They cashed out twelve bricks
of 95 percent pure cocaine at the cost of $17,000 a key.
With that much upfront cash on the table, Juan was more
than willing to personally meet up with the infamous
pair.

They were true earners in his eyes. The pair had
proven they could be trusted. They were soldiers, and
the higher-ups in the tightly run organization had to recognize their earning potential as well. Loyalty and being
true to the game were always looked upon with respect,
and because Greedy and his girl stepped up their grind,
game cashing out the last few runs, Juan promised them
a gravy deal. Without hesitation, he got it cleared the
next flip he would be authorized a double of the order on
consignment.

Juan had been doing business with Greedy almost
three solid calendars and a few months. He'd watched
him grow heavy in the game. Sprouting from mid-level
to major league and a force to be reckoned with in the
underworld of heroin kings, he got money. Greedy was

not just about that life by working hard. He, like just
about everyone from that side of town, was born into the
mixed jive world some sort of way. Whether drug dealer,
drug user, or a cop hell-bent on stopping drugs, that was
the DNA play bloodline in Detroit.

After watching the news report, they each said a prayer
for Juan and Karen and kept that shit moving. They knew
there might be a slight delay in getting a new bag sometime down the line, but thankful to the hustle gods, they
had more than enough to get them through the following
months. They decided to step on the close-to-pure product several good times the night before to stretch the play,
just in case. Worst-case scenario, if it was their people
that got hemmed up, whenever the new point person
would get at them, they'd be more than ready to honor
their financial obligation to the organization.

Nevertheless, Greedy and Gigi were celebrating their
new deal with Juan by blowing a fat blunt of OG Kush.
Red plastic cups in hand, they slow sipped on 1738.
However, the effects on Gigi's demeanor were far different from that of her better half. While Greedy was
calm, Gigi got off on acting a straight fool. Known for
snapping at bullshit, something minor could, and would,
become major in the mere blink of an eye. One pull, two
pulls, three long good pulls later, she was ready. With
another sip to get her all the way right, Gigi's eyes turned
from light brown to green. Hands planted firmly on her
hips, she directed traffic of who got what product and
how much of it. The workers coming and going out of
the trap to get that work had grown accustomed to her
black-hearted attitude. Most tuned Gigi out, keeping
their eye on the prize: the bag. They had more to stay
focused on dealing drugs in the streets of Detroit, praying
to see another day alive or get pinched, then convicted
and sentenced to the new plantation called Michigan
Department of Corrections.

Greedy sat back. With a devious smirk, he enjoyed the mellow buzz he was experiencing in the midst of it all. After all he'd been through to get to this point, he took in every moment. He was a boss, and no one could tell him differently. His dues had long since been paid in blood, so he earned the right to gloat. Gigi was also elevated by the trees and smooth brown they were drinking as he took delight in her antics. Watching her take control gave him an instant hard-on. He knew they would get off into some real serious sex play later, but for now, it was business first. After tossing his empty cup onto the coffee table, he snatched up the bottle of liquor. Holding it up, he saw there was just enough left for him to get one last shot. Taking the top off, Greedy took it to the head.

Yeah, hell yeah. This shit got a nigga feeling all right up in this bitch! Knowing Gigi had his back, Greedy closed his eyes. He reminisced on what it took for him to be living in the celebration of this moment in time.

Chapter Five

Greedy always counted his blessings. When the bag touched down in the city, he balled out like every other li'l nigga pushing a sack. After days of chasing behind ticket money for the next man, Greedy's time to shine finally emerged. He remembered when his small-time life in the dope game initially changed. His mother couldn't stop him from slanging. She tried everything she could but to no avail. Selling drugs was in his direct DNA, his birth right. Out of options, Greedy's weary-minded mother finally did what she thought was best. If the streets were going to have her son, she'd make sure he was prepared. He would have to do the family name proud. Early one morning she woke him up.

"Damn, Ma. What time is it?" he asked, rubbing the sleep out of his eyes. "The sun ain't even up, and a nigga like me just lay down."

"Look, boy, don't 'damn, Ma' me. And do you think I give two shits about what time you drug yourself in through my front door? You out here making the next family rich while we got bills to pay. You want that life so bad? Well, you 'bout to get your wish." She shook her head while once more demanding he got up.

Once in the car, Greedy's mother pulled into the gas station and filled up. Minutes later, they were on the highway. It would soon be remembered as a road trip that would change both of their lives. She was taking him to see her only brother. Ed was locked up in a federal prison in West Virginia. In the past, she'd urged her son up and down to ride with her to the prison. Yet, he always fought her word for word. This time, there was no discussion. She won, and in some hours, they'd be there.

Unfortunately, Greedy's uncle was doing a nice chunk of time under the RICO Act. Before getting knocked, Ed had been the man. In his heyday, he was legendary, flooding the streets of Detroit and a number of other neighboring states with cocaine and heroin. The government cited all of those allegations, along with numerous other crimes in the indictment papers. Ed had gotten too full of himself. It had caused him to get sloppy. The feds were taking a good long hard look at him. He was the main priority on their radar. Agents were watching his every move. His phone was wired for sound. The case broke open when the phone tap picked up a direct conversation he had about dope. Dumbly as well, he was bragging about murders his crew had definite involvement in.

When the mother and son finally arrived at the prison, they were both exhausted. Greedy's mother told him to go on in the visiting room by himself. She felt he and his uncle needed to talk alone. Greedy argued with his mother saying that they ain't got nothing to talk about alone, thinking he was just going to get the same ole speech he has been hearing from his momma: *You should stay outta the streets, you need to go to school, you gon' end up dead or in prison if you keep slanging dope.* He thought to himself she was wasting his time. He could be back in Detroit shaking the bag, putting money in his pocket instead of being across the country on some type of fake-ass intervention with an uncle he hasn't seen in years and doesn't even know any more, it's been so long.

"Dig, Ma, for real. I ain't tryin'a hear 'thou shall not follow in my footsteps' bullshit from your brother! If that's what the fuck he on, I'm good. I'ma tell him like that too. I'ma gonna put it on the floor with you for the last goddamn time too. I'm gonna do me by all means necessary—with or without your blessing," Greedy growled, looking his momma dead in her eyes.

She took one step forward toward her disrespectful seed. With her hand drawn back, he soon got what was coming next. Before he knew it, his mother had made full contact with the side of his face. Using every bit of strength she could garnish, the heartfelt slap was so hard she'd knocked spit out of the corner of his mouth. He was in total shock and disbelief. Raising his arm, he wiped the spit that was slightly dripping from his chin, then rubbed his stinging jawline. Definitely not in the business of being disrespected by her child, she wasn't done with teaching him that lesson. If looks could kill, he'd certainly be dead as she shot him several eye daggers.

"Look, boy, you must've done forgot who the fuck I am! I'm not one of yo' little homeboys that you call yourself running. I don't give two fucks about how bad you think you is or how much money you claim you got stashed here and there." With a no-nonsense tone, she proceeded to call him by his birth name before grabbing him up by his shirt collar. Once she had a good tight grip, she stood on her toes attempting to bring him down to her eye level. Whispering in his face while still trying not to cause a scene, she and he both realized it was a little too late to be discreet. When she'd smacked the baby-now-turned-man she had given birth to years ago, the guard at the sign in desk and people in the lobby waiting to visit their loved ones took notice. Waiting to see what was going to happen after what came next, a hush fell over the onlookers, and all eyes were glued on them.

Greedy stood with his head down, ashamed, embarrassed, and heated. But he dared not do or say shit else
that may have caused his mother to put on her big red
shoes and red nose and wig, and completely clown on
him. Not to mention run the risk of getting locked up
across the state in a prison lobby, of all places. The middle-aged black woman guard that ran the visitor sign in
desk called them over to the station. She told the mother
and son that any further disruption and they would be
escorted off the prison grounds immediately. Greedy's
mamma didn't apologize for her action to the guard
because she meant and said what she did and would sure
do it again. Truth be told, the guard was a mother herself
of a hardheaded young boy and understood where she
was coming from and would have done the same.

While his mother talked to the prison guard, Greedy
looked around the lobby mean mugging people that were
still all up in his business. Then a different young, burly,
black federal correctional officer came out from behind
the sliding glass doors that led to the inmate visiting
room and called three inmates' last names. His uncle was
one of the three called. Greedy reluctantly follow the CO
through the glass doors after his mother gave him the
"you better take yo' ass on in there" death stare.

Once he was behind the glass doors, he was ordered
to take his shoes and socks off. Then the CO patted him
down, searching him and his belongings for contraband.
When he was told to open his mouth and raise his tongue,
that's when things took a quick, abrupt turn.

"Hold up." Greedy took a step back and put his hand
up. "You done went in my pockets and played with my
nuts. Made me take my shoes and socks off and got me
standing on a piece of paper. Now you want to go all in
my fucking mouth?" He felt degraded and powerless, as
if he was being arrested.

"Sir, if you don't do like I ask you, you won't be allowed in to visit," the correctional officer said, irritated.

I just want to do my eight hours and go home, he thought.

Frustrated and already over the whole visit shit, Greedy opened his mouth for CO to inspect. Seeing there was no contraband in his mouth, he was told to walk through the metal detector. Greedy paused, giving the officer a hard look. He then walked through the metal detector. No alarm sounded so he was given the go-ahead into another set of glass doors that entered into the prisoners' visiting room.

Visitors and inmates could be seen talking to one another, playing board games, cards games, and taking photos with their families. Inmates were allowed five visitors at a time. Some had one person, and others had the limit of five people. Each convict sported brown khakis so they could be identified from civilians. They had their own space and weren't allowed to cross visit. The visiting room rules were given to him on a white sheet of paper in the lobby. As soon as he got into the visiting room with the criminals and law-abiding citizens alike, he balled the paper up, tossing it in the trash. "Fuck a rule," he growled. With a chip on his shoulder, he looked around the room carefully for his uncle Ed. He hoped he hadn't changed much in appearance so that he couldn't recognize him.

Over in the far corner of the visiting room, Ed stood up when he saw his nephew. When they made eye contact, he waved Greedy over to him. Greedy put on a half smile and walked through the visiting room with swagger only a Detroit nigga possessed. Ed gave his nephew a hard manly hug, patting him on the back with both hands.

"You look good, Nephew. Yeah, youngin', I see you shining. You remind me of myself at your age," Ed reminisced praising his sister's boy.

Greedy brushed his shoulders off and tugged at his eighteen-inch gold chain with an old English D iced out. "Yeah, Unc, you don't look bad yo' self. I see you been working out and done grew some dreadlocks. I bet they stank, don't they?" Greedy turned his nose up joking with his uncle.

"Fuck no, nigga. I see you got jokes," he said, laughing, shaking his fist at his kin from across the table. Then he rubbed his hand over his face, and it was like he changed into another person. His expression was different. He had a serious look on his face.

Greedy noticed the change and thought to himself, *Here we go with his preaching shit.* He dropped his head, closed his eyes, shook his head, and slid an inch down in the already-uncomfortable, hard, plastic visiting chair. He then crossed his arms over his chest bracing himself for the sermon. Greedy exhaled the stale visiting room air, opened his eyes, and looked up at his uncle, who was staring at him with his head cocked to the side, snarling. Abruptly, Greedy jumped to his feet, forgetting where he was. The chair made a loud scraping sound on the concrete floor. "Look, Unc, I ain't come cross country to be preached to by you or nobody else."

Inmates and visitors began to stare at them and whisper about them. Ed looked around the room and took notice that all eyes were on them. Infuriated, he turned his attention back to his nephew. He was heated beyond belief. "If you don't sit yo' ass down and stop making a scene up in here, I'm gonna catch another life bit for murder! Fuck is wrong with you, li'l nigga? You trying to front on me up in this visiting room like I won't lay hands on you?" Ed seethed with an even, deliberate tone of voice.

Greedy snapped out of his feelings. Glancing around the room, he reminded himself who he was talking to and

where he was at. He really didn't want any part of what
his uncle had in store for him if he put his hands on him.
"Look, Unc—" Greedy replied humbly.

"Naw, li'l nigga, *you* look," Ed demanded. Resting
his elbows on the table, he then leaned in his nephew's
direction. Greedy followed his lead and leaned in as well
for privacy. "Okay, bet. Now that I got your full attention,
boy, his ain't what you think it is, young dumb-ass nigga,"
Ed remarked, checking the young pup from Detroit. "I
don't give a fuck if you wanna be out in the streets as long
as you make that bullshit worth it."

"All right, then." Greedy was now all in.

"Yeah, you see where I'm at, and I don't regret shit. You
know why? Because I made it worth it. I still got bread.
I'm still living good. I'm still getting pussy. You see that
bitch up at the desk?"

Greedy glanced over at the officer's desk. There he saw
a fine brown-skinned female officer standing on guard
like a hawk. He looked back at his unc like he was shitting
him. "Naw, Unc, you for real?"

"Yeah, I'm fucking her. That's my bitch. She knows I got
long, serious paper. If I didn't, she wouldn't look my way
twice. I want for nothing locked up in here. Nigga, I ain't
ate chow hall food in ten years. My point is, I planned
for the day I got knocked. That means I went hard to get
real money. Fuck that petty money niggaz be chasing
just to go to the club and show out so they can fuck them
hood-raised bitches. I stacked loot and invested it in
businesses. Your momma will tell you if you don't know
or remember. Them people took a lot of money from me
and some houses I had in your momma's and your grandma's name. It was funny to me because they couldn't take
what they didn't know about. That's why I can still live
like a king even up in this shit hole. Now, Nephew, let me
ask you this. You want real money, or you just bullshit-

ting around till you get popped with a sack on the block? Or fuck around and catch a prison number with nothing to show for it?" Still being discreet, Ed waited for his response, looking seriously at his nephew.

"Unc, I ain't playing out in these streets. I done worked my way up to two slabs. And I got like six goons on my payroll. I got thirty thousand stacked up."

Ed liked what he was hearing from his nephew. The seasoned, veteran drug dealer thought there might be hope for him as a money getter after all. On instinct, he decided to give him a shot at the title. However, bloodline or not, the game is to be sold not told. "You got that much cash on hand right now at home?" Ed questioned, with doubt and speculation because busters were prone to lie about how big their bag is. Or how much loot they really be holding, especially these lames he was jailing with.

"Yeah, I do. Unc, I'm not playing. I'm focused. I wanna do it big like you did it back in the day, but better. No offense. You know?" Greedy spoke with confidence, sure of himself.

"I tell you what. When you get home, wire me a thousand dollars a week until you done sent me ten thousand altogether. Then I'm going to hook you up with my plug in Arizona. If you fuck it up once I plug you in, that's on you. They not gonna play no games with you. They will kill your mamma and anybody else, then move on to the next nigga that wanna hustle and grind. So, li'l nigga, don't mess around and get my sister killed on no bullshit!" Ed warned his eager young kin. "So, is you ready to level up or what? 'Cause everything ain't for everybody!"

Greedy was skeptical of his unc's proposal, yet excited as he thought of all the dope he could cop, along with the ton of money he'd make if his fam was on the up and up.

"Okay, then, we good. Bet that up. A thousand dollars a week until I drop ten of them things on you, and I get plugged. Say no more, Unc. It's done soon. As soon as I get to my phone, I can have one of my people wire you a stack ASAP," Greedy vowed, cocky as ever.

"All right, then. I'm gonna slide you this number. Now don't call this motherfucker until I tell you to. I ain't bull-shitting. If you mess around and spook these Mexicans and fuck shit up, it's over! You feel me? Ain't shit pop-ping." Ed had the number written down to the connect on a brown piece of paper towel. He slid it across the table on the low so the other guards wouldn't see him passing what they call contraband. It was against the rules to pass anything to visitors and vice versa.

Greedy nodded in agreement not to call the number until he was given the green light to do so. Ed had given his nephew his blessing, because if any of his kin was gonna play the dope game, he wanted them to represent the bloodline and do it big. Still in teacher mode, he dropped one more jewel on Greedy. He told him that when you come up on that bag, make niggas pay for it. Keep your money stacking up.

"Huh, what?" Greedy looked at him, puzzled. Dumb-founded, he wondered how he could make the next man pay for his bag and their own bag, plus stack up his money.

"I see you sitting over there confused as hell. You wanna know how? Shittt . . . I should charge you for this game too, li'l nigga. But you's family, and I don't want you bumping your head in them streets. See, you'd fuck around, taking more loss like you crazy when you don't have to. So, pay attention, Nephew. When you have a direct line to the work, you set your own prices. See, if you getting slabs for say seventeen thousand, you flip them for twenty-eight or better. It depends on who's buy-ing. Either way, there go free bands that belong to you. That's called your tops."

Greedy nodded at the same time he was rubbing his chin. It was all so clear to him what his uncle was saying. In his mind, the bottom line is he was going to be rich. That day shaped his life into what it is today: a true official force to be reckoned with knowing the plug and the unspoken rules.

Chapter Six

Greedy was brought out of his moment of reflecting. Gigi was going, yelling, and talking a million miles an hour. Something was definitely up. He stood up from his chair. All the workers were shaking their heads like, *oh boy, it's going down now*. With the bottle of 1738 still in one hand and his pistol now in the other, he bent the corner to the living room. There he saw Gigi all in Dirty Mike's face. He'd come up short for the last time, and Gigi, of course, wasn't having it.

"You bum-ass nigga. Fuck you mean you ain't got it? Fuck naw, ain't no making it right. The next flip? Dude, you done flipped your last bag outta this camp," Gigi barked looking at her man for approval.

Greedy nonchalantly said, "Put him down in the basement with the girls. If he can sweet talk them into letting him work again, he still got a job. If not, he 'bout done." He turned the radio up and grabbed the opened bottle of liquor.

Dirty Mike pleaded with Greedy not to send him down in the basement. He resisted at first . . . until he was staring down the barrel of Gigi's forty cal. She marched him to the basement door. "Please—"

"Naw, go on, fuck boy. You wanted this life, now live it."

Dirty Mike opened the door slowly. Full of fear, he looked down the steps. There they sat waiting patiently. Chelle and Jada, two massive female Cane Corsos weighing in at eighty pounds each, both trained to kill on command. Hesitantly, he looked back over his shoulder at the real-life trap queen, thinking to himself, *I'm fucked*. Both anger and fear showed in his eyes.

Gigi took one step back in her pink Air Force Ones. *Click-clack* was the sound her pistol made when she racked it, putting one up top. "Today, you gonna see a real bitch one way or another, up here or down there. And it ain't to get your dick wet." Gigi frowned with attitude pointing her iron at his head. Reluctantly, he descended down into hell one step at a time where his fate awaited him. "Eat!" Gigi ordered her babies and slammed the door shut. She locked it and placed her gun in her waistband. She then pressed her ear to the door. Within a matter of seconds, she heard what sounded like several grown men bum-rushing up the steps on a deadly mission. It was like two lions ripping into a frightened African gazelle on an otherwise quiet summer afternoon. Growls and Dirty Mike's bloodcurdling screams echoed up the basement steps over the radio. They vibrated through the door and walls up into the entire house.

Greedy and Gigi, along with three dudes on their payroll, stood in the trap house kitchen. The worker with a scar across his throat stood back. He looked as if he'd been through his fair share of hood wars and came out on top, but this was different. His face twisted up six different ways. He closed his eyes, and then put his hands over his ears. Dirty Mike's screams were still louder than the radio. Scar Throat had done some unspeakable acts to people, but nothing on this level. He thought the money was gravy he was stacking up fucking with the team for the last three months. But he wasn't with this shit these motherfuckers were capable of. He had made up his mind right that moment, he was done dealing with these bloodthirsty goons, bag on deck or not.

Zack, a trusted soldier, was in the back room weighing and bagging up work. Used to that type of treatment, he rushed into the front room where Greedy, Gigi, and the rest of the crew were now standing at. "Yo, come smoke this shit over! Nigga done got popped with a mill ticket," he yelled as he shot back into the room.

Everybody quickly followed him to the rear room. They all stood posted in front of the seventy-inch TV mounted on the wall, except Zack. He had time-sensitive work to do. He sat back at his work table big enough to seat six people. On the table was a digital scale and two bricks of cocaine broken down into chunks. Ounces of cocaine bagged up for distribution sat to the side. Zack's only job was to break down the work and weigh it up into ounces. He reached down under the table and grabbed a box of baggies and set it on the table. Then he pulled one out of the box. Placing it between both his hands, Zack began rubbing his hands back and forth together until the baggie was static free and easily opened up. He looked up at the TV while he reached and turned the scale on. Then he put a chunk of 'caine in a baggie and set it on the skillet. Briefly, he glanced down at the numbers. They read twenty-eight point zero. Zack smirked. He did his job well, and his eye was always on point.

Greedy and Gigi watched the news like the rest of their counterparts. They'd already seen one report of some people getting knocked earlier that had them spooked. But since they had yet to have official verification it was their connect, they kept it tight to the chest. Besides, that wasn't the workers' business or concern anyways. Listening to the suited up reporter speak, the pair held their breath as the camera zoomed in on the alleged criminal apprehended in the back of the police car. Greedy gripped the neck of the liquor bottle tight and took it to the head. The man's face appeared to be swollen, but it was obvious who it was. His fear from earlier was now a confirmed reality, a hustler's nightmare. The plug had got knocked. Gulping down the liquor, Greedy's throat burned. He stopped drinking, then took two long pulls on the blunt Scar Throat had just passed him. He held his breath letting the THC absorb into his bloodstream. When he felt like his chest was gonna explode, he blew the weed smoke up at the TV. A long gray cloud covered the screen. Dry mouthed, he looked to his side at Gigi with a what-the-fuck expression on his face. She slow stroked his back with her hand, attempting to soothe her man. Discreetly, she nodded her head toward the door so he would follow her lead.

Reeling from alcohol, weed, and the shock of celebration-turned-to-silent-chaos in both their heads, he followed Gigi out of the room. Greedy began setting up chess moves in his head to keep shit in order until he figured out what the fuck truly happened. For the plug to get jammed up with what was reported to be close to half a million dollars, including some he had just given to him less than twenty-four hours ago, was crazy. He knew someone had fucked up big time, and there definitely was gonna be repercussions by the law—and in the streets.

Chapter Seven

Meanwhile, 1,630 miles away, in Laredo, Texas, the Flying J Truck Stop was buzzing. Truckers were pulling out. Some were pulling in to eat, shower, rest, or gas up their rigs. Lot lizards black, white, and Mexican, were out trolling. Not even a half mile away up the road, the Mexican police stood guard over four mutilated bodies. More than likely casualties of the ongoing cartel drug wars. The police on the far end of the city had a shoot-out with some members of the CSI Cartel. Eight officers were killed and one foot soldier. These brutal occurrences had become normal to Laredo citizens. If you lived in Laredo, you are affected by or affiliated with the cartel, one way or the other.

Maria Blanco, however, wasn't affected by the powers that be. She was affiliated. Her father was a top-ranking member of the cartel while he was alive. He raised Maria by himself after the money and drugs drove her mother crazy. She got strung out on dope, and one day, her husband snapped. He shot Maria's mother in the back of the head. Callously, he dumped her body in the desert. Some years later, her father got killed in a gun battle when a cocaine-processing lab was raided by a rival cartel. The only living family she had was her father's brother, Uncle Juan. He ran the over-the-road drug operation from Arizona and Texas to the Midwest. All in the family, Maria waited tables at the truck stop and recruited truck drivers for the cartel to smuggle drugs across the United States.

Maria, however, was tired of the same old day in and day out truck stop job the cartel had assigned her to. She wanted excitement, adventure, and power. More importantly, she wanted in on the family business. Word of her uncle Juan getting arrested with a ton of money traveled fast. Soon after, she was approached by two goons. They had a message from one of the top-ranking Los Zetas drug bosses. A short, dark Mexican with a big stomach and thick facial hair did all the talking. The lanky Mexican with him said nothing and kept looking around suspiciously. Maria was directly told of her uncle's situation up north. And the fact they needed a driver today that was willing to take a load of work to Detroit, Michigan. The job paid $50,000. She could keep twenty racks for a finder's fee. Instantly, she thought of the perfect trucker for the job: Bobby Bands. He definitely could use the money. Maria knew he could because he'd told her on the phone while he was driving to Texas to drop a shipment of dry goods from up north in Michigan. He had serious past due bills on his head. Back home, his taxes were past due and his truck note past due. Without that ticket paid, he couldn't work. Maria was set to meet him at the Flying J Truck Stop before he headed back up north. So this was perfect timing.

Bobby sat at the counter sipping a cup of hot, black coffee waiting on Maria. Excited, she called him and asked him if he wanted to make some quick money. She didn't go into detail over the phone, but she had Bobby's attention. He needed a blessing or bump from somewhere. Exhausted, he sat back. His mind drifted off to when he first hooked up with Maria.

Bobby Bands was new to the trucking game. He had just beaten a federal indictment on a technicality. If he had gone to trial and got found guilty of a Count One:

distribution of dangerous drugs, three to life in prison. Count Two: murder in the first degree, twenty-five to life in prison. Count Three: possession of an illegal firearm, five years in prison. Thanks to sloppy police work and one dead rat that didn't make it to the witness stand, Bobby Bands knew he had to give up the dope game. He knew he had to do something to eat and keep a roof over his head. He chose truck driving, because it would keep him on the road away from the hood and off the feds' radar. He was cool with cutting loose his gold digger bitch who always had her hand out for cars, jewelry, two houses, and the ballers' lifestyle as long as he was free.

This particular day he'd dropped his truckload and went into the Flying J Truck Stop for a hot meal and a cup of coffee. Maria was attracted to Bobby Bands at first sight. He didn't notice how attentive she was while she served him his food due to his lack of sleep. Maria was confused, wondering why Bobby wasn't sweating her like all the rest of the truckers. She had a pot of coffee in her hand as she approached him sitting at the counter eating his burger and fries.

"Would you like another cup of coffee?" she asked him as he took another bite of his burger.

The red meat gave him life again as he looked up. "No, thank you." He looked at Maria closely for the first time since he'd sat down. She had attractive brown skin, long, dark hair, nice-shaped hips and ass, with full lips. He looked at her name tag. "Maria, I think it would be a good idea for me to go get about an hour or two of sleep in my truck. Then come back so you can show me around Laredo. I wanna get to know you both."

Maria's face lit up with a smile as she spoke. "And your name is?" He told her his name. "Nice to meet you, Bobby, where you from?" They gently shook hands with each other as he answered her question. The attraction was evident. She looked at the clock on the diner wall and said, "My shift doesn't end for another three hours. I can do that, show you around town. There isn't much to see but wetbacks and the Rio Grande."

"I'm cool with that." Bobby smiled; then he gave Maria his cell phone number to call him when her shift ended. She typed his number in her cell. Bobby went in his pocket to pay for the meal and coffee after she'd place the tab on the table. He put a fifty-dollar bill on the counter-top and told her to keep the change.

Maria batted her eyes with a girlish smile. "*Muchas gracias.*"

Hours later, Bobby awoke from a much-needed sleep. He was feeling fresher and horny as he thought of his new Mexican female friend. He had showered inside the Flying J before he went to sleep. So all he had to do was get dressed and meet up with Maria. No sooner than he'd got finished, she called his phone. They agreed to meet in the trucker's parking lot. Bobby grabbed an unopen bottle of vodka and some blunts he had rolled up. His rig was parked in the back of the lot away from the other trucks for privacy and less noise so he could rest. On his way through the truck lot, he grew highly aware of his surroundings. The night air was muggy, mixed with the smell of burning diesel fuel coming from idle semitrucks. It was a smell Bobby never got used to. He put his free hand over his nose. Stepping along the gravel, it crunched under his wheat Tims.

Seeing something out of the corner of his eye, he paused. Movement from in between two freightliners caught his attention. It threw him off guard for a split second. A fat white man had a lot lizard bent over. It was light enough to see them, so he knew they saw him as well. But they kept fucking, and Bobby kept it moving. He walked another ten yards. He then saw two big

Mexican dudes with bandannas tied over their faces.
They were speaking in Spanish as the duo pistol-whipped
a man. Bobby couldn't make out if the guy getting beaten
was white or Mexican, and to him, it didn't matter. He
acted as if he didn't see them as well and kept walking.
He knew better than to care. Growing up in Detroit, you
mind your business when you see shit you ain't trying to
see. Your ass will come up dead or missing if you forget
that hood rule. Bobby looked back to see how much distance he had put between him and whatever it was taking
place. He saw the man being stuffed in the trunk of a car
and still kept moving. Laredo, Texas, reminded Bobby of
the eastside of Detroit, so he almost felt at home.

He soon saw Maria. She had on a red sundress and
white sandals leaning against an old blue Chevy pickup
truck. When he got close up on her, he noticed her
face was slightly beat. Her hair was jet-black and curly.
She was even more attractive than he thought.

"Damn, you look like a bag of money, girl."

She blushed, batting her brown eyes at him. "Thank
you, señor." Maria seductively stroked his arm. He
smiled, holding up the bottle of liquor. "So are you going
to get me drunk and take advantage of me?"

"Not unless you want me to."

They both laughed and got in the pickup. Maria and
Bobby Bands drove around the less seedy side of town,
drinking and talking, getting to know each other. Maria
periodically checked the time. Bobby was starting to feel
some type of way. "Dig, what's up, ma? You got to be
somewhere? You keep looking at the time. What, your
dude got you out on a timer or something? I know how
these Mexican guys are about their women."

Maria giggled as she steered the old truck around
a corner toward the Rio Grande border line. "I don't
have a man, boyfriend, and I am not married. Nor do I

have kids. I move how I please." Suddenly, she pulled over on a side street a block away from the border and killed the engine to the truck. She positioned herself in her seat facing Bobby.

He took a gulp of liquor. "Yeah, I can dig that. You move like I move, something like a free spirit. I don't have any of that baggage. That's why I'm a truck driver. You feel me?"

Maria looked in the review mirror. She saw six to eight figures moving quickly toward her truck. Bobby didn't see them coming. However, he heard them jump in the back of the pickup one after another. The truck rocked up and down as the illegal aliens climbed in and sat in the bed.

"*Con rapidez*," the apparent guide of the group repeated in Spanish.

Maria glanced in the back of the truck making sure everyone was in. "Hurry up! Hurry up. Let's go!"

Normally, hood-raised Bobby Bands was ready for anything at any given time. He was trained to go off bell, but this abrupt commotion damn near gave him a heart attack. "What in the entire fuck!" he yelled out, surprised. It was as if a live documentary on the National Geographic channel was taking place right before him.

Bobby quickly scanned all around the area. He was shook thinking the Border Patrol was going to come out of nowhere any second. The Mexican guide tossed Maria a wad of cash. He wished her good luck and disappeared into the night. She stuffed the money in her bra, started the truck, and drove away. Bobby was dumbfounded. Wide-eyed, he looked at the surprise passengers through the truck cab's back window. They all were carrying backpacks with probably their belongings in them and no telling what other illegal contraband. He felt bad seeing the Mexicans tired, dirty, and hungry. Obviously, they had traveled three days and nights ducking Border Patrol, dangerous mountain terrain, and hundred-degree heat with little to no water. That explained the cases of water that he noticed in the truck bed earlier.

Maria bent a few corners and brought the vehicle to a slow crawl. One by one, the people began jumping out of the rear of the vehicle. Just as the guide had done, they too disappeared into the night.

As the two of them rode, no words were exchanged. Finally, Maria pulled over a few miles down the road. Reaching her hand into her bra, she took out the money given to her. She didn't say anything, just smiled. After counting it out under the streetlight, she split the bread she got from the guide with Bobby. That's when he knew he was going to fuck with her the long way. She was crazy, but a hustler. Later that night, the two fucked hard for hours in his truck until the sun came up. From that point on, they established a mutual bond of respect, trust, and feelings that soon became deeper than either of them would ever be willing to admit.

Chapter Eight

Bobby was snapped back to reality when Maria came from behind him. She put her arm around his neck. They got dirty looks from the other people in the diner. The dislike came mostly from the Mexican men. Brothers and the white guys just hated on them because they wish they were getting the pussy. Maria was excited and couldn't wait to tell Bobby about the opportunity to make some real money that they both could use.

"Hey, poppy," Maria hugged Bobby kissing him on the cheek. She paid the haters no mind that were giving them dirty looks and whispering.

"What's up, future baby momma?" Bobby stood up hugging her back. He was glad to see his Mexican *mamacita*. Yet, he didn't waste any time with small talk. He got straight to it. "So, okay, what did you wanna talk to me about?"

Maria hooked her arm around his. She led Bobby outside to the trucker's parking lot so they could talk with some privacy. They walked into the lot near Bobby's truck. Maria had looked up at him and was just about to reveal how they could come up on a lick. Her palms began to sweat because she was nervous to tell him the real deal. Maria hoped he wouldn't shoot her down and tell her no. This was her chance to break out of Laredo and live like the females she saw on Instagram and in music videos. They always had money, dressed up all the time, and kept their hair done and face beat.

I'm just as pretty and sexy as them. I want better than living in this rotten piece of shit of a city.

Taking a deep breath, she barely opened her mouth to tell Bobby the deal when two Mexican females started knife fighting in the parking lot. Maria and Bobby had just walked up to his rig. He heard them before he saw them.

"Oh shit, World Star, look at these hoes!"

Maria turned toward Bobby. With attitude, she cocked her neck to one side and firmly planted her hands on her shapely hourglass hips. She started cussing him out in Spanish. He was supposed to be paying attention to her. Instead, he was videoing two lot lizards cutting up each other. The smaller of the two women told the truck driver she would take less money if he chose her. The thicker woman pulled her knife first. She was for none of that bullshit, stepping on her toes taking food out of her seven kids' mouths she had to feed. She caught the small woman on the arm with the blade, who dropped her ho bag on the ground and whipped out a six-inch knife from her tattered blue jeans back pocket. The women were out for blood. They really wanted to kill each other. They danced around yelling at each other in Spanish. Suddenly, they rushed at each other at the same time. The bigger of the two missed with her blade. However, the smaller woman connected with her steel blade right across her nemesis's neck. Blood squirted three feet from out of the female's neck. Maria and Bobby moved closer to the truck out of sight. Nevertheless, they kept watching to see what was going to happen next. Once the woman realized she was cut, she grabbed her neck and fell to ground. The smaller woman stood over her victim yelling and cussing with such sheer anger and emotion Bobby asked Maria what they were saying.

Maria interpreted what she said with the short version. "She's telling her if she fucks with her again she's going to cut her cunt off and stuff it in her mouth."

Bobby looked at Maria with a shocked expression on his mug. "Wow, the bitch better not come around here no more. Little momma ain't for no games with that blade."

The smaller woman picked up her ho bag off the ground. Brazenly, she marched over to the big lot lizard, hawked a wad on her, then ran off through the lot. She was going so fast you could literally see gravel flying from underneath her shoes. Maria shook her head, then turned and went to climb up into Bobby's rig. Happily, he followed behind her. Maria had on a light-colored pink, short sundress with no panties on. Bobby could see she had shaved her pussy clean just like he liked it. She now had his total attention. Maria grabbed his hands and guided him to the small bed in the cab. He sat down, and she kneeled down between his legs. Maria had a plan to get what she wanted. She would literally use her head to convince Bobby Bands to take the money to do the job for the cartel. On a mission, she unzipped his jeans and slipped her hand inside of them and his boxers. She grabbed his dick. Slowly, she began massaging it. With her free hand, she unbuttoned his pants, all the while she was seductively telling him about how he could get thirty grand for driving a shit-load of drugs up north to Michigan, his home state.

Maria pulled out his dick. Lusting at the head, she gripped it hard, then started to stroke it up and down. Bobby was relaxed. He lay back and let Maria do her thing. She looked him in his eyes. With great skill and ease, she made his dick disappear into her mouth. Bobby was good and hard for her hot, wet, tight throat. He was caught off guard with pleasure. His meat had never been so deep in her head before.

Maria has been holding back on the neck game. He couldn't think straight.

She was putting on a show sucking his well-endowed man meat. After she made him come in her mouth, she swallowed it. But not before showing Bobby his nut inside her mouth like she had been told by the dentist to "open wide." She had sucked his dick before, but this was the first time she drank his protein. She knew how much he enjoyed her head. He had a hand full of her hair controlling her mouth this way and that away. She didn't resist not one bit. Maria's grandmother schooled her well. She always said, "Maria, you were born pretty. Keep your hair combed, a clean pussy, and learn how to suck dick. That's how you get a man's attention. You blow him good. Then you ask him for whatever you want. He can't say no."

Maria wiped her mouth with the back of her hand. Getting up off her knees, she sat on the bed next to Bobby. He had his shirt off, and sweat coated his hairy chest. He put his dick back in his jeans after he pulled them up from around his ankles.

"So, poppy, can we get this money or what? I need it to help my granny. She's not doing so well. She is eighty-two years old, and she stays in and out of the hospital. I could pay off the medical bills and fix the roof on her house."

Bobby sat up and faced Maria. He was confused. "Hold up. Wait a minute. I thought you said your grandmother was dead. You said your uncle Juan is the only person you got left alive that's your blood."

"Fool. Who do you think raised me? My drug-dealing uncle?" Maria remained calm even after being caught in a lie. Rubbing his chest soothingly, she answered, not missing a beat. "No, he didn't. She took me in, and he gave her money to take care of me up until I was old enough to fend for myself. I don't know my mother's family up north in Detroit. I've never dealt with that side for obvious reasons. But if you take the job, I'll go with you, and maybe I'll try to get in touch with my family there. My uncle won't like it, but he's locked up right now, so . . ."

Bobby stretched out on the twin-size bed. Exhausted, he took a deep breath and fell silent. Maria took off her dress and tossed it onto the floor. She lay down next to him and put her head on his chest. His mind was racing, thinking about the things he could do with $30,000. He could catch up on his bills and pay his truck off. Then, thoughts of getting caught up going back to jail forever flashed again—and again—in his head. He shook that shit off quickly. He put both his hands over his face and rubbed his eyes. Niggas back home in Detroit would die for a plug or any type of connection to a bag of this magnitude. He didn't have much to lose and everything to gain if he could pull this run up north off with the shipment of drugs. He took his hands away from his face and sat up. Maria did as well. She looked at him with a mix of anticipation and a sad, pouty face, like a kid waiting to hear yes or no from their parent.

"Fuck it! We both could use the money. And besides, real talk, I'm tired of struggling from fucking check to fucking check. We gonna get this money, but you do know ain't no room for mistakes. You know we dead if shit get sideways and we get jacked or let the police knock us with all their shit. We gotta be beyond careful."

Maria was elated and relieved that Bobby was down with her mission. Now she could finally get out of Laredo, Texas. Her dreams were getting ready to be set into motion. Bobby didn't know Maria had no plans whatsoever of ever coming back. She hopped up, quickly got dressed, and kissed Bobby on the lips. "I'll let them know you'll do the job, but first come out in the parking lot with me. I wanna show you something."

He stood up, zipped his jeans up, and put his shirt on. They both climbed down out of the semitruck. It was a hot, bright, sunny day, already 98 degrees outside. Regular people and truckers were moving about like normally. The sweltering heat was second nature to most. Maria grabbed Bobby by the hand. She led him to the far side of the lot where truckers leave their rigs parked sometimes for weeks on end when they are not on the road. With a humongous smile on her face, Maria walked up to the trailer she was looking for. It was plain white. It didn't stick out or draw attention. When they got to the rear of the trailer, she took out a set of keys. One of the keys went to the heavy-duty master lock that secured the cargo inside. Bobby looked around the lot anxiously, not sure of what all this was about.

Maria unlocked the lock and held it in her hand. "Help me open this door, Bobby."

Bobby grabbed the metal handle. He pulled on the heavy door, slowly swinging it open. Maria grabbed whatever she could and tried to climb up into the trailer.

"Hold on, step back, Maria."

Bobby climbed up inside of the trailer first; then he held out his hand for her. She took his hand and held it tightly. He pulled her 120-pound frame up with little or no effort. Once both were inside, she pulled the door closed.

"Fuck, it's hot as hell in here. Shit! And dark with this door closed." Bobby quickly observed the change in temperature. Instantly, he took out his phone and used the flashlight app to see the cargo. Maria did the same.

The pair had little room to move around. Yet, they managed to work their way to the front of the trailer which was filled with cardboard boxes. Bobby was sweating hard. It was so hot and humid. He focused his light on what was written on the boxes. It read::*Hazardous material handle with care.*

"From here on back is all the real cargo." Maria shined her light on the boxes to show him. Then she swung her light back up front. "All of these have the drugs in them." There were at least forty to fifty boxes the size of a footlocker each they were looking at.

Bobby had been around a lot of dope in his lifetime but never this much. His heart pounded hard and fast in his chest. It wasn't because of fear. He was excited . . . to the point his dick was getting hard thinking about the endless possibilities he could make happen if he made it back to Detroit with this work. Bobby put his light on Maria. She was looking around in between boxes and everywhere else. "What are you looking for?" he finally asked her.

"The papers for the cargo in case the police pull us over. The cartel owns the legit company that makes the real hazardous stuff. Poppy, this isn't the only company. They run cocaine, Mexican heroin, weed, and pills too. They own just about all of Laredo's manufacturing plants and fresh produce companies. You name it. If they don't own it, they strong-arm the company to do their bidding."

Bobby wiped sweat from his forehead with the back of his hand. "Bitch, I might just marry you." He pulled Maria into him with his free hand and started kissing her aggressively. Maria kissed him back equally hard. She felt his hard dick pressing against her. Just as horny as he was, she grabbed it and rubbed on it through his jeans. Maria was more than ready to be bent over and fucked hard by Bobby. He was seconds away from pulling his dick out when they heard some noise outside at the trailer door. It wasn't particularly loud. It was more of a creeping around type of noise.

Bobby and Maria quickly shut off the flashlight apps on their phones. Both remained silent to listen. It was pitch-black inside the trailer. Bobby reached his hand back. Feeling Maria's hand, he signaled for her to stay behind him. Cautiously, they eased back to the door avoiding all the boxes that blocked almost every footstep.

Nearing the rear area of the truck, Bobby stepped over to the side. Taking a deep breath, he pressed his back against metal walls ready for whatever. His heart raced as he wondered what he had gotten himself into dealing with Maria.

The door slowly opened up. A glimmer of light shined inside. With the door now partly open, Bobby could see Maria's face. She'd fallen behind, despite him telling her to keep close. He frantically waved his hand trying to get her to come stand next to him. Neither of them had any idea who it could be or what they wanted. At least Bobby didn't.

Maria tiptoed quickly and quietly over next to him. Bobby tried to step in front of her so whoever would come in would have to deal with him first. Strangely, Maria pushed him back as if she were the man. The two would-be warriors went back and forth arguing in silence as if mime performing on a street corner. Before either of them could win that battle, a man began climbing into the trailer. The mysterious intruder was up on the entrance ledge with the door cracked open enough for his body to slip through. Unfortunately, this would turn out to be a bad day for him. He picked the wrong trailer to invade, no matter who he was.

Maria was used to the heat and the dense humidity that went along with it. By nature, she didn't sweat much. But in this instant, she was damn near drenched in perspiration. Like Bobby, she prayed it wasn't the police, but knew they wouldn't have just "stumbled" upon a back lot closed trailer. It was someone looking for trouble or an easy possible come up. Regardless of who it was or what they ultimately wanted, it was about to go down.

Bobby took up a defensive stance behind Maria. It was too late in the game for him to jump back in front of her, so he allowed her to take the lead. Maria had the heavy three-pound steel master lock gripped with both hands, fingers in the loop of it, ready to strike. She held it up by her shoulder as if she had a Louisville Slugger baseball bat. When the mystery man's head popped in the trailer, he was looking downward. All he saw was Maria's pretty red painted toes in her white sandals. Without hesitation, he glanced up. At that point, the man saw nothing but stars and tasted nothing but his own blood. Maria had the heavy metal lock over her head. Repeatedly, she brought it crashing down on his forehead. As the lock tore through his skin, a huge gash opened. Blood splattered on her manicured toes and feet. That didn't stop or slow her attack down as she kept on her mission, striking him again and again.

Bobby didn't think twice. Automatically, he did what had to happen next. He moved quickly, reaching down, trying to avoid getting hit. He yanked the man up by his shirt before he totally fell backward out of the trailer. Maria finally stepped out of the way. Bobby struggled to drag the invader man with a split open head all the way up into the trailer. Out of breath, he let his body slump over to the side of the trailer. He then pulled the heavy door closed so no random passerby could break the unspoken code of the truckers' lot and be nosy.

Reaching in his pocket, he grabbed his cell. With sweaty and bloody fingertips, he turned on the flashlight app again. "What in the entire fuck, Maria?" Bobby was confused and shocked, attempting to wipe the perspiration from out of his eyes. Easily, he could see Maria was also breathing hard and just as wet faced as he. Bobby stood mute as she rushed over checking the man for any weapons. Behaving as if she'd won the lottery, Maria removed a gun with a silencer on it out of the man's rear waistband. Seductively, she licked the long barrel of the pistol in victory. The seemingly mild-manner female had turned into a cold-blooded would-be assassin in a matter of seconds. His apparent partner in crime had a look in her eyes Bobby had seen before growing up in the streets of Detroit. Sadly, he knew that look all too well. It was that of a person lusting for blood. His perfectly built, good-pussy-having, Mexican mommy was bloodthirsty.

"It's him. I knew damn well it was him," Maria excitedly spoke with the man's blood still dripping from her hands. Then she started mumbling fast in Spanish.

"Who the fuck is he, Maria?" Bobby demanded to know, taking a few steps back, leaning on some boxes. "Some dude you used to deal with that's stalking you now or what? I mean, damn, girl, you went hard. What the fuck! And speak in damn English." Bobby's mind was going in ten different directions. Waiting for Maria to calm down and respond, he bent down over the motionless mystery man. He checked him for a pulse or any sign of life. Bobby easily concluded the man was indeed dead. Maria had sent him to meet his Maker.

Bobby stood up. As he paced in the small area, he shook his head in disbelief. He had just gotten some of the best head in his life, but now he was directly involved in the murder of a man he'd never seen before. Demanding answers from Maria, he had to reconsider getting hooked up with the cartel or her in any type of way. Bobby was from the streets and knew drugs, money, and murder were all first cousins, but this kinda shit was too much.

Maria finally had an excuse that Bobby could make out for her over-the-top reactions and brazen murder. "He's

Miguel, also known as the Lone Wolf. A dirty gang-hired assassin and thug that rivals our Sinaloa Cartel here in Laredo. The ruthless monster has a bounty on his head worth thousands. After all this time, he finally slipped up." With quickness, Maria took out her cell phone. She tapped the camera app leaving smears of Miguel's blood on the screen. She made sure the flash was on so it would take a good clear picture. She was fearless, showing no signs of remorse. Kneeling down close to the assassin's face, she snapped his picture. After that, she revealed some truths about the dead man. "Several days ago, he killed two Sinaloa members. They were brothers. One of them was close, like family, to me. Rest in peace, brother." She crossed her heart looking upward.

"Oh, wow." Bobby continued to wipe his face as he listened.

"Yeah, his name was Pedro. This rotten scumbag right here cracked his head wide open. My friend's brains were hanging out of his skull. Unfortunately, he wasn't dead. He suffered. Miguel made Wan, his brother, eat some of Pedro's brains while he was still alive."

"Are you serious?" He started to understand Maria's rage.

"Yes, Bobby, I am. Miguel was laughing at him like it was nothing. Then he tortured Wan until he gave up the location of a fully packed load just like this one. After that, he cut off Wan's head. That son of a bitch was crazy enough to dump it in front of the police station. He is, or should I say *was,* a real piece of shit, do you not agree?" Maria stood up and spit on Miguel cursing his dead soul in Spanish.

Bobby was flabbergasted. What she had just told him was like some old movie-of-the-week gangster-type bullshit. He had seen as well as heard a lot of wild things in his years of living, but this was over the top. And now, here he was, knee-deep, in the middle. For lack of words, he just nodded.

Maria faced Bobby. She was unmoved emotionally about having just committed murder, let alone seeing the body slumped over in the corner just a few feet away. She was past that and on to something new now, something that was going to benefit them both. "Baby, just so you know, we're splitting the bounty that was on this monster's head. Just like we split the money from them people we helped get across the border. Me and you make a good team. We're gonna make lots of money, and one day, get away from this dusty town and live like rock stars."

After what she'd told him about the crimes her victim had carried out, Bobby knew Maria had to do what she had to do. If it was his homeboy those things happened to, he'd be hell-bent on revenge as well—any way it came. Shrugging it off, Bobby's mind was back on track once she'd told him they'd be splitting the reward money. "Oh, well. Fuck. This ho-ass nigga had that shit coming."

"Come on, let's go get our money for the load we saved and this grimy *pendejo*."

Bobby hopped down out of the trailer first. Then, he took Maria's hand, and she climbed down as quickly as she could. She wiped the blood off the padlock-turned-murder-weapon the best she could; then she clamped it closed and stood a few feet back. The two of them looked at each other and knew they had to get back to Bobby's rig and her place as discreetly as possible. "Look, Bobby, we leave in like two hours. I'll meet you back here after I shower and change clothes."

"Okay, cool, but what about *him?*" He nodded toward the trailer that was serving as Miguel's temporary tomb.

"Don't worry, poppy. I'ma call the guy the organization uses to clean this type of thing up. No worries. I'ma show him the picture I took of him, proof that it's him dead, and collect that money. We out here doing dirt, so we might as well get cashed out for what the dirt is worth. Do you not agree, poppy?" Standing up on her toes that still had blood on them that was now beginning to dry up, she kissed her accomplice on the lips.

Bobby kissed her back. "Okay, bae, go ahead and do what you got to do. I'ma get cleaned up as well. Then I'll drop my trailer and have my truck ready to hook up and go. You just hurry up and get back here. Oh yeah, and damn right, get that money. We need ours, every penny."

Maria went one way, and he went the other toward his rig. He was feeling alive with hunger to get back in the trenches of the dope game with a new look on life and more money than he dreamed of touching in this lifetime. He knew what he was about to do was a major risk, but so was anything worth having.

Chapter Nine

The Federal Correction Institution, Milan, is a U.S. federal prison in York Charter Township, Michigan. The prison is a low-security facility for male inmates. It was high noon and lunchtime inside the prison's infirmary. Only the desk nurse was posted at her station. Her coworkers were gone to lunch. Federal Correctional Officer Santana Crews stood guard at Juan's bedside. Officer Crews was watching the clock on the wall and looking down at the prisoner. Juan was lying in the bed with one arm strapped down. His body was broken up, battered, and bruised. The doctors had his head wrapped up with white bandages that made him appear to be a terrorist that tried to blow some shit up and failed. His left leg was in a cast, and he had a deep cut across his infamous family crest tattoo on his upper arm. Juan drifted in and out of consciousness. Now semialert, he sensed the officer didn't care for him. It was apparent the way he was mean mugging him, but Juan could care less. He had more pressing things on his mind to think about. He wondered just how long they would hold him in this facility. He also knew he ran the risk of being deported back to Mexico because his paperwork wasn't right. Most importantly, Juan wondered what the cartel had to say about his and Karen's unfortunate arrest. He'd thought about her once or twice through this ordeal and hoped she was keeping her mouth shut, at least for her own sake. The cartel had yet to make contact, and he didn't know how to take that—good or bad. Juan's deep thoughts were interrupted when the otherwise secure room door opened. A man wearing a gray two-piece suit walked in as if he owned the place. His facial expression easily read "I mean business."

"Good day, Warden Valdez." Officer Crews stepped back trying to look on point.

Warden Valdez was stern. He didn't make eye contact with Crews. The bigger-than-life figure literally grunted and tossed his head in the direction of the door, signaling Crews to kick rocks and leave the room. Officer Crews knew what that meant. He knew the power the warden had inside, as well as outside, of the building. Crews didn't ask any questions. He just turned and walked out. When the door closed, the warden walked over to Juan's bedside. Momentarily, he glared down at him with contempt.

"Yeah, okay, so what's good, old man? What the hell you want with me?" Unlike Officer Crews, Juan showed absolutely no respect. As far as he was concerned, matters couldn't get any worse than what they already were.

Warden Valdez straightened his tie as he stood tall. He was not moved by the inmate's brazen mouth and attitude. He was beyond used to that behavior over the years and had grown accustomed to brushing it off. "Look, young man, I, myself, want nothing to do with you, but apparently, we have mutual associates. And those are the people that require something from you."

"What you say?" He now had Juan's full attention.

"Yes, they want to ensure that your people in Detroit are in place to receive goods from Laredo. Not to mention pay that advance ticket you yourself vouched for. Your life depends on it since you fucked up and allowed close to a half-million dollars of our associates to end up in the government possession. Not to mention the pipeline had to be refigured." Warden Valdez never changed his expression. His tone stayed even as he reached inside his jacket pocket. Seconds later, he pulled out a cell phone, handing it to him.

Juan knew the cartel's reach was far and wide. However, he was astonished and in disbelief that the cartel had a federal prison warden tied into their web of corruption. With his free hand, he took the phone. Juan knew the warden was correct. He'd been mixed in the business long enough to know the organization didn't play around or tolerate fuckups. He'd firsthand witnessed people and their loved ones paying with their lives for mishaps less than his and Karen's. He knew he had to make things as right as he could if he even hoped to live to get deported. He took a deep breath and tried to adjust his broken body. Juan dialed Greedy's cell number he had memorized. He then said a silent prayer he'd pick up since it was a strange number.

Greedy was sitting outside in front of Talk of the City Barbershop. He was doing his usual, plotting and scheming on various ways to make cash. The fact that he'd hit a major lick was nothing. His uncle Ed had schooled him long ago to never count on just one stream of income. He advised him to have as many irons in the fire as possible if they all made sense and were, of course, profitable. Greedy followed that concept. With his seat reclined, he was waiting on a money drop while smoking a blunt. Snatched out of his concentration on the game, his phone rang. Lifting up, he turned the knob to the right, lowering the sound of the music he had blasting. Picking his cell up off his lap, Greedy looked at the screen. Squinting his eyes, he took a long, hard pull on his blunt, held the smoke in, then exhaled. He didn't know the number. He took another pull, then exhaled a cloud of smoke again. Knowing what had taken place just weeks prior, he took a chance on bullshit and answered the call. Greedy tried to speak, but the good weed had him coughing hard into his phone when he regained his breath. "Yeah, who dis?"

"Listen, my friend. I don't have much time to talk." Juan's voice was weak, but his tone was deliberate.

Greedy was overjoyed he'd decided to pick up the random number call. And more than relieved to hear the voice of his manz on the other end. He felt like the bank had just cleared a six-figure check. "Damn, what the fuck! My dude, I saw the news. That shit had me all fucked up in the head!" He wasn't going to go into detail of what he'd seen on TV or ask unnecessary questions. Greedy was a vet in the streets and knew better. He knew if Juan was reaching out in his fucked-up position, it'd be best to listen carefully to what he had to say.

"Look, that's a mere minor setback. Nothing to concern yourself with, my friend. Only the business we spoke of before this jumped off. Everything is as I said it would be, do you understand? Everything is everything. Someone will be in touch shortly. Just be ready. Keep your eyes and ears open. And listen, don't disappoint me, or it will cost you dearly, my friend, if you do." Juan spoke in a stern voice. Then the phone abruptly went dead while Greedy still had it pressed to his ear. The Detroit-born and -raised thug was unbothered by Juan's threats. He tossed his phone on the passenger seat and once again hit the blunt hard. He turned up the custom stereo and hoped the next connect person the plug sent would be smart enough not to get knocked like Juan's dumb ass.

As the music blared through the speakers, he looked up in the review mirror. Right on time, he saw the drop-off man pulling up behind him in a black Yukon. He got out of the truck carrying a red gym bag. When he got to Greedy's ride, he didn't get in. He didn't say a single word. He tossed the bag through the rear open window onto the backseat and walked away.

Greedy drove away from the curb. Aware of his surroundings at all times, the street-seasoned warrior took notice of a gray minivan with dark-tinted windows. It had slowly pulled out of the parking lot across the way from the barbershop when he did. Now, the mysterious van had gotten behind him. When Greedy bent a couple of corners, the van did too. On his job, Greedy reached for his phone that was on the passenger seat. "Yo, Gigi, heads-up, baby girl. I got visitors. Get them thangs ready."

Laying his cell on his lap, Greedy sped up. He hit the next corner, went two blocks down, and made a quick left. The van driver had stopped even trying to be discreet by now. He was almost on Greedy's bumper. Greedy was calm. He was deep off into the game and lived the life. He hit the blunt one last time and tossed it out the window. When he got to the middle of the block, he slammed down on the brakes. The tires screeched as the vehicle he was driving came to a dead stop. The van stopped behind him, barely avoiding a collision. Cars were parked on both sides of the street. Greedy, along with the occupants of the van, were boxed in. In no time flat, the sliding doors on both sides of the van slid open fast. Two masked dudes in the back emerged with AK-47s. The front-seat passenger, also masked up, jumped out pointing a .40 cal taking the lead. The armed trio was ready for war. They wasted no time attempting to run up on Greedy, undoubtedly to relieve him of the money drop bag.

They were quick, but unfortunately for their families that had to bury them, not quick enough. Four of Greedy's hired killers, along with his bottom bitch Gigi, opened fire on them from both sides of the street. The would-be jack boys' bodies were riddled, taking in bullet after bullet from various guns. The van driver was stunned. He, like his cohorts, didn't anticipate things going down like they had. He tried to throw the van in reverse and get out of Dodge but backed into a tree. Terrified, he got out trying to run. Like his boys, he was cut down. They were all four left in the street to bleed out, if not already dead. Gigi lowered her firearm. She made eye contact with Greedy and winked. Knowing her man was safe, she waved at him, signaling Greedy to get the hell out of the hood and secure the drop-off cash bag. Greedy drove away knowing his girl was the hardest nigga on his team and could—and would—handle the rest.

Without question, Gigi called him thirty minutes later. She assured him the situation was taken care of. "Yeah, bae, that was them ho-ass motherfuckers from the other side of the tracks. You know they always looking for a come up. But they barked up the wrong tree this damn time. We ain't gotta worry about them no more."

"Good, because we gonna be all the way back up in a day or two. The new bag on its way to us as we speak. Juan came through even doe he sitting fucked up," Greedy happily announced.

"Now, see, that's what I call a real plug. This mother-fucker can get popped and still make the bag shake. Good. We almost done with this one we on now, and our money is right. That's good shit, daddy, for real, for real. Well, I got a few more traps to re-up; then I'll meet you at home. All this gun play got my pussy wet, so I'm gonna need you to pop this pussy for me tonight," Gigi said seductively, sitting in her truck, rubbing her snatch box.

"I'll get that pussy out of the pound soon as I get to you. You know how I want it: face down and ass up. Keep it wet for me. I'll call you when I'm on my way home." Greedy hung up the phone and blazed up another blunt.

Chapter Ten

Somewhere in an unknown location run by the DEA, Karen sat in a gloomy cell. With no windows, the eight-by-twelve confinement area had a table and two chairs. She sat in the chair facing the door with a small window. She could see people walking by every so often. Beet red in the face from crying for the last three days, she'd had little to no sleep. Since she and Juan had been apprehended at the hotel with the money, they'd been on her nonstop.

DEA Special Agent Blane looked through the small window at Karen. He entered the interrogation room. He had a folder in hand that he kept notes in. Sitting down, he opened the folder and removed a pen from his button-up white shirt. "Now, let's go over what you've told me so far."

Karen was sobbing hard as she tried to speak. "When can I go home? I have done nothing wrong. I've told you all I know." Wiping her face with both palms of her hands her head was spinning.

The agent stared at her blank-faced for at least a good five minutes. He then tugged at his necktie, unloosening it. It was obvious he was growing impatient with Karen and her declarations of innocence. He knew she was lying, and he wanted her to give up information that would put Juan and possibly his affiliates away for the rest of their lives. However, Karen was sticking to her story that she knew nothing about the money in the duffle bag. And she didn't have any idea whatsoever where it came from. She claimed she'd been dating the man in question, Juan, off and on for three months. He called her and asked if she would like to take a ride to Michigan with him to visit family and friends. Her story was when he went to see his people, she stayed in the room alone until he returned. Karen said she never ever noticed a duffle bag until they were leaving the hotel room.

The agent leaned forward resting his elbows on the table. "You know you're facing thirty years hard federal time, don't you? So let's cut the act like you so innocent. We know all there is to know about you," he barked out, tired of the game she was trying to run. Annoyed, he shuffled through the folder. He located her federal information packet the government had gathered since she'd been detained. He began reading out truths after truths. "Well, let's see just how innocent you have been. You grew up in Iowa, Nebraska." He then told her what high school she went to and when her mother died, she was thirteen. At age fifteen, she landed in a group home for sexually abused girls. "Yeah, that was when your father, the pedophile, had his way with you after your mother died and you got pregnant with his child. It says here when you delivered the baby he fathered, you reported him to authorities at the hospital. He's still serving time on a sixty-year sentence that he got." The agent was callous in intentions as he momentarily looked up, knowing he was breaking Karen down. Seeing tears form in her eyes, he continued.

"You've been arrested for prostitution in eight states across the USA. In Florida, the police have been looking for you since 2010 in connection with a homicide of an off-duty police officer that liked to pay for your pussy on his downtime. Your prints were run through the system two days ago, and guess what? Bingo! We got a match that came back to you, Karen. So if you want to keep this dumb little white girl act up, I'll get the paperwork started to transfer you to Florida. Or you can give Juan and his people up, and you could be placed in the witness program under our protection." The agent had a smirk drawn on his face. He sat back in his chair feeling as if he'd slayed a dragon. "Well, what's it gonna be, Karen? I'm tired of messing around with you."

Karen was as pale as a ghost. Her eyes were the size of a half dollar. She was twisted up mentally that the government had dug up most of her dirty secrets. On everything she loved, she had no idea the trick in Florida that she killed was a police officer. Not wanting to get caught up, she didn't stay around long enough to find out exactly who she'd murdered. That same night, she'd gotten on the Greyhound bus bound for Arizona, never looking back. Karen got chills. She had flashbacks of getting in the man's car after they agreed on a price for head only. He then drove to an isolated area. However, that's when he got violent. The man began smacking and punching her in the face and head. He strong-armed Karen to have sex. Thank God, she somehow got a hold of a screwdriver on the rear floor board of his car. Defending herself, she stuck him over thirty times in the face and neck, killing him.

Karen was at a loss for words. She was trembling and needed a cigarette badly to calm her nerves. Her voice cracked, and she stuttered as she struggled to speak. The agent waved his hand, signaling her to be quiet for a moment. He was far from being done with letting her know what he knew. She'd wasted his time long enough with the denial game, so now it was time to play hardball. It was obvious that he was breaking his prisoner down, yet he had to drive home the point that these charges she was facing were serious and not going to go away on their own. He went back in the folder ready to expose more harsh truths. She cried harder, and snot ran from her nose as she braced herself. The agent then produced a photograph. It showed two teenagers dressed in prom attire. He slid it across the table.

"Here you go. That's right, Karen. Take a good, long, hard look."

Karen sat up straight in her chair. Picking up the picture she did what was asked. She studied it hard through her teary vision. Her heart damn near stopped. A lump grew in her throat. It was her baby girl she had given up to the state of Iowa. "She looks like me and my father." Karen sobbed, unsure how to feel at the moment.

The agent laid it on thick, hoping to get her to flip on Juan and the cartel. His goal was for her to say she'd become a snitch for the federal government. "Look, if you want, I can arrange for you both to be reunited. Maybe begin a new start on life together in the program under government protection. I can make that happen, and that murder charge can disappear with your old life."

Karen wanted to be with her child more than anything in the world. For years she'd lived with a hole in her heart longing to have her child. Now was her chance to make it right and finally see her baby girl. She knew it could possibly cost her her life if the organization caught wind of her plans, but Karen felt the risk was worth it just to meet her daughter. Out of choices, she wiped the snot from her nose with her open hand. "Okay, I'll do it. I want the witness protection program for me and my daughter. I want immunity in writing for everything now and in Florida. I'll take the stand and testify about everything I know."

The agent stood up trying to hold his excitement in. "Listen, you better not be shitting me around on this. If you do, I'll make sure you never see daylight again." The special agent in charge turned and hastily exited the small room, leaving Karen there sobbing and staring at the photo. Five minutes later, he returned into the interrogation room. "Hand over the picture, Karen. It goes back in my records. But play your cards right and you'll be taking new family photos with your daughter real soon."

Karen reluctantly handed over the picture and folded her arms. She slid down some in the hard metal chair. As the door closed behind the agent, her mind raced with what consequences the cartel could—and would—make her face when they found out she flipped. Her head dropped. She buried her face in her hands and began to sob once more. "Oh my God, what did I just do?" For once, she was glad the police were on her side and would protect her.

"Hello, yeah, it's me."

"Yes, my friend. How did it go?"

"Unfortunately, just as we knew it would. The disloyal bitch folded. I showed her that fabricated picture of who she thought was her daughter. She bugged out and flipped. She promised to give me Juan and everyone else she knew of." The special agent shook his head while he spoke. "Hell, I'm quite sure if I press the whore anymore, she'll tell me who really shot King and Kennedy."

"Well, we know what must be done."

"I already know, sir—no loose ends need to unravel in the wind."

"Exactly. Consider her no longer an asset but a major liability. I trust she will be dealt with accordingly."

"Of course, consider it done. But what about our other 'situation'?"

"No need for concern. Our mutual friend Warden Valdez had Juan handle those two calls, so we're good all the way around. Like Karen, Juan's contract with us is to be immediately terminated as well. For now, the pipeline is once again secure on all ends, and that's what's most important. However, we have yet to find the leak in our midst that turned them in. That housekeeper story can't be true. That's a front for whoever the rat is. But we'll keep looking until we discover who it is."

"I understand. Say no more." Ending his conversation, DEA Special Agent Blane placed his private line cell phone back in his inner jacket pocket. Having completed the task of seeing if Karen could, and would, stand tall if need be, he plotted on the arrangements to have her and Juan transferred from prison . . . and relocated to unmarked graves somewhere in the middle of nowhere.

Chapter Eleven

All went as planned. Bobby and Maria met back up like they had agreed to do. She had their bounty reward money in a bag. She had been hailed as a hero for bringing down Miguel who had long since been a thorn in the side of the organization. However, she didn't have time to live in that celebration. More work needed to be done, and more money to be earned. Maria was blessed when her beloved uncle called. She saw the strange number pop up on her screen and started not to answer, but she was glad she had. Their conversation was brief. Juan informed her of the Detroit man's name and his number to call once they were thirty miles outside of Michigan. Juan's final words were for his niece to stand tall and continue to represent the infamous bloodline they shared and the family crest tattoo. Juan had her word. Then the line went dead.

Bobby hooked his rig up to the hot box trailer in less than twenty minutes. Shortly after that, the pair was on the road headed to Detroit. It would take twenty-three, maybe twenty-four hours if they drove nonstop. Although the two had anticipated stopping along the way, Bobby had his mind focused on getting the dope to Michigan as quickly as possible. He had just tucked his share of the reward away in the rear of his cab, making him want even more to stack with that cash. So even if it means bodies falling by the wayside along the way, he would make it back home to collect. Bobby wasn't like Maria. He didn't have nor understand family loyalty. But he understood money. And to him, the come up was all that mattered, not what it stood for.

Maria sat in the passenger seat with one bare foot up on the dashboard and the other tucked under her ass cheek. She'd showered and changed into a pair of pink cotton booty shorts and a matching sports bra. She fixed her hair up into a genie ponytail. It was so long it rested over her shoulders. Maria was relaxed thinking about how cute she was going to be when she came back from shopping buying all the latest high-end name brand clothes and shoes. She was finally on her way out of that dusty town. Maria idolized the Instagram models she saw on social media. She yearned to dress just like them and drive hot cars like a true boss bitch, as most rap lyrics would say. She looked over her shoulder at the handmade bag her grandma sewed for her. It was filled with her share of the money for killing Miguel, and she had Juan's blessings. Everything was great in her life and about to get better. All she needed now was to get to Detroit.

Maria put her hand over her mouth and yawned. She was drained and decided to grab a blanket from the back to put over her legs. The air-conditioning inside the cab was on high. She made herself comfortable in the seat and drifted off to sleep. A few hours into their trip had gone by. Suddenly, her relaxation and pleasant dreams were interrupted. Her cell phone was ringing as it lay positioned in between her legs. Rubbing her eyes, Maria glanced at the number. Her heart started to beat fast. A lump lodged in her throat. She panicked. Maria knew it was the cartel's boss's number. Before leaving Laredo, her people advised her to keep her phone on at all times because he or someone would be in touch.

Bobby glanced over at Maria. "What's wrong? Who is that calling you?"

"Oh my God, it's jefe calling. They told me someone from the organization would be calling, but I didn't expect for it to be him personally."

"Okay, then, it's him. Answer it and see what's up," Bobby urged taking his eyes off the road for a split second to look at her.

Maria pressed the talk icon on her phone and spoke in Spanish. "Hello, Jefe."

"Hello, Maria. You have done well over the years since you were a little girl to aid the cartel. Your father would be proud to see the woman you have grown into. And your uncle Juan oftentimes sings your praises. I must say your time has finally come to join the family. We want you to eat as we eat. Want for nothing that money can't buy. You can rest assured your enemy is my enemy. He who is my foe, blood runs from his veins until he is no more. Do you accept my embrace, Maria?"

Maria was humbly stunned. She was at a loss for words. The cartel boss of bosses himself had just formally asked her to become official. Maria came back to her senses and finally replied, "Of course, yes, I will eat at your table. It would be an honor to give my all to the organization, even my life, Jefe."

They ended the conversation. The ultimate deed was done. Maria was now down in the books for being damn near untouchable to most. Regretfully, the young female had no idea the man who'd just blessed her had just ordered her uncle Juan's death just as he allowed her father's death to be excused years earlier.

Bobby didn't understand much Spanish but could tell by the expression on Maria's face that whatever just happened was epic.

After hours on the road, avoiding contact with the state boys through several jurisdictions and sleeping in truck rest areas, they were almost there. Drinking a cup of coffee, Maria was admiring the early-morning scenery. With his baseball hat turned backward, Bobby soon announced the words she had been waiting to hear.

"Hey, baby, you might wanna put that cup down and make that call."

"Huh, what call?"

"Girl, I know we been on the road, but don't dummy up on me now. Make the call to your contact person in the D. Let them know we right outside of Michigan and heading in."

"Oh my God, are you serious?"

"Yeah, girl, so make that call. I'ma pull over at the next exit and get some gas and take a shit. After that, we back on the road."

Maria took a small piece of paper out of her wallet. Tapping in the numbers, she placed the call. One ring, two rings, three rings later, Greedy answered. After a brief time talking, they agreed to meet in the Mexican Village area of Detroit. Once there, they could sit down and discuss the collection of funds and transference of product.

Crossing the state line into Michigan, Bobby jumped off of I-75 on got on I-94. They needed to stop by Metro Airport. There were various rental car companies on the premises. Seeing how she had to meet up with the contact person, Maria couldn't very well drive up in a huge semitruck filled with illegal drugs and other contraband. Amazed with all the regular people coming and going around the airport, she knew she'd made the right decision to get out of the Laredo truck stop area that had become home. Picking out a midsize vehicle, she signed the paperwork and drove off the lot. Trailing behind

Bobby, he soon pulled into a motel located right outside of Detroit. They had made it. The mission was almost accomplished. Slowly, the trained driver pulled his rig alongside many others. To anyone passing by, his truck and he seemed like any other truck and any other weary, over-the-road driver.

Maria let him check into the motel room. With the key in hand, Bobby walked to the lower-level room while she slowly drove waiting to park. Once inside the room, each used the bathroom. Bobby fell onto the bed, and Maria joined him. After taking a short nap, she would call Greedy and tell him a definite time to meet up at the restaurant and Bobby would stay with the load.

Chapter Twelve

Greedy received the meet up time call he'd been waiting for. Although shocked earlier when finding out his new plug connect was a female, he rolled with the punches. To him, money had no restrictions on it. If you were eight to eighty, blind, crippled, or crazy, he'd get money with you if you were a hustler. Arriving at Los Galanes a few minutes ahead of time, he and Gigi ordered chips and salsa. He kept an eye on the door. Even though he'd fail to tell the caller his girl and partner in crime would be joining them, everyone in the cartel knew they moved as one. Ten minutes after the chips had arrived, a female wearing a powder-blue shirt with a kitten on it strolled through the door. Greedy easily recognized what she had on. "Well, damn!"

"Damn *what,* nigga?" Gigi turned to see what had his interest.

"I know damn well this ain't the new connect." Greedy stood to his feet so Maria could see he was wearing the Spartan green fitted D cap. He waved her over, and the introductions were made.

After they all ordered food, the details were hashed out. Maria was beautiful, but like Gigi, played no games when it came to business. She wanted to assure her new "friends" that all was well with the flow of the product, and things, for the most part, would not change. She was in town not to just drop off product, but to pick up the ticket money on the fronted product Juan had vouched for. She didn't mention Juan's name, and neither did Greedy or Gigi. When all the particulars were established about what motel to meet up at and what time, they enjoyed their meals. Maria made small talk. She asked a few questions about the nightlife in Detroit and what the casinos were like she'd heard so much about. Greedy was all in telling the Mexican beauty this and that, and she continuously flipped her long, flowing hair over her shoulder.

Gigi sat back, not saying much. She had been with her man long enough to tell when some other bitch had him acting goofy or wide open. Whereas part of her wanted to smack the shit outta Maria for being all extra, she was forced to respect that she was indeed the new connect and the key to the pipeline. However, as far as Greedy was concerned, she'd deal with him later.

It was nearing seven in the evening. The sun was still shining bright. It was thirty minutes before they would meet back up with Maria and her counterpart. Reaching for a bottle of water, Greedy swallowed three Tylenols. The right side of his temple was pounding. He had migraines in the past, but this one was courtesy of Gigi. Ever since leaving the restaurant, she'd been talking shit, going hard. Normally, he was used to hearing her mouth, but this time, it was different. This time, she was furious, breathing on him about his apparent behavior at the restaurant. She kept at him asking why he seemed so fascinated with that stringy-haired Mexican bitch. For some reason, Gigi hated Mexicans but never let it stand in the way of doing busi-ness . . . before now. It was bad enough Maria was flirting with her man, but this asshole had the nerve to seem to be open to it. Gigi lost control of herself and her emotions. A few times she even hit Greedy on the back of his head to get his attention when she felt as if he'd tuned her out. She reminded him that Maria was just another whore with a slit. Nothing more, nothing less.

Greedy soon caught on to what the problem was as they got in the car. Gigi was a boss bitch. Everyone they'd come in contact with respected her and her gangster. They knew she was a force to be reckoned with. However, Maria was one as well. She was nothing like Karen was to Juan. She was the leader, the key point person; plus, she was more than easy on the eyes. Gigi didn't like either of those qualities in another female, especially one dealing with her man.

Greedy wanted to keep the peace. His main objective was to stay making money and maintain an open line to the plug. All of that female jealousy shit was for the birds. He told Gigi that he'd fall back and let her go into the motel room for the money count. She agreed, shut her mouth, and drove off.

When the longtime devoted pair pulled up, Maria and Bobby were just coming back from McDonald's. He had slept all day and half the evening since they arrived. However, he was now wide awake and alert. Maria introduced Greedy and Gigi to Bobby. Not knowing what to expect, Bobby played it cool. He was born and raised in the city, so he already knew Detroit niggas could get grimy. Although he didn't have a gun, he feigned as if he did. He knew his rig was holding the drugs and without the go-ahead from Maria, they'd stay in there.

Money bag in tow, Gigi followed Maria into the other room Bobby had rented as well. The men stayed back in the parking lot to watch out for both their girl's safety and best interest. Once inside, Maria started back with the idle chitchat about this, that, and the third. After ten or so minutes of counting, she had Gigi heated. No matter what she tried, Maria's mouth was going a mile a minute.

"So, how long have you and him been together?"

"Why you need to know all of that?"

"I was just asking. Well, are you married?"

"Excuse me?"

"I mean, he loves you, right?"

"Of course, Greedy loves me. What the fuck kinda question is that?"

"Well, when a man truly loves a woman he marries her, yes?"

"Girl, let's just count this money and handle this business." Gigi was getting more aggravated with each passing moment. She knew Maria was the direct connect to the plug, but this was becoming all too much to take in.

"Okay, what you call it, soul sister? We count."

Soul sister? I swear to God I hate these wannabe black wetback bitches with a passion. If this bitch say one more thing about me or Greedy's relationship, I'ma bug out.

Twenty minutes more passed. Both females seemed to be back on their best behavior. With only three more small bundles of money to count, Maria couldn't keep quiet. "So you and your boyfriend makes lots of money, I see." She put an emphasis on *boyfriend*.

Gigi was no dummy and caught the dis. That was all it took. All bets were off, plug or no plug. "Look, bitch, you got me fucked up. I tolerated your ass earlier at the restaurant because you might not have known better. But now you stepping all the way outta line, and I ain't with that shit."

Maria was beautiful, but far from a coward. It was in her DNA to brawl if need be. And if Gigi was willing to step up, she'd be more than happy to meet her halfway. She liked Bobby, but she was just testing the waters to see how other guys from the D got down. Truth be told, Maria went both ways when she felt like it. And she had been even willing to see how Gigi was laying too—until she starting being so defensive about her so-called man. Not bothered about the female's name-calling, Maria just giggled as she bent over to get her lipstick out of her purse. "Wow, he must really have a huge dick to make you wanna fight over it!"

Gigi snapped. As she mean mugged Maria ready to pounce, she noticed a unique tattoo on her lower back. It was one that was all too familiar to her. Gigi's grand-mother, mother, and aunts spoke often about that very design. It was one she and everyone else in their family were trained to beware of. Now, here this smart-mouthed bitch representing the cartel was a few feet away begging to get killed. Dropping a stack of hundred-dollar bills to the floor, Gigi pulled out a knife she always kept tucked in her bra. Creeping up on Maria while she was still bending over, Gigi was not interested in making this a fair fight. What was about to take place was deeper than money and drugs. This was about family respect. "So you part of the infamous Lopez Family line, huh?"

"Yeah, what you—"

Before Maria could finish her sentence, Gigi had slit her throat without thinking twice. Not being able to even stand, Maria used both hands to grab her neck. Her jaw dropped open as if she wanted to scream out for Bobby but couldn't. Her eyes grew big as tears poured out of the corners. The thick black mascara she had on ran down the sides of her face. All her dreams of getting to Detroit and living a new life just ended. All her plans of going on shopping sprees and living large were done. She trav-eled all this way and didn't even get a chance to find her deceased mother's family. Maria had been a real hustler and loyal to the cartel since birth. She had seen and had done a lot of wrong in her life, but this was never how she envisioned taking her final breath. Maria had three seconds left in the land of the living for a quick "Hail Mary" before she was gone.

With the bloody knife still in her hand, Gigi stood menacingly over her victim. She quickly snapped out of her rage coming back to reality. She'd just killed the damn connect! Gigi knew there were going to be consequences for her actions down the line, but now, she had to immediately put Greedy up on what she'd done without Bobby knowing as well. Gigi texted him their private code: 921. He'd know some bullshit had or was about to jump off. He'd be prepared either way it went. Seconds later, someone knocked at the door. Gigi stood close asking who it was. Greedy replied that it was him and Bobby. She looked through the peephole seeing that her man was standing behind Bobby, so it was all good. She knew the routine. Slowly, she opened the door and braced herself for chaos to ensue.

Chapter Thirteen

Bobby stepped inside first as Gigi hoped he would. Once Greedy entered and closed the door, he pulled out his gun. Gigi then started explaining. Bobby heard nothing she was saying. He saw Maria slumped over on the floor and hoped that she was playing. She had to be. Only a short time ago she'd been laughing and joking, telling him all the things she planned to buy with her newly acquired wealth. He rushed to her side. Getting down on both knees, he scooped up Maria. Her arms flung out to the side and her head tilted back. It was then that he and Greedy saw the huge gash across her throat. Momentarily, both men were speechless. They'd heard no arguing out in the parking lot. There were no signs of a struggle, and the money appeared to be neatly stacked and rubber band bound on the bed.

"What the hell happened? Why did you do this? What in the fuck!" Bobby was in shock as he fired off question after question, not waiting for a response.

Greedy was pissed and on the same thing as Bobby. He wanted to know what'd gone down so drastic that caused Gigi to do what she obviously had done—killed the connect and probably any chance, hope, or prayer of ever getting a bag from the cartel again. That was, if they both lived to see another sunrise. "Yo, damn. What in the fuck happened in this son of a bitch? Why you do that to that girl? I know you wasn't still on that bullshit from earlier."

Gigi had killed before, with no remorse or purpose. But this time was much different. Although she wondered if her man or Bobby would understand, this was bigger than drugs and money. She'd killed Maria on point and principal. "Listen, bae," she tried to reason with Greedy who now stood mute with his gun still on Bobby. "That bitch last name is Lopez."

"And . . . so?"

"Look on her lower back. She has that tattoo I told you about."

"Huh, tattoo? Gigi, what in the fuck is you talking about?"

Bobby had tears in his eyes as he still held on to Maria's lifeless body. "You mean the one she said was her family crest or something like that? What about it? What the fuck that have to do with your ass?"

In any normal situation, Greedy would chin check the next man for breathing on his girl like that, but all things considered, he wanted to know that answer as well. "Well, what the fuck?"

Gigi took a deep breath as she started to explain the strange but true connection she and Maria had. "See, listen, when I was a young girl, my mother's sister ran off with this man. He was scum. That shit had my grandmother's heart aching for years behind the bullshit. It was some fucked up Mexican she started dealing with. My mother said he had her strung out on drugs. Then the dirty bastard killed her. My people told us all while growing up that any of them Mexicans with the last name Lopez that ran with the cartel wasn't about shit and definitely wasn't to be trusted. Well, that bitch's last name not only was Lopez, she was proudly wearing that murderous family crest tattoo like she was untouchable. So, see, I had to kill the bitch for having a tainted bloodline."

Greedy said nothing. He just stood staring at Gigi knowing this time she'd crossed the line. She and her bad attitude and fairy-tale stories of yesteryear were going to probably get him, his mother, uncle, and entire generation slaughtered behind this.

Bobby gently laid Maria down on the carpet. He was hurt. He was confused, and now he was infuriated as he stood to his feet. "You stupid-ass little wannabe tough bitch. Do you even realize what in the fuck you just did, huh? Do you?"

"Yeah, I do," Gigi defiantly barked back. "I killed a family member of the monster that killed my aunt. So it is what it is."

"You dumb hood rat. You right, you did kill a family member of the man that killed your aunt—their *daughter*, you fool! Your *cousin!* Maria told me the story of her parents while we were on the road. That's why she said she volunteered with the cartel to be the Detroit connect. She wanted to come here and search for her family that she'd been robbed of so many years ago as a small child."

Gigi for once in her life was speechless. Not only had she murdered her own cousin in cold blood, she'd fucked up the pipeline and money. At this point, she didn't know what to do or what to say. Greedy, however, no matter how pissed he was, had to think quickly. He had to make some tough decisions if he wanted to stay alive, let alone maintain his kingpin status throughout the city. The cartel was not for games. He'd seen hustlers come and go over the years for calling themselves fucking over the plug. But Maria Lopez dead in the middle of the motel room was a major fuckup, a major fuckup with the plug of all plugs. Lowering his gun, Greedy asked Bobby on a scale from one to ten how bad he thought this was. Bobby kept it brief. He informed Greedy that he himself was terrified to even walk outside the room. He'd spent a lot of

time in Texas near the border. He'd witnessed unspeakable acts that he prayed would never be his fate.

"We all dead. Period." He paced the floor as he kept
looking over at Maria. "Them motherfuckers don't play,
and we can't hide. Damn, bitch! You done got us all
killed! Maria was into this shit deep." Bobby lunged at
Gigi, but Greedy held him back.

Just then, Maria's cell phone rang. The room grew
silent. It rang once more, then a third time. No one
moved. No one said a word until it stopped. Bobby went
over to Maria and slid the cell out of her rear pocket.
Before he could check the call log, the cell started to ring
once more. "Oh, shit! It's them probably wanting an
update. So fuck the dumb shit. I ain't do nothing; she did.
That's *your* girl, not mine. I'ma just tell them what happened and that's on y'all."

Greedy stopped Bobby from answering the call. "Wait
a minute, hold tight. Maybe we can both make a few
moves and be all right behind all this."

"Be all right? Dude, I ain't do shit—she did." He pointed
at Gigi who was still stunned about Maria's true identity.
"They gonna kill her first when the shit do hit the fan."

Greedy started thinking about his uncle Ed and the
day he'd gone to visit him. He swore he'd never let him
down for hooking him up with the plug. He promised to
protect his mother and siblings from harm or any negative fallout that came from the game. Up until this point,
Greedy had kept his word, and it was bond. It was his
word that kept his territory strong. His word that had
his workers' loyalty, and his word that had Juan get the
cartel to front him all the extra product that made him
who he was. Greedy's lifestyle flashed before his eyes.
He was not done living and not done making money. He
craved slanging dope and was not willing to give all that
up—not now, not ever. He had to make things right with

the cartel. He had to do something major to show he was still worthy of their favor. Seconds later, out of nowhere, Greedy smashed the side of the gun against Gigi's skull. Dazed, she fell to the ground. Like a gazelle, he leaped on her, striking her once more. Bobby stood well over to the far side not knowing what was about to happen next. Greedy dragged Gigi over to the side of the bed. Snatching two pillows off the bed, he told Bobby to turn the television up loud. Bobby wanted to get out of the room and get some air anyway and figure out his next move. He couldn't believe Maria was gone, but she was. As he passed by the television, he did as he was asked. An episode of *Law and Order*, of all shows, blasted through the speakers.

Greedy and Gigi had come up tighter in the streets and the game. She was, without doubt, one of the realest niggas on his team. If he rocked, she rolled. She had his back time and time again. But this and what she did would not be overlooked by the cartel. Before he placed both pillows on her face, he explained that he was sorry and had no choice. "My bad, baby girl. You always been a rider for daddy, and I appreciate the fuck outta you. But with me, it's always gonna be money over bitches when the bag is in." Just like that, Gigi was dead lying next to her long lost cousin. Greedy prayed the cartel accepted his sacrifice and knew his loyalty was true.

Bobby Bands was devastated. He finally found the courage to answer Maria's cell. He swiftly told the caller what had happened. He knew better than to leave anything out. Jefe claimed to be all right with what jumped off and how Maria's death was paid back in blood. But with the cartel, one never knew. He had strict details on how everything was going to go as far as the load was concerned and them getting all monies owed. They'd send someone to pick up Maria's body, clean the room thoroughly, and transport her back home. Sitting around the main table, high-ranking members tried to speculate on just who the original leak was in the organization or pipeline that set all this madness in play in the first place. Some thought it was Greedy and ordered him watched.

Meanwhile, on the west side of Detroit, Marisa the housekeeper sat in front of the television. Ironically, she was watching the same episode of *Law and Order* that was on in the motel room. Just receiving another self-ordained degree in Crime TV, it would only be a short time before the dizzy, paranoid-minded old bitch believed she'd seen another dead body stuffed in a duffle bag, setting off a new chain reaction of wild and crazy events.

The End